G000115826

The
Best Seller

R S J STEEL

Copyright © 2017 R S J STEEL

All rights reserved

Cover design by Antoneta Wotringer

Cover images by Pixabay and 123RF

Independent Publishing Network

ISBN: 978-1-78808-126-9

With many thanks to Dave Kimber,
for technical advice.

POST SCRIPT

Edwin Strong opened a new document, pushed his glasses up on the bridge of his nose with one finger, frowned and started typing.

Someone once wrote that the only satisfactory beginning to any story is the first chapter of Genesis. I can't remember who, but I've a feeling they were right. However, to narrate the following events as clearly as possible, I think it will be adequate to begin in September 1985, in a Hoomloft Hotel in Amsterdam, seven miles from Schiphol Airport.

Edwin paused and smiled. Perhaps as the hotel and airport were both in continental Europe, he could make a joke about it actually being eleven kilometres rather than seven miles. His dad would certainly make that joke. But then again, his dad wouldn't be writing a report on a murder investigation, and he suspected that that sort of writing was traditionally light on humour.

Six months earlier Edwin Strong himself wouldn't have been detailing the circumstances of a death — he

1

would have been writing an essay on Postcolonial Literatures and Theory, or some such topic, in a large hall in Bristol with dozens of his peers. The hall would have been slightly too warm, and the tense silence that the exam began with would have gradually defrosted into a carpet of very faint background rustles, scratches and creaks as papers were turned, pens were pushed across them and chairs were absent-mindedly moved to better positions. Edwin continued tapping away on the rather elderly PC keyboard.

This particular Hoomloft Hotel, in September 1985, was hosting the first of several annual conferences sponsored by West German firm Jurgen IT, exploring the fledgeling area of the use of personal computers in commerce. In recent years, the worlds of business and finance had watched with interest as massively expensive supercomputers had been used to perform astonishingly complex processing tasks, and it hadn't taken them long to realise that with the advent of the first home computers, very useful processing power was available at a fraction of the cost. This particular conference was aiming to bring together some of the leading lights in the areas of information technology, business in general and finance in particular, to see what resulted. And if Jurgen IT happened to sell more of their own distinct brand of home computer as a result, well so much the better.

The fact that Edwin was using a PC for such a processing-light task as composing a text document, was indicative of an era in which the computer was taken for granted. It was 2016. And the fact that the keyboard on which Edwin was tapping was elderly, in 2016, was indicative of the fact that he worked for an outfit that was down at heel. This firm was Parker Investigations, an agency based in a rather run-down office spread over two floors behind a shop at the top end of South East London's Lordship Lane.

Among the many delegates at the conference were several from the UK, including the owner of Northington International, Tony Northington.

This was accurate as far as it went, but what wasn't so apparent in 2016 was that in September 1985, Northington the man, and Northington the business, had been one and the same entity. But Edwin captured the essentials as he continued.

Northington International was a small operation in 1985. Records of any employees have since disappeared. The business was involved in financial brokerage, and the owner, Tony Northington, also had a keen interest in the emerging field of information technology. So on paper, he was the ideal attendee at Jurgen IT's conference. During the course of this event, he met a young woman named Holly Hall.

Edwin stopped typing for a minute, and looked out of the window, through the grubby net curtains, at the small scrap of garden below. The shop downstairs owned the garden, and there had been talk of making some sort of feature of it, though at the moment it was rather neglected. He turned back to his keyboard.

In Amsterdam Tony Northington gradually realised how ill-suited he was to the event he was attending. And as the extent of the mismatch dawned on him, he spent less and less time in each seminar. He would find a seat near the back, and as soon as he felt he had a handle on the direction the session was taking, and established yet again that it was either far too technical for him or geared to a different business sector, he would slip out and create his own agenda. He didn't want to cut the week short, having paid for it, so he gradually found himself spending more and more time relaxing, unwinding and taking in some of the sights of Amsterdam, after a quick assessment of the opening section of the talk on offer that day.

As he quietly opened the door on the Wednesday morning to get away from yet another impenetrable topic, he found he wasn't the only one leaving. He held the door open for a young woman who was studying, with a frown of concentration, the clipboard she was carrying. She absently nodded her thanks to Tony, but as soon as they had both exited the room and shut the door, she threw herself down on a comfortable chair in the foyer area, slapped the clipboard onto the table beside her, raised her eyes heavenward for a couple of moments, and then began to laugh. 'What on earth was all that about?'

Her English was perfect, as was her smile, and her tone towards Tony was deliciously conspiratorial. 'If I have to sit through another one of those, taking notes, I don't know what I'll do! I'm Holly, by the way.'

'I'm Tony. Tony Northington. Pleased to meet you.'

They shook hands.

'Pleased to meet you too, Tony Northington. Really, have you any idea what all that was about?'

Tony smiled back. 'No idea at all. Even though this was the option I thought I had the best chance of understanding this morning. Luckily I'm here on my own

4

behalf, as it were, so if I don't understand what's going on I just have to lump it. I don't have to carry a clipboard to make notes on, and I don't have to try and look like I've just been called away on important business to leave a seminar. By the way — you know they provide a synopsis of each session? You might find it cuts down your note-taking time.'

Tony went over to a table bristling with conference literature, and selected a couple of type-written and photocopied sheets. He came back and gave one to Holly. 'There you go. One for you, and one for me. I'm afraid I'm a serial offender, so I know all the short cuts.'

'Oh, that's amazing!' Holly quickly scanned the document and her smile grew even bigger. 'And you say these notes are available for all the different topics?'

Tony nodded, mirroring Holly's smile.

'Fantastic,' she said. 'I'm now going to be able to do my whole day's work in about ten minutes, for the rest of the week. I owe you big time!'

'No, not at all. Happy to help. You'll have more time for sightseeing now.'

'It wouldn't really feel like sightseeing for me — I live here.'

'But your English is perfect.' Tony was puzzled.

'Thank you. That would be because I *am* English. But I do live here. If you're wanting to have a look around, though, why don't I give you the benefit of my local knowledge?'

Holly's smile maintained its perfectly welcoming curve. And was it Tony's imagination, or did Holly shift her hips ever so slightly, and almost accidentally flick the top button of her blouse as she said, 'What would you like to see?'

She then broke the awkward pause decisively.

'Come on. Let's go to the flower market.' She glanced at her watch. 'They'll just be clearing away now, so we might pick up some bargains. My apartment needs brightening up. You can watch me haggle in Dutch, and see if it's as perfect as my English.'

Tony had by now recovered his composure. 'That sounds like a very constructive plan! Let's do it! Let's go to the flower market, I mean, of course.'

'Of course,' Holly replied.

Tony reddened.

'But well done for clarifying that,' she added graciously. And then immediately back in conspiratorial mode, 'Amsterdam is *such* a confusing city. I'll look after you.'

The trip to the flower market went well. Holly negotiated vigorously, translating as she went for Tony's benefit, and as the market was winding down for the day after its dawn rush hour, she ended up with a couple of large and varied bunches of flowers, at the cost of only a very few guilders.

'Do you mind if I take these home straight away? They need water as soon as possible.'

'No, of course not. I'm intrigued to see where you live. Do you live alone?'

Again Tony felt his cheeks stupidly reddening, as they walked along. He was sure Holly noticed.

She replied in a completely neutral tone, 'No. I live with my husband, Vincent. He's a native.'

And then with a slightly roguish inflection, 'But as

chance would have it, he's away on business at the moment. In the U.S.'

'The U.S.? What business is he in?'

'He's an academic. He's at a conference on International Relations.'

A brief pause. Tony decided against using her mention of international relations as a springboard for a waggish comment.

'Anyway,' Holly continued, 'we turn left just here, and it's along there on the right.'

They continued in silence.

But by the time they had climbed the stairs and entered Holly's apartment, she had recovered her chattiness.

'Make yourself at home. I'll get these in some water. Do you fancy some coffee? I'll put the percolator on.'

She busied herself in the small kitchen while Tony lowered himself onto the sofa, and gradually relaxed. This was certainly better than struggling through yet another dull talk. Jeanette would be glad to hear he wasn't working too hard. She often suggested he should take things more easily. Though maybe he wouldn't tell her absolutely all the details.

Just as he was thinking this, Holly came out of the kitchen again with a small tray holding a very continental looking percolator, a jug of cream and a couple of mugs. She bent down slightly too low to put the tray on the coffee table, waited slightly longer than necessary before rising again, and looking up before she did so, caught Tony staring rather too obviously. Yet again he felt himself blush, and rather disconcertingly Holly didn't react at all, but simply served up the drinks and sat down in the chair opposite. They chatted of this and that while they drank their coffees. Tony found his rather bitter, but didn't like to mention it. Looking back later, he thought this small moment of commonplace social deception probably marked the beginning of a lengthy process during which the straightforward, hard-working Tony Northington gradually disappeared, and was replaced by a caricature, or shell, of the man he used to be.

They finished their drinks and the conversation died away. Holly picked up her mug and Tony's, and put them back on the tray. This time she slowly, deliberately bent over to pick up the tray, watching Tony's face all the time. As before his eyes flickered downward, and as before his cheeks flushed. She didn't say anything but took the tray into the kitchen.

When she came out again, Holly walked straight over to Tony, held out her hand to help him up, and keeping hold of his hand, led him unprotesting across the room and through the only other door into the bedroom.

CHAPTER 1

Jeanette Northington rang the bell, and seconds later Hunter was in the room.

'You rang, Miss Jeanette?'

She liked being called Miss; it made her feel much younger than her 60 years. (It had taken her a long time to persuade him not to always call her Madam.)

'Ah, Hunter. Amelia is coming round shortly, and so is Miss Raestock from the office. Would you be able to bring us some refreshments at about half past three? And if when you bring them you could stay for a bit, hopefully by then we'll know what we want to do, and we can see how it will work for you.'

Hunter's expression flickered ever so slightly, and Jeanette's heart sank.

'But don't worry about getting the door. Amelia may still have her key, and I'm happy to greet Miss Raestock. Thank you Hunter.'

He bowed very slightly and withdrew, his face inscrutable once more.

Jeanette moved round the spacious living room, straightening a couple of cushions and moving the potpourri from the coffee table onto the hearth. They would need the table, perhaps. She would have to remember to move it back later, or Hunter would flinch again. She smiled to herself as she completed these few preparations. How could it be that someone with her background could be so ineffective with servants? And then the doorbell brought her back to the present. As she walked across the hall, she could see silhouetted in the frosted glass of the big front door a slight figure with an outrageously large hat.

'Amelia, darling!' She opened the door and greeted her daughter. As she did so, she saw her other guest coming in through the gate from the pavement.

'Mother.' Amelia walked past her, without a hug, and disappeared into the living room. Jeanette waited by the door for Molly Raestock, and the two women shook hands slightly awkwardly.

'Thank you for inviting me. It can be a real treat to get out of the office sometimes!'

'Not at all. Come in, come in. We're just in the front room here. You've met Amelia before, haven't you?'

Amelia nodded to Molly Raestock, who smiled back at her.

'Hello, Amelia. Nice to see you.'

Amelia had already settled herself in one of the big comfortable armchairs facing in towards the coffee table and the fireplace, her hat cast carelessly on the floor beside the chair. She was wearing a squarish, smock-like dress, in a pale beige, with a darker diagonal stripe. She was also wearing a rather sulky expression.

'Do take a seat, Miss Raestock.' Jeanette gestured vaguely at the remaining chairs and the sofa. Molly sat down next to Amelia, with her handbag next to her. She smiled brightly at her hostess.

'So, we've got to organise a dinner party!'

'Well, yes, I thought it would be nice to have some sort of celebration...'

Amelia briefly raised her eyebrows. Jeanette continued.

'Hunter's going to bring in some refreshments about half three, so if we can have some sort of overall plans for the evening by then, that would be great.'

'An hour and a half?' said Molly, looking at her watch. 'We should certainly be able to generate some ideas and make some decisions in that time. Do you want to kick things off, Mrs Northington? After all, it's your husband whose achievement we're celebrating.'

Again, a twitch of Amelia's eyebrows.

'Yes of course, and please, Miss Raestock, do call me Jeanette. You've worked for Tony so long, you're like family.'

Practically a snort from Amelia at this, and then a comment. 'I don't want to be pushy, Mother, but can we get on with this? My one creative suggestion, for what it's worth, is that everything is kept as simple as possible. Father's not a great one for family occasions.'

'Oh, but dear, there will be people from the office as well,' Jeanette said. 'That's partly why Miss Raestock has so kindly agreed to help out.'

'Ah. If it's a work do, then maybe he'll take a bit of interest. Still, my idea would be to keep it simple.'

'But an OBE! It's such a big thing! I know he's got the

evening free, and how often do we do something like this? No, I absolutely insist we plan something really special. I know it's not like me, but I really want to put my foot down on this occasion. We shall plan an evening to remember.'

Amelia slowly smiled, for the first time.

'Impressive display of enthusiasm, Mother! Go on then. Maybe we could plan something.'

'Well I do feel strongly about this, dear. I want to organise something really special, that everyone will enjoy.' Here Jeanette faltered a little. 'And I'd really like Tony to enjoy it too. Though you know what he's like.'

The vigour had gone out of Jeanette's voice, and there was a moment's silence, as Tony Northington's wife, daughter and office manager mused on what he was like.

The Northington's Hampstead home was very generously proportioned. The mantelpiece in the living room was on such a big scale that Jeanette had had to search very hard to find a clock that wouldn't look too small on it. None of the clocks in her own family were quite right, but eventually she found a French one with a glass-covered open mechanism that looked perfect. And just as the chime of this clock had finished striking half past three, Hunter's knock was heard at the door. He entered with a trolley that was a size up from the normal hostess trolley, with an extra compartment at the bottom and a bold, rather masculine styling. Hunter was still, to tell the truth, slightly embarrassed to be seen pushing it. He was more of a tray man.

He had been making a special effort to ensure he maintained his self-composure, no matter what plans he was to be presented with this afternoon, but when he had realised that in order to serve the refreshments himself, he would have to use this cart, his poise had received its first blow. It received its second when, as he passed Jeanette her cup of tea, he noticed how many pages on the coffee table in front of her were covered in her writing. However it rallied somewhat when he noticed that Amelia no longer looked sulky, and even seemed slightly animated. Hunter had always had a soft spot for Amelia, despite the fact that she had left home so long ago, visited so infrequently and often looked so angry.

When he had served the three women with tea, and offered them biscuits and small cakes, which they all declined, he pushed the trolley into a corner of the room and hovered unobtrusively for a moment until Jeanette said,

'Hunter, do come and sit down. We're about to unload the results of our planning on you, so the least we can do is ask you to join us for refreshments first.'

This was very unconventional, absolutely not something Hunter felt comfortable with, and a third blow to his equilibrium. But he had expected this one might come, and he had arrived prepared.

'Thank you Madam, Miss Jeanette. I took the liberty of bringing for myself a small flask of coffee, which if you insist, I will gladly drink with you.'

Amelia spoke. 'Come here and sit beside me, Hunter.'

'Thank you, Miss Amelia. I will.'

There was an awkward pause, then Jeanette and Molly began to speak at once.

'Do you know we—'

'I'm impressed that—'

'Sorry, after you.' said Jeanette.

'Oh,' said Molly, 'I was just going to say how impressed I was with how much we managed to get planned in the end.'

'Well, so was I,' said Jeanette. 'It must be true!'

'Don't worry Hunter,' said Amelia. 'You'll be able to do your end of it no problem. And at least you didn't have the chore of planning too.'

'Thank you, Miss Amelia. I'm sure you'll all have come up with some admirable ideas.'

But Hunter was worried. And when the drinks were finished, and he had cleared the cups away, and the aimless small talk, trying to paper over the social cracks, had run its course, Jeanette returned to the business of the day.

'So,' she began, leafing through the papers on the coffee table, 'Let me talk you through what we've planned. And please, everyone feel free to jump in and correct me if I've written it down wrong, or, Hunter, if it doesn't seem feasible. We're going to have the meal here. We'll use the big dining room at the back, and assuming the weather is fine, spill out into the garden as well, when we're not actually sitting at the table. We'll aim to start at seven with drinks and canapés, then sit down to eat at eight. We'll get a pianist in to play jazz in the background, and maybe a cello too.'

Amelia interrupted. 'Don't you mean double bass? With the piano, for the jazz?'

'Yes, maybe I do,' said Jeanette. 'The one like a big violin. Then after the main courses we'll have a couple of speeches, a special vegetarian, gluten-free cake that everyone can enjoy, and drinks in the garden, with the lights on.'

The other two women nodded their agreement.

'And these are the dishes we thought we could have. Lots of variety, including all Tony's favourites.'

Jeanette handed the final page to Hunter, who so far had succeeded in maintaining his equilibrium. He read it, and courteously handed it back.

'That all looks a most delicious variety,' he said. 'Who are you getting in to prepare it?'

'Well,' Jeanette began, 'I was hoping that as we won't be that many in number, just immediate family plus four or five from the office—'

'You're going to do it of course,' interrupted Amelia. 'It's your job, isn't it?'

Hunter looked taken aback. 'Well, Miss Amelia, I have over the years, due to changing fashions, added a certain amount of food preparation to my duties—'

Jeanette's phone rang loudly, bringing conversation to a halt.

'Oh, it's Tony. I'd better take this. Sorry. Excuse me.'

She quickly slipped out into the hall, and carefully touched the screen to accept the call. Before she could say anything, her husband spoke.

'Is Molly still with you?'

'Hello, dear. Yes she is.'

'Well she's not answering her phone. Can you get her to ring me?'

'Yes of course. We were just planning the evening when we're celebrating your—'

'Ah yes. About that. You don't really need me to be there, do you? The thing is some more issues have surfaced with the new product, and we have so little time left to get it all absolutely bomb-proof before it goes live.'

'Tony, you know how rarely I ask you a favour, but couldn't you, just this one time, put your family first? Even just for me?'

'Yes, of course, but, well — look. I'll see how we're getting on.' There was another phone ringing in the background now. 'Sorry, got to go. Get Molly to ring me.' The line went dead.

Jeanette smiled ruefully. Actually that could have gone much worse. She went back into the front room, to find that in her absence Hunter had left the room, saying that he was being expected to do far more than was reasonable. Amelia said she had told him not to be silly, and then he had simply stood up and gone.

'Oh dear,' murmured Jeanette. 'I do wish that you would leave dealing with Hunter to me, dear. I know how to—'

'Oh don't be ridiculous, Mother. He has you wrapped around his little finger! You treat him like a spoilt child!'

'No, that's not true, Amelia. Remember I deal with him on a daily basis, not just occasionally, when you turn up.'

'Oh! So now you think I don't visit enough! And I've made a huge effort to be here today! Well maybe I won't be free for the actual evening!'

'You sound just like your father. He's just told me he might not be able to come either!'

Amelia grabbed her hat, glared at her mother, stormed out of the room, and seconds later Jeanette and Molly heard the front door slam.

'Oh, and he also asked me to get you to ring him,

Miss Raestock,' Jeanette added forlornly. 'What a family you must think us.'

Molly Raestock smiled kindly. 'Not at all. I'll ring him later. Don't worry about that.'

She reached into her handbag, and took out an A5 notebook, and a small packet of tissues. She handed the tissues to Jeanette, and opened the notebook. 'I've got some great caterers we've used for office events. I'll ring them, and if they can't do it, they'll know someone who can.'

Molly made a few brief notes, and took pictures of Jeanette's handwritten pages with her phone.

Jeanette had dried her eyes. 'Thank you so much, Miss Raestock. Molly. I'm sorry. I mustn't keep you. Are you sure you're happy to talk to the caterers?'

'Absolutely. It's what I do. And I'll ring Tony now. Don't worry about it. It'll be a great evening.'

Molly smiled reassuringly as she left, but once the front door had closed, her smile quickly faded. She got out her phone and rang Jeanette's husband.

CHAPTER 2

Tony Northington woke with a start on the morning of the investiture ceremony. He hadn't slept well, and it took him a minute or two to clear his head. His phone helped with this process by buzzing intermittently as the day's emails started to arrive. He always left his BlackBerry set to vibrate — he hated the intrusion of ringing or beeping, but didn't want to miss anything by putting it in silent mode. And as soon as he was out of the shower, Northington began reading his emails, as he was dressing. This Best Seller project was getting more and more complex in the planning, but at the same time, he kept seeing more and more possibilities of it working spectacularly well, and making his company huge sums of money. Some of the messages were irrelevant, and he instantly deleted them, but a few were more time-consuming.

Jeanette was being rather time-consuming this morning too, Tony thought. It wasn't as if *she* was being awarded an OBE. All the dresses she was showing him still looked just as fine as they had done the last time she had asked him. Now they were sitting eating breakfast together in rather frosty silence, Jeanette wearing the white dress with the pale blue and lemon flowers that Hunter had been glad to be able to reassure her looked "eminently appropriate", and Tony munching toast and frowning though his reading glasses at the precise wording of a sentence in an email from the company lawyers.

At half past eight Hunter came into the room and announced that the cab had arrived. Northington liked the down-to-earth image that a Managing Director travelling by cab projected. It also gave him a great excuse for packing his wallet with twenties, which never failed to give him a feeling of satisfaction. He slurped down the remnants of his coffee and Jeanette stood up and smoothed her dress down. As she reached for her hat from the dresser, Tony, thinking to lighten the mood, asked her when she was getting changed. She didn't reply, but a slight change in the colour of her cheeks and a slight compression of her lips let Tony know he had misjudged things, again. But as they got in the cab, Jeanette said, 'I don't want to nag, but have you got your tie?'

'Yes. In my pocket.' Northington liked to have an open collar as much as possible, and always kept a tie in his inside right jacket pocket to put on at the last minute, just before it was needed.

'Where to, guv?' asked the cabbie.

'Buckingham Palace,' said Tony Northington.

For the last month, since the news of his forthcoming investiture had been announced, he had endured constant inquiries as to when he would be visiting the palace. But it was only as the words left his mouth that he suddenly had a sinking feeling. In his other inside jacket pocket he had safely stored the final letter confirming all the details of the ceremony. As Jeanette got in the cab, he reached into this pocket. Nothing there. The sinking feeling was now tinged with panic. He quickly searched through the other pockets. No paper in any of them. The cab was just starting to move.

'Hang on a minute. I just need to get something,' he said in the general direction of Jeanette and the cab driver. The taxi jolted to a halt again, and he got out. He trotted laboriously back up the drive to the house, where Hunter was surprised to see him reappearing so soon, and looking so anxious.

'I've lost the fucking piece of paper with the fucking details on it. Where is the fucking thing...'

He was rummaging in the papers on the dresser in the hall. Hunter stayed calm but immediately set off upstairs, calling over his shoulder, 'I'll have a look in your other jackets, sir.'

As Northington got to the bottom of the papers on the dresser, his phone buzzed. He whipped it out of his pocket, saw it was Jeanette calling, and violently pressed the button to reject the call.

'Fucking woman!' he muttered.

Hunter descended the stairs at an impressive speed, holding a piece of paper.

'Sir I think this may be what you're looking for? It was in the inside left pocket of your other navy jacket.'

Northington looked at it, and grabbed it. 'Yes, this is it. Thank you, Hunter.'

His eyes flickered rapidly right and left as he scanned the first few lines, then stopped half way down and opened wide as his mouth clamped tightly shut. He opened his mouth again just enough to say, 'Fucking Windsor Castle,' before clamping it shut again, as he folded the paper into the correct pocket, and slammed the door behind him on the way out.

Hunter's mouth relaxed into a wry smile. The lads at the Cross Keys would enjoy this one.

'Tony, I'm so sorry. I just didn't realise. I didn't think you had two jackets so similar, and I didn't think about the pockets.'

Northington ignored her. He leaned forward to speak to the driver.

'Do we have to be on the North Circular? Aren't you people meant to know all the short cuts?'

The cabbie, who was listening to LBC, looked up, eyebrows raised, nonplussed. 'See that sign on the partition? The one that says that if you have a preferred route you should tell the driver at the start of your journey?' Then his face relaxed into a good-natured smile. 'To be fair though, this is pretty slow. I was going to stay on it till the M4, but I can hang a right on Western Avenue, and then back down the M25.'

Tony sat back in his seat again. 'Just as long as we make it by ten. That's the absolute deadline.'

'I'll do what I can, guv, I'll do what I can.'

Jeanette was now completely silent. Tony looked at her, and something about her expression made him sit up. 'What is it? What are you thinking?'

Jeanette replied in a small voice, 'Was there anything

else in your other jacket?'

'No, just my tie.' Tony quickly checked the pockets of this jacket. There was no tie.

'There's no tie in this jacket,' he said, ominously quietly, to Jeanette. 'You've managed to find possibly the only jacket in the wardrobe that didn't have a tie in the pocket.'

Jeanette's voice was even smaller as she replied.

'There might have been a tie in the pocket when I picked it out of the wardrobe, and I might have taken it out, and put it on your tie shelf.'

'The tie shelf,' Tony said in the same quiet, even tone, 'is where I keep the spare ties. The garish ones. The outlandish ones. The Christmas present ones. The ones I never fucking wear, as they're not conveniently in my inside right jacket pocket.'

Jeanette shrank back in her seat. 'Maybe we can ring Neville? He might still be at home. Perhaps he could bring a tie?'

Tony's phone was in his hand and ringing his son's number before his wife had finished speaking.

'Neville? Have you set off yet?'

'Yep. I'm nearly there. I thought I'd take a cab. The driver knows some blinding short cuts.'

'You don't have such a thing as a spare tie on you?' Tony was staying remarkably calm.

'Well funny enough, I looked out a rather natty one from my tie shelf, as today's a special occasion, and let me just check — yes! My normal one is here in my inside right jacket pocket. Don't tell me you've forgotten your tie?'

Tony Northington ignored the question. 'You're a

life-saver. Not my life though.' He looked at Jeanette. 'Look, we'll meet you at the entrance.' He fished out the paper, and peered at the details. 'It just says here that the entrance will be clearly signposted.'

'OK. I'll be there in a minute. We're on Birdcage Walk now. Literally thirty seconds away.'

'Neville! It's Windsor Castle! Fucking Windsor Castle! It says it on the invite! Didn't you read the fucking invite?'

'Oh no. That rings a bell. But everyone's been asking me when I'm going to the palace for weeks now, I just—'

'Windsor Castle. Get your driver to use his blinding short cuts. And bring the tie.' Tony ended the call, pressing the button with unnecessary force. He glared at his wife. She still looked uncomfortable.

After a brief silence, she said, 'I think I'll just ring Amelia to check she's going to the right place.'

Tony snorted. His BlackBerry buzzed yet again and he opened up yet another email, as Jeanette carefully found her daughter's number, and called it.

'Amelia, darling, just checking you're OK?… Yes, lovely... And it is Windsor Castle you've arrived at, not Buckingham Palace?... No, no, just wanted to make sure.'

Jeanette mouthed the words to Tony, 'She's there already.'

Then back with Amelia, 'That's splendid dear. We're running just a little late, but we'll—'

Suddenly Tony reached over. 'Here, give me your phone a minute.'

Jeanette handed it to him.

'Amelia? Your father here. Look, can you find a tie

shop, and get me a smart tie? Yes, you'll have plenty of time... Of course I'll reimburse you. Or your mother will, actually... It has to go with a navy suit... No, not that sort of navy suit. I'm not a fucking sailor. Just get a fucking tie.'

He wrenched the phone away from his ear and jabbed at the red symbol to end the call. His finger slid on the screen and he needed another attempt before the faraway sounds of his daughter's protests were silenced.

'Right,' Tony muttered, 'all my offspring are now bringing me ties. Surely between them...'

He lapsed into silence, frowning blankly at the advert on the cab's partition.

Tony, Jeanette, Neville and Amelia Northington were ushered up the magnificent staircase with the other recipients and their guests. Despite his striking new red tie, and the knowledge that he now had another one in his pocket for emergencies, Tony felt positively shabby as they passed the line of household cavalry in their ceremonial attire. At the top of the stairs, the recipients were separated from the guests, and Tony found himself in a large room with dozens of strangers. He felt at a bit of a loss, as these days the only time he met anyone he didn't know would be for some very specific business reason. For a moment he almost relaxed and started to chat to someone, but then he pulled himself together. He would have enjoyed that when he was younger, he was sure, but these days he had other priorities. Instead, he got his phone out again, as it had buzzed at least twice since they had arrived in Windsor.

Shortly, the assembled recipients were talked through

the procedure, and given detailed instructions as to the protocol. Tony took it in, his mind on auto-pilot. He still had a couple of un-answered questions about the company's new project, that he really needed to talk through with Alastair as as soon as possible. Though actually, Neville might have some insight into whether those concerns had already been addressed. He'd ask him as soon as he got a chance. They'd probably be able to get a moment before leaving Windsor. In fact they could share a cab back to the office. Perfect.

The investiture ceremony began.

Before he knew it, Tony Northington was at the head of the queue. A man next to him liberally decorated with gold braid said, 'Go on,' and gave him a gentle push forward.

He walked in a stately fashion to the front of the room, racking his brains as to whether there were any other possible issues he hadn't thought about. The speed and security of the internet connections were obviously going to be paramount, in order to maintain the lightning fast reactions to market stimuli that the system depended on. There would have to be at least one completely separate backup network in place, and easy re-routing of everything.

He had arrived in front of the Queen, who was standing on a dais, and she was leaning forward and pinning the medal on the little hook that had been attached to his jacket earlier.

In terms of the speed and reliability of the actual information that would be reaching them from the overseas markets, there wasn't a lot they could do.

The Queen shook his hand.

The system was designed to work in a completely integrated way, and compensating software kicked in if the feed from one or more market went down, or was subject to interference.

'Is it technology?' she asked him.

'Technology relating to financial markets, yes, your Majesty.'

Just at that moment Tony's BlackBerry buzzed. He froze. Just one buzz though, and he relaxed again. Only an email. He would have hated to miss a call.

'Where would we be without it?' The Queen smiled at him.

'Yes ma'am,' he said.

Tony moved on, but already he was miles away. The algorithms that controlled the rapidity of the new system's response to external financial events — they were the real beauty of the idea, and potentially also its weak point. This carpet he was walking down now, for example. It was comfortable, but not fast. They needed speed, but just enough 'give' to provide a natural feel, and no alarmingly rapid swings. Tony smiled absently at Jeanette as he passed her. He didn't notice Amelia or Neville.

CHAPTER 3

The double bass was lying on its side in the corner beside the baby grand in the big dining room. Its cover had been tucked away under the piano, and it was connected by a lead like an umbilical cord to a small amplifier. The musicians were nowhere to be seen. The chef and the waitress, who had been sent along by the catering company, were busy in the kitchen, the waitress having first made sure the table was set properly, rather to Hunter's annoyance. Hunter himself had briefly stepped out into the warm summer air of the back garden, ostensibly to check the lighting, but in reality to get away from the caterers. He knew he'd have to be back inside soon enough, when the guests started arriving.

Tony was upstairs in his room, changing, having just arrived back from his regular Saturday stint at the office in Holborn. He found this a very productive time to work, due to the pleasing emptiness of the building. He had a lot of his best ideas on Saturdays. This particular

Saturday though, the building hadn't been empty, as he had insisted on a troubleshooting session with the team that were preparing to launch the Best Seller. They had a simulator version of the software that they could put through its paces by inputting various combinations of factors, both historical and fictitious, and then see how it responded. This afternoon's results had been reassuring for Tony, though he wished they'd been able to stay a bit longer. He kept thinking of new variants they hadn't yet tested to exhaustion.

Jeanette, like Hunter, had wanted to get away from the preparations in the kitchen, and had chosen the living room for her escape. She was wearing the same dress she had worn at Windsor Castle the previous week, to try and give a sense of continuity, but she rather hoped this evening would be a more relaxed and enjoyable affair. Most of the other recipients of decorations had gone off immediately after the ceremony to celebrate with their guests, but of course Tony, and in fact Neville as well, as she had realised with disappointment, had insisted they needed to be back in London as soon as possible.

Jeanette glanced at the clock. Ten to seven. People would be arriving any minute now. She must go and get the musicians to start. And just as the thought crossed her mind, she heard the doorbell, and almost immediately from the next room a few tentative chords on the piano, evolving into a tune that sounded vaguely familiar. She relaxed a little. Tunes that sounded vaguely familiar were exactly what she had hoped jazz musicians would provide. Now she could sense the double bass was playing as well, though not exactly notes — surely those were too low to be actual notes? Jeanette quickly glanced at her reflection in the mirror, and reassured by what she saw, went out into the hall where Hunter was just welcoming Molly Raestock, and the waitress was hovering with a tray of champagne flutes.

'Miss Raestock, lovely to see you,' said Jeanette. 'Do come in and have a drink.' She leaned a little closer in and said in a lower voice, 'And the caterers have been simply great so far. You would hardly know they're here!'

Molly Raestock replied with a smile, 'Very happy I could come, Mrs Northington. And I'm glad you like the catering company. I trust your husband's back from work?'

Molly's presence had also been required at the afternoon's brainstorming session, to help with any resulting planning that needed coordinating.

'Yes, he's changing, I think,' Jeanette replied. 'I'm sure he'll be down any minute.'

Even as she spoke, Tony appeared at the top of the stairs, and began to descend. His smile seemed a little forced, but when he got down to the hall he welcomed Molly courteously enough. The doorbell rang again. Hunter opened it to reveal two men, perhaps in their fifties, one carrying a large bunch of flowers, and one a card. Jeanette was closest to the door.

'Alastair! Lovely to see you. And Gerry, so glad you were free.'

'Honoured to be invited,' Gerry Kennedy replied, with a charming smile.

His partner Alastair Forth, just nodded. Tony came to shake hands with them.

'Alastair. Gerry.'

Gerry took a glass of champagne from the tray, and moved away from the door, greeting Molly Raestock warmly. Alastair asked quietly if there were any soft drinks. The waitress, after quickly glancing at the tray and realising there were none on it, excused herself and disappeared into the kitchen. She returned a minute later with a couple of glasses of orange juice and a sparkling mineral water added to her selection of drinks, and a polite apology.

'Not to worry,' said Alastair. 'Thanks.'

The doorbell rang again. Again Hunter opened it. A young man stood there, with short blond hair and wearing a very stylish looking linen jacket. He had a bottle with him. Tony saw him and preempted Hunter's welcome.

'Jasper Felder! Come on in! Make yourself at home. Not literally, of course.' He laughed rather awkwardly at his joke, though Felder didn't smile.

Jeanette shook the young man's hand as he entered. 'Hello Jasper. Nice to see you again. Do have a drink.'

Now he smiled. 'Thanks Mrs Northington, I will. What a beautiful home you have!'

'Oh, thank you. We were very lucky when we bought it all those years ago. I'm very attached to it, though we don't really need somewhere this big anymore.'

'Ah! I like the music! Is that *Stella by Starlight*?'

'Oh, gosh — I really don't know. It certainly sounds familiar, though.'

The hall, though spacious, was filling up now. And before the door could shut behind Jasper, another voice was heard from outside.

'Don't shut it! We're here! Sorry if we're a bit late.'

Neville Northington pushed the door open, and joined the throng in the hall. In his wake came his wife, Louise.

'We had a bit of a mix-up with the baby-sitter,' Neville explained.

'Well, when I say *we*, I mean...' Here he made a humorous grimace in the direction of his slight and pretty wife.

She smiled a self-deprecating smile. 'Yes, I'm afraid I got the time wrong—'

'Louise told the sitter the wrong time. She asked her to be at ours for seven, though we needed to be *here* at seven! I ask you! But you know, I drove like the very devil and,' — here Neville checked his watch — 'I do believe we've made it!'

He took a glass from the tray and raised it towards the group facing him.

'Cheers! Here's to Father's OBE. He's probably saying it stands for Other Buggers' Efforts. He's right! Has he been saying that?'

'I don't think he's really mentioned it,' Jeanette murmured vaguely. 'But nice to see you again, darling.'

'And I'd only just got in from the office,' Neville was still addressing the room. 'But I got straight on the phone to the baby-sitter and...' He moved off towards Molly, who as the first to arrive was now furthest from the door.

Jeanette seized the chance to greet her daughter-in-law. 'Louise, lovely to see you. How is little Josh?'

'Oh, he's very well thanks. He's so lovely.' Louise's face relaxed into a smile, and Jeanette smiled back. 'I sort of don't like leaving him with a baby-sitter, mainly because I miss him! Very soppy of me, I know.'

'Not at all, dear. I completely understand it.'

Neville was raising his voice over the others again. 'I say! Now that everyone's here, we can go through into the back garden. It's a lovely evening. We don't have to stay cramped in here!'

'Though Amelia hasn't arrived yet,' Jeanette said to Louise, looking at her watch. 'I hope she comes. She had a bit of a falling-out with Tony at the investiture ceremony. It was all a bit embarrassing.'

Louise sympathised. 'Neville said something about that. He gave the impression that he had managed to pour oil on troubled waters though.'

'Hmm,' said Jeanette. And then as the doorbell rang again, 'Maybe that's her, now.'

Hunter, who was quite enjoying his limited duties of simply opening the door every couple of minutes, performed this function again. It wasn't Amelia, but a thin, grey-haired priest, who smiled warmly at the assembled company.

'Father White! Do come in,' said Jeanette. 'I'm so glad you could come. This is Neville's wife, Louise. Josh's Mum.'

'Pleased to meet you, Louise,' Father White said. Then turning to Jeanette, 'I hope I'm not late? And sorry I'm not wearing anything smarter. I came straight from a visit.'

'No, not at all,' Jeanette reassured him. 'Amelia hasn't arrived yet. Do help yourself to a drink.'

People were starting to drift out into the garden now. Tony was the first out, a champagne glass in each hand, deep in conversation with Alastair. Neville had finally stopped talking, and was standing rather awkwardly beside Gerry Kennedy, and nodding slightly too much, while his eyes flitted here and there as the other man talked. Jasper was chatting quietly to Molly Raestock, an enigmatic expression on his face.

Father White was now talking to Louise about her son. 'Yes, Jeanette has shown me pictures of him. He seems a sturdy little chap!'

Louise beamed with pride. 'He's simply wonderful,' she replied. 'Neville gets annoyed with him in the night, but I never mind him waking. I relish every moment I spend with him. Probably a bit selfish of me, really.'

Father White smiled. 'I'm sure it isn't. It sounds like he has a very caring mother.'

Neville's voice could be heard calling out, 'More champagne over here, please!'

The waitress hurried over to oblige.

Jeanette, sipping her drink carefully, was starting to relax.

The doorbell rang again at five to eight. This time there was a short pause before the door was opened, as Hunter had been shepherding the guests in from the garden to the dining room. When he opened it, Amelia was on the doorstep, looking rather dishevelled, and clasping by the hand a young man Hunter didn't recognise.

'Hallo Hunter, old bean,' she said. 'This is Ken.'

'Ben,' said the young man.

'Ken has come to enjoy the party with me. I'm pretty sure Dad will welcome him in. Pretty sure. Pretty sure indeed.'

'I'll let Mr Tony know you've arrived,' said Hunter impassively. He turned away from the door to find

Jeanette approaching.

'Miss Amelia,' he announced, with the faintest raising of his eyebrows.

Jeanette passed him and went to the door. 'Hello, dear, come on in,' she said. 'And I see you've brought a friend.' She peered at the young man. 'I don't think we've met? I'm Jeanette.' She smiled and held out her hand.

'I'm Ben,' said Ben, shaking hands. 'Nice house, man!'

'Ken's coming to the party to keep me company,' said Amelia. 'He likes parties. Aren't you going to offer us drinks?'

'Yes, of course. There's a waitress somewhere with a tray.' Jeanette looked round. 'But actually, we're just all going in to eat. Come straight in. I'm sure Hunter will set a place for your, er, your friend.'

Hunter acknowledged this request with a brief nod and moved to carry it out.

Jeanette, followed by Amelia and then Ben (who emitted sporadic low whistles at the fixtures and fittings), led the way into the dining room, where the musicians were now playing a version of *Caravan*. Everyone was noisily sitting down, looking for their names on the cards by each seat. This was one of the things Jeanette, Amelia and Molly had put a lot of effort into. They had tried to work out a seating plan which alternated family and office connections, with Tony and Neville representing both. But Tony had taken for himself the seat in the middle of one of the long sides of the big oval table.

'Alastair,' he called above the music. 'Come and sit at my right hand. And Jasper, over here, on my left.'

Neville was frowning. Tony continued, 'Neville —

you sit straight opposite me. And we'd better have someone to take notes, just in case. Molly — you'd better sit next to Neville, just there. Right!'

Tony looked round at the others. 'The rest of you, sit where you like.'

Jeanette demurred. 'But Tony dear, we've worked out a seating plan. This isn't a business meeting, you know!'

'Of course not. But I'd like to have my team around me, just in case.'

Tony laughed. 'And in any case, this is my home, my business, and also, may I remind you, my OBE!'

Neville smirked and turned to Molly, who was just sitting down next to him. 'It stands for Other Buggers' Efforts!'

Then he turned the other way to where Gerry Kennedy had taken a seat. 'I said it stands for Other Buggers' Efforts! No offence.'

Gerry said, 'Nothing to do with me.'

Neville tried to explain. 'No, I didn't mean it was your efforts, I meant, oh never mind.' He flushed slightly and turned back to talk to Molly.

Gerry smiled and raised his eyebrows discreetly at Alastair, who was listening to Tony tell a story he'd heard before.

Jeanette persisted a little with the seating plan, speaking loudly to be heard over the music, which seemed to have reached a rather boisterous section. 'But, dear, there are little name cards at each of the places...'

Tony picked up the card in front of him, which said Father White. He glanced round the table, and then threw it a couple of places to his right where the priest was just taking a seat. Father White good humouredly set it neatly in front of him. Hunter had now brought in another chair, and the waitress had set another place, between Jeanette and Amelia, which Ben squeezed into.

'Nice chair!' said Ben.

Everyone was now sitting down, and Tony's action with the name card had sparked some copycat moves, adding to the party atmosphere the piano and bass were generating. The music rose to a climax, and then stopped abruptly, just after a reiteration of a section that Jeanette thought she had heard before. As it did so, the waitress appeared with the first plates of the starter. She approached Jeanette and said,

'I've got the vegetarian one here — who is this for?'

'That'll be for me,' called Amelia, who had overheard. She then turned to Ben. 'You're not vegetarian, are you?'

'No,' said Ben. 'Only on aeroplanes.'

The waitress gave Amelia her starter, burrata on yellow pepper coulis, and the first of the regular starters went to Ben, who was, yet again, impressed. 'Thank you very much,' he said with sincerity.

He had never eaten quail before, so assumed it was chicken. He had never eaten lobster before either, but recognised that.

'By the way, Ken' said Amelia, 'Can you pass me some wine? I'm still thirsty.'

'Sure thing, man. Red or white?'

'I don't mind. you decide,' said Amelia.

The pianist and bass player had been conversing together in low voices, and now began a rather relaxed version of *Have You Met Miss Jones*. The waitress kept bringing in starters, and very shortly Hunter appeared, to decant the wine, and proceeded to make a circuit of the table, filling any empty glasses.

Ten minutes later, as *Days of Wine and Roses* began, the starters had been finished, and conversations struck up again. The waitress shortly reappeared and began removing plates. Tony had now noticed Ben for the first time.

'I say, Amelia, you haven't introduced your friend. Jeanette didn't tell me you were bringing someone?' He frowned at his wife.

'Oh, it was a bit of a last minute thing, you see,' Jeanette replied.

'Sorry Father,' said Amelia. 'I didn't think I needed permission. This is Ken, and he's very kind to me.'

'Ben,' said Ben.

'Ken agreed to keep me company tonight, as he likes my company.' She glared defensively round the table, then raised her glass in a toasting gesture.

'We all like your company, dear,' said her mother, rather uncertainly.

'I like your company,' said the grey-haired priest sitting next to her. He smiled kindly as he said it, which rather threw Amelia.

'Of course we all like your company!' bellowed her father. 'Stupid girl.' he said under his breath to Jasper Felder on his left. Jasper sniggered.

'Why don't you tell us about the investiture ceremony, Tony?' asked Molly, perhaps thinking to change the subject.

'Yes do,' agreed Jasper. 'I'd be thrilled to be invited to the palace.'

'Well, it's funny you mention the palace,' began Tony, relaxing into his anecdote.

As he spoke, Alastair listened intently, with a half smile, while Jasper's focus was absolute. Neville, across the table from them, began to frown as he sipped his wine and watched them hanging on his father's every word.

Louise, who had heard a version of this story several times from her husband, turned to Molly on her left. 'It sounds so stressful! I'm quite glad I wasn't there. I'd probably have messed things up in some way!'

'Oh I'm sure you wouldn't,' Molly reassured her. 'With a big occasion like that you'd have been very organised.'

'Do you think so? Yes, I suppose maybe I would. Don't tell Neville, but the reason I booked the sitter for seven tonight, was that he told me we needed to leave shortly after seven. He doesn't remember that of course. You won't tell him I said that, will you?'

'No, of course not,' said Molly. She looked at Louise. 'I'm very discreet. I have to be.'

Louise smiled. 'Thanks,' she said, quietly.

Days of Wine and Roses having drawn to an emphatic conclusion, the musicians had another one of their brief chats, that always seemed to involve some laughter, and then launched into *What's New*.

'Oh, listen! I like this one,' said Tony. 'It's called *So What*. It's by Howard, er, Parker. Excellent.'

'Isn't this *What's New*?' Alastair asked. 'Doesn't that other one have a sort of bass bit at the beginning?'

Tony turned and glared at him. 'Do you always have to be right about everything?'

'Well, no, but I think I'd recognise *So What*.'

'So What?' shouted Jasper. 'Does it matter?'

He looked around the table for appreciation. Tony began to smile. Alastair shrugged. Jasper began drumming his fingers on the table in time to the music.

The main course was now arriving, the waitress now being assisted in this task by Hunter. Once more the vegetarian portion for Amelia came first; an aubergine parmigiana.

Ben whispered to her, 'See, your dad makes sure you're served first. Actions speak louder than words.'

Amelia whispered back rather louder, 'No, Ken. It's because I'm vegetarian I get served first.'

'Oh. I see,' said Ben.

And then his own main course arrived. Beef. He knew what that was. Doubtless cooked in a special way. And though the spinach under it looked rather wilted, he tucked in manfully.

As Tony was taking his first mouthful, the double bass started playing a line which was unmistakably *So What*. Tony spluttered in his eagerness to point this out to Alastair.

'*So What*! It's *So What*! I told you it was *So What*! Sorry Neville, did that get you?'

'Not to worry,' Neville replied as he wiped his glass and the edge of his plate.

Alastair said seriously, 'Well, it might just be a quote from *So What*, not the actual song.'

Just at this point the pianist interspersed the bassist's meanderings with what were very definitely the iconic response chords from *So What*, before returning to the melody of *What's New*.

'See?' gloated Tony, as he heard the two distinctive chords. '*So What*. Case closed.'

'Well,' began Alastair as *What's New* sounded clearly round the room. He thought for a minute, then said, 'So what,' and tucked into his food.

'*So What,*' muttered Jasper with a grin. 'I said it was.'

Two tunes later, and once again the plates were being cleared away. As the final chord of *If I Were A Bell* died away, Jeanette seized the opportunity.

'If I could have your attention just for a moment. To go with the dessert, which is a chocolate mousse, I'd like to announce that I've managed to get one of Tony's favourite dessert wines, Schiava. It's difficult to get hold of, so I hope you enjoy it.'

'Hear hear.' said Tony.

'Speech!' said Neville.

'No, dear,' Jeanette said, leaning across Gerry Kennedy to speak to her son, 'I just wanted everyone to know it was a special—'

The rest of Jeanette's sentence was lost under the opening chords of *Satin Doll*, and the resurgence of general conversation. When she relaxed back into her seat again, Ben, on her left, said,

'Nice speech, man.'

Jeanette turned away from him immediately, to Gerry on her right.

'Gerry, I'm so glad you could come.' She smiled brightly.

'It's a pleasure to be here. I get to do so few social things with Alastair. And one day we'll do something social that has absolutely nothing to do with work!'

'Yes. I can understand that. The office seems to be absolutely flat out at the moment with this new product. But I expect you hear all about that at home.'

'Well, very little, actually. Alastair's very discreet.' He smiled charmingly at Jeanette. 'But I hear enough. And anyway, we do other things together.'

Neville sniggered, and then turned to talk to Molly. Gerry ignored him.

The desserts and the accompanying wine were now appearing on the table.

'You did well with the wine, dear,' Tony called out, then muttered to Alastair, 'Even compliments can be taken the wrong way though!'

Alastair frowned.

'What was that dear?' asked Jeanette, not quite hearing her husband.

'See what I mean?' Tony whispered. Jasper spluttered into his expensive glassful.

'Men!' snorted Amelia, whose hearing was acute.

'Ben,' said Ben.

'Just complimenting you on finding this wine.' Tony replied in a clear voice. 'Absolutely delicious! Thank you!'

CHAPTER 4

The next Tuesday was the day of the final meeting with the Financial Conduct Authority. The senior staff at Northington International who were involved in the new project had been summoned for an eight a.m. meeting, that at this late stage was likely to be simply a pep talk from Tony. The weather had been unseasonably hot, even for July, but just after seven in the morning, as the main doors were unlocked by overnight security for Alastair Forth to enter, the temperature outside was just perfect. The buzz of central London was just at that agreeable level where it radiated energy and optimism, though later in the day, Alastair knew, it would escalate to an incessant, oppressive turmoil. The forecast heat would exacerbate the effect.

He went straight up to his office, initially taking the stairs two at a time, but after the first flight reverting to single steps. Even inside the building, it was hotter than he'd expected today. On the third floor, he crossed the open foyer area and entered his room, on the right, past the second reception desk. It was a strange mixture of order and chaos — his desk was almost empty, and the few items on it (lined notepad, black pen, old fashioned calculator) were neatly arranged in front of his computer monitor. But the rest of the good-sized room had piles of books and boxes of documents stacked apparently randomly, with one whole corner of the floor completely covered in a carpet of papers.

Before sitting down to write his brief summary of the previous month's activity for the finance department, his area of responsibility, Alastair paused, walked over to his window and looked down at the street. He'd been working for the same company, and in fact the same man, for thirty years now. The work had always suited him, but how much longer could he stand the man? And what was he prepared to do about it? It was one of the few things that he and Gerry struggled to discuss rationally, partly because of Gerry's previous company having been clients of Northington International, and his current one being direct competitors. Alastair turned from the window and back to his desk, and as he did so, the thing solidified in his mind as 'a problem', and suddenly he felt sure he could sort it out. Sorting out problems was something he enjoyed. He looked at his watch, realised there was no immediate rush to finish the summary, sat down and began making some rapid notes.

Tony arrived shortly after, but he paid no attention to the beauty of the early morning and dived straight into the building. He was wearing his lightest cotton shirt, and an unlined light-weight fresco suit, that despite looking very sharp (and costing a lot) was incredibly comfortable, even in the hottest temperatures. When Neville arrived, he was similarly attired, as was Jasper.

As they all convened in the small meeting room just before eight, Alastair noticed his colleagues' choice of clothing. He frowned.

'What's with the tropical suits?'

Tony looked confused. 'Didn't you get the message? The air-conditioning isn't going to be working so well today. Hopefully Hobbes from the FCA will be itching to get away by mid-morning. Molly should have emailed you.'

'I got the message,' said Neville, with a grin.

'So did I,' said Jasper.

'This is ridiculous,' said Alastair. 'How hot is it going to be?'

'Difficult to say,' replied Neville. 'The hotter the better, really.'

'You'll just have to sweat it out,' said Tony unfeelingly. 'As soon as the guy goes, we'll crank the air-con up again.'

'Have I got time to run out and get something cooler?'

'Hobbes is due to arrive at nine, and his initial talks will be with myself, and you, as finance director, so, no. But when Molly arrives, give her hell for not copying you in, and maybe she'll send out a girl for something. Anyway, back to business. As far as I can tell, we should be getting the all-clear for our new product today, but let's just go over a few important points. I know we've all referred to it as the Best Seller, but obviously I don't need to tell you that today we will be exclusively calling it the Connected Chain Bond. In my talks with the FCA I've not sensed any opposition to the concept, but if any of you are being pressed on the possible risks of it either spiralling out of control, or being cynically manipulated to maximise profits, the thing to do is to point them to the security software. Explain that the override function will kill any excessive swings, and that the auto-report facility goes further than any other financial product on the market by creating permanent records of every transaction, timed to the microsecond. Neville, and Jasper — you're all over the technical side of that, right?'

'Certainly. I can talk about it for hours,' said Neville.

'However hot it gets,' said Jasper, with a sly look at Alastair.

Tony continued. 'And if they ask what sort of product needs these elaborate precautions, the line to take is that in our view, all investment vehicles should be safeguarded in this way. We're leading the way in risk management. That sort of thing. Look, we've all been over this before, but are there any more questions?'

He looked around the room quizzically. 'Right. I'll see you two later. Alastair — let's make sure we have the paperwork we'll need in here.'

Neville and Jasper left the room.

Alastair said, 'Can I have a quick word first?'

'Of course,' said Tony, glancing at his watch, and starting to leaf through his pile of papers.

'This probably isn't the best time to bring this up,' said Alastair, 'but this air-conditioning stunt is, for me, something of a last straw.'

Tony looked up. He was used to Alastair being the voice of reason and moderation, but today there was something in his tone of voice.

'Carry on,' he said, carefully.

As Jasper and Neville were leaving the meeting room, Molly was arriving. Her office overlooked the third floor reception area, and from it she supervised the activities of the two receptionists, as well as generally managing the offices and taking care of the more delicate tasks that Tony entrusted her with from time to time. Neville slipped in to her office as he was passing.

'Molly, I'm afraid I've got a confession to make. The email about the air-conditioning problems that I asked you to send for me, was missing one name. Alastair's.'

'Oh dear! That's unfortunate.' Molly was moving purposefully round the room, making sure everything was in its place for the day ahead.

'The thing is,' said Neville, 'it's absolutely my fault, but would there be any chance you could cover for me? Things are a bit stressy with him at the moment, and I don't want to cause any more friction.'

'That really isn't fair,' said Molly, straightening up and frowning at Neville.

She was about to say more, but they both became aware of raised voices from outside her office. Molly marched to the door and opened it. The sound was coming from the meeting room, and they could both hear two distinct voices, each trying to shout over the other.

'But the room's soundproofed!' Neville was shocked.

'How loud must it be in there!' Molly was impressed.

The meeting room door swung open violently, and Alastair strode out, red-faced. He stopped near Neville and Molly, gripped the material of his suit and held it out towards them as if for inspection, shrugged as if asking for an explanation, then stalked off down the corridor and went into his own office, slamming the door behind him.

Neville and Molly looked at each other.

'I think you got away with it,' said Neville.

Hobbes arrived at nine sharp, with two others from the Financial Conduct Authority. Tony came down from the third floor to greet them in the entrance foyer.

'Good morning, Tony,' said Hobbes.

'Morning Hobbes. Perfect timekeeping!'

'Thanks. And I think over the past few months you've met both my colleagues? Angela, and Achim?'

'Good to see you again.' Tony shook their hands. 'I must apologise for the heat — the air-conditioning isn't pulling the temperature down as much as it should at the moment. Hopefully we'll get it sorted soon.'

Tony handed the team their temporary security passes and smiled cheerfully as he led them to the lift. 'We'll be on the third floor today. I feel sure we'll be able to give you any information you still need.'

Alastair rose from his seat to greet them when they arrived in the meeting room. He still looked flushed. Tony made the introductions, asked Molly to organise some coffee, and helped everyone get seated and comfortable.

Hobbes kicked off the session. 'We've studied the documentation you gave us very carefully, and in principle, as I've indicated in our previous discussions, we think the product is sound, and doesn't contravene any regulations. But we have a couple of areas of concern.'

Tony nodded. 'If there's anything we can clarify, we

will.'

'I understand that this financial product is modelled on the Whole Chain Investment Strategy that you've used successfully for years, enabling clients to invest simultaneously in all the different components, and companies, involved in the manufacture of one particular product. So that if the product is successful, you get a return on every stage of its manufacture, but if it dies a death, you would have to be extremely unlucky to lose your shirt.'

'Spot on,' said Tony.

'Absolutely,' agreed a straight-faced Alastair.

'Talking of shirts, do these windows open?'

'Really sorry, they don't,' said Tony. 'Oh, here's our coffee. Sorry Hobbes, you carry on while I hand these round.'

'Thanks.' Hobbes added milk to the coffee Tony had given him, and gave it a quick stir. 'And now you're adapting this concept to apply it to complex financial products, rather than the manufacturing sector, with the same basic aim of maximising profit and minimising risk.'

'That's it,' said Tony. 'Milk, Achim? Cream?'

'No thanks, just as it comes.'

'There you go.'

'Well our concerns about this Connected Chain Bond are mainly to do with the potential for excessive swings. I know that the software you put in place with the manufacturing version has worked well, but in that product you're dealing with traded commodities, fundamentally. We feel that the types of financial entities you are seeking to chain together now, make this a wholly different type of exercise.'

'Well, if I could address—'

'Sorry Tony, please let me finish. We have in fact been given by the FCA board the authority to licence the product as it stands, but for my peace of mind, and I know I speak for my colleagues too, we'd like more reassurances as to how your security systems would work in practice.'

Angela Parkes and Achim Nasir were nodding.

'Well,' said Tony, 'Maybe if Alastair talks you through the financial — no, even better. Let's go straight to the modelling stage, and I'll get Neville to come in here and run the simulations for you. Any scenario you can dream up, we can replicate it and see how our new product might react.'

Tony was off his seat and out the door and into Neville's office. His son was seated at his desk with one of the receptionists leaning across it.

'Neville!' Tony barked. Neville's head jerked up from what he was carefully inspecting.

'Get in the meeting room with the simulator software. Impress them.'

'That'll do for now,' said Neville to the girl. 'But I'll need to look at those messages again later. Off you go.'

He unplugged his laptop from his desk, grinned at his father, and said, 'Lead on.'

CHAPTER 5

By mid-morning, the London heat was baking the pavements. However, as Amelia came up out of Holborn tube station into the bustle of Kingsway, she was thrilled to be out in the fresh air again. The tube was very convenient, but in the summer the conditions could be almost inhuman. As she waited to cross the road onto High Holborn, she thought about the sort of fuss animal rights groups would make if livestock were transported in such high temperatures, and with so little fresh air. The green man appeared, and she followed the crowd across the road. She felt bad about her behaviour at the party at the weekend. And now she was going to make amends.

Across High Holborn, up Southampton Place and finally left into Barter Street. The perfect name, she thought, for a road housing the offices of Northington International. She hadn't been there for a long time, and was surprised by how much security there was. Despite Amelia explaining who she was at the front desk, the rather blank-faced man made her wait while he rang upstairs, first to third floor reception, and then to Molly Raestock's office. The reply he received from Molly was obviously satisfactory, as he pulled out a large pad of daily passes for her to write her name and time of arrival on. He didn't seem bad-tempered, but when Amelia wrote 'Father' in the section on who she was visiting, he made her start again. This time she wrote 'Mr Anthony Northington OBE' and she could see the security officer didn't like it, but couldn't really object. The pass had to go on a lanyard round her neck, and then she was allowed through the barriers.

On the third floor there were two more reception desks. Why two? thought Amelia to herself. The girl at the first one was very friendly, but said she thought Mr Tony was in a meeting at the moment. As she said this Molly's door opened at the other end of the foyer area, and Molly appeared in the doorway, on the phone, but waving Amelia towards her. After replying in the affirmative to the reception girl's offer of coffee, Amelia followed Molly into her office.

While the phone call lasted, Amelia glanced round the room. It contained a surprising amount of dark wood, that somehow contrived to look more oppressive than expensive, and a light carpet. But Amelia's eye was immediately drawn to the pictures on the wall, and she moved in for a closer look. There were three of them, all representations of animals, but with their natural hide replaced in the image by a synthetic covering. They were reproductions rather than original artworks, but Amelia found them intriguing. She subconsciously fingered her visitor's pass as she examined them.

'What do you think of the pictures?' Molly was off the phone now.

'Oh, hello Molly. I like them. I find them interesting. Though if I'm honest, I'm surprised to find them in your office.'

'Very perceptive. They weren't my choice, but your father's. He prides himself on buying bits of modern art. You can probably tell he doesn't spend much on them though. Occasionally he tells people he has a daughter who's a successful contemporary artist.'

'Really? I don't think I can remember a single conversation with him when he didn't suggest I got a proper job. How strange.'

The girl from reception now knocked on the door, entered with a coffee, and discreetly slipped out again. Amelia took a first sip, still standing looking at the pictures, while Molly said,

'So, I'm guessing you're here to see your dad. He's officially got meetings all day, but may get a gap at some point, and also,' here Molly pulled her collar away from her neck, 'as you may have noticed, the air-con isn't working as it should. I think he's hoping that will speed his meetings along.'

Amelia frowned. 'Could you call him and see if he can spare me a moment? I'd really appreciate it.'

Molly looked uneasy. 'He did give me strict instructions that he shouldn't be disturbed. The meetings are to do with the new product that...'

Molly saw the look on Amelia's face, and quickly added, 'But obviously family is different. Just give me a minute.'

She left the office. Amelia was frustrated with

herself. Of course he'll be busy. That's what people do at work — they're busy. I must just get over myself. But Molly was back in no time, with a smile.

'Good news, Amelia. They're breaking for refreshments in ten minutes, and probably stepping outside for some fresh air. I'm sure if you were in the foyer here you could grab a word with him.'

'Oh that's brilliant. Thanks so much.'

Amelia spent the next ten minutes in the foyer area, sipping her coffee and examining the slightly duller, more corporate prints on those walls, and briefly trying to peer through the window into Neville's office. The glass, however, was tinted sufficiently to make this impossible.

Eventually the meeting room door opened, and a small group came out. Neville was there, deep in conversation with a couple of men she didn't recognise, as they walked over to the lift. Her father was next out of the room, with a rather plain woman in her mid-forties. Tony was talking animatedly to her, but she seemed fatigued. They were heading for the lift door too.

'Father,' called Amelia.

Tony turned round, eyebrows raised, a fixed smile on his face. 'Amelia! How nice to see you. I'm afraid I'm pretty tied up at the moment, though.'

He took a couple of steps in her direction, his eyes making emphatic signals that Amelia chose to ignore.

'I literally just want thirty seconds of your time,' she said.

'Well, to be honest, today isn't a great day for it, I've got this—'

'Dad, she's gone. The woman got in the lift and it's

gone.' Amelia took a deep breath to steady herself. 'It won't be back for perhaps a minute. Will you talk to me in that time?'

'I've missed the lift! Oh, all right. Talk to me as we walk over to it.'

'Well, thanks for the gracious welcome.' Amelia's good intentions were dissolving rapidly. But she pulled herself back from the brink. She spoke again with an effort at self-control.

'I wanted to apologise for being rude at your party.'

'Apology accepted. I didn't want to be there either. Is that all?' Tony looked at his watch. But Amelia's composure held.

'And I wanted to invite you to the opening night of my new exhibition, in September.'

'Ah. That's not great timing, I'm afraid. My new bond goes live on the 19th, and I couldn't really justify taking time off so close to that date.'

The lift had now arrived again, and Tony got in as he finished speaking. 'But thanks for inviting me, and all that, er, sort of thing.' He was stabbing at the lift buttons now as he talked.

'Hope it goes—'

The lift doors had shut on him. Amelia stood there, cold with fury. The receptionists very professionally ignored her. Then she heard a man's voice.

'It's Amelia, isn't it?'

Jasper had stayed in the meeting room for a couple of minutes to let the simulation software run to the very end of its current projection, and then reset it. He had closed down the software, and was wandering out of the room, when he saw Amelia. He walked towards her.

'Are you OK? I think you've just missed your father.'

'I didn't miss him. I just wasn't *trying* to kill him this time.'

'Oh dear! Sounds serious. Come and cool down in my office.' Jasper smiled and leaned towards her. 'Don't tell anyone, but I've got a portable air-conditioner in there.'

A reluctant smile appeared on Amelia's lips. She followed him into his office, which was very near the lifts. It was noticeably cooler, and as Jasper closed the door, he motioned for her to take a seat in one of the two comfortable leather chairs opposite his desk. As she sat, her eyes flicked round the room and she noticed some more intriguing modernist prints.

'How can you stand working with him?' she eventually said. 'All my life I've tried to connect with him, but he's always too busy. And if anything, he's getting worse as he gets older. And then when I visit his work, I find he's accessorised the building with his idea of contemporary art, and apparently tells people his daughter is a successful artist. Though I guess if you're connecting with him at work, you might not have the same issues. Adequate as a boss, definitely not as a father.' Amelia re-crossed her legs, and sighed. 'I'm sorry to take this out on you. We've only met a couple of times. But he makes me so mad.'

She sank down in the chair. Jasper waited till he was sure she had finished. When he spoke again, his voice wasn't completely steady. He paced around as he talked.

'I'm so sorry to hear that. I obviously can hardly know what he is like as a father, but I sort of hoped that would be where his good side would come out.'

He cleared his throat.

'You've spoken frankly to me in confidence, so I'll return the compliment. At one point I thought he and I could have some sort of friendship — I thought he saw me almost as one of the family. He spotted my potential when I arrived in London from the Netherlands, fast-tracked me for promotion and got me involved at the highest level, along with your brother. And then I made the mistake of bringing up the subject of my relationship with him. He was furious. He said a lot of things, but basically he wanted me to know that work was where it started and finished. I was younger then, and completely devastated.'

Jasper stood still now, and stared out his window. 'So I know a little bit about how you feel.'

'You know why I came?' Amelia sounded calmer now. 'I just wanted to invite him to my new exhibition. He said it was bad timing, and he wouldn't be able to make it.'

'When is it?'

Amelia smiled. 'September. It opens on the evening of the second. It's just some more of my pickled machines. Live electronics suspended in a solution of cetohyde, so they'll still work, but look like they're under water.'

Jasper had his phone out. 'Well I can definitely be there, if you'd like me to be? I know it's not the same as family though?'

'I'd be delighted,' said Amelia. 'That'd be lovely.' She smiled warmly now. 'Thanks.'

'I'll look forward to it,' said Jasper.

From the lobby outside his office came the sound of Neville Northington telling an amusing anecdote. Jasper winced.

'I'd better go,' he said. 'Stay here till you're cool.'

And he was gone, back to the group, back to the humid heat of the meeting room and the simulator software.

Amelia had stayed for about half an hour in Jasper's office after he had left. The portable air-conditioning unit had done a very good job of cooling the room, and with it, Amelia's disturbed psyche. She often found it hard to be philosophical about things, and she always found it hard to be philosophical about the way her father treated her. As she thought about it now, she realised that possibly it was entirely appropriate to be angry about the way he constantly dismissed her, rather than bleakly accepting. This realisation didn't make her any less angry, but it meant that at least she didn't add to her overworked emotions a sense of guilt at being angry. She savoured this feeling for a while. Maybe she was growing up. It was probably time — after all she'd soon be thirty. And to nip in the bud the guilt she started to feel about not having a mature attitude till she was nearly thirty, she got up and left the office.

Mid afternoon, back at home, and going over some of the practical arrangements for her exhibition, she had a call from Ben. They chatted for a while, then on the spur of the moment she suggested he bring some food round that evening and cook it for her, as she was working. Ben sounded a little confused, but agreed.

He arrived about eight, with a bottle of wine. 'It's white, my favourite,' he announced.

He had remembered that Amelia was vegetarian, and

so had brought a frozen packet of mixed diced vegetables for them to share, and a beef pot noodle for him. Amelia, busily experimenting with exhibition layouts on squared paper, with small card rectangles representing her display tanks, laughed when she saw what he had brought.

'That will be lovely, Ken. The kitchen's just through there. Pour me a glass, will you? I'll keep going at this till the food's ready.'

She went back into the front room where she was working, and could just hear a quiet, 'Ben,' from Ben in the kitchen. He was very sweet. Very sweet and very young — she didn't actually want to find out just how young.

The food, when it arrived, was surprisingly tasty. The mayonnaise and grated cheese helped, as did the pepper that Amelia ground over her plate, and as did the wine.

'Thanks, Ken,' she murmured as she snuggled up to him on the sofa. 'You did well. That was delicious. Be a dear, and fill my glass, will you?'

Ben stopped fiddling with the buttons on the TV remote and reached for the nearly empty bottle.

Her phone rang. Mr Anthony Northington OBE, the screen said. She pressed the reject button. Her warm and relaxed mood instantly disappeared. It was replaced by a painful tension in her chest, and a bitter taste in the back of her mouth.

'Hurry up,' she snapped.

Ben looked hurt. Amelia winced. What was she doing, talking to him like that? She sounded just like her father. And as quickly as it had come, the tension eased as she said, 'Sorry Ben. I've had a bad day.'

'Ben,' said Ben, automatically.

They opened another bottle, and Ben found a programme about Rembrandt. 'Hey, this guy's an artist. You like art, don't you?'

'I love it.' Amelia smiled.

Her phone beeped. A text. 'Sorry, Ken, just let me read this and I'll be with you.'

It was from Tony. She got up and wandered into the kitchen as she read it.

Your mother has suggested that I may be able to make your exhibition opening after all. Thought you'd like to know. TN.

The painful tension was back, as was the bitter taste at the back of her throat, as was a strangely specific desire to kill her father, by choking him. And along with these feelings came a girlish pleasure, a shy excitement, that her dad was going to come to her exhibition. She leant over the sink, holding her head in her hands. She read the text again, experiencing the same conflicting sensations.

Standing upright again, she looked on the top shelf. Plenty more bottles. Then another though occurred to her. She quickly ran upstairs, and rummaged in the back of her top drawer. Yes. She took the small plastic bag downstairs, and cleared a space on the kitchen table.

'Ken,' she called through to the next room, 'Change of plan. We're going out. And I've got a treat for you here first.'

'Ben,' came the reply. 'Just coming.'

He shuffled through in his socks. 'Wow!' he said, and his eyes lit up.

Then a flicker of concern crossed his face. 'You

haven't forgotten you're a vegetarian, have you?'

'No...' Amelia looked up briefly at Ben, puzzled.

'OK. Just checking. I just assumed that vegetarians couldn't... Or maybe wouldn't... Oh, nothing... '

Amelia ignored him now. She had a kitchen knife out and was marshalling powder, and harrying stray clumps into formation.

'Right. Here we go.'

CHAPTER 6

It was now the second of September, and despite the beautiful late summer sunshine, the Chromium Gallery in Pavilion Road had its blinds drawn by late afternoon. This particular day had in fact been so hot and oppressive that people had been complaining of headaches and forecasting thunder since breakfast time. But the gallery had been a hive of activity since well before then. Its previous exhibition had only just closed, and the exhibits removed overnight. Amelia's pieces had been arriving since first thing, and the gallery had hired in extra help to get everything set up in the short time available. The advance planning had been meticulous, and so far everything was going smoothly.

The blinds had been drawn as the electricity supply to the final pieces was being connected. It was only possible to check that all the visual elements were working as they should, by checking each exhibit both in bright daylight, and in more subdued lighting conditions. Laurence, the gallery owner, had been hugely supportive of Amelia ever since her last exhibition, and as the room was darkened, he was sitting beside her on a leather sofa at the side of the exhibition space, encouraging her to take a few minutes out before the adrenalin rush of the opening evening. So they were ideally positioned for the change of ambience created by the darkening of the room. The building was well air-conditioned (and of course humidity-controlled), and though by this time of day the sun's rays were no longer shining directly into the west-facing room, there was still some heat from reflected light that was cut off as the blind came down.

The very pale grey of the walls had appeared almost white in the bright sunshine, but now the faint colouring became a living shadowy presence at the edges of the space. Darker hues seemed to be rippling up and down the vertical surfaces, perhaps generated by faint imperfections in the smoothness of the plastering. The ceiling retreated from view with the fading light, creating a sense of openness and expansiveness. But strangely this was immediately supplanted by a feeling of intimacy and closeness, as the possibility of the roof being infinitely high was replaced by an awareness that it might be creeping closer, in a comforting way.

After the blind was fully lowered, and everyone's eyes had adjusted, the electricity supply to the exhibits was finally switched on. In a quiet room, with the effect of the darkness magnified by the recent presence of bright light, the impact was astonishing. Like a city seen at night from the air, like a Christmas tree in a darkened room, like phosphorescent sea creatures seen from a small boat on a warm night, the transparent tanks containing the circuit boards and components blinked and twinkled into life. The two sophisticated urbanites were suddenly in fairyland. Laurence was entranced. Amelia, who should have known what to expect, was completely undone. The pieces had all been designed from a slightly cynical and avowedly intellectual point of view, and she simply wasn't prepared for how pretty the overall effect was. As Amelia relished the enjoyment of this sensation, she was transported back to childhood, and almost with a child's perspective she said to Laurence,

'I hope my mother likes this.'

He squeezed her hand briefly. 'She'll absolutely love it.'

'And my father's coming too.'

Amelia had been aware of this all day, as she supervised the final setup, but had thrust the thought to the back of her mind. Now though, she let the idea take on solidity, and she savoured it for a moment. It felt good.

'He'll love it too,' said Laurence.

By eight o'clock, the gallery was buzzing. Amelia and Laurence had combined address books when they sent out the invites, so everyone — from the great and the good of the contemporary art world, to Amelia's oldest friend Cheryl, from primary school — was there. Ben was mixing indiscriminately, enthusiastically pointing out that Amelia had organised the exhibition all by herself, and that he'd been there as she had moved little models of the pieces round, to work out where they could be best positioned.

Champagne was flowing, and Jeanette had loaned out

Hunter for the evening, as she felt he added a certain gravitas to any event. So he was moving through the crowd, discreetly replacing empty glasses with full ones. One of Amelia's art school friends had gone on to work as a DJ, and as the evening wore on he was there with his special play-list of tunes, that had either been created or treated so that all the sounds were either very low or very high in pitch. This left the frequencies used for speech acoustically empty, meaning that despite the exciting feeling of energising music playing, conversation at a normal volume was possible.

At Laurence's insistence, Amelia had hiked her prices significantly since her last show. And at Amelia's insistence, Laurence had replaced the traditional little red sticker indicating a piece had sold, with a small adhesive circuit board, that displayed a bar code. By nine thirty, Amelia noticed with a thrill of surprise, many of the pieces already had these in place.

By ten thirty, some of the earlier attendees had left, and Amelia was surrounded by a hardcore fan base of friends and family. As the gallery was very much in a residential area, it had an eleven o'clock curfew for evening events, so people were starting to talk of where to go next.

Jeanette said, 'Well I haven't got the energy I used to have. I'll leave you young things to it, and head back to Hampstead. Hunter will escort me safely home, I'm sure.' She glanced across to where he was unobtrusively loading a tray with empties.

Amelia suddenly realised with a sinking feeling she hadn't seen Tony all evening.

'What about Dad? Did he have to leave early? I don't

think I saw him at all.'

Jeanette looked embarrassed. 'Well, dear, I've got a feeling that he had a last minute engagement. He did come home, but was muttering something about a conference call.'

'At this time of night?' Amelia was indignant.

'You've got to remember, dear, he phones people all over the world. Who knows what time zone he—'

'I've got to remember no such thing. Hang on a minute. Are you saying you don't think he came at all?'

'Well I'm not absolutely certain he didn't, but to be honest, no, I don't think he did come.'

Cheryl from primary school chimed in, 'Well, surely he's allowed to miss one every so often?'

Amelia turned to face Cheryl. 'Do you remember seeing him at any of my exhibitions? Ever?'

Cheryl didn't.

Ben tried to be conciliatory. 'Well, let's think of a really great place where we can continue the evening.'

Neville barged his way into the group. He looked rather merry, as did Jasper , who was with him. Amelia could also see Alastair hovering just behind them, though not looking so merry.

'Well done little sister! I insisted the guys from the office came. They think the show is brilliant. Don't you guys? Go on, tell her.'

Amelia preempted them. 'Did you insist your managing director came? Did you? Because he didn't, you know.'

Neville looked rather taken aback. Jeanette tried to calm Amelia.

'I'm sure he had a legitimate excuse, dear.'

Amelia stared hard at her mother. She was trying to work out if Jeanette really believed what she had just said. She had never known her to consciously tell a lie. So she was not surprised when Jeanette qualified her statement.

'At least he may have done. I can see why you're upset. He did say in the end that he would be here.'

Amelia smiled grimly. 'He did indeed, Mother. Though I think he's better off elsewhere now. The only drink I'd offer him now would be — here she looked round for inspiration — a glass of the cetohyde from one of the exhibits.'

'I bet that tastes pretty nasty,' said Neville with an unpleasant grin.

'Oh I've no idea what it tastes like, but it's actually poisonous,' gushed Ben. 'It has to be ordered specially and stored in a locked cupboard, it's so poisonous.'

He glanced round to see who he'd impressed.

'Oh Amelia, I'm sure you don't mean it,' murmured Jeanette.

'I certainly do. And I challenge any of you standing round here to say you've never thought of killing him. Apart from you, Ken, of course. You haven't known him long enough.'

There was a chorus of protests against any intention in that particular direction, and a quiet 'Ben,' from Ben.

The mild-mannered Father White had now joined the group. He was always a keen judge of character, and the fact that Jeanette seemed to include him in all sorts of family occasions made Amelia well disposed towards him. Maybe he could explain the twisted way in which Tony's absence during the evening was such a bad thing, and yet now his presence in her head, haunting her thoughts, was also a bad thing. Then again, maybe not. He was only a priest.

But just now there was partying to do.

'I don't believe any of you,' she said. 'But before we're all serving life sentences, let's grab a couple of cabs and hit the town.'

The party trooped out into the street, a tiny but energetic rabble, and began casting this way and that for taxis. As the confused group swirled around, the first heavy drops of rain began to spatter on the dry tarmac around them, rapidly increasing to become a deluge.

CHAPTER 7

By the 19th of September, the date of Northington International's new product launch, the weather had cooled a little. There was a slight crispness in the air, and a sense of nature taking stock, gathering in what resources it could, and bracing itself for what lay ahead.

But on the third floor of the Holborn office, in Tony Northington's inner sanctum, the mood was expansive and optimistic, and if there was any bracing, it was in anticipation of plenty, and if there was any taking stock, it was only literally. There was however a crispness in Tony's white shirt, just in case of any media opportunities.

It was ten o'clock in the morning, and the company's new Connected Chain Bond was due to be issued onto the markets at midday. There had been a few nervous moments with the FCA first thing, as Hobbes had been in touch to raise some last minute concerns about the transparency of the connecting mechanism. Tony had been forced rather into the role of salesman at this point, as he 'didn't have at his fingertips' the precise technical details Hobbes was seeking. But what he did have was a good track record of successful, responsible products, including the Whole Chain Investment Strategy, which was as close a product as it was possible to get, at least in concept. And he did also have great skills both with clients and interfering regulatory authorities, so eventually, having made a couple of concessions involving increased reporting of short term results, and providing within one week exact technical details of the connecting mechanism which concerned Hobbes, the clearance for the product launch was given. He was confident that Neville and Jasper between them could come up with answers which would reassure the FCA.

As Tony put down the phone, he stood up and walked to the window. He looked down at the street, with a deep feeling of satisfaction, and suddenly had a sense of déjà vu, which he couldn't quite place. Then it dawned on him. This was exactly what successful businessmen were always shown doing in films, to symbolise their achievements. Even though his office was only on the third floor (he wasn't keen on heights) the pedestrians down there looked pretty small. He laughed suddenly at the extra metaphor that had occurred to him. Tony Northington, a giant among men. Maybe he could consider moving his office up a couple of levels. There were eight to choose from, after all. A bigger room might be a good idea too. Though then he'd have to get more art for the walls. That reminded him — Amelia's exhibition. He must remember to text her and say that something important had come up on the night of her launch. Wouldn't do to neglect his own family. Then an even better idea occurred to him. He strode back to his desk, and buzzed for Molly. A minute later she knocked at his door. When she didn't immediately enter, he barked,

'Come!'

'Sorry,' she said as she came in, 'for some reason I was thinking of Mr Neville, and he doesn't like me to open the door till he gives the all clear. What can I do for you?'

'I'd like you to get me one of Amelia's pictures from her new exhibition. For my office. That wall over there has some space.'

'Certainly Mr Tony, I'll try. I'll get in touch with the gallery, and see what I can find. What sort of budget were you thinking of?'

'Just a small one, really. Whatever the smallest one costs. We have a decorating budget, or you could see what's left in this year's art investment account. Use your initiative.'

'OK.' Molly made a few notes. 'Was there anything else?'

'No. Nothing more.' Then Tony's face relaxed into a broad grin. 'Only that we've got the final go-ahead for the Best Seller! That's all!'

Molly didn't look as impressed as Tony had hoped. In fact she looked rather concerned.

'But I thought that was signed off ages ago?'

'Well, there were just a couple of things that concerned the FCA, but that's all sorted now. Nothing to worry about.'

Molly still looked worried. 'Mr Tony, I don't want to push my nose into other people's business, but is everything all right? You know everyone talks to me, so I can't help knowing that Neville and Jasper seem a little bit uneasy with each other, and as for Alastair, he seems to be in a sad little world of his own these days. I mean, they all do their jobs well, brilliantly in fact — I never have to remind them about deadlines or anything like that, but, you know... And now hearing you say there had been some issues with the BS Bond—'

'The what?'

'Sorry. The Best Seller. Surely you know everyone calls it the BS Bond?'

'No, I didn't,' replied Tony. 'But that's actually quite funny. Carry on.'

'Well, all this just made me wonder if there was some sort of trouble, that's all.'

Tony thought for a minute, then started slowly walking round the room as he talked.

'I've always been very frank with you, and it sounds like everyone else has been too. And I can assure you there's no trouble at all. The new bond, the BS Bond, (here he grinned) has been okayed. Jasper and Neville sparring — that's just testosterone, and that sort of competitiveness is good for maintaining standards. As for Alastair, I might as well tell you that he challenged me recently with some concerns he had about my running of the business. He didn't like my answers, and to my disappointment hasn't stopped sulking since. But the bottom line is, as you say, they all do their jobs extremely well, so all is good.'

He was at the window again now, and turned round and smiled. He looked briefly at his watch.

'We've less than two hours now till the launch, and

I'm planning a brief Occasion in the third-floor foyer here, so if you could make sure that all heads of departments, and their assistants, are here at about a quarter to twelve, that would be fantastic.'

He thought for a minute. 'I want enough people there so it looks full. Make sure the more positive people come.'

By 11.50 the open area in front of the reception desks on the third floor was crowded with employees happy to take a bit of time away from their desks. Molly had done her job well, and there was a buzz in the air. Tony stepped out of his office to address them just as Neville was arriving in the lift. A compact PA system had been brought into the foyer, and Tony spent a bit of time getting the little microphone clipped to his lapel, and checking he was connected. He didn't think his voice needed any amplification, but the speakers were vital for the second part of his Occasion.

'One, two, testing, testing.'

The assembly became much quieter, and Tony climbed onto the dais that had been rustled up.

'Ladies and gentlemen, unaccustomed *as I certainly am not* to public speaking, (a few sniggers) I find myself slightly nervous today. Nervous, you ask? Tony Northington, nervous? (a few more sniggers) Who was that laughing? (mock outrage) Take those peoples' names, Miss Raestock! (more laughs) You'll be relieved to hear that, no, I'm not finally losing it. And no, I'm not getting timid in my old age. The nerves in fact are purely nerves of excitement, as our new Connected Chain Bond goes live in, oh, about six minutes now.'

At this point Tony looked at Jasper, who was

presiding over the PA system, and briefly raised his eyebrows. Jasper nodded, his attention flicking back to the watch that he had set in front of him, and to the music app on his phone, which was connected to the speakers.

'Excitement,' continued Tony, 'to be in the driving seat of a company that can launch a product that is known in advance as the Best Seller. Excitement about the profits we're going to clear. And excitement about—'

At this point Tony's phone buzzed in his pocket. He paused to see if it would continue vibrating, and would therefore be a phone call. It did. He got his phone out — the screen said Jeanette. She never rang him at work — it must be something very important. He suddenly remembered the moment when he hadn't checked his phone when talking to the Queen, and felt extremely noble as he quietened the crowd with one hand, turned his face away and said in a low voice,

'Hello, what's wrong?'

'Oh hello, Tony. I'm sorry — I've rung you by mistake. But how nice that you picked up my call. What are you up to at the moment?'

Tony turned back round to the group of expectant employees, and smiled, still on the phone.

'Actually, I'm just in the middle of making a speech.'

As Jeanette replied, Tony furrowed his brows in mock despair, and mouthed the words, *'It's the wife,'* to the delight of those assembled.

'Oh, that's nice,' she said. And then, 'What, you're making a speech this very minute?'

'Yes, this very minute, dear.'

This time his expression feigned exasperation, and

the bursts of laughter this evoked in his audience must have been audible to his wife, as she immediately hung up.

Stung at no longer having the game on his terms, Tony muttered, 'Stupid woman,' as he pressed the lock button on his BlackBerry and put it back in his pocket. Due to his lapel mic, this comment was clearly audible throughout the foyer, and Tony, embarrassed and cross now, swiped at the mic angrily. Jasper, who hadn't been listening to Tony at all, but had been concentrating intently on his part of the presentation, which depended on split-second timing, now pressed play on his phone.

The distinctive opening musical salvoes of Europe's The Final Countdown now filled the area. This deflected attention from Tony, who had finally succeeded in extricating himself from his wiring, and now turned smartly and disappeared into his office, slamming the door behind him.

By the time the song was drawing to a close, he had recovered himself sufficiently to reappear, smiling, and chant along with the countdown from ten to one that Jasper had overlaid on the song's outro, and to grab again the tiny microphone from where he'd tossed it to proclaim at the very end,

'The Connected Chain Bond is live now! Let's sell some BS!'

And then he quickly disappeared back into his room.

CHAPTER 8

November began with an unusually mild day. There had been plenty of mist around all morning, spreading right into the centre of London, but the ambient temperature was comparatively high. Molly Raestock was in her office after lunch, and had just slipped her shoes off. Open on her computer monitor was some email correspondence between Northington International and the FCA, but open in a window obscuring it was a video of a kitten and a puppy running round and round in circles. Most of those whose offices were on the third floor were out of the building this afternoon, and she was taking the opportunity to relax a little. The clocks had just gone back, and though this made the mornings lighter, Molly knew she'd have to brace herself for when she would look out the window about five o'clock, and find it virtually dark outside. The front of her desk was panelled, so any visitors to her office would not know that she had slipped her shoes off, nor that she kept a little footstool under there, for occasions such as this.

She was beginning to breathe more slowly, with her eyelids just beginning to droop, when Samantha on reception buzzed through to her.

'Molly, there's someone at downstairs reception with a delivery for Mr Tony. Some artwork, I think they said. Shall I ask them to come straight up?'

'Oh thanks, Sam. Yes, just get them to come on up. It'll be the new thing for Mr Tony's room. I think it will fit in nicely. Can I leave you to supervise it?'

'Yes, of course,' said Sam, pleased with the responsibility.

'Lovely. You do that, and I'll come and have a look when I've finished what I'm doing now.'

Molly put the receiver down, adjusted the back of her office chair to a slightly less business-like angle, and let her eyelids succumb to gravity.

She awoke with a start some time later, with a stiff neck, a very dry mouth, and a sudden sensation of panic, as her room was almost completely dark. As she shifted from her uncomfortable position, her feet slipped off the footstool, and she almost fell off her seat. This further wakened her, and as she walked across the office to switch the main light on she began to recover her composure.

Lights on, blinds drawn, shoes back on, a glass of water from the dispenser in the corner and a quick freshen up in the mirror, and she felt ready for anything. She had by now established that the time was four-thirty, and that what she wanted most was a black coffee, so she went out into the foyer in search of one.

Sam was happy to prepare the drink, and as she did so, Molly remembered the picture that arrived just before she fell asleep. Sam gave her the coffee.

'Oh thanks, Sam. That's lovely. Did they get the picture up OK?'

Sam frowned. 'The picture?'

'Yes. You know, it was arriving just as I went — just as I carried on with my work. Did they hang it OK? I hope it was obvious where it went?'

Sam's frown deepened. 'I hope I haven't messed up. You'd better come and have a look.'

With a feeling of unease Molly followed Sam into Tony's office. Unlike his son, Tony never left his room locked during the day. There was a very obvious blank space on the wall, and just under it, wrapped carefully in cardboard and bubble-wrap, something that looked rather like a small desk, or a table football set without the handles.

'Oh! What have they sent us?' said Molly.

She approached the object and picked up the docket from the top of it.

Chromium Gallery, Pavilion Road. Amelia North — Life's Bright Idea.

'OK,' Molly said slowly, 'this title matches the piece I ordered. But why would a picture be on legs?'

'Shall we open it up?' ventured Sam.

'Let's do it,' said Molly. 'I'm intrigued.'

The two women began peeling off the tape holding the bubble-wrap in place, and then the cardboard packaging. First the legs were revealed — striking constructions made of what looked like perspex, with strands of naked copper wiring encased in them, and terminating in substantial feet which all seemed to be fitted with the sort of socket a kettle had. Molly and Sam looked at each other.

'Well, we might as well finish unwrapping it,' said Molly.

They removed the final layer of card from the top to reveal an oblong tank, made of the same perspex as the legs, filled with a transparent liquid and an assortment of what looked like electrical components. Some were arranged in the shape of a traditional light-bulb, while others were piled, seemingly randomly, in one corner of the tank. A slim leaflet was taped to the top, and some sort of tap, or valve, could just be seen on the bottom.

There was a knock at the open door. Molly and Sam turned round to see Jasper there with an inquiring smile on his face.

'What's going on?' he asked. Then spotting the discarded packaging, he said, 'Ah! There's been a delivery. How exciting. What is it?'

'Well, maybe you could tell us,' replied Molly. 'I ordered a piece of art from Amelia's new collection on Mr Tony's instructions, and they've sent us this strange contraption, whatever it is.'

Jasper's smile broadened. 'I think I can help you. I went to the opening night of the show, and all the pieces were somewhat like that one.'

He came a bit closer, and had a look. 'They plug into the mains — look that might be a socket on its leg — and all bits of circuit board come to life, and twinkle, and some of them move around.' He pulled the leaflet off the top of the tank and started looking through it.

'The ones in the show looked very striking. A lot of them were considerably bigger than this, too.'

'That figures,' said Molly. 'This was the cheapest one

I could find. I just assumed it would be a picture. I'm too old fashioned, I suppose.'

Jasper put the leaflet into his pocket and bent down to examine the sockets on the legs.

'Let's plug it in, and see what it looks like. All we need is a kettle lead. Sam, could you fetch one?'

Sam nodded eagerly, then frowned. 'Where will I find one?'

Jasper and Molly looked at her.

Eventually Molly whispered, 'On the kettle,' and Sam ran off to fetch it.

Jasper was taking charge. 'Can we pull it out from the wall just a bit? I think that might look good.'

He and Molly managed it between them, and then Sam entered again with the lead.

'Here you go,' she said.

Jasper connected it to the closest leg of the piece, and then plugged the other end into the mains socket. 'I tell you what, why don't we switch the lights off first, for maximum effect?'

Molly did so, and after a short pause, as their eyes grew accustomed to the gloom, Jasper reached down again and and switched the socket on.

To begin with, nothing happened. Then all at once, the components that formed the light-bulb shape began to emit light in various ways. Some were fitted with tiny LEDs, others had miniature display screens and yet others had a sort of phosphorescent glow that came and went. The pattern in which the lights appeared and disappeared seemed too organised to be random, but it was very difficult to pin down any exact sequences. Then things started happening in the heap of components at the corner of the tank.

Everyone's attention was attracted by various tiny movements in the pile, and gradually the pieces near the edge of it began to move away from the others. Some had legs like tiny crabs, some had wheels, and some had no visible means of propulsion, yet seemed to move smoothly and easily through all three dimensions. The pile gradually diminished as the little fragments of circuitry extricated themselves, and one after another began to move around the tank. As with the lights, their movements didn't seem haphazard, and yet it was almost impossible to mentally superimpose an overall structure on the choreography. And as with the lights, the desire to work out the patterns became so strong, that it was very difficult for the viewers to tear their gaze away. Also, as Amelia herself had realised only just before her show began, the combined effect of the lights and the movement, seen through the unusual filter of a layer of transparent liquid, was extraordinarily pretty.

'It's beautiful,' whispered Sam.

'It's absolutely gorgeous,' breathed Molly.

'It's very cleverly designed,' said Jasper, quietly.

Suddenly the three of them were aware of a fourth presence in the room.

'But what is it?' asked Tony Northington, reverently.

No-one had noticed him enter, but he too was staring, transfixed. The blinds had not yet been drawn in his office, and the street-lights and distant illuminated skyscrapers seen through the window made a very effective and appropriate backdrop for the piece. Molly was suddenly nervous.

'It's from Amelia's show. Remember, you asked me to

get something.'

'Yes, I remember,' said Tony. His eyes were still fixed on the moving and twinkling lights in front of him. 'I knew she did contemporary art, but I didn't expect this. How long has she been making things like this?'

'Her last exhibition apparently contained some similar items, but wasn't as sophisticated,' said Jasper. He too was keeping his eyes firmly on the display. 'That was a couple of years ago now.'

'It's very beautiful,' said Tony. 'Though obviously don't tell Amelia I said that.'

After another minute of silent gazing, he reached out and switched the lights on. He then moved across the room to close the blinds. The illumination levels of Amelia's piece increased in line with the background lighting, but the magic moment was over.

'I hope we put it in the right place?' asked Molly.

'Yes, yes, it's fine there.' Tony's voice was business like once more. He looked at his watch. 'Well, clocking off time, if I'm not mistaken.'

He smiled brightly round the room. 'Thanks for your help setting it up. See you all tomorrow.'

Jasper, Molly and Sam filed out of Tony's office. Jasper headed back to his room in silence, and Sam went to get her coat, after checking her reception desk one last time. Molly went back into her own room, and sat down in her other chair, the one facing the desk. She still felt slightly jet-lagged after her unplanned sleep, and sat there musing, for some time, before reverting to her usual brisk manner and getting her things together, ready to go home. As she left her office, she noticed Tony's light was still on, and a casual glance was enough to establish that he was standing staring at his daughter's creation. Molly smiled, and walked over to the lift.

CHAPTER 9

Despite the weather being cold and wet on the day of the Northington International Christmas meal, things started well. Tony had warned Jeanette that Alastair had been bad tempered for months now, and that his tactic was to ignore it. But when he and Gerry arrived at the Northington's house, they couldn't have been more charming. Jeanette bumped into Tony upstairs as she was putting their guests' coats in a spare bedroom.

'Alastair's being absolutely lovely,' she said. 'What were you saying about him being grumpy all the time?'

Tony frowned, and followed her into the room. 'Well, it's a funny thing, that. About a week ago he came into work all smiles, and has been behaving like a normal human being again ever since.'

'Well that's great. I'm pleased,' said Jeanette.

Tony sighed and sat down on the corner of the bed.

'Yes, it's less wearing, certainly. But don't get too excited, as Jasper's been a bit odd recently, so just bear with him if he starts getting cranky. He's come to me a few times wanting to speak privately about personal matters, but even if I humour him, he just tends to get upset. I'm beginning to wish I didn't rely on him so much, particularly with this new product we've launched. Neville says he knows just as much about the technical side as Jasper, but I don't believe him for a minute. Still, if it carries on being as unprofitable as it is at the moment, it's not a problem I'll be worrying about for long.'

He sat frowning, and staring at the carpet.

Jeanette was taken aback by her husband suddenly confiding in her. It had been years since he had talked to her about anything that mattered to him. What a shame he should choose a moment when as hosts, they really should be with their guests. Her marriage often felt like it had been on one long downward trajectory over the years, but every so often she felt sparks of hope. After a brief silence, she said,

'I don't want to stop you, dear, but we probably need to go downstairs.' She smiled gently at him.

'Oh, sorry,' said Tony. 'I'd forgotten you were still here. Let's go.' He got up without looking at her, and headed straight for the stairs. Jeanette followed, at a distance.

Hunter had just opened the door to Neville, who then accidentally shut it in Louise's face. He was very apologetic.

'I'm so sorry. I think it's because it's still technically part of the working day, so you didn't cross my mind.'

Louise didn't really seem reassured by this. Neville hastened to fetch her a stiff drink.

'Get that down you,' he said, thrusting a large tumbler

of whisky into her hand.

'Thanks,' said Louise, 'but you know I don't really like whisky.'

'It's Christmas!' said Neville. 'Just drink the stuff!'

Then he paused, and continued in a gentler voice. 'Here, let me take your coat. You remember Alastair, and Gerry? I'll just put these upstairs.'

As Neville disappeared with their coats, the doorbell went again, and Hunter opened the door to Jasper and Molly, who had shared a cab from Holborn. Jeanette greeted them both warmly.

'Oh, I see you were able to get the same waitress again!' said Molly, looking past Jeanette, and through towards the kitchen.

'Yes — she's called Hannah, and she's very nice.'

Jasper smiled at Jeanette. 'You know, it's only been a few months, but I'd quite forgotten how beautiful your home is.'

'Why, thank you. That's very kind.'

Face to face with him, Jeanette found it hard to credit Tony's earlier concerns about Jasper. 'Do come and have a drink. Make yourself at home.'

A log fire was burning in the front room, and there were a selection of drinks on the sideboard. Jasper poured Molly a glass of of sherry, and took for himself the whisky that Louise had abandoned. Hunter was opening the front door again. It had begun to rain. Amelia was on the doorstep.

'Hunter, how lovely to see you!' She flung her arms around him and kissed him firmly on the cheek, to his obvious embarrassment.

'Miss Amelia, you're very welcome. Do come

through and have a drink.'

'Don't mind if I do, Hunter, don't mind if I do.'

She sashayed through the doorway, and bumped into her mother.

'Amelia, darling! How nice to see you. Are you all right?'

'Yep. Never been better. Well, hardly ever, anyway. Hunter said something about a drink?'

'Yes, of course. Just behind you on the sideboard.'

Jeanette returned to the entrance hall, where Hunter was once again on door duty. This time when he opened it he saw a rather bedraggled Father White, who was facing away from the door, staring down the front path. Hunter gently cleared his throat. The priest turned round and made an apologetic gesture.

'I'm sorry. How rude of me!'

'Do come in, Father White.'

'Thank you, Hunter. Your courteous welcomes are sometimes the highlight of my day.'

Tony Northington's feelings were mixed as he stood by the log fire, clasping a large glass of red wine, and glancing round the room at the assembled company. He'd received more reassurances just this morning from Hobbes at the FCA, that he was very happy with the progress so far of the Connected Chain Bond. This was fine, but the reason Tony had been so keen to get it all signed off from Hobbes's pedantic meddling, was that he thought the profits for his company would be suspiciously large. And so far they had been, if anything, suspiciously small.

Tony had grilled both Neville and Jasper

individually, just in case they had been carefully re-routing income streams out of sight of the regulators, but they both seemed convincingly baffled by the lack of results from the carefully planned scheme. Jasper had seemed particularly frustrated with it, and the two men had achieved what was nowadays a rare moment of bonding, over their mutual frustration. This hadn't lasted of course, as Tony had hinted to Jeanette earlier, and he was currently struggling to see any valid future for Jasper at Northington International.

Hunter was now calling the guests through into the dining room to eat. Tony stayed where he was for a minute longer, though taking a judicious step away from the flames behind him. He noted sourly that Father White was here again — he had just re-entered the room in fact, talking quietly with Molly Raestock. Every time they had people round, there were clerics everywhere, he thought. The fact that in reality it was always the same cleric usually reassured him, but today it seemed to make his presence more sinister. To be fair, this particular cleric didn't try to push his outmoded view of reality down anyone's throat, but again, today, this suddenly seemed a calculated subterfuge. With a start Northington noticed that everyone had now gone through, and with a grunt he followed them.

This time there was no seating plan, and Tony, as the last to enter the room, found himself in the uncomfortable position of having to sit between the two people he least wanted to talk to. On his left was Jasper Felder, and on his right, Alastair Forth. To his relief though, he was facing Neville, and he thought he could get through at least the main course talking to his son.

Then maybe he could suggest everyone changed places for the dessert.

Hunter seemed to be in his element. The food he had prepared was traditional Christmas fare, but well cooked, immaculately presented and in generous portions. He was enjoying Hannah's assistance, and the pair of them were keeping an eye on the state of everyone's plates and glasses. For some time there was no conversation at all, and the sound of steady munching competed with the quiet, Christmas-themed background music. As the plates grew emptier, talking resumed. Hannah was bringing in more helpings of ham, and offering them round.

'Thanks, I'll gladly take another slice,' said Louise. She was sitting next to Jeanette.

'Do you really need it?' asked Neville from across the table. Louise coloured.

'Well, of course she doesn't *need* it, dear, none of us do,' said Jeannette.

'*She* certainly doesn't,' said Neville. 'I know it's Christmas, but really!'

Louise put down her cutlery, wiped her mouth on her napkin, stood up and left the room. There was an uncomfortable silence.

'Maybe you'd better see where she's gone?' said Tony to his son.

Neville stared back at him belligerently, and said, 'Maybe she can look after herself. She's a big girl. More's the pity.'

He stretched out his fork to spear another sausage, then, sensing the irony of this, put the cutlery back down on his plate, and sat there defiantly. Jeanette got up and followed her daughter-in-law out of the room, with a single despairing glance at her son. There was a moment's silence round the table. Then, just as it looked like Amelia was about to say something, Neville pushed his chair back noisily and also left the room.

Hannah had been hovering with the last plate of ham, but chose this moment to make a discreet exit. Above the sweet sound of choirboys' voices, a low murmur could now be heard coming from the kitchen. Feeling that it was up to him to move things on a bit, Tony remembered his plan of swapping seats between courses. He abruptly stood up.

'Right,' he announced, 'let's all move round a bit so we can talk to different people over dessert.'

Everyone was glad to be distracted, and began to move round, some purposefully and some vaguely. Eventually people began to settle in new seats, but Tony noticed that Molly had ended up still sitting next to Father White.

'Molly,' he called across, 'You're still next to Father White.'

'Why, so I am,' she replied, sounding surprised.

'If you just move two seats to your right, to that empty chair, then I think we'll be all set when the others come back in.'

'Of course. No problem,' said Molly, moving, however, two seats to her left.

Tony frowned. 'That's your left,' he said.

'No, no — I moved to my right. But maybe it looks like my left from where you're sitting?'

'You moved to my right, which is your left. Don't tell me you don't know your right from your left?'

Tony's expression of astonishment was only partly put on to amuse his guests.

'Oh, of course,' Molly said, smiling again after a brief frown of concentration. 'You're right. Or maybe I should say — you're left! My one area of weakness!'

She laughed, and Tony laughed too.

'I had no idea you struggled with that,' he said. 'But no need to move. You're fine where you are now.'

He smiled appreciatively at this woman who over the years had taken his notes, kept his secrets, defused his moods and made his phone calls. He felt a warm glow inside that wasn't all due to alcohol. She was like a right hand man to him. He glanced instinctively at the dark eyes and weary look of his actual right hand man, Alastair, as he thought this. Tony stood up again, and signalled for silence with his knife on a nearby glass.

'While we wait for our temporary absentees, I'd like to propose a toast. To the woman with only one fault. Molly Raestock!'

'MOLLY RAESTOCK!'

Molly was pleased but embarrassed.

'No, no, I've got lots of faults. Honestly. Too many to mention.'

Her protestations were dismissed by all present. The mood of the meal had changed, as the guests, relieved to have an opportunity to be light-hearted, vied with each other to make Molly more and more extravagant compliments. Tony noticed Jeanette in the doorway, and waved her in. She was followed by Louise, who looked drawn, and Neville, who still looked defiant. They made their choices of the available empty chairs, and their glasses were passed to them from their previous seats.

'We were just toasting Molly,' explained Tony, very pleased with himself, as he sat down.

'Come on, while we're waiting for dessert — Hunter! Where's that dessert? — let's have a few more toasts. Go on, someone else propose one.'

He looked expectantly round the table. To his surprise, Alastair stood up immediately with a smile.

'I'd like to propose a toast to a man with only one fault.'

'Only one *what*?' shouted Neville. Alastair was unfazed.

'A man with only one fault,' he continued. 'Though that fault is a big one, admittedly.'

'He's got a *big one*?' said Neville, sotto voce this time.

'The fault, as I say, is a big one, as the fault he has got, is me. I'd like to propose a toast to the epitome of charm, and the last word in generosity. Gerry Kennedy!'

'GERRY KENNEDY!'

'Oh, that's so sweet,' said Amelia under her breath.

Gerry just sat there quietly, looking up at Alastair, and gradually big tears began to roll down his cheeks.

Amelia now stood up, as Alastair sat down.

'To the best mother anyone could wish for. Who's given up everything for her marriage, and for her family. To Mum! Jeanette Northington!'

'JEANETTE NORTHINGTON!'

Hunter and Hannah were now starting to bring in plates with tiny steaming individual Christmas puddings. But the mood for toasts was still there.

Neville looked like he might rise, but Amelia wasn't sitting down just yet.

'And to the best father anyone could wish for, who's

also given up everything.'

Tony felt a resurgence of the warm glow that had kindled his toast to Molly. He prepared to stand up and return the toast.

'FATHER WHITE!' Amelia turned and nodded, with a bright smile, at the priest, whose mild face regarded her with a look of surprise as she sat down.

'Father White!'

A slightly subdued response this time as people realised that this was actually something else, masquerading as a toast. But Tony had got to his feet before he was aware he had misread the situation. He half sat down, before realising that two could play at that game. Summoning a broad smile, he indicated the small Christmas tree perched on a coffee table at the end of the room.

'Ladies and gentleman, I hope you've had a chance to enjoy something from her latest exhibition. To the greatest artist this side of, oh, the table. AMELIA NORTH.'

Tony's smile had turned into something rather grimmer as most of his guests responded, in a slightly confused manner, 'Amelia North!' and a few, 'Amelia Northington!' Tony sat down heavily, and folded his arms. Then he noticed that Jasper was rising.

'Thank you Jeanette for your kind hospitality. Thank you for providing the delicious Dutch beer.'

'But I didn't provide any—'

'I know. I'd like to propose a toast to our fine company.'

'*My* fine company,' muttered Tony.

'Our fine company that has stood the tests of time, of

market swings, of oh, all sorts of tests. So I propose a toast. To Northington International, and its inspirational father-figure, Tony Northington!'

Felder stared at Tony for a minute, and then smiled. 'Come on, see if you can repeat all that!'

His manner was playful, so the guests began to relax, and parroted back a fairly good rendition.

'To Northington International, and its inspirational father-figure, Tony Northington!'

This tongue twister was a good stress-reliever, and there was a buzz of laughter as Jasper sat down. Tony however wasn't laughing. Jasper's manner had him constantly on edge these days. Tony stood up yet again.

'Well, that's probably enough speeches!'

But Neville was now standing too.

'Just one more,' he said.

'Oh, all right.' Tony sat down again, crossly.

'To the woman I'm sorry if I offended.'

Everyone waited for a snappy sound-bite for them to repeat as the toast, but Neville was sitting down again. That was all they were going to get. So there was an awkward and shambling attempt at, 'To the woman I'm sorry if I offended.'

The buzz of laughter had now been replaced by a strained silence, and as Tony racked his brains for another ice-breaker, Father White stood up.

'I know my place here is far more tenuous than anyone else's, but my vocation maybe puts me in an appropriate position to propose a toast to the spirit of the season.'

His calm voice and demeanour brought a fresh sense of poise to the table. Everyone was listening as he carried on talking.

'To the spirit of new beginnings.'

His gaze took in all those round the table as he continued.

'To the spirit of peace on earth.'

His calmly roving eyes included Hunter, and Hannah, who were hovering, one just inside, and one just outside, the door.

'To the spirit of goodwill among men.'

Was it Tony's imagination, or was the priest looking particularly at him at this point?

'To the spirit of joy to the world.'

Father White's smile seemed sad and subdued as he quietly proposed the final toast.

'Merry Christmas, everyone!'

'MERRY CHRISTMAS, EVERYONE!'

Hunter dived in with the final puddings, and Hannah brought some more bottles in, as the atmosphere began to regain some sort of normality.

CHAPTER 10

It was Friday 23rd December, a dark and wet afternoon, and Northington International's Holborn offices were almost empty. Most of the staff hadn't come in at all, and Molly Raestock was just tidying her desk. It was now nearly three o'clock in the afternoon, and she reckoned that if she played her cards carefully, Tony would be very happy for her to go home now. She took the two documents that needed his signature, walked across to his office, knocked on the door and entered.

To her surprise, despite the gloomy weather, the light in Tony's office wasn't on, and neither was the desk lamp. Even Amelia's Life's Bright Idea piece wasn't switched on. Tony was sitting in his chair, staring rather vacantly at the wall.

'Are you all right?' Molly asked, concerned. Tony slowly turned round and looked at her.

'Yes, I'm fine. Just thinking. Always a bad idea.'

'Would you like me to turn the light on?' asked Molly.

'No, it's fine. I'm just musing on things. Has Jasper gone home?'

'Yes, he has. Just about everyone on this floor has. There's a team on the floor below finishing that latest report for the FCA, but I believe they're nearly done now. I sent Sam and Ellie home at lunch time.'

'Good, good, that's fine. Why don't you go too?' said Tony. 'I think we're all finished, really.'

'Well, if you could just sign these two lease documents that we discussed earlier, I'll get them in the post as I go. I think the Post Office will still be open.' Molly brought the documents across the room. Tony had to switch his desk lamp on to see where to sign them, and the room suddenly looked much more cheerful. Molly, relieved that her work was nearly done, walked over to Amelia's piece with the idea of turning it on too, as her final constructive contribution for the year. But when she got to the socket, she realised it was already switched on, though nothing was lit up or moving. Tony had affixed his signature to the documents now, and looked up to see what Molly was doing. She looked at him quizzically.

'Ah, yes, that has stopped working.'

'Oh dear,' said Molly. She was worried that if she expressed any detailed concern she'd be drawn into another task, but then she realised there was probably nothing to be done, so close to Christmas. So she continued.

'Have you asked the gallery about it? They should be able to get someone out to fix it.'

'Oh no, I don't want to bother them,' said Tony. 'I don't want to bother Amelia, either. You know she's spending Christmas with Ken's family this year?' Tony suddenly looked old, and vulnerable. 'And if I'm honest — I occasionally am, you know — I don't want her to know that I actually like the piece. Sometimes when everyone's gone home, or early in the morning, I lock the door, turn the lights off and just sit here staring at it. At Life's Bright Idea.'

'I'm sure she'd be delighted to know what it means to you.'

'She's not talking to me at all at the moment,' said Tony. 'And until the thing stopped working, I didn't realise that I would miss it.'

'I'm sure we'll be able to get it working again,' said Molly. 'If you like, I'll make the necessary phone calls to the gallery.'

Tony looked up.

'In the new year,' Molly added hurriedly.

'No,' said Tony. 'It's actually been quite instructive to me having it sitting here, inanimate. I'd like to leave it like this for the time being.'

Then he seemed to pull himself together.

'Right. Enough of this. You run along home, Miss Raestock. Molly. Have a wonderful Christmas, and by the way, I meant every word of my toast.'

'Thank you,' said Molly simply. She turned and left his office, remembering the newly signed documents, and closed the door gently behind her.

CHAPTER 11

The Times, London, Tuesday 7th March 2017

Tony Northington OBE, who has died aged 60 after a brief illness, was a pioneer in the field of financial technology, and the owner and managing director of Northington International. He is survived by his wife Jeanette, his son, Neville, who works for Northington International, and his daughter, the well known contemporary artist Amelia North.

An exhausted-looking Neville Northington was on the phone in his office.

'Look, Sheldon,' he was saying. 'You've done well for me over the years. And I hope I've kept up my end.'

After a short pause, Neville heard the distinctive, weary tones of Sheldon Haynes replying. 'Even by ringing me, you're behaving in an uncharacteristic way. I feel very cautious about this idea.'

'You know what's happened. Of course I'm going to

behave in an uncharacteristic way. It would be astonishing if I didn't.'

'OK. That's a fair point. I still don't like it. Do you not think this is one project that really should be done by the book?'

'Sheldon, I know why you're saying all this. You're covering your back, in case it all goes tits up. Believe me, it won't. All I need is for you to be in your office between three and four o'clock tomorrow afternoon, to accept the assignment that my colleague Miss Raestock will offer you. Don't tell me you're too busy?'

'You know very well my availability depends on my fee,' said Haynes.

'Your fee will be the usual.'

'In the usual format, and with the usual records for Parker?'

'Absolutely. And, if you think about it for a minute — if I was guilty I wouldn't be booking an investigator, would I?'

Sheldon Haynes cleared his throat, and said, ' Okay. I still don't like it, but I'll do it.'

Then the line went dead. Neville put his phone back in his pocket, and stood for a while looking out the window. Then he unlocked his door, and went out into the foyer. As he did so, he saw Jasper disappearing into his office across the hallway. He knocked on Molly's door, and entered. Sam was in there with her.

There was a moment's uneasy silence, then Neville said, 'Miss Raestock, can I see you in my office when you have a minute?'

As he left the room he tried to catch Sam's eye, but she wouldn't look at him.

Tony's funeral service had been the previous day.

Hunter had filed in with the family, and sat in the second row. The Golders Green Crematorium was packed and hushed as the Northingtons entered. Jeanette stood tall and straight as she led her son and daughter to the front. Louise was with a grim-faced Neville, and Amelia, who looked completely washed out, had Ben with her.

The imposing bulk of Tony's coffin maintained a sense of his presence throughout the brief service. In a slightly unusual twist, Jeanette, Amelia and Neville all contributed brief readings, while it was left to Father White to provide the eulogy. He spoke in a simple and unaffected manner, fully aware of the unbelief of the man he was eulogising. He spent a long time emphasising that the most significant things about Tony, such as his parents, his abilities, even the timing of his birth and death in the context of both global history, and in his immediate culture and community, were things that he had had no control over. And then he pointed out that the things about Tony that made him specifically him — here he asked the congregation to recollect some of his unique characteristics — were in fact things that in themselves could not die.

Hunter found this rather distasteful. Why not stick to religion? He fancied he could hear some shuffling at this point. And when the priest finally said something overtly religious, Hunter realised that this, too, was problematic. 'Flesh and blood cannot inherit the kingdom of God, nor does the perishable inherit the imperishable'.

Surely this excluded everyone from the kingdom of

God, he thought, even if such a thing existed? Hunter was surprised no-one had noticed this before. He went to surreptitiously change his watch from his left to his right wrist as an aide memoir, as he wanted to remember this point for one of his occasional casual demolitions of religion in the Cross Keys, but he found he'd already changed it. Oh yes, that had been to remind him of a joke he had thought of earlier when he had put some throat lozenges in his pocket, to dispense in case of need, as you 'didn't want any more coughin' at a funeral'. So now he discreetly turned his watch upside down as well. He thought he might be able to word that joke a little better, but he often found that a great way of saying these things occurred to him spontaneously after about the third pint.

He now realised everyone else was standing, and stood with them. The strained silence stretched out, and then the coffin began to slide behind the curtains. There was a sudden outburst of sobbing from, to his surprise, Molly Raestock, who was in the row behind, and a couple of places to his right. Just as Hunter was wondering whether she was not embarrassed to cry when Tony Northington's family were stoically dry-eyed, he felt his own eyes hot and prickling, and before he knew it, sensed two long trails of moisture on his face, a solitary heavy tear on each cheek.

He carefully reached into his pocket for a tissue. His fingers searched carefully, but to his frustration, found only throat lozenges. Molly was still sobbing, but quietly now. And just as Hunter thought how much more dignified that sounded, to his dismay a single massive sob racked his own body. This seemed to have a destabilising effect, for now he could see Jeanette's shoulders shaking, and Amelia had tissues pressed firmly to both eyes. Hunter clasped a hand to his mouth to stifle any more sobs, and then had the bright idea of very deliberately taking one of his throat sweets. People would now just think he had a strange-sounding cough. And the tears on his cheeks would soon dry.

Afterwards, at the Polton Hotel, Hunter felt rather out of place amongst the mourners. He knew many of the family, and a good handful of those from Northington International, but he found himself gravitating more and more to the fringes of the assembly. He eventually found somewhere comfortable to sit and think, in a sort of conservatory, tacked on to the back of the building. He was clutching a pint of bitter, and a very tasty ham sandwich. The weather was still cold enough that no-one was outside in the hotel's compact but beautiful gardens, apart from a few hardened smokers clustered in a corner. Hunter noticed that buds were starting to appear on some of the trees, despite the slow start to spring. He became aware of someone sitting down beside him, and turning, saw Father White. He too was holding a pint glass, and nodded companionably.

'Hunter,' he said.

'Father White,' replied Hunter gravely. He racked his brains for a conversational gambit appropriate for a priest. None suggested themselves. But there was always the weather.

'Cold for the time of year, isn't it?'

'Freezing,' the other man agreed. 'Tell me,' he said, turning to Hunter, and suddenly animated, 'do you know that poem called The Cremation of Sam McGee?'

Hunter stared at him. 'Funny enough, I do.' He took a deep swig of his pint, and continued. 'It doesn't however strike me, if I may say so, as a very priestly poem.'

'Nonsense,' said White, briskly. 'It's very human, and anything to do with people, or the world we live in, or of course the divine, is legitimate fodder for us. Hopefully we can make things clearer rather than more obscure. Not sure I did very well today though.'

Now it was the priest's turn to drink deeply. Hunter waited politely for him to continue talking.

'I feel it's always important to give some sort of global context for life, and death, but of course most people just want to pay their respects, and express their grief. I'm not sure I succeeded at either aim today.'

'No, you did very well,' said Hunter, hoping he wouldn't have to elaborate. White smiled.

'Thank you. But Sam McGee — that poem brings together lots of conflicting feelings, in a very focussed way. Maybe that could have inspired me to take a different approach.' He frowned and examined his half-empty pint.

Hunter was frowning too. He was dragging up from the vaults of his memory vaguely remembered lines. Eventually his face lit up, and he assumed a slightly sing-song voice, as he declaimed,

'Some planks I tore from the cabin floor, and I lit the boiler fire;

Some coal I found that was lying around, and I heaped the fuel higher.'

He stopped abruptly, feeling somewhat uncomfortable. But the priest was delighted.

'That's the one,' he said. 'I like the next bit —

something like,

And the heavens howled, — no — *scowled, and the huskies howled,* — that's right — *and the*

wind began to blow,

It was icy cold, but the hot sweat rolled down my cheeks, and I don't know why — hang on, that doesn't fit. Maybe the line ends with *know*? Anyway, I love the vividness of what that language expresses. The biting cold, the searing heat, the down to earth practicalities and then the surprising tears.'

'Sweat,' corrected Hunter. 'Sweat, not tears.'

'Yes, it says sweat, but surely that's his way of passing his weeping off as something else?'

There was a moment's silence, both men staring out at the garden. Then White continued.

'But I feel for the family today. I'm sure I'm giving away no priestly secrets,' he grinned briefly at Hunter, 'if I suggest Tony Northington wasn't universally loved. But the sudden removal of anyone, even someone you struggle with, is always hard to cope with. Another drink?'

'Don't mind if I do,' replied Hunter, revising upwards his estimation of the priest. One more drink, then maybe he should see if any of the family needed his assistance, and if not, excuse himself. He glanced at his watch. It wasn't on his wrist, and he experienced a moment's panic before remembering he'd moved it, in order to remember something. He looked at the other wrist. Midnight! That wasn't right! Then he remembered he'd turned it upside down as well. Half past six. That was better. He began to chuckle to himself. That was a better story than the ones he'd been trying to remember. He'd tell Father White when he returned.

CHAPTER 12

As Hunter opened the door, Neville pushed past him without saying anything, and went straight into the front room. It had been a cold March so far, and there was a fire burning on the hearth. The mantelpiece was completely covered with sympathy cards of various tasteful or tacky designs, as was the sideboard.

Jeanette was sitting upright in a chair by the window. Her face looked pale, and this paleness was accentuated by her black dress. On her lap she had a wooden writing board, with an address book and a pad of writing paper on it. She looked up calmly as her son entered.

'Mother,' he said, with a nod, as he took up a position with his back to the fire.

'Hello, dear,' said Jeanette quietly. 'How are you doing? Is Louise here?'

'I'm fine. Or I will be. Louise is meant to be coming under her own steam, but I just had a missed call from her, so who knows what's gone wrong now. You know what she's like.'

'That's a little harsh,' said Jeanette. 'Things are difficult for her too, you know.'

Neville looked coldly at his mother. 'Are you going to step into Father's shoes, and start trying to control everyone? I hope not.'

Jeanette winced, and shook her head slowly. 'No, dear, of course not. But if you don't mind me saying so, why do we have to go through this process? Especially so soon? I find your plan a little heavy-handed. Everyone's very tender. We've all been bereaved in one way or another.'

Neville's expression didn't change. 'We have indeed. You, for example, have lost someone who you've known two-thirds of your life, who you never saw eye to eye with. I have lost someone who's been the background to my whole life, as well as a boss, a colleague and an industry leader. So if I'm OK with it, I think everyone should be.' He thrust his hands firmly into his pockets, as if to end the discussion. Jeanette sighed resignedly.

Out of the corner of his eye Neville saw Louise coming up the path, and just behind her, a cab stopping at the gate. 'Here they come,' he said.

In ones and twos, with serious faces, and some visible signs of distress, once more the family and close colleagues of Tony Northington gathered in the house he had so recently vacated, until eventually the front room was full. Jeanette hadn't moved from her chair by the window, seemingly content to greet everyone from there. And Neville had maintained his position by the fire. This enabled him to get a good view of people entering the room, and to assert, he hoped, some sort of dominance over them at a early stage.

Hunter was very discreetly taking orders and making drinks for everyone who arrived, as well as opening the door and having just the right blend of gravity and warmth in his welcome. Neville noticed how well he was doing this. He assumed his mother would wish to keep him on, but he wondered if Hunter might fancy a change of scene. Then he remembered the rumours of Hunter's lack of discretion at The Cross Keys, and put the thought from his mind.

Some time after all those invited had arrived, the door bell went yet again, and after answering it, Hunter came and whispered briefly in Neville's ear. Jeanette shook her head despondently as she watched this.

'So. If I can have your attention, please.' Neville's brusque opening remark certainly achieved its aim. 'You all basically know why I've asked you to be here today, but I'd just like to go over it again, as I know there's some unhappiness about it. Obviously we were all close to Father, to Tony Northington, in one capacity or another. Some of us in more than one.'

As Neville spoke, his gaze drifted across the faces in front of him. He sensed sadness, fear, suspicion and some outright hostility. Interesting.

'And equally obviously, after his sad departure from us—'

A sudden sob from Jeanette, who was rapidly comforted by Amelia, sitting next to her.

Neville continued. 'As I say, after this sad departure, he was deemed to have died of natural causes. Heart failure, that the hospital were powerless to reverse. But what I am suggesting is that there is a possibility of foul play.'

Now Jeanette was crying in earnest, and mutterings were heard from various parts of the room. Alastair Forth spoke up. 'Neville, if you think there is such a possibility, wouldn't that have been spotted at an early stage?'

'Not necessarily. Lots of things can cause heart failure.'

'Things that are unknown to medical science?' asked Amelia.

'Well, possibly,' said Neville. 'But let me continue.'

Alastair spoke again. Neville couldn't quite identify the expression on his face, but it made him feel uneasy.

'Isn't this assembling of everyone who knew Tony well, and threatening them with some vague accusations, just a way of bullying us? Of trying to assert your position?'

'Please just let me finish,' said Neville. 'As I say, I think there may be such a possibility, but I certainly don't want to cause a media ruckus by suggesting anything of the sort in public.'

Several people now tried to speak at once, but Neville stilled them with his impassive expression and down-turned, outstretched palms.

'So what I propose is to appoint a private investigator, to look into the circumstances of Tony's death, particularly in relation to the people closest to him.'

Alastair spoke again. 'So you want us all to be investigated? Is that what you're saying?'

Neville stared levelly back. 'Do you have a problem with that? Anything you'd rather keep hidden?'

'No, of course not.' Alastair coloured a little, but then continued. 'But why should we trust a private detective who, I assume, you have appointed?'

'Good question,' replied Neville calmly. He felt he was back on safe ground here. 'I anticipated that particular concern, and basically pulled a random private investigator out of the Yellow Pages. Then Miss Raestock visited and engaged him. I was a bit concerned subsequently when I saw the stature of his firm, as to whether he would be suitable, but then I thought that the best guarantee of fairness is an impartial appointment.'

Father White, who Jeanette had insisted should not be left out of this grim meeting, now spoke quietly. 'So this investigator is going to report to whom, may I ask?'

'To me,' replied Neville.

There were howls of protest round the room. But the priest carried on calmly. 'But I assume he'll be investigating you as well?'

'Of course not,' scowled Neville. 'It was my idea.'

'Forgive my impertinence,' White continued, 'but I have a feeling the only way most of us would agree to this plan of yours, would be if we were all in it together.' He smiled sweetly. 'I'm sure none of us has anything to hide.'

'I want to talk to my lawyer first,' said a stony-faced Alastair Forth.

Neville raised his eyebrows. 'Objection noted,' he said calmly. 'But if the rest of you are happy to continue, I think Hunter is with our detective in the next room as we speak. HUNTER! Could you bring in —'

Here Neville took a sheet of notepaper from Molly Raestock, and his face went pale. His fingers quivered, and he swallowed hard. But he rallied himself, and read out slowly,

'Edwin Strong.'

He turned to Molly, his pale face rigid, and held the paper out to her interrogatively. She frowned back, shaking her head, and looking puzzled.

The door opened, and Hunter entered the room followed by a young man, a boy almost, with a slightly chubby face, rather over-long hair and a straggly beard. He had glasses on, was wearing jeans and a sweatshirt, and had an amiable smile.

'Hi, everyone,' he said. 'I'm Edwin.'

Neville, who had recovered some of his composure, strode over to him, and seized him by the hand. 'Hello, Edwin. I'm Neville Northington. I'm the person responsible for engaging you.'

'Excellent,' said Edwin.

There was a moment's silence. Then Neville said awkwardly, 'Well, I think that's probably all we need to do today.'

'Certainly not,' protested Alastair. 'He needs to be briefed for his investigation in front of all of us, and to our satisfaction. If you can do that, I will immediately withdraw my objection.'

There was a murmur of assent around the room. Neville briefly shut his eyes, as if suffering from a headache. Everyone was looking at him expectantly. He opened his eyes again, gave a strained smile, and said, drily, 'Yes, of course, that would be a very transparent way to organise things. Thank you Alastair.'

'So what do you want me to do?' asked Edwin, taking from his pocket a small notebook and a pen.

'Well,' began Neville in a colourless voice, 'you may be aware that my father, Tony Northington, very recently passed away after a brief illness. His death was attributed to heart failure, and I want you to make absolutely sure that there was nothing suspicious about it, specifically with reference to the people in this room.'

Hearing the proposal put this baldly, there was another undercurrent of dissent, until Alastair added, 'Including Neville himself.'

'Yes,' said Neville, 'of course including me, for transparency's sake. And I hope I needn't tell you how important it is that the media shouldn't get hold of the story.'

'That's fine,' said Edwin. 'Confidentiality is one of my firm's watchwords, I think.'

'You think?' said Neville. 'You're not sure?'

'No, I'm pretty sure it is,' said Edwin.

'How long have you worked at this firm?' asked Neville.

'Oh, about six months,' said Edwin. 'I'm the intern.'

Neville's eyes involuntarily closed again.

'Well,' said Alastair, pleasantly. 'We look forward to working with you on this matter, to put Neville's mind at rest.'

He gave the young man one of his business cards, and excused himself.

Jeanette now rose, and went over to where Edwin Strong was standing.

'Hello, Edwin. I'm Jeanette Northington, Tony's widow.' She paused, and looked down for a minute. 'Gosh — I think that's the first time I've had to introduce myself in those terms.'

'I'm very sorry for your loss,' said Edwin quickly. 'It must be very difficult for you. Miss Raestock spoke very kindly of you when she engaged me.'

'That's very nice of her,' said Jeanette. 'But you must just feel free to get on with your job. I'm sure we'll all help you as best we can. It will help reassure Neville.'

Conversations were now beginning around the room, and under cover of this general background noise, Neville approached Molly Raestock. He kept a fixed smile on his face as he hissed,

'Who the fuck is this?'

Molly looked uncomfortable, but replied in a slightly less aggressive whisper, but with the same fixed smile, and with what conviction she could summon, 'I did exactly what you asked when I went to the agency.'

Her conviction started to falter though, as she continued. 'When I got to the top of the stairs, you told me to turn right, and I did. There was an office there, and this young man was in it, and I engaged him, as you asked.'

Molly's voice still retained some defiance as she finished. 'If this isn't who you were expecting, I'm very sorry.'

Neville didn't reply, but gazed blankly round the room. They must have changed offices. That's the only way this would make sense. He suddenly noticed both Louise and Father White looking at him. He turned to Molly, and spoke in the most relaxed tone of voice he could manage.

'Thanks very much for all your help.'

He made an effort to nod politely to her, then walked over to talk to his wife.

CHAPTER 13

On the next Monday morning Edwin Strong was uncharacteristically early for work. He had found the previous Friday's meeting rather overwhelming, and after a fidgety weekend, had slept badly on Sunday night. So when, at about half past six he finally realised he wasn't going to get any more sleep, he thought he might as well get on with his day. A brief shower, so as not to wake the family he lodged with, a leisurely breakfast in silence, and then, leaving the house just as he heard the first signs of life from upstairs, the forty minute walk to the office. It was one of the first really spring-like days of the year, and Edwin felt his spirits rise as he crossed the park.

The entrance to the offices of Parker Investigations was through a nondescript door with an entry buzzer and peeling grey paint, next to a traditional greengrocer's shop. Edwin twisted his key in the lock, and pulled the door towards him just the right amount to enable it to open. He passed the cubbyhole on the ground floor that was the office of his boss, Parker, and pressing the timer switch at the foot of the dark staircase, jogged to the top before the lights could go off again. He turned to the left at the top of the stairs, wrestled briefly with the lock on this door too, and finally entered his own room.

He'd been unsure what direction to take the previous year when his degree had been drawing to an end. He knew he wasn't going to set the world on fire with his results at the end of the course. But he had a quiet confidence that at least some of that was down to weaknesses in the selection and teaching of the syllabus, rather than in him, the student. So when he'd seen the small notice advertising the position of intern with a firm of private investigators, the adventurous side of him had jumped at the chance.

He had been put through his paces in this very office, by Parker himself, and the firm's only other employee, Sheldon Haynes. A bored-looking Parker had asked a few commonplace questions, familiar to interviewees the world over. In fact he had showed remarkably little curiosity for a man whose profession was investigation. At this point Edwin had felt the interview wasn't going well. Then Haynes took over, and talked Edwin briefly through a 'real world' problem, which he asked Edwin to suggest solutions for. Edwin might have struggled, if he hadn't recognised the setup instantly from the writings of Sir Arthur Conan Doyle. As it was, his only problem was to make it seem like he was momentarily struggling to think of possible answers. The interview perked up after that, with a round of general observation questions. What colour is our front door? How old would you say Parker is? ('Hey!' objected Parker.) What buses stop directly outside this office?

And finally the practical test. Sheldon Haynes had taken Edwin outside, indicated a random middle-aged woman some twenty yards in front of them, and told him to find out what he could about her. He was to report back to Haynes in The Plough, in one hour's time. Strong reappeared in forty-five minutes with her name, age, date of birth, occupation, professional qualifications, the names of her children, and the same information for her husband. When Haynes, who was clearly not on his first drink of the afternoon, asked Edwin with some surprise how he had obtained the information, he felt quite justified in replying that he would rather not divulge that. He had a feeling that approaching the woman once Haynes was out of sight, as he had done, and explaining the whole situation to her, relying on her sympathy, wouldn't cut much ice.

And when he had passed the information on to Sheldon Haynes, he had simply nodded approvingly, without bothering to check its accuracy, and bought the newest employee of Parker Investigations the drink of his choice, which turned out to be cider, before they returned to the office.

Edwin had started work at the beginning of September, and found his feet quickly. His first genuinely investigative assignment happened within days of starting the job, when he was required to monitor the comings and goings from a betting shop, looking for one person in particular. He thoroughly enjoyed the combination of excitement and idleness. And as time went on, Parker, and more directly Haynes, discovered that Edwin's unassuming way with people made him a huge asset to the company.

The salary was minimal, and the hours could be unpredictable, though this was something that Edwin found he could use to his advantage, but the expenses were generous on the occasions when he was out and about, and Edwin had felt that in many ways he had fallen on his feet.

Until yesterday. He had been, for the first time since September, completely out of his depth. He had made a few scribbled notes at the house in Hampstead, but found it wasn't really feasible to record things in detail there. He had filled a couple of pages of his notebook on his way home while rattling along the Northern Line, and then on the train from London Bridge. But despite his general optimism, and his buoyant attitude when in Jeanette Northington's home, he felt confused. He had an inkling he had been somehow put in a false position, and wasn't sure what to do about it.

Edwin slung his bag in the small locker in the corner of the room, as he walked across to pull the blind. The bright spring sunshine made the grubby net curtains look even worse that they had done in the darker months. Soon after he had started working there, Edwin had tucked them up round their wire to let a bit more light in, but Parker, on one of his periodic meanders round the building, had objected. Edwin had conceded Parker's point that the nets were important for security, and had then asked if the curtains could maybe be cleaned. Parker said they could, and that was how the matter rested. The rest of the room was adequate, with a solid cupboard, a small bookcase and a substantial desk, in addition to the locker.

But the chair was much more than adequate. Not the client's chair — in Edwin's office this was just a plain metal folding one — but Edwin's own chair. It was covered in leather, was well padded and had generous wings to its back that were very pleasantly supportive. This was the perfect chair for musing, or for dozing, and Edwin had found that so far, the post of intern at a small private investigator's agency involved healthy amounts of both.

It was still only eight o'clock in the morning. Edwin got out the notes he had made on Friday and started looking through them again.

A crime hadn't necessarily taken place, but one was suspected. Suspicion was the bread and butter of the private investigator. So far so good. But those who were suspected of the crime had all been in the room at the time of the suspicion being voiced. This was a very unusual scenario for any sort of investigation, and one more suited for the purposes of fiction. Most of Parker Investigations' clients were very much working behind the backs of others.

The person who was doing the suspecting, the client, was also, as far as Edwin could work out, to be one of those investigated. This was the most unusual point of all, though having had the brief explained to him in the company of all those who were suspected, Edwin understood why the mood of the room had insisted on this. He would have to grill Sheldon Haynes on all these points when he arrived.

The only thing he wouldn't need advice on was the client's desire for complete confidentiality. That was a universal longing of those who approached private investigators.

In the meantime, Edwin, who was still very inexperienced when it came to running his own cases from start to finish, was trying to think of a useful way to organise the information he already had, and that which he needed to acquire. His first idea was to give each person a separate page in his notebook. This would enable him to build up an overview. Then perhaps a separate family tree. But of course some of the people on his list weren't family, but colleagues. A work tree would be required as well. Then a detailed history of the last days of the deceased, including medical records. Perhaps that would be a good place to start in fact, just in case he could rule out foul play instantly.

Edwin leant back in his chair, and stared up at the ceiling.

CHAPTER 14

Sheldon Haynes had also had a rather fidgety weekend. His usual dealer had been rather elusive, and he'd had to get his recreational supplies from another source, who had then proved a little unreliable in the timing department. So a succession of cans of Special Brew had served as something of a stop-gap till early Sunday afternoon, when finally his medicinal stores were replenished. His customary routine, and therefore also his sleep patterns, had been so disrupted over the two days that by the time he rolled into the office at ten o'clock on Monday, Sheldon felt he was suffering from severe jet-lag, in addition to the hangover.

His boss, Parker, didn't look any fresher than Haynes did as he passed his tiny office on the way to the stairs, and the two men grunted monosyllabically at each other as was their custom. Haynes reached his room, opened his blind just an inch, rummaged in his desk drawer for the right type of pills, slouched out into the corridor again to get to the tap in the kitchenette at the end of it, and washed the pills down with a gulp of fresh water from a dirty glass. He swallowed with some difficulty, then refilled the glass and headed back to his office. His chair was identical to Edwin's, but he had a very different method of sitting on it, preferring to cross his long legs one over the other, and then wedge them under the desk in front of him. This position was awkward to attain, and even more difficult to get out of, but Haynes found a strange comfort in being so contorted and constrained at the same time.

He had just closed his eyes and let out his breath with a long sigh, when he heard a gentle knock at his door. He said nothing, but the door opened anyway, and Edwin came in.

'I heard you arrive,' he explained, 'and thought you'd be interested in hearing about the client I went to see on Friday.'

Haynes' eyes remained closed. 'You will most probably over-estimate my interest in everything today, just so you know.' He shifted slightly in his seat, but didn't open his eyes. 'The pills are starting to take effect now though, so, if you can talk very quietly, by all means tell me about your client.'

Edwin told the whole story of his visit to Hampstead, from his being kept in a separate room by some sort of butler type, to being produced before the assembled company like a rabbit from a hat, from the strange mixture of family and colleagues of the deceased in attendance, to the public agreement that everyone in the room should be investigated.

Sheldon Haynes said nothing as Edwin spoke, but, despite the fact that it obviously seemed to be hurting him, he began to smile at a very early point in the story. His smile grew broader and broader, and eventually, as Edwin was drawing to an end, he even opened his eyes as well. This proved too much, however, and he quickly shut them again. Edwin found his reaction disconcerting, as Haynes generally wasn't one of life's smilers. When he had finished he waited in silence for Sheldon to respond, which eventually he did, without, however, opening his eyes again.

'Well, Mr Strong, I think that what we have here is a case of mistaken identity.'

'You mean Tony Northington hasn't really died? Some sort of insurance fraud you mean?'

'When I said mistaken identity, I didn't mean the identity of the deceased. I meant your identity.'

'My identity? What are you talking about?'

Haynes risked lifting his eyelids a little. 'It's extremely simple, and at the same time extremely complicated. Did your client, Neville Northington, seem at all surprised to see you when he announced you to the group?'

'Well, he'd never met me before. But now you mention it, he did perhaps look at me rather strangely, and certainly he then had a whispered conversation with the woman who booked me.' Edwin looked at his notes. 'Molly. Molly Raestock.'

Haynes nodded. 'Believe me, he was surprised to see you. Obviously you don't officially know this, but Northington called me the day before you were booked, and arranged for me to be in between three and four. I'm guessing you were booked between three and four?'

Edwin thought, and then nodded.

'So,' said Haynes, 'for some reason, perhaps through administrative error, you've been booked for this investigation, when Northington really wanted me. I've worked for him before doing routine surveillance and business investigation jobs. He obviously feels he needs someone he knows working for him in this context, but wanted to present it as a completely random appointment.'

Haynes risked a broad grin at this point, though the movement of his facial muscles clearly cut through him like a knife. 'And the funny thing is, he's ended up with a completely random appointment.'

Edwin frowned. 'I don't really get why it's funny.'

'Well, Neville Northington will have some sort of scheme, some sort of angle, with appointing a private investigator, and doing so in public. He'll have a plan, and he'll know exactly what he'll want you to uncover. He would have been quietly confident with me on board, that I would uncover what he wanted me to. He won't be so sure about you.'

'I see. So what looked like a straightforward Intern with Six Months' Experience Investigates Suspected Murder of International Businessman by Close Colleague or Family Member, actually turns out to be more complicated?'

Haynes smiled and nodded at the same time, then winced, and began to rummage in his drawer for more pills.

'Exactly,' he said.

Neville Northington was walking down a bustling High Holborn in his brief lunch break. He had spent the morning alone with the company lawyers, trying to thrash out a public statement on the ownership of Northington International that was both reassuring and broadly truthful. He was fully aware that Alastair and Jasper, who seemed to have closed ranks since Tony's death, were spending the morning closeted together. God alone knew what plans they would concoct between them. He was intensely suspicious of them both.

He swore under his breath as he fished his phone out of his pocket. Sheldon Haynes had always been unreliable, that was his basic personality type, but up till now Neville had been able to use the man's weaknesses to exert something of a hold over him. But not to be in his office when he said he would be! He was now holding his phone against his head, listening to Haynes's answering machine. It was the generic female voice provided by the network. After the tone, he started leaving his message.

'Haynes, you may have just ruined my life. If you can't be in your office when you say you—'

There was now the buzz of an incoming call. Northington pulled the phone away from his ear to see who it was. Haynes. He cancelled his call to the answering machine, and accepted Haynes, who was already talking.

'What are you ringing me for? What in the name of all that's confidential, in the name of all that can stand up as evidence in court, are you leaving a message on my fucking answering machine for? Are you out of your tiny little mind? I don't know what your current scheme is, but you know as well as I do — we do not leave messages.'

'Hang on a minute, I was ringing to tear a strip off you. No-one's going to be looking at this phone call in any court. And they especially wouldn't be if you'd been in your fucking office when you said you would be.'

Neville cut his volume and whispered the last few words, as he suddenly found himself in the middle of a string of children, on a school trip. Some of them were staring at him. He smiled reassuringly and stepped abruptly out of their line.

Haynes sounded angry. 'I was in my office when I said I would be. I didn't leave till after four, when your woman still hadn't turned up. Unless you muddled the days? I wasn't in the office at all on Friday.'

Northington was now confused. 'But you can't have been there. Molly is the most reliable person I know. And you are exactly the opposite.'

'Well she very reliably ballsed this up, if you were counting on her engaging me.'

Neville had now lost some of his confidence. 'Well, what's done is done, and what I'd like to do now is book you as well as that Edwin child. You can keep an eye on him, and point him where I want you to.'

Sheldon chuckled. 'No can do. Have you any idea just how unethical that would be?'

Northington spluttered into his phone in his indignation. 'How dare you lecture me about ethics! I am now ordering you to keep an eye on him, or there will be trouble.'

There was a brief silence.

'So you want *me* to initiate a surveillance operation on one of *my* colleagues, who *you* have engaged to investigate *you*?'

'That's right,' said Neville. He thought it sounded rather odd put that way, but that was in fact what he now wanted. 'I need to be one step ahead of this intern chappie, and you're the man who can help me do that.'

Another idea occurred to him. 'And that will enable me to be very hands-off with the investigation, which will look bloody good at this end. Anyway, drop whatever you're doing, and get your antennae up.'

Northington cut off the call, turned on his heel and headed back to base. He needed another casual chat with Molly Raestock, before diving back in with the lawyers.

Haynes put down his phone. His headache had almost gone, but now he felt it returning again. Bloody Northington. Painfully he extricated himself from his chair, and popping the final two pills from the plastic packet as he left his desk, he headed to the kitchenette for yet more water.

Feeling marginally refreshed, he wandered into Edwin's office. The desk was covered with a litter of pages torn from a notebook. All had been written on; some with several colours of ink. Edwin looked up.

'Hi,' he said. 'I think I'm starting to get a handle on this. I've got one page for each person, and I've written down the main things I know about them. It's not much so far, but I'm slowly getting my head round the size of the task.'

He cocked his head on one side and smiled at Haynes. 'You don't fancy sharing the fee for this and giving me a hand, do you? And by the way, this bloke Northington, he didn't give me a time limit. When I signed the agreement with Molly Raestock, it was an open ended contract. Has he got very deep pockets?'

Haynes nodded. 'Very deep indeed. And they seem to be lined with cash. Make sure Parker sends our invoice out promptly, and in the meantime make sure you take all the expenses you need. As for giving you a hand, I've actually had a job of my own just come in. I don't know if you heard me just now on the phone?'

'I heard something,' said Edwin. 'Good job?'

'Yes, it'll keep me out of trouble,' said Haynes, carelessly. 'But it does mean I'm not so available. What I can do however is give you a bit of time here and there, and because I know some of the people I may be able to point you in useful directions. Unofficially, of course.'

'That'd be great,' said Edwin. 'I'm happy doing the donkey work, if you can give me some pointers.'

Haynes wandered over to Edwin's side of the desk. He nodded approvingly. 'Very organised,' he said.

He suddenly grinned, and this time only a very brief shudder passed through his frame.

'You have no idea how much I'd absolutely love to dive in and help you on this one. But at the moment all I can do is suggest you interview everyone. You're very good at getting things out of people without them even noticing. See how you get on.'

Haynes very deliberately picked up the page with 'Molly Raestock' written in Edwin's childish hand at the top.

'Everyone tells her everything,' he said. He dropped the page again, and walked, still rather gingerly, out of the room.

CHAPTER 15

Edwin got through to Molly Raestock on the phone almost immediately. One of his fledgling theories about detection was that people gave him more useful information when they weren't on their own territory. So after a brief greeting he initially suggested meeting in a neutral venue.

'I was wondering if we could go somewhere and grab a coffee perhaps? I find I listen better somewhere busy.'

'Oh, I think you'll find it's busy enough for you here at the office. You see, I haven't really got the time to go off anywhere at the moment. We're rushed off our feet.' Molly's voice on the phone sounded strained.

'I'm happy to arrange it for outside work hours,' suggested Edwin. He suddenly had a vision of how much work might be required simply to organise times and places to talk to all the people he needed to talk to. Still, that was part of the job. But Molly now seemed to be having second thoughts. 'Well look, can we arrange it for lunchtime — say Friday? — and if I find I really can't spare the time, we can go for out of hours.'

'That sounds good to me,' said Edwin. 'I can meet you at your office at, say, one?'

'OK. Friday at one. I'll see you then.'

Edwin wrote the appointment in his diary. One down, eight to go.

Molly put the phone down, leaned back in her chair and closed her eyes. She wasn't looking forward to meeting Edwin. She became aware of someone entering her office, and she opened her eyes. Neville was just shutting the door behind him.

'Come in,' she said. 'Can I help you?'

'No, not really. Just wanted to rehearse our position for the tame detective.'

'Ah. He's just been on the phone to me. I tried vaguely to put him off, but now have a provisional meeting Friday lunchtime.'

'That's fine, don't try and avoid him. It's important to look innocent.'

'I am innocent,' bristled Molly.

'Yes, yes, I know. That's why it's important to look innocent.'

Molly narrowed her eyes. Through years of working devotedly for his father, she had gained a tolerance for Neville Northington, but she felt very little warmth towards him. And since his father's illness and tragic death she had somehow felt even less well disposed to him.

'The thing is,' Molly said, 'Everyone tells me everything. I simply have no idea how much of that everything I should tell the sleuth when he grills me. I'm sure he'll be very courteous, but he'll expect me to tell him some things about everyone.'

'With respect,' said Neville, 'I think you're wrong. He will want to talk about you. Any fishing for information about anyone else should be dismissed out of hand. Do you understand what I mean?'

'Are you saying that I'm meant to be a suspect myself?' The idea was completely new and shocking to Molly.

'Of course not. You didn't kill my father, did you?'

'How can you even ask such a thing?' Molly's face was turning bright red.

'No, of course not. Don't get upset. I was just pointing out you have nothing to worry about. But just talk about yourself.'

Neville winked and was gone. Molly sat staring at the door as it closed.

Edwin got up and looked out his window through the grubby net curtains at the depressingly small scrap of garden below. There were a couple of green shoots of something beginning to emerge from what looked like a pile of rubble. He took heart from this.

Before trying to arrange any more interviews though, he bent his mind to the issue of medical records. He would certainly ask Neville Northington for copies of his father's records, but just on a hunch he knocked on Haynes's door again, and went in. The detective seemed to be snoozing peacefully, but one eye opened as his colleague entered. The other eye opened too, without any visible signs of distress on the part of its owner. Sheldon Haynes was on the road to recovery.

'Sorry to butt in again so soon,' said Edwin. 'I'm just thinking about medical records, and wondered if there's a way I can get hold of them, other than through the family.'

'Yes, that's a very good idea. Obviously ask the family for the records, but I have a contact who has a fair degree of access to NHS... Oh. Would it have been NHS or private? Though I'm not even sure if that would make any difference. I'll get him to look into it, though I guess it might be a while before I hear anything back.'

'That would be fantastic,' said Edwin. 'If you don't mind.'

'I don't mind at all.'

Back in his room, Edwin fired off a string of emails, all broadly similar, to various Northingtons and employees of Northington International, requesting availability for interviews. He cross-checked his sent emails with the list that Neville Northington had given him, and realised he'd missed one name — Father White. Edwin remembered meeting him. He had seemed a pleasant, mild man, typical priest really, but then Strong remembered the rather perceptive look in his eyes, that seemed to indicate a strength of character inappropriate for a man of the cloth. He copied the body of his email onto a new message with Father White's address, altered the name at the top, and pressed Send.

Time for some refreshments, he thought. Office etiquette at Parker Investigations dictated that whoever was running an active case would step outside mid-morning and mid-afternoon to fetch coffees and pastries. These would then be added to the case expenses. Edwin knew what Haynes would want, but as he passed

Parker's office on the ground floor he knocked gently at the open door, then discreetly looked the other way as Parker replaced the bottle in his bottom drawer.

'Coffee? Tea?' he asked, staring at the filthy hallway ceiling.

'Oh, thanks,' replied Parker. 'Perhaps just a small bun? You know the ones with icing, and a cherry?'

'Yes. An iced bun. I can get that.'

'And a small coffee. Black. No milk. No sugar. As it comes. And, actually, on second thoughts, scratch the bun. Just the coffee. A small one.'

Parker smiled politely at Edwin, who grinned back and set off to the Blessed Hope Bakery down the road. It had turned into a lovely day, and he almost caught himself whistling as he walked down the street.

There were a few people in front of him in the shop, so Edwin had time for a leisurely examination of the delicacies on offer. The iced buns looked particularly good today. He might have one himself. How was it that glacé cherries looked so much better than fresh ones? The croissants also looked mouthwatering. They were gleaming just enough to look moist and sweet, but not so much that you could doubt their essential lightness and delicate flakiness. And then those custard tarts! The visible contrast between the smooth cool stillness of the custard, and the firm fluffiness of the pastry. Even the wrinkled tin foil they were encased in somehow enhanced the aesthetic pleasure by providing another, well, foil. And the little dark sprinkles of...

Edwin realised that the shop had gone very quiet. He looked up, and the girl behind the counter was looking at him pityingly.

'No rush,' came a voice from behind him.

'Sorry,' said Edwin, turning and apologising to the queue. 'I was miles away.'

'I saw you examining those pastries,' said the girl behind the counter, her eyes wide in mock excitement. 'Did you work out which one committed the crime?'

Several months earlier, when Edwin had started coming into this shop on a regular basis to soak up some expenses on one of his first assignments, he had let slip to this girl, who was called Bet, that he worked as an investigator. He had regretted it ever since.

'No,' he said, 'but I've worked out which one I'd like to violently demolish.' Bet looked alarmed.

'By eating it,' Edwin elaborated lamely.

'Oh, you had a lucky escape there,' said Bet. 'I had my finger on the emergency alarm. I was that close to pressing it.'

Edwin forced a smile. 'Three small black coffees and a custard tart, please.'

'Certainly. That comes to — or maybe you could deduce the total?'

'Six pounds, five pence?' said Edwin after a brief mental battle.

Bet was sorting the coffees. She rang the goods up in the till, and it came to six pounds, five pence. She whistled under her breath. 'You're good!' she said, as she held out her hand for the cash.

The voice behind Edwin chimed in again. 'Come on, you two. This isn't a dating agency!'

Edwin coloured and dropped his handful of coins. They spun and rolled all over the floor.

Bet smiled. 'Tell me when you've recovered the

fugitives,' she said. 'Next, please.'

As he walked back to the office, Edwin thought about the effect Bet had on him. He was fairly down to earth around women, and the few girlfriends he had had, tended to leave him for more exciting partners who were prepared to make more of an effort. He generally hadn't worried about them leaving him. Which had tended to make them blame him even more firmly for the end of the relationship. But Bet made him clumsy, and embarrassed, yet at the same time alive and alert.

At university, Edwin had been a keen player of a trading card game called Fantasy Element Compendium. The characters in the game were represented by cards of various colours, which in turn signified some quality of character. So there were red cards, which featured characters with violent tendencies, and black cards whose representatives exuded a paralysing gloom. He wondered what colour of card he would assign to Bet, were she a character in the game. That was a tricky one. Those sorts of games didn't usually have characters like Bet in them. He'd have to think about it. But the idea of representing personalities by colour — that was interesting.

Edwin had to put down his cardboard tray to open the door. He'd seen Haynes do it with one hand, but so far Edwin had never managed that. Coffees distributed, and back in his office, Edwin saw there were a couple of replies to his recent emails already. He ignored them, and clicked onto to the Fantasy Element Compendium website to refresh his memory.

CHAPTER 16

Alastair Forth shook Edwin's hand, as he greeted him at the lift. He offered him a drink, placed the order for coffee with Sam at the second reception desk, and led Edwin into his office.

It was a medium-sized room, with a surprisingly striking pale grey wall colour. Two of the three pictures on the walls were from the Northington International contemporary art collection, while the third was very small, very dark, and to Edwin's untrained eye, simply looked very old fashioned. Alastair noticed Edwin staring at it.

'Do you know what it is?' he asked. A gentle lilt in his voice was the only remaining sign of a Glasgow childhood.

'No,' admitted Edwin. 'Though would it make much difference if I did?'

'Good question.' Forth smiled. 'Even without knowing what it is, do you like it?'

'Well,' said Edwin, still staring at the tiny square of

muted colours with its cumbersome frame, 'I'm not sure that "like" is the right word, but I can't take my eyes off it. I feel like it's drawing me in to some other world, or era, or something.'

Alastair was standing beside him now. He put on a pair of reading glasses while he looked at the picture. 'Yes,' he said. 'I know exactly what you mean. There were a few disparaging comments when I had this put up, but most people soon shut up when they've stared at it for a few minutes.'

Suddenly Sam was there with coffees, and eventually the two men were sitting, facing each other across Alastair's desk.

'So,' said Alastair, 'what can I tell you?'

'Well, you know why I'm here. My approach is going to involve asking everyone some very general questions, and then to go away and collate the information I've gathered, along with the results of some more technical research. I have a colleague who is a devotee of Sherlock Holmes, who would already have deduced any number of things, but I prefer a more direct and simple route to the truth.'

'Well, all the best with that.' Alastair smiled, and then pursed his lips. 'I absolutely guarantee that not everyone you interview will tell you the truth. Certainly not the whole truth.'

'Yes, you're probably right. But even the lies, or half truths that people tell reveal a lot. And even when they are telling the whole truth, the way that people tell it is also very revealing. Anyway, if you're happy for me to proceed?'

'Yes, of course,' said Alastair.

'And are you happy for me to record this conversation?'

Alastair paused. 'Do you have to?'

'No. I can take notes if you'd rather.' Edwin didn't mention the voice recorder that as an employee of Parker Investigations he routinely wore during his working day.

'Yes, that'd be better,' said Alastair. 'And can I photocopy them when you're finished, for my records?'

'Of course. So when was the last time you saw Tony Northington?'

'Well, as you probably know, he hardly returned to the office after Christmas. I've heard he did come in a couple of times, out of hours, so no-one could see how weak he was becoming, but the last time I saw him would have been the Friday before Christmas.'

Alastair looked at the calendar on his desk. 'Friday the 23rd, that would be.'

'And did you notice anything unusual?'

'To be honest, I had been trying to avoid him unless it was necessary. I didn't even speak to him that day, I don't think. I did see him going into his office though, and I remember thinking that he looked tired.'

Edwin was making notes. He was genuinely making them for his own benefit, though he was aware it was all being recorded, as he knew that the process of going through archived recordings was painfully slow.

'Could you tell me why you had been trying to avoid him?'

Alastair paused for a while. Edwin watched his eyebrows contract and then relax again. Finally he replied.

'Can I trust you?'

'What do you mean?'

Forth didn't reply immediately, so Edwin continued. 'You can trust me that any information you give me will only be used in the context of this investigation, if that's what you mean?'

'It's not quite what I meant, but thanks for the reassurance. I think I can trust you.'

Alastair was holding his glasses on the desk in front of him, and as he talked, he fiddled with them, opening and closing them repeatedly, and then holding them by one wing and tapping them gently on his desk calculator.

'I had been trying to avoid Tony because I didn't trust him. I'd worked for him for thirty years. I'd complemented his skills very well, in my opinion, and to be fair, he'd rewarded me handsomely. I'm not short of money. But more and more, I'd been thinking that the way the company was going was not the way I wanted it to be going. This new Connected Chain Bond, for example, which I'm sure you've heard about. The idea itself is just about ethically justifiable, but the way it was developed, and pushed through the regulators, was something I was very uncomfortable with. This sort of thing had been happening more and more over the years. So finally I decided I'd had enough.'

Alastair paused. Edwin, who had been scribbling away on his yellow, lined notepad, paused too, and looked up, expectantly. After a while, he decided a prompt was in order.

'So, you decided you'd had enough. What did you decide to do about it?'

'Well, I decided that I would try and buy the company. And I went and talked to Tony about it.'

Another pause.

'How did Tony react?'

Alastair looked uncomfortable for a moment. Then he replied slowly and carefully.

'He was unhappy about the idea.'

'Just that? Unhappy about the idea?'

Alastair nodded. Still fiddling with his glasses, he got up from his seat and walked over to the small painting on the wall. He put the glasses on again to have another look at it, before he continued talking.

'Yes. He was unhappy about the idea. So since then, I had been trying to avoid him where possible. Of course it wasn't easy, as historically Tony and I had worked very closely together. But I felt it was for the best, while I got together my plan.' Forth's attention now seemed to drift, as he continued gazing at the miniature picture on the wall.

'What plan was it that you were getting together?' Edwin asked, as casually as possible.

Alastair spun round to face him, and removed his glasses again. 'Sorry. I thought I'd explained. My plan to buy the business.'

Edwin looked confused. 'But Northington International is a private company. There are no shareholders. Surely if Tony Northington was unhappy about selling the business, there was nothing you could do?'

'Yes, yes, that's right.' Now Alastair looked a bit confused. 'I was thinking that he might change his mind. And I wanted to be ready.'

'We'd probably be talking about having access to a very large sum of money?' Edwin said, tentatively.

'Yes, pretty large.' Alastair seemed quite casual about it.

'And did you want to buy the business on your own?'

'Either that, or with my partner, Gerry. Latterly my plan was to buy it with Gerry.'

'OK,' said Edwin. 'It's really helpful for me to just get an idea of what was going on behind the scenes, as it were. I'm sure you realise that at the moment there's not even a hint of Tony Northington's death being suspicious. Officially the heart trouble he'd suffered with for several years finally caught up with him. I believe about fifteen percent of those on the waiting list for a heart transplant die before receiving it. And he was one of the unlucky ones. But are you happy for me to have photocopies of your diary for the last year? So from last March?'

Alastair thought briefly. 'Yes, that would be fine. I'll send them over. I guess you're going to very casually ask for access to my bank records as well?'

Edwin smiled.

'No problem,' said Forth. 'And don't worry about making me copies of those notes you've been taking.'

'OK. Final thing for now,' said Edwin. He handed over a sheaf of A4 pages stapled together.

'It's a bit old-school these days, but would you mind filling in this whereabouts chart for the weeks leading up to Tony's death? I know it will duplicate any diary entries, but I'm asking everyone to fill in the same forms, in the same format.'

'Of course,' said Alastair. 'Will that be all, then?'

'Yes, that's all for now,' said Edwin.

Alastair shook his hand, then sat back down at his

desk, already replacing his reading glasses as he did so, and starting to leaf through the papers Edwin had given him. Edwin shut the door carefully behind him. As he turned to walk off, he suddenly frowned in annoyance. He'd not found out what the picture was.

CHAPTER 17

The rendezvous was the main concourse at Euston Station. The time was six fifteen. Edwin couldn't stop himself yawning repeatedly. He had gone to bed early the night before, but had kept waking during the night, worried about sleeping through his four forty-five alarm. Eventually he had got up before it was due to go off. He felt even more obliged than usual to get ready quietly, with the result that everything he did took more time, and when his minicab driver rapped gently on the door he wasn't ready.

But here he was, on the concourse, bang on time. Practically no traffic, and a good run of lights. He looked round for Neville Northington. They both had tickets for the six twenty-five, as due to Neville's chronic lack of free time, Edwin was going to interview him as he travelled to Manchester for a meeting. He had expressed concern about the lack of privacy this provided, but Neville had dismissed his fear, saying he had nothing to hide. Suddenly he saw him, striding briskly across from the main entrance. Neville must have seen Edwin at the same time, as he altered his course to head straight for him.

'Morning.' Neville held out his hand.

'Morning,' replied Edwin. 'Good journey?'

'Yes, fine.' Neville was already scanning the departure boards, and had spotted the platform they needed. 'We're on eight. I've got your ticket too. Let's go.'

As the train eased away from Euston, the two men settled into opposite seats in one of the first class areas. This was Edwin's first time travelling first class, and it gave him a boyish thrill. A year ago his day might have involved a lecture and some reading — now he was travelling Intercity first class from London to Manchester to interview a high-flying businessman about a murder. Or was it a murder?

Up to this point, Edwin realised, he had assumed that it wasn't. That it was death by natural causes. That Neville Northington was both an upset, bereaved son, and a suspicious colleague in a business whose legal ownership still hadn't been pinned down satisfactorily, and who was therefore paranoid about others' intentions. But now he was suddenly aware that, paranoid or not, Neville might be right about the nature of his father's death. After all, he must surely have *some* concrete reasons for his suspicions. And suddenly the ambivalence of the case being possibly murder and possibly not, became a rather sinister additional layer to Edwin's investigations, rather than a dilution of the significance of his research.

All this passed through Edwin's mind as he settled

himself in his seat, and got out his notepad.

'Right,' said Neville. 'Let's start with my mother.'

He looked at Edwin's closed notebook.

'Are you writing this down?'

'Yes, okay. I'll make some notes,' said Edwin, opening his pad to a fresh page and taking the lid off his pen.

'So,' said Neville, 'my parents were married for over thirty years. They were madly in love to start off with, otherwise they wouldn't have overcome the class divide. Mother's family thought that Father was beneath her. And his family thought her a terrible snob, and simultaneously thought him awfully shallow for marrying for money. That's how they saw it, anyway. But he made something of himself over the years, and as he did so, Mother lost interest in him. Sure he had to be away a lot on business, but clearly that's par for the course. And as soon as he had given her two children, she was busy enough. But since Amelia and I had left home, she had no time for him at all. Always nipping up to Simon's farm in Suffolk, or consorting with that priest.'

'Sorry,' said Edwin. 'Simon is?'

'Simon is her brother. He runs what's left of the family estate. Has horses, mostly. But anyway, the more successful Father became, the more distant Mother became from him. Even I could see that, though my perspective may not be completely objective. Factor in the priest, and there you have it. Obviously you never met Father, but if you'd seen how firm he had to be with her, you'd maybe understand a bit more about what my mother is really like.'

Neville Northington adjusted his position in his seat, carefully placed his hands together, fingertip to fingertip, and pressed his forefingers against his lips. Edwin wondered if he had finished. He hadn't.

'Moving on from the murder itself, there are other things it would be good for you to uncover on your way to solving it. Starting with Jasper Felder.'

'I'm sorry,' said Edwin. 'Just to rewind a bit. Am I right in thinking that you are saying your mother murdered your father?'

Neville shrugged. 'Yes, I think it's pretty likely. But if you discover it couldn't possibly have been her, it'll have been the priest on her behalf. Think about it. She inherits his money. She runs off with the priest. End of story. And if you find that both of them are definitely in the clear, then, beneath his calm exterior, Alastair Forth is your man.'

Edwin was struggling to take this all in. 'But why should anyone have murdered him?'

'Did you meet him?'

'Well, no, but—'

'I'll say no more then. So, as I was saying, Jasper Felder. Get some technical assistance (I can give you a few names) and start investigating the way the Best Seller, sorry, the Connected Chain Bond, functions. I worked with him on it, and it's my belief he's incorporated some sort of devious trick to benefit himself at the expense of the company. The FCA have been all over it without finding anything, but then again, the FCA couldn't find their own—'

'Sorry again,' said Edwin. 'The FCA is?'

'The Financial Conduct Authority.' Neville stared at

Edwin. 'God, you've got a lot to learn. If you've got good technical assistance, as I say, from someone who's a programming whizz and understands the electronic banking scene, you may be able to unravel his little scam. Then moving on to Forth, assuming he's not the murderer, I'd really like to know what he and that Gerry of his are up to. Not in that way, of course. I really *don't* want to know what they're up to in that way!' Neville chuckled. 'But I'm sure they've been plotting something. I'm no slouch at body language, and I can—'

He suddenly stopped talking and bent his head down, with his right hand at one side of it, as if to shield his face from view. He then started scratching his head, with his hand in a strange shape, as if pointing or signalling. Confused, Edwin looked around, but saw nothing.

'Are you all right?' he asked Northington.

'Yes, just scratching this... should get it seen to... there. I think that's better.'

Edwin had another look in the direction Neville kept glancing, but still saw nothing.

'Are you happy to continue?' he asked.

'Yes, should be okay now. Where were we?'

Edwin looked at his notes. 'You were just talking about Alastair Forth, and his partner, and suggesting they were maybe plotting something. It would be very helpful for me, if you could give me any more concrete evidence to back up your suspicions. Any documents, conversations, unusual behaviour, that sort of thing. Would you have any of those?'

Neville stared at him coldly. 'Well, I would have thought that was your job, as the investigator. I've already done half your work for you by pointing you in the right direction. Anyway, I don't know what sort of hold Forth had over Father, but it must have been quite considerable, for him still to have that plum job thirty years after being taken on. I'm sure you can squirrel that information out of him. And if not, there are other investigators.'

Edwin's pride was stung. 'Yes, I'll be able to examine all sorts of details, including his financial affairs. In fact, I've started doing so already.'

'Really? You're on to him already?'

Edwin was surprised at how gratified he felt by Northington's eager expression of interest.

'Yes, I've been doing a bit of digging, finding out one or two things. Obviously I can't say what they are till my research is complete, but I've got good access to his financial activities in particular.'

'Oh, you can tell me. I'm paying for the bloody investigation!'

Edwin felt awkward. He hadn't so far found out anything at all suspicious about Forth. The only surprising thing was how much of his income he seemed to give to various charities. So he clutched at this straw.

'There are a few transactions with certain organisations that are rather surprising. I'll be looking at them in more detail.'

'Hmm. Well, I must say you're doing rather better than I feared you would when I first saw you.'

'Thank you,' said Edwin, unsure how much of a compliment this was.

He couldn't help asking his next question with a slight ironic emphasis. 'Are there any other people who you suspect of things you'd like me to investigate?'

His tone of voice was lost on Northington, apparently, as he answered quite seriously.

'Yes, a few more. My sister, Amelia, has had just as bad a relationship with Father as my mother. And she's very emotional. Artistic temperament and all that. Until the will's been clarified, I don't know exactly what she would have stood to gain by his death, but she's so temperamental that she might have done him in just in a rage.'

'But,' pointed out Edwin, trying to be the voice of reason, 'There is still no evidence that it was murder.'

'There will be,' said Neville darkly. 'You mark my words, there will be.'

The train was now stopping at Milton Keynes, and conversation lagged for a while as the carriages lost and then gained passengers. The area Neville and Edwin were sitting in suddenly became busier.

'I'll just take a wander down the train,' said Edwin. 'I need the loo, and I'm going to get a drink too.' He felt obliged to add, 'Do you want one as well?'

'A drink? No, far too early in the morning. But I know what you detective types are like. However if you're going, I'll have a tomato juice. Apparently its healthy. So Louise tells me.'

Edwin Strong slowly made his way through the carriages. The train was moving smoothly, despite already having regained much of its original speed. But he was in no rush to get back to a man who radiated suspicion like Neville did. He used the loo, and then in the very next carriage found the buffet area. Wanting a bit more time to himself, he walked through it, and carried on slowly down the train.

If the people he was passing were characters in Fantasy Element Compendium, he thought to himself, what colour of cards would represent them? That man, for example. Beige zipped jacket, completely blank face as he stared out the window. A grey card, Edwin decided, whatever that meant. But of course he might have a surprising secret power. And how about this woman, talking cheerfully on the phone, but in between sentences mouthing angry phrases at her lively young son, and even miming a threat to hit him? Edwin couldn't recall the colour for a changeable or duplicitous personality. He moved on.

What about the woman by the window over there, again staring out the window, but who looked exactly like the receptionist girl from Northington International? Hang on a minute, that *was* the receptionist girl from Northington International. Edwin was almost completely sure. She didn't seem to notice him as he passed. He couldn't remember her name, but she definitely served him coffee when he was there. Was she travelling to the same meetings as Neville, for secretarial back-up? Or was it just a coincidence?

Edwin had now reached the very end of the train, and turned round to head back to the restaurant car and, eventually, his seat. He looked out for the girl on his way back, and this time he was sure she saw him and immediately looked away. He didn't stop, and didn't say anything, but filed it away for future reference.

So, armed with a coffee and a tomato juice, Edwin arrived back where he had started. Neville was on the phone when he got back, but quickly ended his call, and didn't seem inclined to talk about it. And Edwin didn't mention the girl he'd seen. In fact the momentum of the interview had definitely stalled now, as the neighbouring seats had filled up, and despite Northington's fighting talk about having nothing to hide, Edwin's prediction about a train not being the best place for a confidential interview seemed to have come true. By the time they eventually drew into Manchester Piccadilly, the only further ground they had covered was that Neville had reluctantly taken one of Edwin's whereabouts questionnaires, and equally reluctantly agreed to give the young detective access to his bank accounts. Edwin had to remind him that the terms of his engagement meant Neville had to be investigated the same as everyone else.

'Ah, yes, of course,' said Neville. 'We've got to make it look convincing. I get it. Though clearly, if I was guilty of anything, I wouldn't have started this investigation.'

And then they were both off the train, Neville to get a cab to his meeting, and Edwin to get the next train back. Though he did make a point of loitering for a while, for long enough to see the girl from Northington International exit through the barriers after him, and head over to where Neville was waiting in the cab rank. He couldn't hear their conversation from where he was, but thought the embrace they shared looked more affectionate than business protocol strictly permitted.

CHAPTER 18

Thursday morning found Edwin Strong slumped in his comfortable office chair, feeling at a bit of a loss, and staring blankly at the ceiling. Molly Raestock had just emailed to postpone tomorrow's interview. He found this surprisingly disconcerting, perhaps because Sheldon Haynes had hinted that she might be central to the investigation.

Edwin didn't like this vacant feeling. He worked best when there were a variety of ideas and options floating in the air like butterflies, and all he had to do was net one, and have a look at it, to see if it was what he was looking for. He often found that even a butterfly that didn't fit the bill often led him to one that did, but he was now finding that a butterfly which postponed its interview seemed to drive all the others under cover.

His youthful and energetic nature soon tired of this dejected mood however, and Edwin levered himself upright, and began pacing round the room. Even a bit of movement helped, and almost immediately Edwin found ideas, half-ideas, and tenuous associations beginning to cluster on the edges of his consciousness. Never mind about Molly Raestock for now. His time spent with both Alastair Forth and Neville Northington had provided him with plenty of scope for research. He'd looked through Alastair's returned whereabouts chart, and it certainly tallied with his diary entries. But it would, of course — that would have been how he had filled it in. Edwin wondered how he could double-check these details. Maybe the swipe card system installed at the office would have some useful information. He'd ask Dave about it when he spoke to him next.

Dave Clark had been one of Edwin's friends in Bristol, who had been an extraordinary computer whizz. He hadn't achieved spectacular results in his studies, but the stories of his hacking and programming activities were legion. He was also Edwin's only friend who had his own personalised greeting, the Dave Clark High Five. Edwin had got him to agree in principle to help him with the technical side of his investigations, and he was going to speak to him as soon as he had a better idea of exactly what needed doing. That might even be this evening, as this afternoon he was due to talk to Jasper Felder.

Edwin got out the sheet of notes he had made about Jasper. There wasn't much information on it, apart from a couple of remarks about Neville's suspicions that he had interfered with the workings of the Connected Chain Bond in some way.

All Edwin's note-taking was done on yellow paper with black ink, as he found it easier to read, but in the case of Jasper Felder, without even having met the man,

Edwin had a feeling that the colour somehow suited his character. We're back to Fantasy Element Compendium again, he thought with a smile.

It was nearly time for a mid-morning break, but having done it every day this week so far, Edwin was determined not to run for coffee yet again. After all, Haynes had a live case as well — that was the reason he couldn't help Edwin more. Let him go.

So to keep himself busy should Sheldon look in, Edwin returned to his chair and had another look at the details of Fantasy Element Compendium online. There were useful guides as to what various colours represented in terms of basic personality type, and then, by accident, he stumbled across a site which had templates for creating your own cards.

Edwin selected a background colour of yellow, copied a photo of Jasper Felder from the Northington International website and pasted it in position on the card template. He leant back to study the effect from a distance, and smiled. This was good. There were sections for ratings of various abilities, and room for a couple of explanatory sentences as well. He'd fill those in later.

Just as he was in this position of leaning back and smiling, Sheldon Haynes, on his phone, poked his head round the door of Edwin's office, and mouthed the words 'Small black coffee please', pointing apologetically at the handset clamped to the side of his face.

Edwin sighed and pursed his lips. Then he remembered Bet, and at the same moment remembered that in many firms the junior member of staff always gets the drinks. So why not.

'Hello Jasper. Are you good to talk?'

Edwin was still in his office, and was talking slowly and clearly to his ancient desktop computer. It was so old he had to use a separate desk microphone for Skype.

'Yes, that's cool,' said Jasper. 'I've just had breakfast, and don't have any meetings till after lunch.'

Jasper was in New York, where he had been since Tuesday, attending a conference on financial technology. He was finishing off his short trip by having a couple of meetings with independent companies providing investment services.

'Okay. Well, thanks for sparing the time. I wanted to start by asking you a bit about your background. Where you were born, and brought up — that sort of thing. And then how you came to be involved with Northington International.'

Skype was very useful, but almost immediately Edwin was regretting the decision to use it. He thought he detected a wary look pass over Jasper's face, but the poor quality of the connection, or perhaps of his machine, meant that he wasn't sure.

'Yes, sure, I can talk about that.' There was definitely a trace of something in Jasper's accent that wasn't a Skype issue.

'I was born in Amsterdam, in 1986, and grew up there, studying computing and then working for Rabobank, still in Amsterdam, till I answered an advert from Northington International. At that time they were looking for someone fluent in Dutch. I applied, and I presume my background in both computing and banking sealed the deal. I initially worked on some tentative joint projects with companies in the Netherlands, but they didn't last long. Tony took me under his wing after a while, and I progressed rapidly through the company. Most recently I've been working on the Connected Chain Bond, heading up the technical side.'

'Can I ask how long you've been in the States? Were you, for example, still in London for Tony Northington's funeral?'

Edwin watched Jasper leaning forward to adjust his laptop and then almost immediately the picture froze. It stayed that way for a couple of minutes, occasionally flickering and jumping to a slightly changed image, but staying basically static. Then it resumed normal service.

'— and I've been here since,' Jasper was saying.

'I'm sorry, I missed most of that,' said Edwin. 'Dodgy connection. But no matter, I'll get that information from you later. I'm really interested at the moment in the personal side of all this. Perhaps you could tell me something about the nature of your relationship with Tony Northington.'

Again Jasper seemed to lean forward, and again the screen froze. But this time the hiatus didn't last nearly as long.

'— was very helpful. So I found myself very quickly progressing on the programming side. In a sense I was just the perfect fit, with the right genetic make-up to be able to learn and apply computing skills to the thorough understanding I already had of banking and investments.'

Edwin felt frustrated to be missing so much, but thought it better to keep moving for now.

'How many people in the company would have a similar level of programming expertise to your own?

How many people, for example, would be able to understand every step in the structure of the Connected Chain Bond?'

There was another pause, but this time it wasn't due to a technical hitch.

'Oh, there are quite a few, I'd say. Ten? Twenty? Neville Northington understands it much better than I do, for example.'

'Really?' said Edwin, genuinely surprised. 'He gave me the impression that you were the only one who was completely au fait with its workings.'

'No,' said Jasper, dismissively. 'He's just being modest. He's all over that code.'

For the first time in the interview Jasper smiled, though perhaps rather coldly. Edwin continued with the technical angle.

'In terms of programming languages, what do you mainly use?'

'Well, primarily Java, but also a lot of Python for prototyping, and C, when it's required.'

Edwin thought Jasper seemed to be relaxing a little.

'My personal trademark is using an unnecessarily complicated mixture of languages. I like to keep people on their toes.'

He grinned.

'That's great,' said Edwin, who was rapidly losing interest in this very unsatisfactory interview format. 'When do you return to the UK?'

'I'm scheduled on a flight next Tuesday, but I've got plenty of leeway with my visa, so I'm keeping my options open, depending on how my meetings go here. Being more on the technical side, it's not often I get to travel, so if I can make the most of it, and have constructive meetings at the same time, well, can you blame me?'

'No,' said Edwin. 'I certainly can't. But if you're going to be there for a while, do you mind if I email you a whereabouts questionnaire? If you could just fill that in, I hopefully won't need to bother you again while you're in the States. And thanks for already completing the bank forms. Very helpful.'

'No worries at all,' said Jasper, smiling. 'Just ping it over.'

'The only other thing,' said Edwin, 'is your diary. Could you scan your diary entries for the last year, and send them to me? I appreciate you probably won't have last year's with you, but even just this year for now, and the rest when you're back.'

Again the Skype image froze on the screen.

'Why won't Parker buy a proper computer,' muttered Edwin under his breath. But when the picture started moving again, it was as if he'd missed nothing.

'I'm afraid I'm one of the modern generation who doesn't use a diary,' said Jasper. 'Sorry about that.'

'Electronic schedule records are fine,' said Edwin. 'Any format.' And then quietly, and trying not to move his lips, 'Any format apart from Skype, that is.'

'Ok,' Jasper said. 'I'll get something to you. Will that be all?'

'Yes. Thanks for your time. I hope you have a successful trip.'

'I'll do my best.' Jasper reached a hand out, as if towards Edwin, and his image disappeared from the screen.

Very unsatisfactory, thought Edwin to himself, leaning back in his chair. He had jotted down the names of the programming languages for Dave's benefit, but apart from that he had picked up no new information, and due to the technically erratic and intrinsically impersonal nature of the connection, very little feel for the essence of the man who was Jasper Felder.

He pulled up the Fantasy Element Compendium page he'd been playing with earlier, and sighed as he realised how little he could add to the card he'd been creating. In the Special Powers section however, he added Java, Python and C. And then, as an afterthought, Dutch.

Sheldon Haynes was in his favourite contorted position, awkwardly squashed into his comfortable chair, when after a perfunctory knock, the door to his office opened, and Edwin entered. He looked gloomy, thought Haynes. Poor kid.

'How's it going?' he asked.

'Oh, so-so. I've just interviewed Jasper Felder via Skype. Very unsatisfactory method — I don't recommend it.'

'Don't worry. I wouldn't use it even if you did recommend it.'

'But despite the weakness of the method, the odd thing was he was nothing like I expected.'

'What did you base your expectation on?' asked Haynes, shifting his position slightly in his chair, and indicating the client chair, should Edwin wish to sit down. Edwin shook his head.

'Probably on what I heard from Neville Northington,' he replied.

'I see,' said Haynes.

'But what I wanted to ask was, have you had any feedback from your hospital contact yet? I know it's early days, but I could do with finding something suspicious.'

'Sorry, I haven't heard anything so far. Have you talked to the office manager woman yet? Molly Raestock?'

'No. She's had to re-schedule the appointment we made for tomorrow.'

Haynes' eyebrows flicked upwards a little. 'Is that suspicious?'

'Not really. She had to make an emergency dental appointment,' said Edwin.

'That old excuse. Tell me — have you done any actual sleuthing? Any snooping around? Any not trusting a word anyone tells you, and looking for clues?'

Edwin looked uncomfortable. Haynes thought he could safely push it a bit more.

'You've just told me that what Northington led you to expect, and what you actually found, didn't tally.'

'It's not exactly a smoking gun,' said Edwin.

'No, but it's suspicious. Any other discrepancies of that type?'

'Well, Alastair Forth wasn't really how Northington portrayed him either.'

'There you go,' said Haynes.

'My assumption is that Northington believes the worst of everyone, and therefore they're never as bad as he makes out. Though occasionally,' Edwin continued more thoughtfully, 'occasionally I get the feeling that he might be right. But surely not about everybody? It just doesn't make sense.'

Sheldon shrugged. 'I'll gently nudge my hospital contact. But in the meantime, I suggest you become more suspicious. What's your next step?'

'Well, I'm meeting my computer expert tonight, and then tomorrow I'm going to talk to the widow. Who, incidentally, Northington is also suspicious of, even though she's his mother.'

Haynes raised his eyebrows fully and snorted. 'Good grief. Still. Just remember, sleuthing is the way forward. Let me know how you get on.'

Edwin met Dave Clark in The Plough after work, and greeted him in the traditional way, with the Dave Clark High Five. Dave's eyes lit up as Edwin explained that the drinks would be on him. Or rather, on his firm. Or rather, on his firm's client.

'You've fallen on your feet!' said Dave, impressed.

'Yes,' agreed Edwin. 'The money's terrible, but there are perks. There you go. A pint of Tree Shaker. Cheers.'

Edwin felt his spirits rise as he cautiously took his first sip. 'Here's to old friends,' he said.

'Old friends,' Dave echoed. 'So tell me what you need me to do.'

Edwin tilted his head towards an empty table in the far corner of the pub, and Dave, nodding, followed him over. They sat down, and Edwin began talking quietly.

'Well, there's something I'd like you to look into. It's a software package that controls a complicated financial product, which according to my client, has been doctored by one of its designers. I've talked to the man he suspects, and I don't share his suspicion. But I'm being paid to research these things. Though actually, thinking out loud, it's nothing to do with the original investigation. Anyway, what do you need to know in order to access this software, and to tell me if there's anything suspicious about it?'

'This is just up my street. What I need is for you to point me to the product, point me to the company that makes it, to tell me any more information you have, and then to stand back in amazement.'

'That's my man,' said Edwin. 'Make sure you keep track of your expenses, won't you? And I can pay you a good hourly rate too.'

Dave's eyes lit up, and suddenly Edwin felt a bit apprehensive. 'You will be able to do it, won't you?'

'If I can't do it,' said Dave, 'you won't have to pay me a thing. Tell me what you've got, and if I can't get anywhere by Monday, I'll gracefully withdraw, humiliated and shamed.'

'Well I'll still be happy, I mean *my client* will still be happy to pay you for your expertise. He gave me the authorisation keys that are needed to log on as him, if that helps.'

'Yes, that will save a lot of time.' Dave Clark looked thoughtful. 'You know, no offence and all that, but would you mind if I went straight off after this drink and got cracking on it?'

Edwin laughed. 'Some friend you are!'

Dave looked crestfallen.

'Of course I don't mind,' Edwin continued. 'It's helping me enormously having you on board with this. The sooner the better!'

Edwin fished a sheet of his yellow paper from his

pocket. It had many lines of his handwriting on it, done to an uncharacteristically neat standard.

'This is all the info I've got. I can email it to you if you'd rather?'

'A handwritten copy is good, thanks. It's more cloak and dagger to avoid leaving an electronic trail with emails.'

'Exactly what I was thinking. And talking of leaving a trail, I do need you to sign this disclaimer for my boss.' Edwin now pulled a printed page from the same pocket. 'Just on the off-chance that you drag our firm through the dirt by your clumsy and illegal methods, we use this to prove we know nothing about you.'

'Even though we'll both have signed it?' asked Dave, glancing through the document.

'Even though that.'

'Blimey. And did you take my advice and record your Skype conversation?'

'Yes, I did, but the whole thing was a bit of a washout. Connection kept dropping. But I can always look back over it if I feel I need to.'

'Cool.'

Conversation now drifted into more general matters. Who was doing what now. The current success and lack of success among their university peers. Who had been lucky enough to be able to stay in Bristol and who was back living with their parents. But the time flew by, and without even staying for a second drink, Dave headed for the bus stop, itching to get started on his project.

Edwin, heading the other way off down Barry Road, felt much better than he had done for a while. With Dave on his side, and Sheldon Haynes looking out for him as well, he thought his investigation was now on a sounder footing.

CHAPTER 19

On Friday morning, at nine o'clock, Edwin again walked up the drive of the house in Hampstead. It looked bigger in daylight. In fact all the houses in the road looked big. And as this was one of the most expensive areas of London, they must cost an absolute fortune. He rang the doorbell. The door was opened by the same impressive looking man who had opened it last time. Suddenly Edwin felt like a child who has accidentally kicked his ball into a neighbour's garden. Please don't let his voice squeak.

'Hello, I've got an appointment to see Mrs Northington? To talk to her?'

The impressive looking man didn't have the opportunity to reply, as the woman he had come to interview appeared at the far end of the hallway, and began speaking immediately.

'Hello, do come in. It's Edwin, isn't it?'

She was tall and slender, and though Edwin knew she was sixty, he didn't think she looked it. Her hair was very fair, though perhaps there was some grey in there too? He wasn't sure. Now he felt like a boy who was obliged to make conversation with his friend's mother.

'Hello Mrs Northington. Thanks for making the time to see me.'

'Well, I didn't have much choice, did I?'

Edwin made a rueful grimace, as Jeanette Northington indicated the door of the room at the front of the house.

'We can talk in here,' she said. 'I'm sorry, that sounded rather impolite. I know you're just doing your job, and it's Neville who's put us all in this awkward position.'

'I'll try and make it as painless as possible,' said Edwin. 'I've just got a list of basic questions that I'm asking everyone. It shouldn't take too long. And can I just say again how sorry I am for your loss.'

'Thanks for your sympathy,' said Jeanette. 'But, to be honest, there are benefits to being a widow.'

'Oh?' said Edwin, surprised.

'Yes. The main one is that I don't have to live with Tony Northington any more.' Jeanette must have noticed Edwin's shocked expression. 'Don't worry, I didn't kill him. Though do please investigate me anyway, just to keep Neville happy. You never met Tony, but he could be a most unpleasant man. Most difficult and most unpleasant. Of course he wasn't always like that, or I wouldn't have married him. When I met him he was quite charming. Well, in fact all his life he was quite charming. But he was less and less charming to me.'

Edwin and Jeanette had been standing just inside the door of the living room. Jeanette moved as if to sit down, then suddenly stopped, and said, 'How rude of me. I haven't offered you anything. Would you like a cup of tea? Coffee?' Then she suddenly smiled. 'Orange squash, maybe?'

Edwin laughed. 'I'm not as young as I look. Well, maybe I am. But, yes, I'd love a cup of tea.'

'Great. We can talk better with tea. Let's go in the kitchen.'

Jeanette led the way out of the living room, down the hallway to the far end, and into a spacious kitchen which overlooked the well-tended back garden. The man who had opened the door to Edwin was sitting at the kitchen table, with a mug in front of him and a copy of The Times.

'Hello,' said Edwin, awkwardly.

The man ignored him, and instead addressed Jeanette. 'Would you like me to move, Miss Jeanette?'

'No, Hunter, you stay here. I'm just going to make a couple of mugs of tea, and then young Edwin and I will take them elsewhere and talk.'

As Jeanette busied herself with the kettle, mugs and tea bags, Edwin looked around the room. It was very homely — surprisingly homely, he thought, for such an impressive house. The man Jeanette called Hunter watched him with what Edwin felt was disapproval. Well, let him disapprove, thought Edwin. Fair enough, really. He'd probably disapprove if he was in Hunter's position.

The tea made, Jeanette handed one cup to Edwin.

'Right,' she said. 'Follow me.'

She led the way back into the hallway, and seemed to be heading for the living room again. Then at the last minute she suddenly turned the other way.

'Let's go in here. This was Tony's office for many years. It's almost as he left it, though Neville's been endlessly in and out looking for papers.'

The room they went into wasn't large, but had a good many filing cabinets along one wall. The only window, on the opposite wall, gave a side view of the house next door. Edwin hoped he wasn't going to have to start hunting for documents here. There would be thousands. The enormity of his task smote him yet again. Jeanette was still talking.

'It's strange coming in here now. Tony didn't like me in this room when he was working on something, and he certainly didn't want me coming in here when he was out.'

'Did he work from home a lot?'

'More and more, over the years. When he was younger, he would have been out at the office all the time, or making trips abroad. Though I never liked him doing those trips — he tended to come back in a bad frame of mind. But latterly, he didn't work quite such long days, but made up for it by shutting himself in here for hours on end doing goodness knows what.'

'A bit of a workaholic?'

Jeanette nodded grimly. 'The original model. It's probably fair to say he had a chip on his shoulder, which was exacerbated when we got married. He felt my family looked down on him, and certainly his family made it very clear they considered me a bit of a snob, and him an opportunist, for marrying into my family.'

'And do you think this was a motivating factor in his relentless work ethic?'

'Certainly to start with. He was quite open about that. I've no idea more recently, as he wasn't open about anything, really.'

Jeanette sat down on her late husband's chair. 'In the early days, even when he was busy, he'd still have time for me. He'd make time, and we'd talk through everything. But yes, that drive to make something of himself was always there, pushing him on. I do regret not being more emphatic in my attempts to reassure him that he didn't need to do anything. That I was very happy with him as he was.'

Edwin stood quietly listening.

'When I was pregnant with Neville, for example, he couldn't have been better to me. But looking back at that time, I felt I had now got all I had ever wanted, while he was obviously thinking that things were just starting off. Maybe he thought he had to try and get all *he* ever wanted, and make sure it was more impressive than what I wanted? Maybe he was competing with me? I just don't know.'

Edwin wasn't sure whether to say anything. Jeanette seemed lost in her own thoughts now, as she sat there, her mug of tea still steaming between her cupped hands. Edwin took a sip of his.

'Then when Neville was a tiny baby, he went away to that conference in Denmark or somewhere, and when he got back, I remember thinking how hard he seemed. Hard, and a bit shallow, maybe. He didn't change completely overnight, but really ever since then, his hardness, his shallowness, his driven-ness, all separated him from me. Sad really.'

Jeannette looked up. 'Right,' she said, more briskly.

'You'll have some specific questions you'll want to ask me. Let fly with them, and I'll do my best. I tell you what — I'll show you round the house as we talk.'

So the widow and the detective climbed several flights of stairs, and started at the very top. From a couple of the windows on the highest floor there were spectacular views across London. And even the spare bedrooms that obviously weren't used that much, had an air of warmth and welcome, despite also looking very modern. Edwin noticed this.

'Nothing to do with my official questions,' he said, 'but I'm intrigued by how you've managed to make the whole house both welcoming and stylish. It's not really my thing, but I've noticed before that often houses which are very well decorated are also rather impersonal. I hope you don't mind me asking?'

'No, not at all. But I honestly don't know the answer. Though people are genuinely welcome here. Welcome to visit, welcome to stay. And as far as the decor goes, I've had plenty of time to consider it, and no real budget constraints, though actually I haven't done anything terribly expensive.'

Edwin nodded thoughtfully. Then he said, 'While we're up here with this spectacular panorama of London, I've got a question about the overview of your late husband's life. Neville seemed to suggest to me that there were several people with a strong motivation to do away with him. Would you agree with that?'

'Oh, certainly,' said Jeanette immediately. 'As I think I said, even I am finding huge benefits to life without him.'

'Will there be financial benefits?' probed Edwin.

'In theory I would have thought that I would inherit half, and Neville and Amelia the other half. I believe Neville has a lawyer looking at the will as we speak. You probably know more about that than I do.'

Edwin felt another twinge of apprehension, and Jeanette continued talking.

'But financial benefits wouldn't have motivated me to kill him in any case.'

She paused. After a minute she continued, frowning, and talking more slowly, as if she was piecing her thoughts and feelings together as she voiced them.

'Maybe aesthetic benefits might have motivated me. And after all, his actual death wasn't violent or ugly. So if I had no check on my behaviour beyond that of style, I might have chosen to do away with him in a non-offensive manner, to remove his coarse influence from my elegant world. It's possible.'

Jeanette seemed to suddenly snap into a brighter mood now. 'Come on,' she said. 'Let's go down a floor.'

As Edwin followed her down the stairs, his footsteps noiseless on the thick carpet, she kept talking.

'As far as other people go, the most obvious person with a financial motivation would be Neville himself. Though of course that is dependent on the outcome of the company ownership issue. I think Alastair Forth had some sort of issue with Tony, and actually, his partner...'

Jeanette's voice, which had up till now been strong and relaxed, now faltered.

'His partner?' prompted Edwin.

'His partner has worked for a couple of other companies with some sort of competitive interests with Northington International.'

Jeanette's voice was almost back to normal.

'And Tony had been getting very suspicious about that, I think. Oh dear, I don't want to put Alastair in an awkward position.'

'Don't worry, Mrs Northington. The best thing is to be as clear as possible. If there's nothing in it, there will be no repercussions for him.'

'Yes. I see what you mean. I'm sure it's nothing.'

They entered the room at the front of the house on the first floor.

'This was our bedroom,' said Jeanette. 'Nice and big, with a dressing room for me, and a bathroom each.'

Edwin noticed a booklet on one of the bedside tables. Jeanette saw him look at it.

'That was Tony's side,' she said. 'He started looking through that in the evening before going to sleep, in the last couple of weeks before he went into hospital. I was so pleased, as he and Amelia never got on. So she was very touched when I was able to tell her that he'd been leafing through the catalogue for her recent show every night.'

'When you say they never got on,' said Edwin, 'I'm sorry to put this so bluntly, but would you say Amelia might have been motivated to kill him?'

'Oh, yes,' replied Jeanette immediately. 'I'm sure there were loads of times she would have wanted to. But suddenly, and violently, and in the heat of the moment. And even if there was anything suspicious in Tony's death, it certainly wasn't something sudden or violent.'

'I see,' said Edwin, making a mental note nonetheless.

They moved on through the other bedrooms.

'Seeing all these beds,' said Jeanette, 'you're probably

trying to work out how to politely enquire about my love life with Tony.'

Edwin coloured.

'So to avoid you having to ask, I'll tell you it disappeared very rapidly after our children arrived. I did make an effort, but despite sporadic bouts of enthusiasm, Tony's mind was on other things. That's what it felt like anyway. I gave up suggesting it in the end. There's only so much pleasure a girl can get out of it when her partner's thinking about something else. I'm not aware of him having affairs, and from my point of view, it wasn't something that occurred to me to look for until I was that little bit older, and by that time I'd seen that sort of thing go badly wrong for so many of my friends, that it wasn't hard for me to avoid any entanglements.'

Jeanette smiled. 'And you can probably see by the fact that I used the word 'entanglements', what I think of the idea.'

Edwin had regained his composure. 'Thanks for telling me, though strictly speaking it wasn't on my list of questions. Perhaps it should have been. As you know, I haven't been doing this very long. Though I've got a more experienced colleague backing me up, and giving me lots of advice.'

'A good way to learn,' said Jeanette. 'But I've got to say, you're good at inspiring confidence in the person being questioned. Though maybe I'd feel differently if I had something to hide.'

'Well, I'm glad you've nothing to hide,' said Edwin, trying to laugh off his embarrassment at being complimented. 'That brings me on neatly to my next point, which is that I'd like copies of your diary entries and bank statements for the last year. Would that be okay?'

'Yes, fine,' said Jeanette. 'Would that be my engagement diary, or my Dear Diary diary?'

'Both would be brilliant,' said Edwin. 'Could you scan them and email them over to me?'

'Possibly,' said Jeanette. 'But it'd be much quicker if you just took them. When you've finished, or scanned them, just send them back, would you?'

'Yes, of course,' said Edwin.

They were now back on the ground floor, and had finally returned to the living room.

'Is that all for now?' asked Jeanette.

'Yes, you've been very helpful,' said Edwin.

'I'll just go and get those diaries.'

Jeanette left the room. Almost immediately the front doorbell rang. Edwin could hear Hunter opening the door.

'Good morning, Father White. Are you all right?'

There was a sudden crumpled thud, and a muffled expletive from Hunter. Edwin jumped up and went out into the hall. The priest had collapsed right in the doorway, and Hunter was bending over him. Edwin ran over to them.

'What happened?'

'He just crumpled in a heap,' said Hunter. 'He must have rung the bell, then collapsed against the door. He was leaning on it as I opened it. Could you help me move him into the living room?'

Edwin had very little knowledge of first aid, but vaguely remembered something about not moving people. 'Should we move him at all?'

Before Hunter could reply, Jeanette had reappeared, with her two diaries. When she saw what had happened she very calmly put them down on the hall table and crouched down beside Hunter.

'He's breathing,' she said. She took the priest's wrist between her fingers. 'Pulse very faint. Hunter, can you ring for an ambulance? And then bring a couple of blankets.'

Edwin took off his hoodie, and gently placed it under the fallen man's head. Jeanette didn't notice. Her troubled eyes were fixed pleadingly on his face.

'Come on, come on. You'll be all right. Come on. You'll be all right.'

CHAPTER 20

This is a very bad idea, thought Edwin.

The Hoxton bar was absolutely heaving. It was packed with people mainly of his own age or slightly older, and throbbing with a solid wall of music. At the far side of the room, he caught sight of Amelia Northington. She had her eyes shut, and was dancing uninhibitedly to the pulsing rhythm. Edwin, leaning his elbows on the bar that filled one entire wall, watched her for a while. He hadn't been able to buy his favourite cider, so had had to make do with a beer, the name of which he had been unable to hear over the music. It was better than he had expected though, so he thought he might have one more, before trying to cross the room and speak to her.

He suddenly realised that Amelia had spotted him, and was making her way over. He waved at her rather awkwardly. She greeted him loudly, when she got within a few feet.

'Would you like a drink?' asked Edwin.

'Pardon?' said Amelia.

'I said, would you like a drink?' he repeated, as loudly as he could.

Amelia said something unintelligible, but as she said it she nodded, and Edwin, noticing the empty wine glass in her hands, and noticing the colour of the dregs at the bottom, put two and two together, and ordered her a large red wine.

'Do you come here often?' he asked her, while waiting for their drinks. Amelia just laughed.

Well, thought Edwin, she probably can't hear what I'm saying anyway. I'd better stick to clichés — that's my best chance of being understood. The wine arrived, and another beer for Edwin. It turned out not to be the same one he had ordered previously. Never mind. A cautious sip revealed it to be good, so he took another sip, with more confidence. Amelia said something to him but he couldn't hear her at all.

'Shall we go somewhere else?' he shouted.

Again, Amelia just laughed. Rather than replying, she hooked a finger into his top, and walking backwards, pulled him on to the dance floor.

This is completely hopeless, thought Edwin. I'm never going to get a proper interview done here. So I might as well enjoy the evening. He took a large gulp of his pint, and started to move in time with the music. His questions would last.

By two o'clock in the morning, Edwin and Amelia were walking, arm in arm, along Hoxton High Street. Edwin's ears were ringing. But not so much that he couldn't hear Amelia's question.

'So what did you want to ask me?'

Edwin burst out laughing. 'What did I want to ask you? I can't start all that now! You must be joking.'

'No, I'm serious,' said Amelia. 'You've been to all this effort to come and interview me — the least I can do is try and answer your questions. I tell you what, let's go back to my house, and we can talk in more comfort.'

Edwin tried to work out whether this was a good idea or not. But the part of him that he would have used to decide whether it was a good or a bad idea, felt rather sleepy and disorientated so he had to guess. He guessed it was a bad idea, but then thought that as he'd had a couple of drinks, he probably wasn't making good decisions, so concluded it was a good one.

'Yes, that's a great idea,' he said. 'I'll come to yours and ask you all the questions I've got.'

'Lovely,' said Amelia. 'We just need to take this next turn on the right, and it's only about twenty minutes walk.'

Edwin wasn't quite himself. He felt a bit queasy and kept walking slower and slower. Amelia was holding him by the hand and guiding him carefully in the correct direction. They seem to be taking rather longer than twenty minutes. But eventually they stopped outside a Victorian terraced house.

'Here we are,' she said triumphantly. 'This is it.'

She rummaged through her handbag and pulled out a bunch of keys. 'I think it's one of these,' she said. 'I'm not sure which one.'

Suddenly she sat down on the doorstep. 'You'd better choose one,' she said. 'You're the detective.'

Edwin said groggily, 'I'm not feeling at my very best, but I'll have a go.'

He selected a key at random, and tried it in the lock. It wouldn't go in. He tried another one, with the same disappointing results. He sat down beside Amelia on the doorstep.

'Are we locked out?' she asked.

'Technically, no,' said Edwin. 'But practically, yes.'

'Right,' said Amelia, tucking her feet under her, and stretching her arms round her knees. 'You'd better interrogate me here.'

'Okay,' said Edwin.

This really seemed like a bad idea, but again he remembered that his judgement was impaired by the effects of alcohol, so it might well be a good one. It was very late at night, and in a residential area, so he'd have to whisper. Right. Here we go.

'Where were you on the night of the sixth of March?' he asked.

'The sixth of March this year?'

'That's right. This year. Where were you?'

'I've absolutely no idea. Does it matter?'

'Probably not. Were you cruelly murdering your own father, by a devious means that is untraceable, and looks like heart failure?'

'No. I think I'd probably remember if I'd done that. Pretty sure.'

'Yes, you probably would,' whispered Edwin. 'Just out of interest, how do you feel now he's died? I heard you two didn't get on.'

'Oh, I hated him with a passion,' Amelia whispered back. They were sitting side by side, leaning their backs against the front door, their heads close together.

'I hated him with a passion, and yet I always longed

to impress him. To impress him so much he would suddenly become warm towards me, and hug me gently, and tell me how special I was to him.'

Amelia now sat up straighter, and her voice grew louder as she said, 'I'm so glad he's dead.' Her voice rose to a wail as she continued. 'And I miss him with all my heart.'

There was a noise of a window being opened across the road, and a voice called out, 'Give it a rest. Some of us are trying to sleep.' The window was slammed shut again.

Amelia was on her feet immediately. 'Takes one to know one,' she shouted into the darkness.

Edwin had jumped up too. 'Shhh,' he whispered. 'It's pretty late now, I think. Let me try those keys again. There's probably a scientific way to find the right one.'

'Good idea,' said Amelia. 'If it helps, it's the key with the yellow plastic cover.'

Edwin had a look at the bunch of keys. 'Yes, that helps,' he said. He inserted the key with the yellow plastic cover in the lock, turned it, and the door opened.

'Science,' he solemnly announced. 'The scientific method. Never fails.'

Amelia stumbled past him into the house, and as Edwin remained standing uncertainly on the doorstep, called back to him, 'Are you coming in or what?'

Edwin's phone was ringing somewhere, but he couldn't find it. It was Sunday afternoon, and he was still at Amelia's house in Hackney. He was feeling rather fragile, and the muffled ringing sound was distressing him in two ways simultaneously — by aggravating his headache, and making him worry that he might be missing an important call. His searching revealed that the phone wasn't under any of the sofa cushions, though it didn't sound very far away. His answering facility wasn't activated, and the phone kept ringing and ringing.

Slowly and painfully Edwin lowered himself to the floor and ignored the pounding in his head as he squinted into the darkness under the sofa. There was a luminous electronic glow, and he clenched his fists in triumph. He reached under and pulled his phone out. Just as he did so it stopped ringing. Edwin looked at the screen. Three missed calls, all from Dave Clark. He settled himself back on the sofa, tried to relax his neck, and called Dave back.

'Dave. Sorry I missed your call,' he said.

'No worries. Three calls, I think it was, but never mind. It's not important. I've only accessed all the software associated with the Connected Chain Bond. That's all.'

'You star. That's amazing. I must apologise as I'm not feeling 100 per cent today. Can you remember at all why I asked you to do it?'

'Hope you feel better soon. You asked me to find out if there was anything suspicious about it.'

There was a pause. It all came flooding back to Edwin, and he suddenly felt rather nervous.

'I remember now,' he said.

Another pause. Dave's really milking this, thought Edwin.

'Well? Did you?'

'Yes, I did find out, and yes, there is something rather suspicious about it. It's complicated to explain, but basically I noticed that the software is generally very neatly and carefully put together. Really impressively elegant coding. But there are a couple of points where there is a seemingly random duplication of a line of code. It seems like this only happens for variable instantiation, so in normal circumstances this would simply be irrelevant — it might slow down the program a bit, but not have any other outcome. But whoever wrote the software has created their own compiler to make an incredibly tiny change to the programming language that's being used in those sections. And the change they have made means that those particular repeated lines of code can, if you know what instruction to use, open a whole other hidden area of the program. These other areas have been written in a rather more casual fashion, as if they were purely for private use, and not intended for anyone other than the coder to see.'

'Wow,' said Edwin. 'So you're absolutely sure this isn't just a careless accident?'

'Absolutely,' said Dave. 'These areas have clearly been designed to be hidden from general view, but contain working code. I'm not entirely sure yet what the overall purpose of it is, but the one clear function I have been able to establish is one which relates to routing money through bank accounts.'

'Can you tell who's written the code?'

'Well, no. But what I can tell you are details of the bank accounts that the routing codes are programmed to use. At the risk of stating the obvious, those bank accounts might lead you to the coder, or coders.'

'So it could be more than one person?'

'From the consistent style, I'd say it's more likely to

be one person, but there are two different accounts embedded in the code.'

'Mate, that's all amazing. That's loads to think about. But something else that's just come to mind — I'm in the middle of researching people's movements, and wondered if you would be able to get inside the office swipe card system? Is there a way of finding out who checked in and out, and at what times?'

'I'll certainly have a go. If it's connected to the main office system it shouldn't take too long. By the way, what do I do about invoicing?'

'Actually — I don't know. I'll ask my boss tomorrow morning, and get back to you.'

'Cool. I'll let you know about the swipe stuff, and get you those bank account numbers. I tell you what — I'll send you them when my invoice gets paid.'

'Whoa Dave, that sounds a bit harsh!'

'Surely there'll be no problem? You said the money would be good?'

'Yes, of course, though I don't know how long payment will take. But I'll find out in the morning, and get back to you.'

'OK mate. Speak soon.'

Edwin hung up. His head was spinning. Amelia came into the room.

'Everything all right?' she asked.

Edwin stared at her blankly for a minute before replying. 'Yes, fine.'

'It's just what you were talking about — it sounded a bit worrying.'

'No, no. Everything's fine.' Edwin felt uneasy. How much had she heard?

Amelia sat down beside him. 'Look, I know we don't know each other very well, but if you've got money troubles, I'd be happy to help. Seriously. I had a very successful exhibition last autumn. Don't be embarrassed.'

'No, really, I'm fine,' protested Edwin. 'I was just talking to a friend of mine from uni.'

He tried desperately to remember what he had said to Dave that Amelia might have overheard.

'He's in a spot of bother, so I said I'd help him out. That's all.'

Amelia didn't say anything. Edwin couldn't quite interpret her silence.

'I think I need a glass of water,' he said.

'Help yourself. In the kitchen,' said Amelia.

Edwin got up and went through to the kitchen. He found a heavy glass tumbler with a small chip out of the rim on the draining board, and filled it from the tap.

'You don't have any aspirin, do you?' he called through to Amelia. She came into the kitchen, and found some in a drawer under the worktop.

'There you go,' she said. Edwin picked up the tumbler he had filled, and Amelia's eyes opened wide in alarm.

'No! Don't use that one,' she said sharply. 'Where did you find it?'

'It was just here on the draining board,' said Edwin. 'What's wrong with it?'

'Why on earth was it on the draining board?' said Amelia. 'Sorry — this is the glass I use for small scale cetohyde experiments. Checking out how things will look. It should be put away in that cupboard up there.'

Edwin looked blank.

'Cetohyde. I use it for my artwork. It's a liquid which

allows electrical circuits to operate while submerged in it. It's an insulator, you see. But it's also poisonous. It has those skull and crossbones warnings on the bottles.'

Amelia stood for a moment, unmoving, then reached into another cupboard and fetched Edwin a clean glass which she filled from the tap. She emptied the chipped tumbler out, and wiping it on some kitchen paper which she then threw in the bin, put it back in a high corner cupboard. Edwin took two aspirin, and thinking to lighten the atmosphere, sniffed his glass suspiciously, then looked at Amelia and grinned. His attempt at humour was wasted on her. She waited while he washed the pills down.

'Look, I don't want to rush you, but did you get everything you wanted?' She seemed preoccupied.

'Yes,' said Edwin. 'I got most of it last night.'

He glanced at her, but she was looking out the kitchen window now.

'And now I've got your bank details and the scans of your diary, so I think I'm done.' He hovered awkwardly. 'Well, thanks for your hospitality. I'm sure I'll be in touch again at some point.'

'Yes, that would be fine,' said Amelia with a strained smile. She followed Edwin to the front door. He picked up his jacket on the way.

'Bye, then.'

'Bye.'

The door had hardly shut when she got her phone out, and started scrolling through her contacts.

CHAPTER 21

Neville Northington was sitting in his living room, flicking through the channels on the TV. He had just heard the front door open and close, as Louise came in from a Sunday afternoon trip to the park with little Josh. Neville had been dozing in an armchair, but now he felt like he needed distracting. There didn't seem to be anything he wanted to watch, though.

His phone rang, and he saw to his surprise that it was Amelia calling.

'Hello? Amelia?'

'Listen. I've just had that private investigator kid round, and I overheard him on the phone to someone else. It sounds like he's suspicious about something at NI. I thought you ought to know.'

'Ahhh!' Neville chuckled. 'You weren't to know this, but I specifically asked him to look into that. Don't worry, I think it's probably good news. But thanks for letting me know.'

'Oh.' Amelia sounded deflated. 'It all sounded very

dodgy, what he was talking about. Something about code by more than one person? And then some story about the office swipe card system?'

'No, you needn't worry,' said Neville. 'All of that is fine. Thanks for letting me know, but you really don't need to worry.'

Neville casually pushed some of Josh's toys out of the way into the corner of the room with one toe. 'And are you all right, Amelia?'

'Yes, yes I'm fine.'

He thought she sounded distracted or stressed or something. Women, he thought. Artists, he thought. Women artists worst of all, he thought. 'OK. Well, nice to chat. I'm sure we'll see each other soon. See you. Bye. Cheers. Bye. Bye.'

So the young investigator was earning his money. Excellent. Neville picked up the remote again.

Louise came into the room, carrying Josh on one hip and holding her phone to her ear with the other. Josh looked like he'd been crying.

'Just a minute,' Louise said into her phone. 'Here, Neville, can you take him for a minute? He's a bit grizzly.'

Neville shrugged reluctantly, and Louise set the little boy on his lap. As soon as he realised his mum was setting him down he took a deep breath and began to wail. Neville put down the remote, held his son with both hands, and began to jiggle his knees up and down. Louise put her phone back to her ear, and immediately headed out of the room.

'Sorry. I'm back with you now,' he could just hear her saying as she shut the door behind her.

Neville's son, sitting on his knee, kept crying. Neville tried jiggling his knees faster. Josh cried louder. Neville stopped moving them completely, and immediately Josh stopped crying. Neville couldn't help laughing, so suddenly had Josh stopped. Josh's face, bright red and covered with tears, was immediately split by a huge grin.

'Good boy,' said Neville. 'What a good boy you are. Mummy will be back in a minute.'

And sure enough, a minute later Louise came back into the room. But she was pulling her coat on again.

'I'm off out,' she said. 'I'm not sure when exactly I'll be back, but you can put Josh to bed if I'm not in by seven.'

'Woah, hang on a minute,' said Neville. 'Where are you off to so suddenly?'

'Well, if you must know, I'm just going to be interviewed by that private investigator you hired.'

'What, now? On a Sunday afternoon?'

'Yes. I was talking to him, trying to find a time, and suddenly it occurred to me that this was the perfect time, as you are around to take care of Josh. I'll see you later. Bye.'

And Louise was gone. Neville jumped up, as if to protest, and as he did so Josh began to cry again. Women, he thought, bitterly.

Edwin had felt so excited by Dave's feedback about the coding clues he had uncovered, that, despite his headache, he had been inspired to ring Louise from the bus stop he was waiting at on his way home from Hackney. He hadn't been unsettled by Amelia's brusque manner as he left, rather, he was relieved to go. He wasn't exactly sure of the precise ethics concerning investigators spending the night in the homes of people they were investigating, but he had a feeling that it was better he didn't prolong his time there. Louise had seemed eager to come and talk to him, so suddenly he had the feeling that his work was starting to achieve some results.

When he arrived back at Parker Investigations, he found her already waiting outside. As he wrestled with the locks, she apologised for being early, explaining that she had misjudged just how close the office was to her home, and thanking Edwin for fitting her interview in at short notice.

'Not at all,' said Edwin. 'It happens to be a good time for me too.' He led her up the stairs to his office, and unlocked the door.

'What are the chances of your office being so close to our home, though?' said Louise, surprised.

Edwin gestured her into the room, and indicated the client chair. As he sat down on his own chair, he said, 'Well, I presume that's why your husband started using our firm.'

As the words left his mouth, he remembered that officially his firm had been appointed at random. But Louise didn't seem to notice.

'So what do you want to know?' she asked. 'I might as well tell you up front that I'm not best pleased with Neville at the moment, so I'm not currently inclined to lie on his behalf, as wives are supposed to.'

'Oh,' said Edwin. 'Well, really the only reason I'm talking to everyone is because of Neville's suspicions, not because he himself is suspected of anything.'

Edwin remembered the attempts Neville had been making to pin blame on other people, and the suspicious coding in the product software, the existence of which Neville had seemed to have been aware of, though he was accusing Jasper of creating it. Maybe this was in fact a golden opportunity to probe a little.

'Look,' he said. 'I'll ask you the same list of questions I'm asking everyone, and if anything relevant comes up in other areas, then I'll maybe ask some further ones. Fine by you?'

'Fine by me.'

Sitting facing her across his desk, Edwin talked Louise through her relationship with Tony Northington over the years, her movements around the time of his death, and how she felt now he had died. She was very happy to give Edwin access to her diaries and laughed sardonically when he asked about her bank account. She gave him the details anyway, and then the conversation turned naturally to Neville.

'You know Northington International had a brand new product which came out in the autumn, that Neville had been very involved in planning?' Louise asked.

Edwin said that he did.

'Well, I think something went wrong about that time. I don't know what, but he changed from being just a bit appalling, to completely unbearable.'

Edwin muttered something sympathetic.

'And I've got a strong feeling he's been having an affair.'

Edwin couldn't think of anything to say.

'There are lots of little bits of evidence, insignificant on their own, but put them all together... I saw a friend of his in the park earlier this afternoon, and his discomfort and our very stilted attempts at conversation were the final straw. But still, I've no actual proof.'

Edwin tried to bring the conversation back to the matter in hand. 'Talking of suspicion, has Neville always been as suspicious of other people as he is at the moment? When I talked to him, he suspected almost everyone I mentioned, of something or other. Though not you,' he added hastily.

'I'm not sure,' said Louise. 'I think that's just his personality. Though he was perfectly charming to me when I first met him. A bit like you,' she added with a smile.

'Oh. Thanks.' said Edwin. 'It just occurred to me he might be trying to distract me from investigating him, by pointing out other people who needed an eye kept on them.'

Louise frowned. 'Though if he didn't genuinely suspect them, why on earth go through the charade of appointing you to investigate everyone? No offence, of course.'

'None taken,' said Edwin, remembering his conversations with Sheldon Haynes.

'You know, I've just had a brilliant idea,' said Louise. 'I'd like to engage you as well, to investigate whether or not Neville's having an affair.'

'Oh,' said Edwin, frowning, 'I'm not at all sure that's a good plan.'

'Why ever not?' said Louise. 'It's perfect. You're already in place, being a private investigator, so he has to answer your questions. He won't be aware that you are also working for me.'

'But if he is having an affair, and you challenge him with the evidence, he's bound to know it came from me, who he has employed to work for him. I'm afraid it's not a good idea.'

'It's not a good idea, it's a brilliant idea,' insisted Louise. 'We can find a way round that obstacle easily enough. Please say you will do it?'

Her smile became even brighter, and she clasped her hands together.

CHAPTER 22

Another Monday morning, another knock on Sheldon Haynes' office door. He heard it dimly through the fog of his Monday morning state, which was worse than usual, as he had come into the office especially early today to have a quick snoop around Edwin's room, and particularly his computer. Sheldon wasn't a talented or enthusiastic user of technology, but he certainly knew how to install a password over-ride package in a PC. He had discovered enough to find that Edwin had been making progress, of a sort, and it was a dead cert that it would be him at the door, eager to discuss his progress.

'Come,' said Haynes, without opening his eyes.

'Oh, hello.' It was Edwin's voice.

'Well?' said Sheldon.

'I just wanted, if you've got time, to update you on how I've been getting on with this Northington business, and ask your advice.'

'Okay. Fire ahead.' Haynes' eyes were still closed. 'I'm all ears.'

He heard the sound of Edwin walking across the room, moving the chair slightly and sitting down. He heard Edwin telling him in general terms about the conversations he had had so far. He heard Edwin telling him about his friend Dave's research into the software coding and about the suspicious functions he had discovered. He heard Edwin telling him that Dave had found some bank account numbers covertly connected to the software, and that he would only tell Edwin what they were when his invoice was paid. He opened one eye at this point. He heard Edwin telling him that Dave was also trying to gain access to the office swipe card system. Haynes couldn't stop his lips curling into a grin at this point. He finally heard Edwin telling him about his interview the previous day with Louise Northington, and her offer to engage him additionally to find out if Neville was having an affair. Sheldon Haynes now opened both his eyes.

Just at that point Edwin's phone rang. He looked at the screen.

'It's Dave,' he said, apologetically. 'Do you mind if I take it?'

'No, no. Take it.' Haynes was grateful for the opportunity to close his eyes again.

'Hi Dave. How are you getting on?'

The answer was only audible to Sheldon as a tinny nasal sound. He sighed and leant his head forward so that his chin rested on his cupped hands.

'Right,' Edwin was saying. 'I'll see if I can get hold of that at my end. And I was just about to discuss your invoice procedure with my colleague.'

Haynes snorted slightly.

'OK. I'll be in touch. See you. Cheers. Bye. Bye.'

'Well,' said Edwin, now addressing Haynes, 'he reckons he's got good access to the swipe system. His only issue is connecting the individuals to the card codes — apparently that information isn't stored anywhere on the database, as far as he can tell.'

'Well if their system is as vulnerable to hackers as it seems to be, they did well to keep it separate.'

'Exactly,' said Edwin. 'I'll see if I can get the details from someone in the office. Molly Raestock, maybe, if I ever get to talk to her. But look, Sheldon. What shall I say to Dave about invoicing? Can we get him paid quickly so I can get those bank details? And also, what about Louise's proposition? Can I seriously work for her at the same time as her husband?'

Sheldon Haynes, eyes now both fully open, sighed deeply.

'Look, to be perfectly frank, there is a bit of a can of worms here, and I'm not sure I want to open it. If it looks complicated to you, it looks even more complicated to me.' He closed his eyes again, and pressed his fingers to his temples. 'I'm trying to think of a compromise that won't scupper either of us, yet will still enable us to get the information we need for the long game.'

'I genuinely don't know what you're talking about.'

'No, I don't suppose you do. Just at the moment, it's better that you don't.'

Edwin shook his head as he looked in confusion at his colleague. Haynes sat up. He seemed to have come to some sort of decision.

'Right. How much money does your friend need?'

'Well, I said he would get a good rate. And he's

probably done, I guess, about fifteen hours work? Twenty hours?'

'What job does he do at the moment?'

'Works in a computer repair shop.'

'OK. So get him to write a meaningless invoice to Parker Investigations, you keep it, and give him five hundred quid cash. That's twenty-five an hour for twenty hours. And Neville Northington won't know that you've found anything out about the software. Or indeed the swipe cards, if that leads to anything.'

'But why on earth shouldn't he know? That's what he's paying us to find out.'

'Take my advice,' said Haynes. 'Wait till you know where this evidence points, and then decide whether or not to tell him.'

'That's ridiculous,' said Edwin.

'You won't have lost anything. You have some scraps of evidence that on their own, lead nowhere. Wait till you've been able to draw some conclusions, before you start deciding what exactly to do with the evidence.'

Edwin didn't seem convinced. 'Well, leaving that to one side for the minute, what about the offer from his wife to try and find out if he's been having an affair?'

Haynes gazed at his young colleague for a while, weighing things up in his mind. Eventually he grinned. 'Why don't you do it. Get her to pay you, in cash, up front. No paper trail. It should be an easy job now that you've got inside access to so much of his life. But be extremely careful. And under no circumstances did I know anything about this.'

Edwin shook his head doubtfully.

'Usually I'd be happy to take your advice,' he said.

'But this time I'm not so sure. Why can't you tell me... Oh, never mind.'

Edwin stumped out of Sheldon Haynes' office, the grumpiest Haynes had ever seen him, but twenty seconds later he was sticking his head round the door again.

'Sorry to be rude,' he said. 'I guess it's my turn to get the coffees again? The usual?'

'Don't mention it,' said Sheldon. 'The usual, thanks.' He winked. 'Good boy.'

Edwin closed the door carefully behind him, and Sheldon Haynes waited for his footsteps to die away, before picking up his phone and dialling Neville Northington's number.

'Hello. Can you speak?'

'Sheldon.' Northington answered his phone immediately. 'Yes it's a good time for me. You have some news?'

'Well, nothing too exciting,' said Haynes. 'I came in early this morning and had a good look at Edwin's progress, and he hasn't got very far. But he has found someone who will get stuck into the software issue you mentioned to him.'

There was a pause in the conversation.

'Is that all?' said Neville.

Sheldon couldn't quite analyse Northington's tone of voice.

'Yes,' Haynes continued. 'Judging by the notes he's made, he's interviewed a good handful of people, with still a few to go.'

'Right. No more progress than that?'

'No, not as far as I can see,' said Sheldon. What was Northington getting at? Haynes carried on anyway. 'But while I'm talking to you, where exactly are you hoping the software investigation in particular will lead him? Are you able to give me any pointers so I can help guide him in the right direction?'

'Does he listen to you?'

'Yes — he's a good kid. He was in here earlier, just asking my advice about a couple of things.'

Haynes immediately wished he hadn't said that. And Northington pounced on it immediately. 'About what sort of things?'

Sheldon knew that Northington would spot a blatant lie immediately, so he told some of the truth.

'He said your wife had offered to engage him to find out if you were having an affair. He wanted to know if he should take the job.'

'The bitch. What did you advise him?'

'You know me. I advised him to do it, and ask for cash. You'll be pleased to hear he didn't like my advice.'

Northington snorted.

'So,' Haynes continued, 'to repeat my question, what do you want him to find out? With the software? Or for your wife?'

'I can't talk any more,' replied Neville Northington, 'I've got to go. But keep a closer eye on him. He can take the extra job if he wants. She's not going anywhere.'

The line went dead.

Sheldon Haynes sat absolutely still for quite some time, replaying the conversation in his head. Then he reluctantly plugged the recorder he was wearing into his computer, and downloaded the day's audio files so far. It wasn't hard then to find the conversation he had just had with Northington. He listened a couple of times. There was no doubt about it. He had been expecting the phone call, and the news he had been expecting was not the news he got. What exactly had he got wind of, and how on earth had he got wind of it? Edwin Strong was young and naive, but generally had good instincts. When he came back with the coffee, Sheldon thought, he would pry a little. Then he remembered Edwin's voice recorder. At the risk of wasting a lot of time in a tedious fashion, he could scroll through his colleague's conversations on another early morning visit.

Haynes was just groaning at the thought of another early start, when Edwin appeared with his drink.

'There you go,' he said cheerfully. 'By the way, I rang Dave on my way to Bet's, and he's thrilled with the cash offer. He's texted me the numbers already. Thanks for the advice.'

'No worries,' said Sheldon. He frowned. 'What is "Bet's"?'

Edwin coloured. 'Oh, just the bakery down the road.'

'It's not called "Bet's", is it?'

'No, that's just the name of a girl who works there.'

Light dawned in Sheldon's eyes. 'Ah,' he said. 'I was going to ask you as well—'

'What?' said an embarrassed Edwin, already halfway out of the door.

'Oh nothing. It can wait. Just be careful, that's all.'

CHAPTER 23

Later that morning, Edwin embarked on the journey by bus, train and tube, that would take him to the offices of Northington International. Although he had a future interview lined up with Molly Raestock, that wasn't the reason for his visit, which was technically unscheduled. This presented him with a difficulty at the main downstairs reception area, as security weren't keen to let him in. It took a call to Molly to gain him admittance, with a visitor's security pass displayed on a lanyard round his neck. Molly met him when he came out of the lift on the third floor, and Edwin thought she looked rather flustered.

'Hello, Edwin. I think I must have written down the wrong day — I wasn't expecting you.'

'I'm sorry, I popped in for something completely different, actually.'

The agitated look immediately disappeared from Molly's face. Edwin winced with the realisation that his sudden appearance could create such stress for a person.

'I just wanted some information from the office records. To do with the swipe cards.'

'Oh, of course.' Molly was smiling warmly now. 'I'll just — come over here with me — introduce you to Sam. Sam, this is Edwin Strong. Edwin, this is Sam. Edwin's doing some research for Mr Neville at the moment, Sam, so if you can give him the details he needs, I'd be very grateful. Now if you'll both just excuse me...'

Molly headed back to her office and shut the door behind her.

Edwin had only half heard what Molly had said, as when he had seen Sam, he had immediately recognised her as the girl he had seen on his train journey with Neville. Right, he thought to himself. At least some of this is becoming clearer.

'Hello, Sam,' he said, with a bright smile. 'Nice to meet you. What I'm after is the details of who has which swipe card.'

Sam stared at him slightly blankly. Edwin tried again.

'Every swipe card has a number on it, and I need to find out which number corresponds to which member of staff. Do you have that information?'

He kept smiling, in what he hoped was an encouraging manner. Sam's hand instinctively strayed to the blue desk diary in front of her, and then she drew it back as she said,

'I'll just go and have a quick word with Miss Raestock, if you'll excuse me.'

She disappeared into Molly's office. Where Edwin was standing, his body was between the reception desk and the door of Molly's office, so he felt quite safe in slowly reaching forward and opening the desk diary. He tried the front few pages, and then opened the back of the book. Stuck inside the back cover was a printed sheet of names and numbers. This looked like it might be exactly what he was looking for. His first thought was to get out his notebook and jot down the relevant numbers. His second was to get out his phone, and take a picture of the whole sheet. His third thought, and the one he acted on, was to quietly read out the numbers of a few relevant people, knowing that it was all being recorded by the tiny microphone clipped in its position under his shirt. He read out Neville's number, and Jasper Felder's, and Tony Northington's, and was half way through reading out Alastair's, when he noticed that, on the opposite side of the third floor foyer area, opposite Molly's office, someone was looking out at him through the vertical blinds in their office. Edwin's heart missed a beat, but he didn't panic. He finished reading out the number marked Alastair Forth, and carefully closed the book again. As he did so he simultaneously heard the door of Molly's office opening behind him, and saw the door of the opposite office open, and Alastair Forth himself come out. Sam came up to him from behind.

'I'm sorry for keeping you waiting. I'm afraid I don't have access to those numbers, but Molly said she'd look them out for you, and have them ready for when you have your meeting with her. I hope that's okay.'

'Yes, of course,' said Edwin. 'That's fine.'

As Sam was talking, Alastair had been casually walking towards them.

'Good morning, Edwin,' he now said. 'Did you get what you came for?'

'Well, no,' said Edwin, unable to stop himself blushing slightly. 'Unfortunately not.'

'Oh, I'm sorry to hear that,' said Alastair, in a completely neutral tone of voice. There was a short pause, then he turned and went back towards his office. Edwin thanked Sam for her help, and headed for the stairs.

During the return journey, the order of tube, train and bus now reversed, his discomfort at being caught out by Alastair gradually faded. And he allowed himself to feel more and more pleased with himself for getting hold of at least some of the swipe card numbers. When he arrived back in his own office, he looked at the data Dave had sent him, and played back the recording of himself quietly reciting the numbers. He quickly found the number that correlated to Neville Northington, and looked along the chart to the day Tony Northington died. Neville's diary and whereabouts chart had affirmed he had been in the office all day, until he got the phone call telling him his father had just died. But according to the swipe card record, Neville had left the office mid-morning, returning just after lunch.

Edwin double checked the numbers. Then he double checked his record of what happened when. There was no mistake. Neville Northington had lied about his whereabouts at the time of his father's death.

There was a knock at Edwin's door. It opened, and Sheldon Haynes came in. He tossed a sheaf of papers on Edwin's desk. 'There you go.'

But there was an unaccustomed hesitancy in his voice as he continued.

'The medical records, as promised. Officially all

natural and above board. But my man did a bit of prying, and discovered that this sort of heart failure always, absolutely always, responds in some way to the tried and tested medical processes. Defibrillation, for example. But in this particular case, there was no response whatsoever to the procedure. The doctors on the scene are inclined to put it down, off the record, to faulty equipment. On the record, it was just an unfortunate statistic. But something very strange went on there that day.'

'Oh shit,' said Edwin.

'Exactly,' said Sheldon. 'Last time I saw you, I told you to be extremely careful. I'm not really sure what words could make that advice stronger, but whatever they are — those words.'

Haynes, with a slight sympathetic compression of his lips, turned and left his colleague to his thoughts.

CHAPTER 24

Edwin Strong had hardly slept at all. Ironically, for someone who worked in an office where petty cash was liberally dispensed, he didn't have the available funds for a rush-hour train, so after an early breakfast, he spent the first part of the morning fidgeting in his room. By the time the first cheap train was due, he was on the platform at Nunhead Station. Shortly afterwards, he was on the train to Sevenoaks. Thirty-five minutes later he was on another train, this one due to pass through Robertsbridge fifty minutes later. And an hour after that, he was walking in the fresh spring sunshine along a series of country roads, each turning taking him onto a narrower and less well maintained stretch of tarmac. The last corner saw him turn on to an unmade road and head slightly uphill. He paused, turned and looked back.

He had left Robertsbridge well behind, but could see it nestled just below the curve of the opposite hill. The freshness and greenness of the fields and hedges around him made them look almost artificial, they were so bright. And he could smell occasional sweet waves of something delicately fragrant. He couldn't quite place it. Suddenly it clicked — bluebells. He heard his phone beeping, and tensed instantly. Then slowly a smile spread over his face as he realised that it wasn't his phone — it was a bird singing somewhere nearby. He laughed out loud, then got his phone out and turned it off. That was better. He kept walking in the direction he had been going, with a new spring in his step. Soon the birdsong he had heard was augmented by another sound, the clucking of chickens, and a minute later he rounded a final corner and found himself in his parents' front yard.

Gareth and Sally Strong had moved out of London and down to East Sussex just as Edwin was starting primary school. They had bought a dilapidated bungalow with three acres of land, some of it wooded, with the aim of doing it up, selling it at a profit, and moving on to another project. But they had quickly found that as soon as they moved out of London, the drive to renovate dried up. They had gradually relaxed into a slower pace of life, and a simpler way of living. When Edwin was happily settled at school, Sally started taking piano pupils again, and Gareth started doing fewer journalistic pieces, and spending more time writing his mildly successful series of whimsical time travel books.

Edwin had had what is described as an idyllic childhood, but then by the time he was in his late teens, he was absolutely ready to leave home, especially for somewhere more bustling and metropolitan. Bristol had been a great place to be a student, and then he had seen his move to the bright lights of London as another step forward, or upwards. And how much more forward, or upward, could you get than working as a private investigator, albeit at the level of intern?

But just now, just at this particular moment, Edwin felt a huge surge of relief at being somewhere that he could be, effectively, a child again. Just as that thought clarified itself in his head, his mum walked round the corner of the house carrying a pair of gardening gloves in one hand, and a single egg in the other.

'Edwin! What a nice surprise! Are you not working?'

'Not today,' said Edwin. They exchanged hugs.

'I won't disturb your dad just now, but he should be in for lunch shortly, then we can all catch up.'

'In for lunch? Where is he?'

'Oh, he's just writing. He writes in the caravan these days. It's up in the top field, and he keeps shifting it round a little bit, because apparently having the light just right is very important.'

Sally laughed so infectiously that Edwin found himself joining in.

'Like an artist would?' he asked.

'Exactly like an artist would.'

Sally led her son into the kitchen. The bucket in the far corner was still there.

'I see you haven't got the leak fixed yet,' said Edwin, smiling.

'No,' said Sally. 'It's difficult to get motivated. And it's not that bad, as it only leaks when it rains.'

'Fair enough,' said Edwin. 'I guess Dad's too busy writing to fix it.'

With perfect timing Gareth Strong came into the kitchen.

'But maybe he's got time to fix it now. Hello Dad!'

206

'Edwin! Have they given you the day off?'

'Well, sort of. I'm in the middle of... But I've come to visit you to take my mind off it.'

Sally started getting some lunch things together, while Gareth and Edwin sat down at the table.

'Bit stressful?' asked Gareth quietly.

Edwin nodded. He didn't trust himself to talk. Ridiculously, he felt his lower lip trembling. His father immediately launched into a long and involved anecdote about how the parts of his latest volume which the editor wanted to cut, were parts that were extremely important for furthering the plot. Edwin was grateful. By the time he had eaten, and enjoyed a warm and wholesome atmosphere accompanied by friendly and inconsequential conversation, he was feeling much better.

Sally looked at him critically. 'You look very tired, dear,' she said.

'Yeah, possibly. I didn't sleep well last night.'

'Is London still terribly noisy?'

'Yes, it's pretty noisy, Mum.'

'Tell you what,' said Gareth, 'let's have a walk round the fields, and if you fancy it, you can have a doze in my van. It's very comfortable for that. Not that I ever do,' he added, with a quick glance at Sally, who briefly raised her eyebrows.

'Okay,' said Edwin. 'Lead on, McDad.'

As the two of them walked slowly round the perimeter of the Strongs' land, they talked. At least Edwin talked — his father mostly listened, only interrupting to clarify the odd point. Every so often Gareth Strong would pause to fiddle with a bit of fencing, or to pull up some weeds that were getting in the way of something else, or to pick a couple of mushrooms, which he put in a plastic bag he had pulled out of his back pocket. And Edwin kept talking as his dad kept his hands busy, until he had outlined the whole of the Northington affair as it appeared to him. Even the act of having to verbalise what was inside him helped ease his troubled mind, and so when they arrived at the part of the top field where the caravan was currently standing, Edwin felt relaxed enough to accept the offer of a comfortable place to snatch forty winks. The caravan was tiny, but cosy, and free from distractions. Gareth left him to it, and continued on his circular walk, clasping his carrier bag.

Edwin awoke in the late afternoon, feeling much refreshed. He wandered back down the field towards his parents' house. As he got close, he could hear the sound of a piano being played rather inexpertly. He went into the kitchen, where his dad was doing a crossword. Gareth smiled when he saw his son, and put the kettle on. He sat down again while it heated up, and leant over to Edwin, passing him the biscuit tin.

'I'm sure you probably don't want advice, and also you probably don't need it. But I'll give you what I've got anyway. You need to do this investigation on your own terms. I don't like the sound of the guy who's employing you, and I get the impression you don't much like him either, and if he fires you, I'm guessing you won't be devastated. So make your decision as to how you're going to work, and stick to it. Also, your colleague is an old hand and seems to know more of what's going on than you do. Get him to tell you what the deal is. I don't know how you'll do that, but I'm sure you'll be able to think of a way.'

The kettle boiled, and Gareth made two cups of tea.

'Thanks, Dad,' said Edwin.

Father and son sat and sipped their drinks, the silence broken only by the muffled sounds of Sally's current pupil in the next room, who was currently struggling with a contrary motion scale.

'I'm glad I'm a writer,' said Gareth Strong.

It wasn't till much later that evening, as Edwin was nearing his home station of Nunhead, that he finally turned his phone on again. Apart from being a bit sleepy now, he felt better than he had done for ages. He looked up and down the train to check, and not seeing a conductor, slowly and deliberately put his feet up on the opposite seat, and stretched his legs out luxuriously. What an amazing feeling. One day he would open a Spa business where the only relaxation facilities would be sets of railway carriage seats, which you were allowed to put your feet up on. He was sure it would do a roaring trade.

His phone had been buzzing with a few messages, and when it finally settled down, he had a look at what they were. A missed call from Parker Investigations. A couple of junk emails. And a text from Amelia Northington.

'Father White has died. I don't know what to do.'

CHAPTER 25

Edwin didn't sleep much better that night, and again, when he woke, it was early. He was normally very careful not to disturb the people he lodged with, but this morning he found in himself a strange new combination of tension and carelessness, and made himself breakfast without his usual early morning tiptoeing around.

During the night he had spent his wakeful periods fretting about the Northington situation, now with the added complication of Father White's death. But something in what his own father had said about doing the job on his own terms had somehow liberated him a little, so though he was still worrying, he was also making some concrete plans of his own.

He had exchanged a couple of texts with Amelia, which had clarified little, beyond the fact that Father White had died of heart failure, in hospital, and that she was in pieces because of it. He needed to talk to Jeanette, he thought, but wasn't looking forward to the conversation. He remembered how close she had been to

Father White.

So at eight thirty, acting quickly before he could change his mind, he rang her number. She answered almost immediately.

'Hello, Jeanette. I assume you've heard the sad news about Father White?'

'Yes,' she replied quietly. 'I was there.'

'Oh, I'm sorry,' said Edwin.

'I'm glad you rang. Is there any chance you could come round?'

Edwin thought quickly. Why not? 'Yes, of course. I'll be a couple of hours, but I'll see you soon.'

Why would she want to see him? He had no idea. This felt dangerously like drifting along at the whim of the Northingtons again. But it also seemed like a good opportunity to find out more about this new and unexpected death. He recalled Neville's dark warnings about Father White, that he had dismissed at the time. And in a direct blow to his ability to complete his current job, he obviously now wasn't going to be able to interview the priest. He would chase up the progress of his other outstanding interviews on his way up to Hampstead this morning.

The day had started slightly chilly, with a fresh breeze, but a blue sky that, in Edwin's mind anyway, held a promise of future warmth. On the train up to London Bridge, Edwin realised that he had been more organised than he had thought — as far as he could work out he only had two interviews that hadn't taken place — with Alastair's partner, Gerry Kennedy, and with Molly Raestock. And both of them were already scheduled in. In his hurry to come out he had forgotten his diary, but he was pretty confident they were both in there.

The walk up from Belsize Park tube was now familiar to Edwin, as was the turning onto Downshire Hill, and the approach up the path to the front door. He noticed that with the warmer weather, the front garden had become more colourful even in the short space of time since he was last there.

He rang the door bell, and after a short while Hunter opened it. There was a change in Hunter that Edwin couldn't immediately put his finger on.

'Is Mrs Northington in? I think she's expecting me.'

'Come in,' said Hunter. 'She's just through here, in the front room.'

Edwin realised what the change was. Hunter didn't seem to resent him any more.

'Can I get you anything?' he said to Edwin.

'No, I'm fine, thanks.'

Jeanette's tired voice came from the living room, 'You couldn't get me a coffee, could you Hunter? Thanks ever so much.'

'Actually, can I have one too?' Edwin asked quietly, as he turned to enter the room.

'Of course,' said Hunter, with a slight twitch of his face.

Jeanette Northington was again sitting in the chair by the window. She looked pale and washed out, but somehow still seemed poised. She smiled a thin smile of greeting. Despite only having met this woman properly once before, Edwin felt that he knew her well. They had, after all, discussed some of the more intimate parts of her life.

'I'm so sorry,' he found himself saying, again.

'It was really awful,' she replied in a flat voice. 'He had seemed fairly stable for a while, and then his heart just gave out. The hospital people did their best, but they said that he just didn't respond at all to treatment.'

Edwin suddenly felt the hairs start to stand up on the back of his neck. Part of him was immediately on high alert as adrenaline coursed round his system, and bizarrely, part of him cheerfully commented on the fact that this was the first time in his life that the hairs on the back of his neck had literally stood up. Jeanette was still talking, but the phrase 'he just didn't respond at all', was ringing in his ears. Gradually he focussed again on what she was saying.

'...him so much already, and I know I'm not the only one. He had such a way with people.'

Hunter was back with them again, carrying a tray with two mugs of coffee, a jug of milk and a saucer of sugar lumps.

'If I may say so,' said Hunter, 'I can attest to his way with people. I had a very moving personal conversation with him myself, at Tony's, that is, not that long ago.'

'I didn't know that,' said Jeanette, looking up at Hunter with interest. 'I thought you had no time for priests?'

'Well, in general, Miss Jeanette, you're right, but I found him to be very human. Very human indeed.'

Now it was Edwin's turn to look at Hunter with interest. 'I wonder, Hunter, if you would allow me to interview you?'

Hunter's eyes opened wide in alarm. Edwin hastened to reassure him.

'Purely because of the breadth of your contact with all

the other people who I am talking to, of course. You might have a sort of bird's eye view that would really help me, if you were up for that?'

'You're not implying that Father White's death was in any way suspicious, are you?'

'Oh, no,' said Edwin. 'Not at all. Not in any way. I was in fact hoping to interview him. Obviously that's not going to happen now. No, I'm looking for the big picture, the overall story. And it strikes me that you might be in a perfect position to help with that.'

'Well, if you think it might be helpful,' Hunter replied, 'of course I'd be happy to make myself available. Let me know when you'd like to talk to me.' He bowed very slightly, and withdrew.

Jeanette looked steadily at Edwin. 'You just told Hunter that Father White's death wasn't at all suspicious.'

'Yes,' said Edwin, uneasily.

'Did you know, that as you said it, your face changed colour very slightly?'

'No,' said Edwin, his face now changing colour very considerably.

'You were here when Father White collapsed, last Friday.'

'Yes,' said Edwin, his face gradually regaining its normal colouring.

'When he was lying there, it struck me how exactly like Tony he was looking. I've no medical knowledge whatsoever, but two more basically dissimilar men I couldn't imagine, and yet when they were, as I now know, dying, there was something about them that was exactly alike.'

Edwin started yet again to mutter some sympathetic

words, but Jeanette cut him off with an uncharacteristically abrupt wave of her hand.

'There are two explanations, I think. One is the philosophical point that however men differ during their lives, and as I say, I knew these men well, and they differed a lot — as death approaches, the differences fade away very rapidly. The other, as I think you already know, is the possibility that the same thing has happened to them both. Two separate hospitals, both saying it's just an unfortunate statistic. Could be chance, of course. But if this was a detective novel, you'd be on high alert, wondering which of your witnesses was going to be next.'

'If this was a detective novel,' said Edwin, with feeling, 'the hero wouldn't be an intern, just out of university with an English degree.'

He thought for a moment, then smiled. 'Actually, my colleague, Sheldon Haynes, would make a perfect hero of detective fiction. He's middle aged, slightly bitter, and as far as I can work out has a rather ambivalent attitude towards the law. I'm telling you this in confidence, of course.'

'Of course.' Jeanette smiled.

'Was that what you wanted to see me about?' asked Edwin. 'About the similarities between the two deaths?'

'It was. I really hope there's nothing in it. But I thought you ought to know. Would you like me to call Hunter? That's a great idea to pick his brains a bit. If he can step outside the box of his training for a while, he can probably tell you more about Tony than anyone else.'

Right, thought Edwin. This is a great chance. The

mention of a detective novel had sparked something in his imagination.

The boy detective faced the aged retainer squarely and uncompromisingly. His eyes, while displaying the freshness of youth, also held a steely determination. The elderly servant quailed at their piercing gaze.

'All right, sir, I'll tell you everything,' he cried.

'Okay. If you're happy for me to talk to him here, that would be great.'

Edwin reached into his pocket for his notebook, and found he hadn't brought it. Just then his phone rang. He looked at the caller ID. It was Gerry Kennedy. 'I'd better take this,' he said, getting up and stepping out into the hall. 'Hello? Gerry?'

'Hello Edwin. Where are you?'

'I'm in Hampstead. Why do you ask?'

'I'm sort of at your office, for my interview.'

'Oh, no,' said Edwin. 'I'm so very sorry. Something came up this morning, and I just had to drop everything. Are you in a rush?'

Edwin was grasping at straws. But Gerry seemed quite relaxed.

'How soon can you be back?' he asked.

'Just over an hour,' said Edwin, optimistically.

'Look,' said Gerry, 'I'll just pop across the street to the library and amuse myself there for a bit. Give me a ring when you get back.'

'Sure,' said Edwin. 'I'll do that. Thanks for understanding. Cheers. Bye.'

He turned to Jeanette, and to Hunter, who had now come into the room too.

'I'm really sorry about the coffee — I'm going to have

to shoot off. I've double booked. I'll ring and arrange another time to speak to you, Hunter, if I may?'

Hunter said nothing, but again bowed slightly, in his dignified way.

And Edwin, unsure if he was doing the right thing, headed off again, back to base, and his rendezvous with Gerry Kennedy.

CHAPTER 26

Edwin found the journey back to his office very stressful. He was trying to plan in advance what extra questions he could ask Gerry, that would perhaps shed more light on what his partner, Alastair, had already told him. And at the same time he was regretting his decision to abandon his chance to talk to Hunter. The tube he had been on had waited for ages in a tunnel at one point, and then the train he took from London Bridge seemed to be on a bit of a go-slow. As he finally got off his bus, just down the road from the office, he remembered to call Gerry, who was in the library, and who still sounded very relaxed, to Edwin's relief. He felt it important to get up to his office before Gerry arrived to talk to him, and he just about managed it. He put the kettle on in the kitchenette along the corridor, before setting out his notebook and pen in an organised looking way at his desk. He was ready.

The knock at the door, when it came, was assertive, yet respectful.

'Come in,' called Edwin.

Gerry Kennedy was in his early fifties, with greying hair that had once been jet black. In profile, he was strikingly handsome, though facing him, Edwin was aware of a curious asymmetry about his features. But it was the sort of flaw that tended to increase attractiveness, and at the very least draw the interest of the observer. Was it that his nose was slightly to the right? Or was his left eye slightly smaller than his right? Maybe that was just the lighting. There was a tang or a frisson of a very slightly flawed, and therefore completely convincing, reality, in Gerry's appearance face on. Then when his absolutely perfect profile was subsequently displayed, the effect was devastating, on both men and women, in both his business and social life. To Gerry's credit, though he was aware of this power, he didn't often consciously choose to use it.

'Pleased to meet you, Edwin.' Gerry strode to Edwin's desk, and stretched out his hand, before Edwin had quite scrambled to his feet.

'Do have a seat,' said Edwin, unable to stop himself staring. 'Would you like a coffee? Or a tea? Or something else?'

'A coffee would be brilliant,' said Gerry, smiling. 'The catering was the only weak point at the library. Just black, please.'

Edwin trotted down the corridor to make the drinks. He thought he would definitely have his coffee black too. He briefly wondered which were the best mugs in the cupboard, and then laughed at himself when he realised what he was doing. He still used the best mugs, though.

He brought the drinks back into his office, sneaking a sideways glance at Gerry's profile as he passed him.

They settled quickly down to business, Gerry answering Edwin's introductory questions promptly and fully. The next questions began to touch on the subject of Alastair's relationship with Tony Northington. Gerry's replies confirmed what Alastair had told Edwin. And then he said exactly what his partner had said, when Edwin had been interviewing him.

'Can I trust you?'

And with a faint sense of déjà vu, Edwin replied as he had previously,

'You can trust me that any information you give me will only be used in the context of this investigation, if that's what you mean?'

'That's good enough,' said Gerry. 'Obviously you will know about the plan Alastair and I had been developing to buy Northington International. What Alastair may not have told you is that we did a fair bit of behind the scenes research. I had been suspicious for some time about the overall performance and structure of NI, as had my colleagues at Eurobank. So I told my colleagues I might be in a position to get some inside information.'

For the first time in the conversation, Edwin thought that Gerry Kennedy looked slightly uncomfortable.

'I did a bit of digging, embarrassingly enough behind Alastair's back, as at that point I hadn't told him of my concerns, and I suppose I thought he might put company loyalty first.' Gerry now looked rather more thoughtful. 'And, if I can carry on thinking out loud, I suppose there was a tiny part of me that feared he was in on it.'

'Sorry, in on what?' asked Edwin.

'Well, on whatever shady dealings were giving rise to our general concerns about Northington International. Financial companies are obviously very competitive with each other, but at the same time we all need the overall impression given by the industry as a whole to be solid and trustworthy. Then Alastair caught me in the act.'

Edwin frowned.

'The act of rifling through his filing cabinet,' said Gerry.

Across the table Edwin's face registered understanding.

'As you can imagine, this led to rather a low point in our relationship. I brazened it out as best I could, but found I could only do so by implying that Alastair was paranoid. This seemed so unfair, I eventually admitted what I had been doing. By that time, the Connected Chain Bond had come out, and Alastair was just as suspicious of that as I and my colleagues had been about NI in general. He felt the published results didn't match the combined profits of the component elements. And he's unbelievably meticulous with his calculations, so felt he had solid grounds for his fears.'

'Surely these things are regulated and monitored?' asked Edwin. 'As a member of the public, please reassure me!'

'Well, they are regulated of course, and the Financial Conduct Authority has to authorise any new products. But as with anything complicated, especially where there are confidentiality issues, there is a limit to how closely the fine details of a plan can be monitored in real time. If there turns out to be a big issue in the future, yes that will come out, but small issues in the present tend to slip through the gaps. Also the structure of the Connected Chain Bond uses some novel approaches to combining the performances of different financial products, so the people designing it will have had legitimate concerns around the area of intellectual copyright, and also the fact that it represents a new way of working, means that those tasked with monitoring it will have had little to compare it with.'

Gerry smiled. 'Does that reassure you?'

Edwin smiled back. He hoped he wasn't blushing. 'Not really. But I think I get the picture.'

'And of particular concern to Alastair,' Gerry continued, 'was the fact that he was suspicious about the product, despite being heavily involved in developing it. He still can't reconcile its apparently mediocre performance with the buoyant returns its component bonds are giving.'

'How good are Alastair's coding skills?'

'That side of it isn't really his thing. He's all about the financial part.'

Edwin nodded slowly. His mind was now turning in a different direction. Travelling back to do this interview, he had planned a sort of information ambush, but now that it came to it, he was reluctant to spring the trap. Partly because he still didn't quite know what he'd be able to glean from any of Gerry's possible reactions, and partly, he had to admit to himself, simply because the man's charisma had him under a bit of a spell. But he stood up abruptly, to clear his head and strengthen his resolve.

'Would it surprise you to know that one of the people

I am currently investigating has suddenly died? In circumstances at least as suspicious as Tony Northington's?'

'Yes, it would surprise me a lot.' Gerry twisted round in his seat to face Edwin, who was now standing behind him, and he certainly looked surprised. 'But, hang on a minute, I thought that it was generally accepted that Northington's death wasn't actually suspicious?'

Edwin found himself wrong-footed. He wasn't sure what to say. Gerry continued talking.

'But who has died now? And how?'

'I'm sorry to say it was Father White. I haven't had access to all the details yet.' Edwin found himself walking back round to his own side of his desk. Gerry's eyes followed his movements. As he sat down again, he said, 'Actually, I probably shouldn't have mentioned that Northington's death was suspicious.'

'Don't worry. You can count on my discretion.'

There was a short silence.

'Are you still considering your plan to try and buy Northongton International together with Alastair?' said Edwin.

Again Gerry looked uncomfortable. 'We'll have to wait and see how the dust settles. Until the detail's of Tony's will are released, the actual ownership of the company is unclear. The day-to-day running is fine; Neville is acting CEO, assisted by Alastair and the young guy, Jasper Felder. Though he's young, Alastair says Jasper was very clued up when they had their own meetings to discuss what was happening.'

'And you'd still consider buying it, even bearing in mind your suspicions?'

Gerry smiled wryly. 'Even bearing those in mind. The company still has a great overall reputation, Tony Northington was very personable with clients, and if there are any dodgy practices or products, those can be dealt with.'

Edwin nodded. 'All right. Fair enough.'

'Is there anything else you need to know?'

'I think that's probably about it,' said Edwin, frowning thoughtfully, and only very occasionally allowing his eyes to flicker over towards Gerry, who was now talking.

'And Alastair has told me about your insistence on diaries and bank accounts. I'm happy to comply, as long as everyone's in the same boat?'

'They are,' said Edwin, with what he hoped was a firm smile. 'They certainly are.'

CHAPTER 27

Edwin had just drifted off to sleep in his office chair, when his phone buzzed. He sat up with a start, feeling very groggy. He picked the phone up off the table, and dropped it on the floor. He reached down to get it, and hit his head on the edge of the desk. Finally he had it. A text from Louise Northington.

I have discovered details of another bank account. May be of interest to you?

He felt a surge of annoyance that she had texted him. He hadn't even agreed to take on her job. Then he suddenly realised that maybe she meant the other bank account, presumably Neville's, might be of interest to him in his original investigation. Yes, that might very well be of interest. He still didn't like the idea of texting back. If he was going to do anything behind Neville Northington's back, he wanted to leave as few traces as possible. He looked at his watch. Three forty-five. Northington would presumably still be at his office, and Louise was presumably just down the road in Dulwich.

If he moved quickly...

It was only a ten minute walk, and for the first time today Edwin noticed the weather. It wasn't hot, but there was definitely a sense of warmth from the sun. As he walked past a tree covered in blossom, he was suddenly transported back to his parents' place. He stopped for a second, and breathed in the scent. It was astonishing how quickly the benefit of that trip had evaporated, he thought to himself. But even as he drank in the fragrance of the tiny petals, and without even knowing what they were, he began to feel a faint resurgence of the sense of poise, or perspective, that he had brought away with him from East Sussex on Monday. Only Monday!

Edwin continued towards the Northington's house, in a more purposeful manner. He was going to get on top of this job, and do it on his own terms.

He approached their home with interest. It was sizeable and detached, with space for several cars at the front, and what he could see of the garden was beautifully maintained. They've probably got a gardener, he thought. He walked cautiously up the path, looking for signs of life, and seeing none. He decided against ringing the doorbell, and tried a gentle knock. There was no reply, so he tried again, a bit harder. Still no response, so he rang the bell.

Almost immediately an alarmed looking Louise Northington appeared through the glass of the door. She opened it, and beckoned Edwin in.

'I couldn't work out who it might be, knocking,' she said. 'Any deliveries ring the bell, and obviously Neville has a key.'

Edwin felt a slight twinge of unease as she mentioned

Neville.

'But come in,' she continued. 'I should have time to show you what I've found before Neville gets back.'

'Is he expected back soon?'

'Well, fairly soon. He finishes early on Wednesdays generally, comes home for a quick meal, then off out to choir.'

'Choir? Neville sings in a choir?'

'Yes.' Louise didn't seem to pick up on Edwin's incredulity. 'He has a good voice, apparently. Right. Come through here with me and I'll show you what I've found.'

Louise led the way through the house. 'By the way,' she asked Edwin over her shoulder, 'why didn't you just text back? I could have just sent you the details.'

'I want to put as little as possible in writing. Especially if I take on the additional work you suggested.'

'Ah. That makes sense.'

They entered a small ground floor room near the back of the house. Louise turned to face Edwin.

'You will take it on, won't you? Surely you could do with the money?'

'Well, cash is always useful,' he admitted. 'But I'm really busy with my main investigation at the moment.'

Suddenly Louise came right up beside him. Don't stand so close to me, he thought, and absurdly that song by The Police started playing in his head, and his subconscious started modifying it.

This girl is twice his age.

She sidled even closer to him, and very deliberately brushed her hand against his.

'I could help you? We could work very closely together, if you like?'

Edwin had read of this sort of thing happening, but had not expected to be so thoroughly revolted by the suggestion. It was not her age — she was very attractive, with a good figure. It wasn't that he was uptight about sex. It was more to do with him in his role of investigator somehow identifying himself with truth, and the seeking and finding of it. Somehow a deep part of himself had become aligned in that direction.

Louise had noticed him casting his eye over her, and responded by gently toying with the hem of her skirt. Despite his revulsion, now a part of his mind began to wander.

Temptation, frustration.

Then he suddenly remembered where he was, and what he was doing, and came back down to earth.

'I don't think that would be necessary,' he said, stepping away from her. 'What was it you wanted to show me? The bank account, I mean, just the bank account.'

She smiled. 'I'm sorry. I don't know what came over me.' She briefly pressed her cheeks with the palms of her hands. 'Right. The bank account.'

Louise opened a cupboard in the corner of the room, which was set up as an office. There was a security box on the bottom shelf, with a combination lock. She punched in a series of numbers, opened the box and pulled out a handful of documents. She briefly looked through them, then selected a couple and handed them to Edwin. 'I think you'll find those of interest,' she said.

He looked at the first page, but before he had time to

take anything in, he heard the sound of the front door opening. They both froze.

'Hello?' It was Neville's voice.

'Stay in here,' hissed Louise, as she slipped out of the room and closed the door behind her.

Left alone, Edwin hurriedly looked around for somewhere to hide. Thank heavens he hadn't responded differently to Louise's unexpected overture. He had no idea if anyone was likely to come into the room, but the window had a protective steel mesh like an old fashioned lift door over it. No escape that way. The only conceivable hiding place was the gap between the large desk and the wall. And the only way it could be accessed was by climbing over the desk and down the back of it. Cursing his foolishness for ever coming here in the first place, Edwin jumped on top of the desk, and began squeezing himself behind it. He had just got himself tucked as far down as he could, when he heard the door opening, and Neville's familiar voice.

'...yes, but I've just got to look through some documents first, and then I'll be right with you.'

He could see nothing, but heard heavy footsteps enter the room. Then Louise's voice came from nearby. 'Come on. You're always working. While Nadia's still out with Josh,' here there was a rustling sound, 'why not look through *these* documents?'

Edwin now heard the same heavy footsteps moving back towards the doorway. His heart rate slowed slightly. Neville spoke again, his voice now thick and unsteady.

'Well I never. I thought you'd lost interest in that sort of thing.'

'I won't lose any interest at all, if you invest just... here.' A bit more rustling. 'Or here.'

An audible gulp from Neville. Edwin wondered if he should put his fingers in his ears. Maybe he *was* uptight about sex.

'Come upstairs with me.'

'Too far away,' said Neville hoarsely. 'In here. Right now. On the desk.'

A slight squeal from Louise, a muffled, 'No, not in there,' and now the sound of the footsteps coming in again, even more heavily, and a sudden bump on the desk.

Edwin tried to make himself as small as he could, and after the sound of the second zip, did actually put his fingers in his ears. He could see a small rectangle of cream coloured carpet, and a dust-covered mains power supply, with two plugs, both switched on. There were a couple of dead flies. He couldn't see where the leads went. There was also some sort of internet or TV cable that disappeared into a small socket on the wall.

Despite the fingers in his ears, Edwin could hear that Neville Northington's vocabulary was surprisingly broad for a high-flying businessman who lived in a well-appointed Dulwich home.

Strong words in the staffroom.

And despite shrinking as much as he could, there was now a remorseless grinding of his shoulders between the front panel of the desk and the wall. It was a good solid desk, and perhaps because of the soft carpet, it was able to develop a good solid rhythm. Unlike the songs of The Police, known for their rhythmic steadiness, whatever piece of music the desk was moving to seemed to have arrived at a section involving a marked accelerando. Edwin was now in considerable discomfort, and abandoning any attempt to protect his ears, braced his hands on the floor and risked awkwardly twisting his neck round to look up.

Six inches above his head, staring straight down at him through the gap between the desk and the wall, with eyes wide open, lips tight shut, and hair swinging rhythmically, was Louise. She too was moving in time to the desk's silent music, and now closing her eyes, perhaps with embarrassment, began to sing along as the final crescendo brought the piece to a fitting climax.

Edwin turned his head back down to face the carpet. He rested his face on his hands. His position was very uncomfortable in more ways than one, but the physical aspect of his discomfort was now asserting its presence more and more forcibly. Louise had tried her best to lure her husband away from this room, to be fair, and if he could just remain absolutely quiet now, Edwin thought, hopefully it wouldn't be too long before Neville's choir rehearsal began.

In the meantime the performance on the desktop was drawing to a close. As Louise sang her highest note, Neville's response was, astonishingly,

Just like the old man in
That book by Nabokov.

Even with his face almost on the carpet, Edwin's eyes opened wide, and eyebrows rose high with surprise. It sounded almost like an allergic reaction.

As the participants in the exhibition above Edwin's head began to disentangle themselves, he seized the opportunity to adjust his position again. He only felt safe with a tiny movement, but even that was a wonderful relief.

'Thanks,' Neville said. He sounded genuinely thankful, but as he carried on talking his voice quickly lost the warmth it started with. 'I'm glad you've still got your enthusiasm. Some women lose it very quickly once they've had children, so I'm told.'

If Louise replied, it was lost in the sounds of rustling and zipping that were also going on. Neville continued. 'Obviously you know I haven't lost my enthusiasm. But I wondered if you'd managed to find out yet whether or not I'd been indulging that impulse anywhere else?'

Behind the desk Edwin froze. The sounds of clothes being adjusted and fastened stopped. Louise's voice sounded thin and tense as she replied.

'What are you talking about?'

'I think you know what I'm talking about.'

Edwin hadn't realised until now that a tie being done up has a slight, but distinctive, sound. But that signature rustling was now audible in the room as a shadowy filigree counterpoint to Neville's voice.

'You know, the boy detective who is blundering around asking obvious questions on my behalf? Has he achieved a striking success researching my private life for you? Video footage maybe? Close ups of—'

'I don't know where you've got that idea from, but it's nonsense.' There was now a hint of steel in Louise's voice as she replied.

And if Edwin had frozen before, he now re-froze, or perhaps super-froze. Where *had* Neville got that from? Obviously not from Louise. And the only people he'd talked to were his dad, and... Sheldon Haynes. Sheldon

Haynes who had worked for Neville Northington before. Sheldon Haynes who Neville Northington had wanted working for him on this case.

Never mind about that now. He had a feeling that Louise's desire to protect him from her husband might be diminishing rapidly.

'It's nonsense and you know it,' she said. 'I'm going to have a shower. You can sort your own tea out.'

The door slammed.

Neville now spoke to the empty room. 'Blimey! What's got into her!'

Then he added, presumably to win the hearts of an imaginary audience with his ready wit, 'Apart from the obvious.'

Excruciatingly for Edwin, who wanted him to leave so he could ease his uncomfortable position, and so he could escape before Louise could come and question his discretion, Neville now began repeating his little joke. He tried a few different versions, presumably trying to get the pacing and emphasis just right.

'Blimey! What's got into her! Apart from the obvious.'

'*Blimey*! What's got into her! (Apart from the obvious.)'

'Blimey! *What's* got into *her*! Apart from the *obvious*, that is.'

Eventually he seemed satisfied with his performance. And presumably he now looked at his watch, as the next words Edwin heard were, 'Shit. Time to go.'

Hurried footsteps, and the door slammed again.

Edwin waited cautiously for a while, listening for any clues. He assumed Neville was heading out of the house, either with or without something to eat. And he assumed it would only be a matter of time before Louise had finished her shower and would be back to demand why he had told Neville about her offer to engage his services. So he had to gauge it just right. Too soon, and Neville might see him, too late, and Louise would definitely find him. She certainly knew where he was now.

So after what he judged to be about five minutes, having heard absolutely nothing during that time, he began to stand up and un-cramp himself. He carefully climbed onto the desk, and off the other side. He then realised he had left the documents Louise had given him in his hiding place, so he bent over the desk, spotted them down there, and reached down with one arm to grab them. He could just reach, if he stood on tiptoes.

He heard the door opening, and rather pointlessly froze again. Louise's voice was quiet and cold. 'Get out of the house. Now.'

'If I can just try and explain—'

'If I can just call the police?'

'I'm going, I'm going.'

Funny you should mention The Police, thought Edwin, as soon as he was safely out of the house, and on his way back to the office. He tried saying it out loud, a few different ways, in homage to Neville.

'Funny you should mention The Police.'

'Funny *you* should mention The *Police*.'

And then, least successfully of all,

'Funny you should mention 1980s pop band, The Police.'

At this point Edwin pinched himself just to check.

No, it wasn't a dream. Right. Back to Parker Investigations, for a word with Sheldon Haynes.

CHAPTER 28

Sheldon Haynes was just thinking about shutting up shop for the day. At the moment his only active project involved him keeping an eye on Edwin Strong, on behalf of Neville Northington. And as Neville hadn't given him much guidance when they had met up, apart from asking to be kept abreast of any developments, Sheldon had let himself take things quite easy. He had enjoyed eavesdropping on the beginning of Edwin's session with Gerry Kennedy today, though he had quickly got bored with Edwin's plodding questions. Once Kennedy had gone, as far as he could tell his colleague had first fallen asleep, and then gone out.

He stretched his arms, and began to unwind his legs behind his desk. He was half untangled from his favourite contorted position, when the door opened and Edwin Strong stood there. Sheldon couldn't quite decipher the look on his young colleague's face. He looked uncomfortable, strangely intense and rather flushed.

'What have you been saying to people?' he said, slightly too loudly.

Ah, that was it. He was angry. Haynes quickly rifled through his memory for an idea of what Edwin might be talking about. He came up blank. Then he realised he couldn't hold this semi-contorted position much longer.

'Hang on,' he said, 'just let me get comfortable again, and you can tell me what you're getting at. I was just getting ready to go home,' he added rather plaintively. He twisted both his legs back under him again, and leaned back in his chair. 'Okay. What's bothering you?'

Edwin took a couple of paces into the room. He didn't know what to do with his hands. He thought he should make some threatening or dramatic gestures, but didn't quite have the nerve. So he just let his arms hang by his sides. 'I'll tell you what's bothering me. I have just been listening to a conversation between Neville and Louise Northington.'

'Wire tap?'

'No. In person.'

'You were having a conversation with them?'

'No. They didn't know I was in the room.'

'Undercover? Impressive.'

'Look, can I just get on with it?'

'Sorry. Carry on.' But Haynes was impressed.

'Anyway, in this conversation, Neville Northington asked his wife how she was getting on with her investigation of his private life. When she denied all knowledge of this, he went on to specify me as the investigator she was using.'

Suddenly Haynes wondered why he always sat in this twisted position. It really wasn't all that comfortable. He shifted a little. Edwin continued.

'And as you are the only person I have told about her offer, apart from my dad, and as you know Neville Northington, you are obviously the person who told him.'

Haynes shifted again. He couldn't quite find that position he liked.

'Well?' said Edwin. 'What have you to say for yourself?'

Sheldon looked down at the surface of his desk thoughtfully. He used the blunt end of his biro to meditatively trace the contour of that little area of grain on his desk that in his mind had always been a primitive map of the course of the Orinoco. He liked Edwin. He certainly didn't want to see him come to any harm. But on the other hand Northington had a certain hold over him. But wait a minute. After all these years, he now realised, he also had a certain hold over Northington, if it came to some sort of stand-off.

It would perhaps mean abandoning his current sinecure, but the thought of throwing in his lot with Edwin and combining their resources to work together, generated in him a sense of excitement that he hadn't felt in connection with work for some time. Decision made.

'Okay,' he said. 'Listen carefully.'

For the second day in a row, Edwin was heading up to Hampstead first thing in the morning. But this time he had slept long and soundly the previous night, partly due to his busy and stressful day no doubt, but also because of his conversation with Sheldon Haynes. The leaking of information was now explained, and the promise of help with what every day seemed to become a bigger and more confusing task, was very welcome.

So it was with rather higher spirits that he approached the Downshire Hill house. The weather was a bit colder than yesterday, and the colours in the garden seemed more subdued than they had been.

Hunter answered the door, as always, and this time seemed genuinely pleased to see Edwin. He led the way into a room at the back of the house which was tucked round at the other side from the kitchen. It was furnished as a small sitting room, with a desk as well, and was pleasingly cluttered.

'Welcome to my humble abode,' said Hunter. He switched on a kettle that was in one corner. 'Do have a seat.'

Edwin sank into one of the pair of upholstered chairs, and got out his notebook and pen. Hunter's attitude to him was again subtly different.

'Tea? Coffee?'

'Oh, coffee would be great. Just black, please. No sugar, thanks.'

Hunter carefully measured out a teaspoon of instant into each of the two mugs in front of him. 'Will... do.'

The kettle was now coming to the boil.

'That chair you're sitting on?' said Hunter. 'French, dating from the time of Napoleon the third.'

Edwin was suitably impressed. 'Wow. Approximately when would that have been?'

'Mid-nineteenth century. There you go, one black coffee.' Hunter settled himself in the other chair, and put his feet up on a low footstool.

Edwin indicated it, and said, 'Napoleon the—'

'So, what would you like to ask me?' interrupted Hunter, cheerily.

'Well,' said Edwin with a smile, 'if you don't mind, I'll start with the questions I've asked everyone else, and then see where we go from there. I'm hoping maybe to jog a memory that could reveal something useful.'

'Ask away,' said Hunter expansively. 'I'm all yours.' He crossed one ankle over the other.

Edwin smiled to himself. Of course Hunter's attitude was different here. This, presumably, was his own room, his personal domain within the house. And also he was off duty, and possessed, or might possess, information of use to Edwin. All attitude-changing factors. So Edwin set about interviewing the relaxed, almost garrulous, Hunter. They talked for an hour, but without anything new coming to light.

Then Edwin asked, 'Do you mind me asking if you think Tony Northington was faithful to his wife?'

'No.'

A pause.

'No, you don't mind me asking, or no, he wasn't?'

'Well, both really. I don't mind you asking, and I'm pretty sure he had some sort of mad passionate liaison years and years ago. Before my time, of course, but I spent a lot of time in his company over the years, mainly in an unobtrusive capacity, and you'd be surprised the things a man lets slip in a relaxed frame of mind. Especially after a drink or two.'

'That's interesting,' said Edwin. 'Do you think Jeanette knew about this?'

'Oh, no. Absolutely not. I'd be very surprised if she did. She was very considerate to Mr Tony, even when he was a bit unpleasant, shall we say, back to her. And every time I told the story of Mr Tony's mad passionate liaison, I'd change the names, to protect those involved.'

'Every time you told the story?' queried Edwin.

'Yes. Well, pretty much every time. You won't believe how much harder stories are to tell when you have to remember to change the names all the time!' Hunter chuckled to himself at the thought.

'So who might you have told the story to?' probed Edwin.

'Oh, just to the lads at The Cross Keys.'

'Right,' said Edwin slowly. 'That's... helpful.'

Hunter suddenly looked concerned. 'Do you think the story might have got back to Miss Jeanette?'

'Oh, I should think that's pretty unlikely,' said Edwin. 'And when you say Mr Tony was "a bit unpleasant", what would that involve, exactly?'

'Oh, just verbal stuff, generally. Abuse and such like. Mr Tony held that women like that sort of thing. I don't think he ever actually hit her. That would be going too far, in my opinion.'

'Yes, that would certainly be too far.' Edwin tried to change tack. 'Can you tell me how much Jeanette saw of Father White?'

'Oh, since he moved to the area, which was probably a good fifteen years ago now, she probably saw him once a week or so.'

'Would this have been at services? Confession?'

'In addition to those. She attended fairly regularly, though she made a very good joke once about not being religious about it. Very funny. But no, she would meet up with Father White either here, or out in one of the local restaurants or cafés. And they were on charity committees together too. Very sad business, him dying like that. Very sad.'

'So in your opinion she would probably have shared a lot of her thoughts with Father White?'

'Oh yes,' said Hunter.

'And would it have been Father White that she confessed to?'

'It would have been either Father White, or Father Brian. Now of course it'll just be Father Brian.'

'Of course,' agreed Edwin. Then he frowned. 'I don't know much about these sort of protocols, but why was Father White not also known by his first name? It was, after all, his *Christian* name.' He hoped Hunter would like his little joke.

'That's not really to do with protocol. It's because his first name is Brian too. Sorry, *was* Brian.'

Edwin stopped making notes. A sudden profound sorrow had welled up within him. He said to Hunter, in a flat voice, 'Thanks for your time. I don't need to ask any more questions just now.'

He hardly heard Hunter's cheery, 'No problem at all. Glad to help. And when I tell the lads at The Cross Keys, I'll change your name.'

I'm not cut out to be a detective, Edwin said to himself, as he shut the gate behind him, and stepped onto the pavement.

CHAPTER 29

'Right,' said Sheldon Haynes. 'Team meeting. Reviewing the situation. Comparing notes. Planning the way ahead.'

He was sitting in his twisted position behind his desk, while Edwin sat on the chair opposite, sorting through a sheaf of papers. Despite his talk of comparing notes, Sheldon didn't have any. He tried to write down as little as possible, ostensibly for security reasons, but this also conveniently saved him time and effort.

'Okay,' said Edwin. 'My pages are now in some sort of order, though whether it's the most useful order or not, I don't know. I'll just plough through the gist of what I've got, shall I, and you jump in when you like?'

'Let's do it,' said Haynes. He was feeling upbeat, in a way he hadn't felt for a long time.

'Right,' said Edwin. 'The official scope of the investigation is to find out if the death of Tony Northington, just over three weeks ago now, was natural, or was caused by one, or more than one, I suppose, of the many people who Neville Northington suspects of something or other. Am I right so far?'

'Yes, but to be fair, it's not very far,' said Haynes.

'And, according to what Northington said when I interviewed him, he's also keen to know about whether his suspicions of Jasper Felder and Alastair Forth are justified. These suspicions seem to be to do with goings-on at his company, Northington International.'

'You're a natural,' said Haynes. 'Specialist subject, the bleeding obvious.'

Edwin glared at him.

'Sorry. Carry on,' said Haynes.

Edwin carried on. 'But these additional points are not actually what I was officially booked for, so I'm inclined to leave them to one side for now, unless they seem directly connected to the main enquiry. And to return to that first point, unofficially Tony Northington's death may still have been natural, but his heart condition very unusually didn't respond at all to any of the treatments used. We have no idea why this would be, or in which direction it would point the finger of suspicion, but at the very least it's strange.'

Haynes nodded, and chipped in. 'Yes. According to my man on the inside, it falls in the same category as a miraculous recovery from a terminal illness. It defies all known observations. So it could, technically, be a miracle — or whatever the opposite of a miracle is.'

'An anti-miracle?'

'Something like that. The other option is some sort of medical negligence, which has been covered up, but covered up poorly.'

'Yes. You read about that sort of thing in the papers.

But it's pretty unlikely, isn't it?' said Edwin.

'Well, my man on the inside, my health secretary if you will, says that knowing what he knows of the team of personnel involved, and the frequency with which these sort of heart conditions are treated, negligence is even more unlikely than a miracle.'

'But at the same time, we know of no means of producing the symptoms as they were described, in such a way as to be unresponsive to treatment.'

'None at all,' said Haynes. 'You can cause heart failure by many different preparations, but they all leave distinctive traces that would have been spotted immediately, and also the medical interventions would have had at least some effect. Maybe not enough to save Northington, but they would have made a measurable difference.'

'So, inconclusive so far.'

'Yes.'

Edwin shuffled his papers, then looked up with a grin. 'Actually, after your surveillance of me, you might know this already.'

'Try me,' said Haynes.

With a face immediately more serious, Edwin continued. 'Were you aware that Father White, who was on my list to interview, has also died, with exactly the same description of his failure to respond to treatment?'

'No, I didn't know that.' Haynes was immediately alert. When he had talked to Smith Wilson, the man who did his hospital research, about Tony Northington's death, he had sensed from Wilson's manner that it was a genuinely unprecedented situation. 'Do you have any more details? What hospital was it? Seriously — if you can give me the details now, I'll get my man onto it.'

Edwin told him what he needed to know, and Haynes extricated himself from his seat, and went out into the corridor. Wilson answered straight away, and Haynes passed on the necessary details. Wilson's professional curiosity seemed aroused, and he promised he'd get on to it immediately, as he was in the vicinity of the hospital. After ending the call, Sheldon stood out in the corridor for a minute, looking out the grimy window. He knew enough about Neville Northington to want to be careful, and he realised that he felt rather protective of Edwin now, despite having previously agreed to spy on him. Eventually he sighed, went back into his office and sat down again.

'Right. He's on the case,' he said. 'Hopefully we'll hear something before too long. Where were we?'

'Well, it looks as if Tony Northington's death might be suspicious, so it's worth looking very carefully at those around him. The trouble is that as we have no idea how the murder, if it was a murder, was committed, we have no idea what sort of opportunity would have been needed, or at what time. And if Father White was also murdered, by the same person, with the same method, why are the time-scales of the two deaths so different?'

'The differing time-scales may turn out to be a feature of this unknown method of killing, when we find out what it is, so let's focus on what we can shed light on. Motive, for instance. What have you learned from your research about motive?'

Edwin shook his head. 'The problem with motive is that everyone seems to have one.'

'Okay, but at least we can dig into those motives and

assess them rationally. And you've been quite thorough with your whereabouts research, so once we get some insight into the mystery method, and what sort of opportunity would be needed to implement it, we'll be flying.'

Edwin cleared his throat and took a deep breath.

'So. Possible motives for murdering Tony Northington might be:

'Jeanette Northington. Her husband was a difficult man by all accounts, including her own. She said he had become more and more difficult to live with, and that life was better without him.

'Amelia Northington. Told me she hated him with a passion, and was glad he was dead.'

'Charming,' said Haynes.

'Though to be fair to her, she also said she missed him with all her heart.'

'Oh, that's all right then.' Haynes was again tracing the route of the Orinoco with the end of his pen. Edwin continued.

'Moving on to her brother. While the current ownership of Northington International is still unclear,' (here Haynes raised his eyebrows) 'Neville has certainly gained control of the company, and may yet be proved to own it outright.'

'Wait a minute. Are you saying that *you* don't know who currently owns the company, or that *no-one* knows?'

'Certainly the former, and as far as I know, the latter as well. The contents of the will haven't been made public yet.' Edwin smiled. 'Have you got a man with the right contacts who can find out what's happening?'

Sheldon Haynes smirked. 'Leave it with me. But even if Neville doesn't own the company lock, stock and barrel, there's certainly some motivation there.'

'There is,' said Edwin, 'but I'm still not convinced that he'd commission an investigation if he had killed his father.'

'Unless he knew his method was foolproof, the sleuth he appointed would be firmly in his pocket, and was using it to deflect suspicion from him if any arose? And in the meantime he might get some useful information on some of his rivals. Too elaborate?'

'Maybe. But at the moment he's the only person who we can prove has lied about his whereabouts, and did so on the day his father died. He said he was in the office, and his swipe card says he wasn't. Does he know we know that, Sheldon?'

Sheldon turned rather pale. 'I imagine he doesn't. I certainly didn't. Where did you get that information from?'

'Oh, I'm sorry. I was sure I'd told you. Dave, who's been looking into the software that Neville wanted investigated, also managed to find his way into the swipe card system, at my suggestion. I then called into the NI office, and that nice Sam on reception left her post long enough for me to me to copy the relevant code numbers from the records.'

Despite his pallor, Haynes was impressed. 'Nice work. Did no-one see you do it?'

Edwin looked uncomfortable. 'Well, actually Alastair Forth spotted what I was doing. And let me know he'd seen it. But I'm not sure he realised what I was doing. And he seems so genuine, and eager to help, I find it hard to suspect him of any criminal activity. The only shady thing seems to be his plan to buy Northington International. He gets rather uneasy when that subject comes up. As does his partner, Gerry.' Edwin now frowned and half-closed his eyes. 'And I wonder if Tony's death will make it more or less difficult for them to buy the business.'

'No idea,' said Haynes. 'As soon as we're done with establishing where we stand now, I'll get on to my legal man. We need to know about the will, and the ownership of the business. But to get back to that original point, you're sure that Neville Northington wasn't where he said he was when his father died?'

'Absolutely sure,' said Edwin.

'So we've got motives for three Northingtons, Jeanette, Amelia and Neville, to have killed a fourth Northington, Tony.'

'And a fifth Northington, Louise, a Northington by marriage, was also interviewed. Though I can't think up any story that would give her a reason to kill her father in law. And within the business, Alastair Forth may have had a bit of motive, certainly personally, and perhaps stood to gain in terms of implementing his plan to buy NI. And his partner, Gerry Kennedy, wouldn't have had the personal motive, built up over years of working with the man, but he certainly seemed just as defensive as Alastair when we talked about the business.'

'And the other employee you talked to? Jasper?'

'Well, his interview was very unsatisfactory. It was conducted over Skype, and the image kept freezing. I didn't learn much. He's sent back a whereabouts questionnaire, bank details and schedule files. I haven't compared them yet with the swipe card records. I'm not quite sure what to make of him really, or why he's on the list to investigate, except for Neville's obsession with the Best Seller product they've been working on. But then, thinking out loud, my man in computing (here he nodded knowingly at Haynes) was very suspicious about the way the software was put together, which is by all accounts Felder's area of expertise. I still haven't had a chance to find out anything about the bank details that Dave found connected to the software. Really, there's quite a lot of research to be done regarding bank details, swipe card records and diary entries.'

'Usually the intern does that sort of thing,' said Haynes, helpfully.

Edwin pulled a face. 'Finally, from the NI office, there's Molly Raestock. For an office manager, she's been very disorganised about speaking to me. She's cancelled twice now, and without suggesting a replacement date. Can *she* be a genuine suspect?'

'Not sure,' said Haynes, thoughtfully. 'More likely she will have been primed to cover for Neville, assuming he needs covering for.

'In fact,' he said, a sudden gleam of enlightenment in his eyes, 'Maybe she's being deliberately held in readiness by her boss, so that her story can convincingly quash whatever has arisen during the preceding interviews. Knowing Neville, that just might be what's going on.'

'Okay. I'll talk to her with that in mind.' Edwin nodded slowly. 'I get it. In your capacity watching me, you would feed information to Northington, so he could prime her with whatever is needed when it comes to it.'

'Exactly,' said Haynes. 'But as I am about to sever my connection, with him, that is not now going to happen.'

'What? You haven't done it already?'

Sheldon Haynes felt rather uncomfortable. He didn't like being scolded by this kid. 'No, not yet. Might be rather a stormy interview.'

But Edwin was now a step ahead. 'I tell you what — don't pull out just yet. Feed him some story just before I interview Molly, and see what she comes up with.'

'Hmm. That would enable us to conclude she was covering for him, but not much more. Who else have you not interviewed?'

'The only other outstanding interviewee is Father White, sadly.'

There was a pause as both men reflected on this disturbing fact.

'However, I did also talk to Hunter, Tony Northington's man. And he certainly confirmed that Northington wasn't too nice to his wife — probably stopping short of physical violence, but pretty abusive. And he suspected him of being unfaithful in the past. But he also confirmed that Jeanette saw a good deal of Father White, and had done for many years.'

Another short pause.

'Right,' said Edwin more brightly. 'I'll get stuck into the bank details and the Connected Chain Bond, and I'll give you this pile of whereabouts statements, and the swipe card details. I only had time to get the code numbers for Neville, Jasper and Alastair, I'm afraid. Well, actually I've got Tony Northington's too, but I don't imagine that will be of use. Also, you had some legal expert you were going to point towards Tony's will, and the ownership of NI?'

'Yes,' said Sheldon Haynes. 'I'll get him onto it. And I suppose I can't put off the paperwork indefinitely. But just before I start, tell me the story again about when you had to hide behind Neville Northington's desk.'

CHAPTER 30

Neville had decided to walk home from the station. It was a good twenty minutes, but the weather was perfect. He knew he should really look after himself more in general, but as yet nothing in his life had given him enough of a jolt to kick-start him into any sort of regular exercise. As he walked, he had a thought. He got out his phone, and rang Sheldon Haynes.

'Hello. Haynes?'

'Yes?' The detective sounded a bit uneasy. Maybe he was losing his edge.

'Just a quick pointer,' said Neville, 'that you need to somehow instill in your tea boy.'

'Go on, then. What is it?'

'He's looking into the way our Connected Chain Bond software is set up, and... actually, let me think how to best put this... I'd be interested to know if... I tell you what, just let me know when he gets hold of any information about it. That's all, really.'

'Okay, said Haynes, slowly. 'I think I've got that.

Report back when he starts making inroads into the Connected thing he's researching.'

'That's it,' said Northington. 'By the way — do you know if he has taken the job my wife offered him?'

'I actually have no idea,' said Haynes. 'I'm keeping a close eye on him though. I certainly haven't noticed him starting any researches in that direction. I'll let you know if I do.'

Northington suddenly realised that he had actually had very little feedback from Haynes. 'And look, I need you to be a bit more proactive in getting hold of information from him. I don't think I'm getting as much from you as I should. This is important to me. Let's meet up early next week, and discuss progress.'

'Let's do that.' Haynes sounded less than enthusiastic.

Northington jabbed his finger on the phone to end the call. He had expected better of Haynes. He'd been extremely discreet and productive in the past. He had been disappointed that Molly had messed up by not booking him for this investigation, but now he wasn't so sure. He looked at his watch. There was time to ring Edwin Strong as well, before he got home. He selected Edwin's name from his list of contacts.

'Hello? Northington here. How are you getting on with the investigation?'

'Oh, hello.'

Neville frowned. Now Strong was sounding nervous too. What had got into the pair of them?

'Well? What have you discovered?'

'Gosh. What have I discovered. Well... well there's quite a lot, really. I've amassed a lot of information, and my next job is to sift through it, and come to some—'

'Sift through it? What kind of namby-pamby way is that to proceed? Now listen to me. Get up off your backside, walk down the corridor and knock on the door of your colleague Sheldon Haynes.'

Neville thought he heard Edwin Strong gasp. He realised that Edwin was probably unaware that he knew Haynes. 'Yes, I know more about you and your business than you suspect. Knock on his door, and ask for his advice. Then follow it. I need results. Got it?'

'Yes, I've got it,' said Edwin.

'And we will meet up early next week and discuss your progress. If you haven't got anywhere, I'll need to review the deal.'

And for the second time in quick succession, Northington cut off a call angrily.

Haynes and Strong looked at each other over the desk. There were times when speakerphone was extremely useful. It was Thursday, and it was now after six o'clock, but the look they now exchanged tacitly acknowledged that this was going to be a day for working late.

'Well, we need to get cracking,' said Haynes. 'Deadline — early next week. See what we can come up with over the weekend, and then work out a plan for what line to take with Northington.'

Edwin shuffled together his pile of papers, and headed off to his own office. Haynes settled back in his chair, but rather than making him look more relaxed, this action, combined with the way his lips were now pursed, and his eyes were narrowed to little more than slits, gave him an increased intensity. He gently massaged his temples for a minute, the aura of concentration round him increasing all the time. Eventually he got his phone out, and scrolled through the contacts till he got to 'Eddie'. Eddie Sharp was Sheldon's go-to guy for anything law-related. He rang the number, and it went straight to voicemail, as it always did. He left a brief message.

'Eddie. Call me. It's Sheldon.'

He put his phone down again, and returned to massaging his temples. He found it helped him think. It wasn't long before his phone rang. Unknown number.

'Hello, Eddie.'

'Sheldon. What can I do for you?'

Back in his office, Edwin looked again at the account documents he had been given by Louise Northington. As he had a lot of details, he didn't think he needed any hacking help from Dave Clark.

Could he just ring up the bank, and pretend to be Neville? Probably best not to even try. That would have a very distinct feeling of fraud. What about trying to access the account online? Technically, that was probably just as fraudulent, but the thought of it certainly didn't feel as bad. Online it was, then.

Edwin went to the bank website, and the login section. Account number — that was easy. Customer PIN — not so easy. Six-digit number. Edwin tried Neville's date of birth, and to his astonishment, this was accepted. But the next page expressed concern that the user was logging in on an unfamiliar computer, and required three security questions to be answered. Edwin sat and thought for a few minutes. He tried to remember the occasions when he had received warning emails, telling him of some unauthorised activity on an online account he was associated with. He tried to remember if any of these had been to do with people accessing his bank account from a different computer. He couldn't remember. He thought some more, and realised that even when he had received those sort of warning emails, usually he assumed they were some sort of scam, just wanting him to confirm his details by entering them somewhere, and he always deleted them, and forgot about them. He hoped Neville Northington took the same approach. It was one thing looking at bank accounts as part of his official investigation when the owners had given him the details — it was quite another accessing an account which the owner had very definitely not given him access to. With that hope in mind, he looked at the security questions.

The first two questions gave him no trouble whatsoever. Place of birth, London. Mother's maiden name, Field. Only the third one gave him pause for thought. Name of first school. Edwin had no idea. But he thought he could find out. He got out his phone, and found Jeanette Northington's number. He opened a new text message.

Hi Jeanette, this may seem a little oblique, but I'm just wondering which was the first school that Neville attended? Can't get hold of him... Best, Edwin.

He felt bad about the 'Can't get hold of him' line, but if pressed on its truthfulness, he could always say that it meant he couldn't get hold of him and ask him this question without opening a can of worms. Life as a private investigator seemed to involve many of these subtle distinctions.

He sat back in his chair, and wondered what to do while he waited for a reply.

Almost immediately, his phone beeped.

Greenvale Primary. Jeanette.

Pleased by the promptness of Jeanette's response, Edwin turned back to the computer and carefully typed Greenvale, and then after a moment's thought added Primary. He pressed Continue, and there he was, logged on to the bank account that Neville Northington had hidden from him.

It took him a moment to get his bearings, as it always did with a new website. There didn't seem to be records of any transactions. He tried clicking on everything that he could to bring up the relevant information, but though there were several different sections he could access, they all led him to the same conclusion — after being opened with a deposit of £1,000 about six months earlier, no money at all had entered or left the account.

Jeanette was in Kettering. She was at the home of Father White's older brother, Harry, paying her respects. Harry was 65, and was still thoroughly shocked at the idea that his younger brother could possibly have died. His death, let alone his sudden death, was not something that was supposed to happen during Harry's lifetime. The curtains were drawn at the front of his terraced house, though he left the ones at the back open. There hadn't been a death in his family for a long time, and he wasn't quite sure of the correct etiquette these days.

A couple of friends and neighbours had dropped round earlier in the day. The two friends who had called had also brought their wives, who Harry hardly knew, so their visits were less than relaxed. The neighbours (from next door but one) had been more welcome, and had left Harry feeling well supported. It was amazing the difference that could be made by a few kind words, the fleeting touch of a hand, a bunch of daffodils fresh from the garden. And the sharing of a cup of tea in such circumstances acquired a mystical, almost a sacramental, significance.

Jeanette and Harry had exchanged a couple of phone calls over the last couple of days, having first met at the hospital, when Harry had arrived a couple of hours after his brother had been admitted. Father White had never properly regained consciousness after collapsing at the door of Jeanette's house, but both Jeanette and Harry had sensed a closeness to the dying man in his final hours. He would occasionally open his eyes, and after briefly staring vacantly, would focus on one or other of their faces before quickly slipping away from them again. During the couple of days of their vigil, the two of them had developed a connection that transcended their differences. Having Father White in common gave them a strong, unspoken solidarity.

But the transition from that almost primordial interconnectedness in the presence of their dying fellow traveller, to a more conventional social bond, wasn't a straightforward one. It had seemed natural for Jeanette to ask Harry if he was receiving visitors, and for him to say that he was, and for her to arrange a vague time to arrive. But almost as soon as she set off, mid-afternoon, having carefully programmed her satnav, she began to wonder if it really was a good idea. However, as she didn't drive that often, and she was going to an unfamiliar destination, her mind was kept thoroughly focussed on the practicalities of getting there. She decided afterwards that if she'd been travelling by some other means, and had had time to think about it, she might have turned round and gone home again.

As it was, that idea of turning round and returning home only occurred to her after she'd parked just outside Harry's house, and before she could act on it, she spotted the glass-panelled front door opening, and the familiar, yet unfamiliar, figure of Harry White appearing in the doorway, and raising one hand slightly in an uncertain wave. After that, there was no option but to lock her car carefully and walk over to exchange a mumbled greeting and awkward handshake with the man she had known less than a week. As she followed him into the house, she had a stern word with herself.

Come on Jeanette. You're here to offer your condolences. This is something you've done many times before, in many different capacities. You are a capable, balanced, woman with — Oh! Look! He smiles in exactly the same way Brian did. Half shy, half sad. How can a smile even look sad? I wonder if his smile still looks like that if he's not sad? Condolences. Condolences. That's what you're here for. Condolences.

Suddenly she realised she had been asked a question.

'I'm sorry, I was miles away.'

'Would you like a cuppa?'

'Thanks. That would be lovely. White, no sugar.'

'Yes, I know.' He smiled again.

Jeanette followed him into his tiny kitchen, and as he set about the ritual of tea preparation, they were somehow transported back to the way of relating they had experienced at the hospital bedside of his brother. Much was unspoken, long pauses were commonplace, and somehow were not at all awkward. They talked in snippets, and half remembered stories, with more smiles than either of them really expected, and sudden gushings of tears, that caught them unawares, and then left as suddenly as they had arrived.

Harry was still in the kitchen, but Jeanette had taken a seat in the front room, when she got Edwin's text. She couldn't think what on earth he would need the information for, but quickly replied. She hoped he was getting somewhere constructive with his researches, and not just investigating things for the sake of it.

Now Harry was back in the room with a tray. There was toast, sausage rolls, cheese, salad, some scones, and a large teapot with a knitted cosy.

'Thanks so much,' said Jeanette. 'This looks wonderful.'

CHAPTER 31

'Hello, Edwin? It's Molly Raestock here.'

It was nine thirty on Friday morning, and Edwin was due to interview her at two o'clock this afternoon. As she talked, he had a sinking feeling.

'I'm really sorry, but I'm not going to be able to make our meeting this afternoon.'

Here we go again, he thought.

'We're chronically understaffed in the office today, and I'm suddenly needed in this afternoon's big meeting, as Jasper Felder hasn't turned up for work today.'

'He's off sick?'

'Well, he just hasn't turned up. And he's not answering his phone.'

'Okay,' said Edwin. 'Thanks for letting me know. Do you want to arrange another time for an interview? Shall we say first thing Monday morning? Assuming the staff crisis has stabilised, of course.'

Molly sounded relieved. 'Yes, yes, that would be fine. I'm assuming Jasper will be back by then.'

'Right. I'll see you on Monday morning then. First thing. In your office?'

'Yes, that's fine. See you then.'

Edwin set his phone down thoughtfully on his desk. He had two frustratingly contradictory worries. One was that Neville Northington was playing him like an expert angler plays a fish, through the medium of his loyal office manager, who so far had proved immune to interrogation. The other was that he would like to know what was going on with Jasper Felder, as he felt he had less insight into him than anyone else he was investigating.

Jeanette woke with a start. Everything seemed wrong. She felt as if she was jet-lagged, and her eyes would hardly open. Normally she rose early; six thirty every day, and normally she felt calm. But today was different. Groggily she reached over to the bedside table for her watch. Nine forty-five. Nine forty-five! That would explain the jet-lagged feeling. Forcing herself into action, she sat up, and swung her legs over the edge of the bed. She almost screamed as her feet touched the floor, and she immediately pulled them back up again. There was something cold, hard and smooth on the carpet. And why was the room so dark? She reached for the bedside lamp, but it wasn't in its usual place. Suddenly she was wide awake, and a little scared. As she regained full consciousness, it all came flooding back. She very deliberately put her feet back down on the floor, padded across to the window and pulled back the curtains. Light came streaming in, and she could now clearly see the modest furnishings and painted floorboards of Harry White's spare bedroom.

Jeanette stood there for a minute, leaning on the bottom of the window frame with both hands, and resting her head against one side of it, the final clouds of sleep clearing from her mind. She looked down into the small garden, a shed at one side, and a vegetable patch taking up the half furthest from the house. She finally raised her eyes, and noticed someone staring at her from the equivalent window at the back of the opposing house. Immediately she pulled the curtains closed again. I'm not really dressed for appearing in public, she thought, with a wry look down at herself. That was the trouble with staying somewhere unplanned.

She put yesterday's clothes back on again, and after a quick wash went downstairs.

'Hello, Harry.'

He was washing a bowl in the sink, but spun round to face her. He smiled in a rather worried fashion. 'Hello, Jeanette. Are you all right? I was just wondering if I should come and wake you.'

'Yes, fine. Just overslept. And I'm afraid I may have given your neighbour across the back a bit of a shock.'

Harry smiled. 'Give him something to talk about. What do you want to eat?'

'Oh, I really must go. I can't possibly impose on your hospitality any longer.'

'It is in no way an imposition.' Harry walked over to Jeanette and gently touched her shoulder. 'Please. Have a seat and I'll rustle you up something before you go.'

Jeanette murmured something inaudible, and sank into a kitchen chair. When was the last time a man had spoken to her that kindly, and insisted on helping her? It would have been this man's brother, that was certain, but she had always been so careful to maintain what she called in her head a 'professional distance' with Father White, that she kept any of his kindnesses at arm's length. With Tony, she had tried very hard to breach his professional distance, but had found that more and more difficult as the years passed. Even her most intimate efforts to love him and be loved by him seemed to end with the sensation of a transaction being completed, a deal of some sort being done, or a service rendered.

A bowl of cornflakes appeared in front of her, and a sizzling sound and the accompanying smell told her that bacon and eggs were in the offing. Jeanette smiled as she remembered she had ostensibly come here to comfort Harry. Good grief. What was going on?

Then she began to quietly cry, sitting there at the kitchen table as the expression she had used in her head, good grief, percolated through to her emotions and began to gently expand and fill her, till she was unable to be aware of anything but grief, multi-faceted and long-standing, but finding its catalyst in Father White's death; and goodness, longed for yet often held at bay, and now communicated directly by the hand of his brother.

'I'm sorry,' she sobbed, as she saw his concerned face. 'It's just, oh, everything.' She smiled through her tears. 'Don't mind me. And seriously, don't burn the bacon.'

Sheldon Haynes wandered into Edwin's room.

'Come in,' said Edwin.

'Very funny,' said Haynes. 'Look. About this Raestock woman. I'm sure there must be a way we can use her to unwittingly give away more about

Northington then he'd like her to. Was it Monday you've re-scheduled her for?'

'Yes,' said Edwin. He thought for a minute. 'Let's hint that we're concerned about his whereabouts at a completely irrelevant time, and see if she comes up with some story covering that date.'

Haynes didn't look convinced. 'Yes,' he said slowly, 'but even assuming that they both fall for it, and come up with a perfect alibi, all that tells us is that he's happy to use her to cover for him, and she's willing to do it. That in itself, doesn't actually prove any other wrongdoing, still less any connected with what we're actually investigating.'

Edwin felt a bit deflated. 'Yes,' he said. 'I see what you mean.'

Sheldon Haynes stroked his chin thoughtfully. 'We'll have to be a bit cleverer than that.'

Sheldon Haynes was in expansive mood.

'Why not, Edwin? Why not indeed? Yes! I'll have one final pint. You're a gentleman. And possibly a scholar. Are you a scholar? You would tell me if you were, wouldn't you?'

Edwin carefully composed his features into a suitably serious expression. Curiously, over the past few hours he'd noticed his features being harder to compose than usual. He frowned at his drink. Must be something in the cider.

'Funny you should ask that, Mr Haynes,' he said as he stood up to make his way back to the bar. 'I *was* a scholar, but I'm not any more.'

He turned and weaved through the Friday night

crowd, leaving Sheldon Haynes sitting at the table in the corner, nodding approvingly at his skilful answer.

There were many more people in the pub than there had been last time he went up to the bar. However, he kept seeing cunning short cuts with his peripheral vision, and he lurched to follow them with what he told himself was more than ordinary skill. But despite cutting the length of his journey by means of this tactic, it seemed ages before he finally found himself coming out of the far side of the crowd. And to his surprise, there was Sheldon Haynes, calmly sitting in front of him.

'Oh. I'm sorry, I seem to have taken a wrong turning somewhere. Let me try again.'

'You can do it,' said Haynes in an encouraging manner. 'By the way, I can't remember if we've come up with a cunning way of trapping you know who, with you know who else's interview?'

'I can help you there. I can remember. We haven't.'

'That's a shame. I was just congratulating myself on being so clever.'

Edwin sadly shook his head. 'No. Sadly, at the moment, we're not clever enough.'

He turned in a dignified manner, briefly stared at the bar, then headed determinedly off towards it.

CHAPTER 32

Edwin had arranged to meet Dave Clark outside The Plough on Saturday at lunchtime, and he did so after the brisk walk across Peckham Rye Park, and up Barry Road. The walk had done him some good, but after the previous night he found he couldn't help shuddering slightly as he stopped outside the pub.

Being greeted with the Dave Clark High Five perked him up some more, and soon he and his friend were heading off down the hill to find a suitable office for the afternoon, after Edwin had hurriedly vetoed Dave's suggestion of The Plough. The next most obvious thing would have been to go to Edwin's own office, but he really wanted a change of scene. As they walked, they talked.

'So,' said Dave, 'how's your investigation been going?'

'Well, to be honest, we're not much further on, though there are definitely some weird things that have been happening.'

'You probably can't tell me?'

Edwin laughed. 'I probably can't. And if I could, it wouldn't mean much to you. Oh, while I remember, here's your next installment of cash.'

He reached in his inside pocket, and handed the envelope to Dave.

'Cheers, man! Amazing. I hope I can help you again! This is a monster job for me. Cool.'

'Since I spoke to you last, have you come across anything else in that software?'

'Nah, not really. But I'm so used to it now that I can run round inside the program, and find all the bank connections, like a laboratory rat.'

Edwin frowned. 'Like a laboratory rat in a good way?'

'In a *great* way.'

They had arrived at the start of the rows of shops and restaurants now.

'These are pretty busy,' Edwin said, glancing in at the windows they were passing. 'Are you hungry?'

'Not really.'

'Me neither. I had a bit of a late one last night, if I'm honest. Coffee is what I need. Look. What about this place?'

Brickworks Coffee certainly had some free seating. In keeping with its name, the decor featured large areas of exposed brickwork, and the tables were constructed of massive slabs of unvarnished wood. Edwin stuck his head round the door. 'Do you have WiFi?'

The tousle-haired teenager wearing a waistcoat and carrying a tray of empty mugs turned to Edwin, raised his eyebrows and nodded. As he turned away and headed towards the kitchen area Edwin heard him mutter with heavy teenage emphasis, 'Of *course* we have WiFi.'

Edwin smiled to himself, and beckoned Dave in. They found a corner where they could enjoy a certain amount of privacy, and Dave got out his laptop. It was large, black with dramatic yellow corners, and sounded very heavy as Dave set it on the table. He also produced a mains lead, and plugged it in straight away.

'Battery life no good?' asked Edwin, casually.

Dave looked up, his blank expression somehow still communicating incredulity.

'With a high performance machine like this, battery life is hardly a priority.'

Of course, Edwin thought to himself, if Dave *wasn't* a computer geek, he wouldn't be any help.

The teenager with the tray was back. He stared at Dave's machine with respect.

'Two black Americanos, please,' said Edwin.

'Cool,' said the waiter. Edwin wasn't sure whether he was referring to the order or Dave's laptop. Either way, he just stood there, staring.

Dave said something to him. Edwin heard him say it very clearly, but didn't understand any of it. The teenager replied, and in the reply Edwin caught only the word Speed. He sighed, and feeling a sudden surge of weariness washing over him, folded his arms on the table in front of him and laid his head on them. 'Wake me up when the coffee comes,' he murmured.

The next thing he knew, Dave was gently shaking his shoulder. 'It's here,' he was saying.

Edwin yawned and sat up. In front of him was a large white mug full of steaming black coffee. Beside him, Dave was staring intently at his screen, sipping his own drink sporadically, and tapping away at the keys of his laptop. Edwin sipped his coffee. It didn't take long before he began to feel human again.

'Right,' said Dave, pressing the final couple of keys with a grandiose flourish. Most of the time he set his fingers down very gently, almost caressingly, but he finished off now with a real sense of power in his touch, like a pianist punching out the concluding chords of a favourite sonata.

He pushed the machine sideways a little, so Edwin could see the screen too.

'Okay, what am I looking for?' asked Edwin.

'Well, in this box, the line with the red writing has, as far as I've been able to work out, the details of the two accounts that the software is meant to route money through.'

Edwin got his folder out of his backpack, and leafed through his papers.

'Right. This is the page,' he muttered to himself.

He looked at the list of numbers. Account numbers, and sort codes. It didn't take him long to find that none of the numbers he'd collected during his investigations matched those embedded in the software.

'No good. No matches,' said Edwin.

'No, I didn't think there would be. Almost certainly, if this is some sort of fraud, these will be just the first in a long chain of accounts, probably some in different countries, that you can only find by accessing them one at a time, and finding where any funds have been transferred to next. It's possible to do that of course, but obviously some countries pride themselves on their opacity to inspection.'

Edwin was disappointed. He took another sip of coffee, and frowned.

'Well, looking at it from the other end,' he said, 'Alastair Forth is certain that the individual components of the Connected Chain Bond are doing much better than its results would lead one to believe. Can we find out if any money at all has been routed out of the system? This is the unofficial part of the software you said you'd discovered, right?'

Dave Clark looked smug. 'This certainly is the unofficial part, and I've already got a way of finding that out.'

He hesitated, and leaned slightly closer to Edwin. 'Look, most of this research I've been doing, you gave me all the security credentials and so on, so you could argue it's pretty much above board, but the techniques I've had to use to find out about the money routing are definitely a bit of a grey area. So do you want me to continue with it? I don't want to compromise your investigation by using methods that are unacceptable.'

'A bit of a grey area? How grey?'

'Well, they're definitely illegal.'

'Hmm. Pretty grey.' Edwin remembered the steps he had taken in order to sign into Neville Northington's online banking, and tried to think of a good way to phrase his next question.

'Are these techniques more illegal than, say, using clever guesses and a bit of inside knowledge to log into someone else's bank account?'

Dave thought for a minute. 'Probably about that level, I'd say. Why do you ask?'

'No reason. I'd say we should go ahead.'

'Okay. But don't say I didn't warn you.'

'I won't.'

Edwin leaned forward and watched, as Dave's fingers began their lightning dance over the keys again. Unlike when Edwin used a computer, there were no images or icons on the screen at any time; just lines and lines of letters, numbers and other symbols.

'There you go,' said Dave eventually. 'These lines from here on down, detail the transfers out of the Connected Chain Bond system, and into this bank account.'

'Ah,' said Edwin, scanning them eagerly. 'So you've hacked into that first account?'

'Well, more or less. That is to say, yes, I have. But you told me to.'

'Yes, of course. Don't worry about that.' Edwin's eyes were still fixed on the screen. 'But these are tiny amounts.'

'They are indeed. That's why I'm not more excited than I am.'

'Right,' said Edwin slowly. 'So we've got half a dozen tiny transactions. Of two pounds each.'

Dave chuckled. 'Two pence matey, two pence. Like the song from Mary Poppins.'

'Oh.' Edwin was thoroughly deflated now. 'So we've broken the law, in order to discover that someone involved with Northington International may have defrauded investors of the sum of twelve pence.'

They both sat back in their seats. Dave sat back too far, and banged his head on the brick wall behind him. For some reason this made him laugh, and Edwin joined in. The teenager was back.

'Enjoying your coffees?'

'We certainly are. How quickly can you get us two more?'

'Pretty quickly.' He just stood there.

Edwin thought he'd try a computer joke. 'Well, I don't think much of your processor speed so far!'

Dave groaned. The teenager flushed and moved off.

'Sorry,' muttered Edwin. And then in a brighter voice, 'But talking of processor speed, how quickly were those six transactions made?'

'Ah. I see what you're thinking.' Dave turned back to his laptop.

'The first one was made at eleven thirty and twenty-seven seconds, so was the second one... the third one... They were all made within the same second.'

They looked at each other.

'Is that even possible?' asked Edwin.

'Well, from a computer point of view, of course! Modern processors can do billions of operations per second. From a bank account point of view, however, too many transactions within too short a space of time would be stopped almost immediately. They have pretty robust safeguards, you know.'

'Okay. Let's look at those lines again. Are there definitely just six transactions?'

'Yes. Just the six,' said Dave.

'What happens if you scroll down?'

Dave scrolled down. 'Ah. That's embarrassing.'

As he held the key down, more and more lines of figures slowly rolled on to the screen from the bottom, and exited out the top. As he watched, Edwin began to grin, and his grin grew broader and broader as Dave kept his finger on the Down arrow, and the figures kept appearing.

'Stop it there,' Edwin said eventually. 'Let's see what time these transactions were made.'

Dave peered at the relevant column.

'We've only got as far as eleven thirty and fifty-nine seconds. That's ridiculous. Is it on the same day? There have been hundreds of transactions.'

He searched for the date. 'Yes, it's all the same day.'

'What day?' asked Edwin.

'Sixth of March. This year.'

'Sixth of March?' Edwin let out a low whistle. 'That happens to be a date that is very significant in this investigation. Curiouser and curiouser.'

He leaned in close to the screen. 'So as far as I can see, they all look like two pence transactions, yes?'

'Yes,' said Dave.

'Can we work out approximately how many there are per second?'

'Approximately? Ha.' Dave's fingers raced over the keyboard as he talked.

'Using the second we want to check, as an exported environment variable, I'll just cat the file...'

Edwin's concentration lapsed, as Dave constructed a single command on the black screen.

'...and pipe it into grep, with a simple regex that looks for account numbers...'

The wide-eyed teenaged waiter was back with their fresh coffees.

'...and then redirect the output into the bc calculator, using bash's globbing...'

He took their empty mugs, and reverently withdrew.

'...to take advantage of the polish prefix notation.'

Dave hit the Enter key.

'Nine,' he said.

'Nine?' said Edwin. 'Couldn't you just have counted them?'

'Well sure, but now we have a generalised solution, which we can apply to arbitrary data sets.'

'Okay, fine. But they're all two pence?'

'They're all two pence.'

'Let's try some other times.'

The fresh cups of coffee were gradually sipped as Edwin and Dave methodically scanned second after second, Dave explaining that now they only needed to change one variable each time, and adding up the total number of recorded transactions. There were almost invariably nine per second, but occasionally eight. They scanned through huge tracts of numbers, and everywhere they looked they found the same pattern. Two pence deposited, nine times a second, all day, and as far as they could tell, every day.

Eventually Edwin opened the calculator on his phone, and starting multiplying the figures.

'Two pence isn't a lot, but that Mary Poppins song was right. If my figures are correct, these tiny deposits happening nine times a second gives a total of about... fifteen thousand pounds a day, or... five and a half million a year.'

'Blimey,' said Dave. 'And don't forget, this is only one of the accounts. I haven't accessed the other one, but it's a fair guess that the same thing is happening there.'

'So that's eleven million a year, potentially. Alastair Forth would be very interested in this.'

Dave and Edwin sat silently looking at each other, their coffees forgotten.

'So we've established the time at which these transactions started occurring,' began Edwin slowly. 'Is it possible to find out where they were initiated from? Where the computer was that set them up?'

'Well, not exactly, but as it was all done online, unless whoever did it cleaned up very carefully... let's see.'

Edwin now felt rather fidgety. Maybe it was the two cups of coffee, he thought, as he took another sip, but he suddenly understood why people began biting their nails. At the same time he resolved not to, if he could help it.

'Dave. Stop me if I'm distracting you, but I thought you said that too many transactions, in too short a space of time, would be stopped automatically by the bank?'

'Oh yes. But all those transactions happened, and did you notice there were never more than nine per second? To me it looks like someone knew the bank's warning system is set to go off at ten. And look! Here's the IP address of the computer which was used to initiate the transactions. Fantastic. Whoever it was didn't put a lot of effort into clearing their trail.'

Dave jotted down a line of figures, separated by dots.

'So does that tell us where the computer was?' asked Edwin.

'No. But if it's a computer that's used by someone we know, we can see if the IP addresses match. I'll just have a look through some of the other information you've given me, and see if I can come up with another one the same.'

'I see,' said Edwin thoughtfully. Relaxing a little now

as he sipped his coffee, he stared out the window at the passers by, out enjoying the warm spring sunshine, and going about their Saturday jobs. He wondered if Bet was working today. He might look in on his way home, though it wasn't really on his route. A couple with a pushchair stopped by the door of Brickworks Coffee, and the woman held the door open for the man, who judging by his body language was pushing the child with an ill grace. As they entered, Edwin choked on the mouthful of coffee he was savouring.

It was Neville and Louise Northington, and presumably that was their son Josh in the pushchair.

Dave turned in concern, and slapped his friend on the back. 'You all right, mate?'

'Yea, sorry. Coffee went down the wrong way.'

Out of the corner of his eye, Edwin could see the Northingtons talking to the teenaged waiter, looking round in vain for a good place to sit in the rapidly filling café, and leaving again. Neville's body language was now even more tense. Edwin had forgotten how close they lived.

'Well look at this,' said Dave, oblivious to the drama by the door. Yet again he slid his laptop across so Edwin could see clearly. 'Is that or isn't it the same as this number?'

He indicated the figures he had jotted down. Edwin, after watching the Northingtons disappear from view, checked them carefully. 'Yes. They're the same. Which computer do they refer to?'

'The one in Neville Northington's office,' said Dave Clark.

CHAPTER 33

Edwin knocked on her door at nine sharp, and she immediately called out, 'Come in.'

He noticed as he entered that she looked tired.

'Good morning, Miss Raestock. Good to finally get a chance to speak to you.' Even as he said it, Edwin realised that this sounded a little pointed.

Molly smiled though, as she stood up to shake his hand, and replied quite brightly, 'Yes, indeed. I'm sorry it's taken so long. You can imagine how busy we've been in the office over the last while. And Jasper is still off, and I haven't been able to get in touch with him at all. I'm a bit concerned about him, but Mr Neville told me not to worry. He made some joke about Dutch people and drugs. Anyway, I shouldn't be wasting your time by going on about things.'

She settled back down behind her desk.

'No problem,' sad Edwin. 'And I'll try to take as little as possible of your time.'

He got out his trusty notebook, and turned to the page

with her name at the top. The early questions covered the usual range of basic information, and then he asked Molly about the last time she saw Tony Northington. As she talked, she gradually relaxed, and her voice became slower and more thoughtful.

'It was the Friday before Christmas, in the afternoon, and I went into his office to get him to sign something. Two documents. And it was a bit strange. He was sitting in the gloom just doing nothing. You have to understand that's very unlike him.'

'Did he seem depressed? Or agitated, maybe?'

'Not depressed — more pensive, I'd say. Certainly not agitated. He had this piece of installation art made by his daughter, Amelia, in his office. You've met her?'

Edwin hoped he wasn't blushing. 'Yes, I've met her.'

'Of course. You'll have interviewed her too. Well, this artwork is basically a tank with pretty lights in it, but it had stopped working. I offered to see if I could get someone out to fix it in the new year, but he refused. He said he hadn't appreciated it till it broke, and that he missed it. He was very mellow, I remember. And this was so out of character it has stuck in my mind.'

Molly stopped talking. Her eyes had a distant look, and Edwin sat quietly. Eventually he broke the silence.

'I know that what happened to Tony doesn't make this seem very likely, but would you say, having seen him in that mood, there was any chance he might have been, or might have become, suicidal?'

Molly laughed, and the distant look disappeared from her eyes.

'I'd say absolutely none at all. I've obviously had the chance to think about it since, and although his mood was a little melancholy, it was really a very realistic melancholy. I got the impression that he was contemplating being a bit nicer, a bit more human, to the people around him. Perhaps particularly to his daughter, who had created the piece.'

'Okay,' said Edwin, nodding, and making a few notes in his book. Without looking up he said, 'On the day Tony Northington died, Neville says he was in the office all day. Would you be in a position to confirm that?' Now he looked up.

'Oh, yes. Definitely he was.' Molly was nodding emphatically.

'Do you need to check in your diary?'

'No. I remember it quite well.'

'I've been asking everyone for copies of their diaries. Just now, it would be really helpful if I could look at your diary entries for that day.'

Molly smoothed her skirt down with her hands a couple of times before replying in a casual voice, 'I don't think I have it quite to hand.'

Edwin frowned as he looked at her desk. 'Isn't that it?' he asked, indicating a large pink diary tucked under her desk tidy.

'Oh, yes.' She laughed. 'I can see why you've become a detective.'

'Just a junior investigator, really. Can I look at the diary please?'

'Of course.' Molly slid the diary out, and passed it to Edwin, reluctantly, he thought.

'Thanks.' Holding his pen between his teeth, he thumbed through the pink book. March the sixth. There it was. Under the date was written, in a clear hand, 'Mr

Neville in office all day, till phone call about his father'.

'Right,' said Edwin uncertainly, 'that seems fairly unambiguous. Though, having said that, could you clarify whether this means that he was in the office in general, or his office in particular, all day, till the phone call?'

Molly replied immediately. 'Oh, in his own office. Definitely. Not really one for wandering round, Mr Neville. Not when he's got that nice office.' She indicated its general direction with a wave of her hand.

'Would anyone else have seen him that day, if he was in his own office?'

'No, quite probably not. I'm the only one who has carte blanche to interrupt him. Though obviously I knock.'

'Obviously. So Alastair Forth, perhaps, or Jasper Felder, wouldn't have gone in to talk to him at any point?'

'No, they wouldn't.' Molly seemed very sure about this. 'But I'm sure you could check with them.'

This was true, and in fact Edwin already had checked with them. Molly seemed the only person who had seen him that day.

Having been unable, with Sheldon, to think of any cunning way of interviewing Molly, this was the only serious point Edwin wanted to establish, now that he knew that what looked like fraud on a massive scale had been initiated in Neville Northington's office, and using his computer, on the morning in question. There remained the question of why the swipe system would say that he was out of the office. Edwin casually brought the subject up.

'You're very organised, Miss Raestock, and you supervise a large office with a sophisticated swipe card entry and exit system.'

Was it Edwin's imagination, or was Molly tensing slightly?

'Have you ever known the movements of the staff to be inaccurately recorded?'

'Gosh, that's a difficult question. We don't often have any reason to check through the records. But I would say that, like any system, it's bound to malfunction occasionally. I wouldn't trust it as much as, say, the testimony of a responsible person.'

She was definitely looking tense, Edwin decided, and also her cheeks had flushed slightly. This secretly delighted him, as he was aware of his own tendency to colour when being less than truthful, and he was glad to find he wasn't the only sufferer. Just out of mischief he left a short pause before carrying on with his questions. He used the time to make some unnecessary notes, and by the time he looked up, Molly's colour had heightened considerably. He affected not to notice, and continued with his well rehearsed queries.

By the time he had finished, Molly Raestock was her normal, businesslike self again. She saw Edwin to the door of her office and they shook hands.

Just then, Neville Northington appeared as if from nowhere.

'Ah, Edwin. Good to see you. If I could have a word with you?'

Now it was Edwin's turn to tense up. He hoped he wasn't going red. That would be retribution on a very swift time-scale.

'Yes, of course.'

He followed Neville into his office.

Neville closed the door behind them. His manner was warm and courteous, as he smiled at Edwin. 'Would you like a drink?'

'No thanks, I'm fine.'

Edwin looked round the room with interest. It was decorated in the company's typical restrained style, with pieces of original art on the walls, as he had also noticed in Alastair's office.

'Do take a seat. I won't keep you long.'

Edwin sat down in front of Neville's desk, and couldn't stop his eyes from straying to the computer monitor on the desktop. Presumably that was the machine...

'I'm sorry to say, Edwin, that I'm going to be dispensing with your services.'

'Oh. I mean, well. But—'

'It's not that you've done a bad job. But really, I think I only initiated the investigation out of a deep sense of grief, and on reflection, I feel that it's not going to get anybody anywhere if we carry on with it.'

'Gosh. Er, well I understand that, of course, and I respect that, of course. I know I haven't actually got any concrete results for you, but I feel sure that—'

'I await your final invoice, and it will of course be attended to speedily. With the invoice, I will expect confirmation that you have destroyed all the personal details that you may have had access to while you were conducting your research.'

Neville stood up. Edwin stood up too. He was sure if

only he could think of the right thing to say, he would be able to get Neville to reverse his decision, but he had no idea what that right thing would be. Almost in a daze, he was escorted to Neville's door, which promptly closed behind him. He walked across the foyer as far as the first reception desk. Sam was standing behind it. She raised her eyebrows very slightly, and smiled knowingly. Edwin paused briefly, again with the feeling that the right comment, even at this stage, might somehow turn everything round in his favour. He tried to remember the sort of things people said in films, or more his area of expertise, in books. Despite spending three years studying them full-time, the words they were packed with now seemed to be deserting him, just when he needed them. Disconsolately he trailed over to the lift, and pressed the button with the downward arrow. He had to wait for a couple of minutes, and in fact was considering taking the stairs, when a ping alerted him to the lift's arrival. It was empty, and he stepped in, and pressed the button for the ground floor. The doors were just starting to close when he was aware of footsteps approaching across the foyer, and Alastair Forth stepped briskly in beside him.

'Hello,' said Edwin.

'Hello,' replied Alastair. He then, as the lift doors closed, put one finger up against his lips, and with the other hand mimed a pair of legs walking forward, and then turning sharp left. Edwin, his eyes wide open with surprise, replied with a silent nod. And after returning his security pass at reception, he exited the building, and turned left. Not knowing what to do next, he kept on in a straight line, at an easy pace. After a minute or so, he paused to tie his shoelace, and looked behind him. He couldn't see anyone he recognised, so carried on again the way he had been going. As he passed the next turning on the left he heard a voice quietly say his name, and there was Alastair Forth, slightly out of breath, beckoning him into the side street. Edwin turned and headed towards him, as casually as he could, and without either of them saying anything, followed him into a café, where Alastair ordered a tea, and Edwin, behind him, a black coffee. He then went and sat at the table next to Alastair in the back of the café.

'Cloak and dagger, eh?' said Alastair quietly, not looking at Edwin.

'Very impressive,' said Edwin. 'Is it necessary?' he asked, hesitantly.

'I don't know.' Alastair now smiled, and looked across. 'In the office it probably was, but not here, I guess.'

He slid over to sit at Edwin's table.

'But it might interest you to know that the reason I knew enough to follow you out, is that all the offices are fitted with surveillance systems, and I just happened to overhear your conversation with Neville.'

'Gosh. The surveillance is set up so you can listen in to Neville's conversations?'

'Well, not originally, but it's a very flexible system that's been installed, and it can be configured in lots of different ways. I only came across it by accident, and I then got one of the computer guys who works with Gerry to come in one weekend and suss it out. I can now use it to my advantage. But enough of that. I overheard enough to know Neville doesn't want you doing any more investigating?'

Edwin took a sip of his coffee before replying. His natural instinct was to trust Alastair, but so far today he wasn't having much time to think.

'Yes. He seems to have had enough,' he eventually said, cautiously.

'You can say that again. Have you any idea why he's chosen this moment to pull the plug on it?'

Right, thought Edwin. I either seek Alastair's help, or give up now. He took the plunge.

'Yes, I think I have. I may have found a reason for the suspiciously poor performance of the Connected Chain Bond—'

'BS,' said Alastair, abruptly.

'Sorry?'

'That's what everyone calls it. BS. Short for Best Seller.'

'Ah,' said Edwin. 'Anyway, I've found evidence which implicates Neville in some sort of scam, siphoning money out of the Connected... the Best Seller. I've no idea how he might know that I've discovered it, but if he does, that would be a very obvious reason for him to want to stop me immediately.'

Alastair's eyes had lit up as Edwin was talking. 'Siphoning money out? How was he getting away with that?'

'The siphoning mechanism seems to be built into the software that controls the way the various investments are connected. I have a colleague who helps me with the technical side.'

Edwin had a moment's unease as he heard himself describing the hacking he and Dave Clark had done as 'the technical side'.

Alastair suddenly looked very serious. 'Do you think you've now got enough evidence to go to the police?'

Edwin's unease was increasing. 'Well, I don't know...'

'Because if you do, that might be our best bet now. I've got to admit, that when I started helping Gerry to investigate his concerns about the company, I got rather carried away, and crossed a couple of boundaries that would make the little bits of evidence we uncovered inadmissible in court. But they didn't amount to much anyway, so that wasn't a great loss. But it sounds like you're on to something really convincing here.'

Alastair was smiling encouragingly now. 'In fact, even if Neville is going to instruct you to stop what you've been doing, and withdraw your funding, there's nothing to stop me engaging you to do exactly the same investigation, and covering your expenses going forward. How about it?'

Alastair seemed to become younger as he spoke. Edwin had never seen him animated before. He hated to have to burst his bubble.

'Yeah, well, I don't think we're really at that stage yet.'

Edwin frowned, pursed his lips and drummed his fingers on his chin. 'In fact, if I'm honest, in our investigations we may also have crossed a certain line that may make it rather awkward to involve the law.'

He kept his eyes focussed downwards, on the laminated top of the table.

'Maybe a couple of lines. Possibly.'

Alastair's coffee mug smashed on the tiled floor into an archipelago of porcelain islands in a dark, steaming, tropical sea. Edwin flinched at the noise, but didn't lift his eyes. He listened as Alastair's chair scraped abruptly on the tiled floor, and as Alastair's footsteps crossed the café. And as Alastair explained to the owner in a terse, angry voice, that there had been a breakage. And as the door closed behind him. When Edwin looked up, there was a ten pound note on the table.

CHAPTER 34

Edwin stumped up the stairs towards his office. Unusually, he barely grunted a greeting to his boss, Parker, as he passed the window of his tiny office. After pausing a moment at the top of the stairs, he turned right instead of left, and shortly found himself in the company of Sheldon Haynes, spilling out the story of his morning. As he talked however, he found his mood changing. Having begun his tale in frustration, and with Haynes having barely uttered a word, he finished talking in a more bullish mood.

'So what if we've been fired, just when we're on the brink of something. Let's ignore Northington, and carry on. Hands up who's with me?'

Sheldon Haynes stuck one hand in the air, then the other, and then casually folded them behind his head.

'Let's think it through, though,' he said. 'I'm only just getting my head round the evidence of the bank transfers. How sure are you that Neville knows you're on to him?'

Edwin hesitated. Haynes continued. 'Because I certainly didn't tell him.'

'Oh,' said Edwin. 'But I can't think why else he would want to call us off.' He frowned.

Just then his phone rang. Molly Raestock, the screen said. Edwin raised his eyebrows, and silently showed Haynes who was ringing, before answering. Molly sounded nervous, and was talking quietly. It took Edwin a moment to realise what she was saying.

'...so when I heard he'd dispensed with your services, I couldn't in all conscience leave it like that. I'd like to revise my statement about the sixth of March.'

'Okay,' said Edwin, sitting down in the chair opposite Haynes, pulling his notebook out of his pocket, and finding the page he had made his most recent notes on. 'Talk me through it again.'

'Right,' said Molly. Edwin heard her taking a deep breath before continuing. She was still talking quietly, but seemed calmer now. 'I remember it fairly well, as by the end of the day it was etched on all our memories, for all the wrong reasons. I got in to the office at my usual time, about a quarter to eight. I like to get everything nice and organised before the day starts properly, as by about nine o'clock I'm normally flat out, dealing with whatever comes my way. Mr Neville's hours are generally pretty varied, but certainly that day he came in not long after me, say by about a quarter past eight. He came into my room about that time to tell me that he was going to be unofficially out of the office from mid-morning.'

'Right,' said Edwin. 'So he wasn't in his office all day?'

'No. He was only in for a couple of hours.'

'I see,' said Edwin. 'Was this something he did often?'

'Maybe every couple of weeks. Occasionally twice in one week, then not again for a while.'

'And can I ask you why he would take unofficial absence from the office?'

Molly's voice became even quieter. 'He had an understanding with one of the girls from the office.'

'Ah,' said Edwin. 'And every time he was unofficially absent, was this always for the same reason?'

'Well, I don't know the exact reason every time...'

'Miss Raestock, come on. You've got to be as open and frank as possible. It's the only way we'll get anywhere.'

'Yes, I know,' said Molly. 'Of course I don't want to be obstructive or anything, but I still don't like to paint anyone in a bad light.'

'I'm sure you don't. But it is possible that painting someone in a bad light may stop them from being painted in an even worse light. So were his unofficial absences from the office always for the same reason, as far as you know?'

'As far as I know, yes.'

'Always the same girl?'

'Really, I don't think I would know that sort of thing,' said Molly.

'Let me put it another way. Are you aware of any occasions when Neville took unofficial leave, and Samantha Jones wasn't off sick, or absent for other reasons?'

'Samantha Jones? How did you know? But if you put it that way, no, I'm not aware of any other occasions.'

Molly sounded almost relieved. 'In fact,' she continued, 'though I'm sure he's had the hots for some of the other girls in the office before, this is the first time I'm aware of him acting on it.'

'Thank you,' said Edwin, 'that's very helpful. Tell me — is Miss Jones at work today?'

'Yes. If I look out to the foyer, I can see her.'

'Okay. Would it be possible for you to get her to come into your office now, so I can speak to her?'

'I suppose so. I could cover her reception desk. It would look very odd though. People would talk.'

'Let them,' said Edwin callously. 'This is important.'

'And Mr Neville would — hang on a minute — I can see him just heading for the lifts. Sorry to be so pathetic. Right, he's gone. I'll go and get Sam for you.'

Edwin waited for a minute or so, and a new voice came on the phone.

'Hello?'

'Is that Sam?' said Edwin.

'Yes. Who am I speaking to?'

'My name is Edwin Strong, and I work for a firm of private investigators.'

'Oh!'

'No need to worry. I just need to ask you a couple of questions, if that's okay,' said Edwin.

'What's it to do with?'

'I need to establish some corroborating evidence, to back up what I've been told by someone else.'

'Am I in trouble?' said Sam.

'Not as far as I know. I just wanted to ask you if you could talk me through your day on the sixth of March.'

'This year?' She laughed.

'That's the one,' said Edwin.

'How can I possibly remember what I did on the sixth of March?'

'Does it help you remember if I tell you that it was the day Tony Northington died?'

Silence.

'Sam? Hello? Can you tell me what you were doing that day?'

'I don't feel comfortable talking to you. Shouldn't I have a lawyer present, or something?'

'You don't need one,' said Edwin, crossing the first two fingers of his free hand as he spoke. Across the table, Haynes had his head on one side as if he was listening, though Edwin wasn't sure what he could hear. Edwin continued talking. 'Would it help if I told you that I'm trying to verify something that Neville Northington told me? And that he suggested I get in touch with you?'

'Did he indeed? The bastard. Happy to drop me in it when it suits him.'

Another silence, then Sam spoke again. 'I'll tell you what I was doing, off the record. But if you want an official statement, I need a lawyer.'

'That's fine. Talk me through your day, if you could?'

'Well, the previous evening I would have had a text from Neville saying he'd be free that day, and might I possibly be feeling ill enough to stay at home. Look, are you sure this isn't going to get me into trouble?'

'It's no part of my plan to get you into any sort of trouble,' said Edwin.

'Right.' Sam hesitated, then continued. 'So I replied that possibly I could. And first thing that morning, the day that Mr Tony died — the sixth, was it?'

'Yes, the sixth.'

'First thing that morning, I rang in sick, with my back. I tidied up the flat, and had that all done by about half nine. Then I sat back and waited for Neville.'

'What did you do while you waited?'

There was a moment's silence on the other end of the line, then a chuckle.

'Oh yes, I watched TV. I remember Homes Under the Hammer came on after a while. That would have been at ten.'

Edwin made a mental note.

'And then,' said Sam, 'he arrived while that show was still on.'

'So that would have been approximately what time?'

'Well, it finishes at eleven, so maybe twenty to? Ten to?'

'Okay. Then what?' Edwin immediately wished he hadn't asked.

'Doggy fashion, mainly. He likes that. My flat's not big, but we got around it. I can't believe he told you to ring me!'

'How long did he stay?'

'Oh, he made a day of it,' said Sam. 'Including a nap after.'

'After?'

'After lunch. Then we were back at it, like a couple of star-crossed lovers, till he got the phone call.'

Edwin flinched at the use of Shakespeare's simile in this context, but let it pass.

'What phone call?' he said.

'To tell him that Mr Tony had died. He was a bit confused at the news. He didn't seem to know how to react. He kept asking the hospital if they were absolutely sure they'd got the right person. Then when the call ended, he drew himself up to his full height, by the window, and said in a loud voice, 'The Northington is dead. Long live the Northington'. Then he collapsed into my arms, and cried like a baby. After a while he was calmer, and went back to the office from here. I presume he then went on to the hospital.'

'How confident are you with the timing?'

'My timing's very good. He wouldn't have kept coming back if it wasn't.'

'Sorry,' said Edwin, 'I meant the timing of his coming to... arriving at your flat, and leaving again?'

'Oh. Pretty confident. He definitely arrived before eleven. I can't swear what time he left. I'd guess a bit after four.'

'Okay. That's been very helpful indeed. Thanks for your time, and your, er, frankness.'

'I still can't believe he told you to talk to me. Up till now he hasn't stopped talking about being discreet. I'll discreet him.'

She ended the call.

'Well, well, well,' said Edwin, leaning back in the chair. 'Did you get the gist of that?'

'Molly's changed her story?'

'Indeed,' said Edwin. 'Apparently Neville left the office mid-morning on the sixth of March, to visit Samantha from reception, who wasn't at work. And she confirmed the story.'

'But hang on,' said Haynes, frowning. 'That still doesn't get us anywhere. His swipe card has already told us he wasn't in the office all that day, but now we have a witness, or maybe two, saying he was with some girl, and therefore not at the hospital, administering some deadly and untraceable cocktail of drugs to his father. And then on the other hand we have the evidence of the computer activity in his office in the late morning, that began transferring a torrent of tiny sums from the Connected Chain Bond. The Best Seller.'

Edwin frowned. 'The whole thing stinks,' he said. 'And while I'm in that mood, despite having just been sacked, I'm going to ring Northington up, brazen it out a bit, and say that I owe it to everyone who's been interviewed to take my researches to their conclusion. And that whatever that conclusion is, I will be letting everyone know. See how he reacts. And the other thing I'm going to do is to get Dave Clark to see if the swipe system at the hospital picked up any relevant information on the sixth of March.'

A smile slowly spread across Sheldon Haynes's face. He nodded slowly and leaned back in his chair.

'Do it,' he said quietly. 'Do both things. But ring Northington now.'

Edwin got his phone out quickly, before his confidence could evaporate, and found Neville Northington's office number. He pressed Call.

Northington sounded annoyed. 'Look, this isn't a good time. You know you're not working for me any more? If you've got any administrative questions please ring Miss Raestock. Thank you.'

'Just a minute.' Edwin was pleased to find a new note of authority had entered his voice. 'I don't think I had a chance to really explain my position, when I was with you this morning.'

He left a pause now. Neville didn't say anything. Edwin continued.

'The investigation I've been conducting, at your request, is starting to show signs of bearing fruit. I can't, in all conscience, simply abandon it at this point.' He left another brief silence.

'Hang on a minute,' said Neville. Edwin heard his voice, away from the phone, apologise to someone else, and ask them to come back in half an hour. There was the sound of a door shutting, and then Neville was back.

'So what are you saying?'

Was it Edwin's imagination, or did Northington sound rattled?

'I'm saying,' Edwin continued, 'that I'm starting to uncover some interesting facts, so I don't want to simply drop what I'm doing. Even if I were to close the investigation, the current results of my research would have to be released.'

'Released how? What do you mean, released?'

He definitely sounded rattled.

'Well, released, in the first instance, to yourself, as the initiator of the investigation, and also to all the other people who agreed that they would be investigated. At the current level of evidence the police probably wouldn't need to be informed. Not just yet anyway.'

The longest pause yet.

'Look I'm a businessman,' said Neville. 'You've got a business head too, or you wouldn't be doing this job. What, do you estimate, would be the cost of simply losing all this evidence?'

Edwin's eyes opened wide, partly for the benefit of Sheldon Haynes, sitting watching him.

'It's not a question of money.'

Haynes grinned.

'But,' said Edwin, 'our firm has certain ethical standards, concerning full and frank reporting of discoveries, and maintaining records that are carefully backed up.'

Haynes was wincing and making a wavering gesture with one hand.

'Bollocks,' said Northington.

'Not bollocks,' said Edwin firmly. 'You booked me to make public what was hidden, and I'm going to make public what was hidden.'

Sheldon's eyes were now wide open, and his hand was firmly over his mouth, as Edwin continued. 'I thought it was only fair to clarify to you where I stand.'

The longest pause yet.

'Right,' said Northington. 'I'm not sure I completely believe your disdain for cash, as you've been very prompt with your billing, and not exactly stingy with your expenses, but there's too much at stake to risk it.' He now lowered his voice. 'I understand from sources of my own, that you've managed to get hold of some of our office swipe card records. And that you're aware of a discrepancy. I suspect I know which discrepancy that is, and why it seems suspicious. I don't actually know how the recording of it came about, because I thought I'd got that covered, but now you know about it, I'd better come clean. I think I now have to admit that I wasn't actually in my office all day, on the day my father died. But I do have an alibi. It's an alibi I hoped I wouldn't have to use. Which is why I asked Miss Raestock to say that I was in the office all day. You'll understand this when I tell you that I was visiting one of our receptionists at her flat that day.'

'Right,' said Edwin slowly. 'You're talking about Sam?'

'How did you know?'

'I'm an investigator.'

A snort from Northington. 'Okay. Yes. I'm talking about Sam. She should be able to confirm that I was at her flat that day. In fact I was there when I got the phone call from the hospital.'

'How long would you say you were there?' asked Edwin, looking at his scribbled notes.

'I came in to the office first thing, but didn't stay long. I guess I was out again by about ten.'

'And about what time do you reckon you would have arrived with Sam?'

For the first time, Northington chuckled. 'I remember that. It was definitely before Homes Under The Hammer ended — whatever time that would have been.'

'Okay,' said Edwin slowly, as he made a note. 'But is there any reason why I should believe what you are now telling me, rather than what you initially said?'

'Well, because it's true! Do you think I would admit to having an affair with a secretary if it wasn't true?'

'You might think it would be a convincing alibi, and likely to be believed, if it obviously cost you something to reveal it. And you might think the personal cost was worth it, if it cleared you of accusations of more serious wrongdoing.'

'That's all nonsense. I'm not that sort of person. I may not treat my wife in absolutely the very best way, but I certainly wouldn't kill my father.'

'I see,' said Edwin. 'I'll bear that in mind. And in the meantime, I'll carry on following up the new information I've discovered about the Connected Chain Bond.'

'Wait a minute. The information you've uncovered is to do with the Best Seller?'

'Yes.'

'But why didn't you say? Have I just told you... No!'

'Don't worry,' said Edwin, with an uncharacteristically sardonic smile. 'What you've just told me is still very relevant.'

'Okay. But why did you not stop me, if you were actually talking about... ' He ended the call.

Haynes and Strong sat for a moment, looking at each other across the desk.

'I certainly got the gist of that,' said Haynes.

'Yes,' said Strong, thoughtfully. 'Though I'm not sure how far we've got. Apart from the fact that Neville is very keen to prove he wasn't near the hospital on the day his father died. I'll message Dave Clark.'

CHAPTER 35

Sheldon Haynes breezed into the Gut and Garter with a cheery nod to Mike, the landlord. His eyes flickered restlessly round the dimly lit room, till they spotted Eddie Sharp's newspaper in a gloomy corner, hiding Eddie Sharp's face from general view. He walked over, and without preamble said, 'What are you having?'

The paper didn't even twitch. Eddie's voice came from behind it. 'Pint of the black stuff, if you don't mind.'

'Okay. Seen our man yet?'

No reply. Haynes waited only for a second or two before heading for the bar. It was probably a silly question. But when he returned carrying two pints of Guinness, the newspaper was down, and Eddie was sitting chatting in a relaxed fashion to a large, red-faced man wearing a dark suit with his tie wrenched loose, and his shirt collar open.

'Sheldon!' Eddie shouted cheerily, as Haynes approached with the drinks. 'Have you met Trevor Turtall? Trevor — this is Sheldon Haynes. An old friend.'

Turtall stretched out a massive hand and enveloped Sheldon's in it. He nodded solemnly.

'What will you have, Trevor?' said Eddie.

'Oh, I don't know that I'm really all that... thirsty. Oh, go on. Maybe a dry white... wine.'

'Large or small, Trevor?'

'As I say, I don't feel too... dehydrated. Maybe just a... bottle.'

'Lovely,' said Eddie. He looked up at Sheldon. 'As you're on your feet?'

'Of course,' said Sheldon. So this was the famous Trevor Turtall, he thought to himself, as he made his way back to the ancient bar, and waited to catch Mike's eye. Over the years Eddie Sharp had introduced Haynes to a few lawyers, but none of them with as big a reputation. Turtall's massive fleshy frame concealed a piercing intellect, that swung whichever way it was paid to, and the curious way he talked was apparently very effective in court. Interesting that he should represent Neville Northington.

Sheldon returned, armed with the opened bottle, and a solitary glass, to find Eddie in the middle of an anecdote.

'...you'll need to give me more information than simply that there's a problem with a drip in the office, or I won't know whether to call Facilities or Personnel!'

Haynes joined in with the laughter, as he decanted the wine. Turtall accepted a glass with a grave bow, and took an exploratory sip.

'Good god, man, it's... corked!'

'Is it?' said Sheldon, confused. Was it possible that a

bottle with a screw top could be corked? He glanced from Turtall to Sharp, and something in their silence, and their serious expressions suddenly told him he was being teased. He smiled wryly. They both howled.

'I'll take it back,' he said, with a smile.

But the bottle was being held just out of his reach by the heavyweight lawyer.

'I meant to say, it's... corking!'

More splutters of laughter. Haynes tried to join in, and started pouring his Guinness down his throat to help. He briefly closed his eyes. This was going to be a long lunch break.

In the office on his own, Edwin still had a nagging sense of unease about Jasper Felder. He knew Haynes was dismissive of Felder's significance, but then again Haynes hadn't spoken to him. He remembered with misgiving the Skype conversation they'd had. He had recorded the whole thing on the clunky Parker Investigations PC at Dave Clark's suggestion, and had watched it back a couple of times without feeling any better about his interviewee. And then there was his sudden disappearance from Northington International.

Edwin looked at his watch. Just after one o'clock. What if he went out, grabbed a sandwich, and headed off in search of Felder while he ate it? Technically he would be on his lunch break, so he wouldn't be wasting anyone's time by indulging a foolish whim. And anyway, it was his operation. He could run it as he saw fit. Although Neville Northington hadn't officially reinstated him, their last conversation had ended with him apparently resigned to the fact that Edwin would be continuing his investigation. That was enough to be going on with. Grabbing his hoodie, he skipped off down the stairs, calling out a greeting to the shadowy figure of Parker in passing.

What better place to get a sandwich than the Blessed Hope Bakery, he thought, as he saw its familiar frontage approaching. Unusually for lunchtime, it was almost empty, and when he saw that Bet wasn't behind the counter, he turned away, and was about to leave. But Joyce, the smiling Ghanaian lady who ran the bakery, had spotted him.

'Young man! She's not here today! Did you just come in to see her?'

Edwin knew he was blushing, but turned back into the shop. 'No, no. I'd like a sandwich please, actually.'

Joyce beamed at him. After a few seconds of silence she said, 'Shall I choose the filling?'

Edwin felt his flush deepen. 'I'll have that one, please,' he said, pointing quickly and at random.

Joyce looked where he was indicating. There was a plastic tub full of what looked like stewed beans. Joyce looked back at Edwin, and for a moment her smile wavered. 'You want red red? Red red in a sandwich?'

'Please,' said Edwin. 'Is that okay?'

Joyce's smile was back. 'It's more than okay. It's delicious. Though I must tell you, you're the first person to have it in a sandwich. Wait till I tell Bet! She'll be impressed by how adventurous you are!' Joyce laughed long and loud, as she coaxed the thick stew between two slices of bread. 'I'll just put it in one of these trays. Otherwise it'll soak through. Do you want a fork?'

'Thanks,' said Edwin.

Without reddening any further, he paid for the food, and left. It was a good walk down the hill towards the station, and he stopped every so often to take a mouthful of his meal. It was rich and spicy, and the bread enabled him to finish every last trace, but it definitely wasn't a sandwich. He was finally able to laugh at himself as he threw the empty carton in the bin by the station, but his laughter was tempered by the thought of Joyce telling Bet what he had ordered.

One train and one tube later, he was walking down the street in Islington where Jasper Felder lived, trying to look casual. This was the part of being a private investigator that he had no training in, and very little confidence. He reckoned he was good at talking to people, and establishing trust with them, but this sort of thing, where you turn your collar up, and pull the brim of your hat down...

Matching the action to the thought, he pulled his hood forward over his eyes, as he passed what he reckoned was the front door of Felder's flat. Yes, number forty-two. First floor flat. He risked a glance upward as he walked along, but saw nothing. He carried on to the end of the street, stopped and crouched down to untie, and then re-tie, his shoelace. He saw a post box across the street, and after checking elaborately for traffic, crossed over and took an imaginary letter from his back pocket, and posted it. Then he walked back down the street the other way.

And this time, just as he was nearing the part of the road he had a special interest in, Felder's front door opened, and Felder himself came out, dressed in an overcoat, wearing dark glasses and carrying a holdall over his shoulder. Edwin knew he should do his best not to draw attention to himself, yet he wanted to stop and stare, and then follow Felder, wherever he was off to. Bizarrely, the first idea his subconscious suggested was to pretend to trip over a loose paving stone, and lie motionless on the ground. What he actually did was to keep walking normally, take the first turning on his side of the road that he came to, and almost immediately turn round and stop, peering back from behind a tree.

Jasper Felder was heading down his street, in the direction Edwin had originally come from, walking briskly, the holdall now held in his right hand. When he judged Felder was a safe distance in front, Edwin eased out from behind the tree and followed him, staying on the other side of the road. Felder never once looked round. Just before he got to the main road, he took a turning on the left, that led to a square with a small park in the middle. The park had railings all round it, and an open gate which Felder went through, immediately turning right, and disappearing from view behind thick shrubbery.

Edwin hesitated momentarily, before cautiously following through the same gate. He also turned right onto the narrow tarmac path which led between dense bushes, but Felder was nowhere to be seen. The outside world of London streets and busy people rapidly faded away, in the presence of unaccustomed greenery and unaccustomed quiet. Rounding a corner, Edwin saw Jasper just disappearing round a curve of the path a little way ahead. He was now holding a phone to the side of his head, and already Edwin fancied he could hear him talking. He began to walk rather more quickly, to try and get closer to him.

The path between the bushes continued, without yet breaking into open grass. Edwin reckoned they must be nearly at the other end of the park by now. He began to walk even faster. The path twisted sharply to the left ahead of him, and just as he got to the turn, he suddenly heard a voice, and stopping immediately, realised that he was almost on top of Felder. The other man was just on the other side of the shrubbery, off the path on the left hand side. The bushes were thinner at this point, and Edwin thought he might have just pushed through them. He was sitting cross legged on the grass beside his bag, with his back to the path, and therefore Edwin, and talking quietly into his phone.

Standing stock still, Edwin could hear his own breathing very clearly, and felt the beating of his heart as an additional sound. He gradually stilled himself though, and began to focus on Jasper Felder, seated on the grass not six feet from him. He could hear Felder's end of the phone conversation very clearly.

'...so I thought this might be a good opportunity. Would that work for you?'

Felder sounded subdued, thought Edwin. But he didn't seem ill.

'Yes. I could be with you very soon. To be honest, it's all turning into a bit of a nightmare here.'

Actually, thought Edwin, he sounded upset.

'I know,' Felder was saying, 'this must be very difficult for you too.'

Edwin wondered who was on the other end of the line. As Felder sat there, now listening, now talking, he seemed to gradually droop, and was now resting his head on his free hand.

'Yes, I know, but I'm fed up with it. It would be lovely just to see you again.'

Edwin was maintaining his static position, and hoping that no-one else would come along the path.

'Right. I'll be with you as soon as I can. Bye. Love you, Moeder.'

Felder laid his phone down on the grass, and sagged even more, till his forehead was almost touching the grass. Then, in a surprisingly sudden movement, he grabbed his phone, got to his feet, and slung his holdall over his shoulder. He looked about him with a frown, and Edwin had a momentary panic — first that he'd been spotted, and then that Felder was about to head back onto the path that Edwin was still standing on. But with a brief sigh, he turned and walked the other way across the grass.

Edwin watched from his hiding place till Felder was almost out of sight, and then headed back the way he had come, trying to match his pacing to what he estimated Felder's would be. And by the time he reached the gate, he discovered that he had judged it well. Felder had now left the park, and Edwin just caught sight of him turning the corner back onto the road he lived on. He hastened after him, and when he got to the junction saw the familiar holdall heading away from the flat, and towards the main road. Edwin continued to shadow Felder, trying to keep a safe distance.

When he got to the main road he turned right, in a purposeful manner, and after waiting briefly for the lights to change, crossed over. Edwin didn't cross with him, but stayed on his own side, slowing his walk as necessary, and taking an interest in the shop windows next to him. Felder stopped at the first bus stop he got to, and sat down in the shelter, with his head leaning forwards. The dark glasses successfully obscured his eyes, but it looked like he was staring at the ground.

Edwin carried on walking up his side of the road, and pressed the button for the pedestrian crossing a little further on. As he crossed he rapidly tried to think of a plan. He wanted to find out where Felder was heading, but didn't think his sleuthing skills were up to getting on the same bus. Now on the same side of the street as Jasper, he halted in front of an estate agent's window. Out of the corner of his eye he saw his quarry stand up. And then a bus passed him, slowing as it approached the stop. With the beginnings of an idea Edwin got his phone out, switched it to silent and then locked it. He started running towards the bus stop. He noticed there was another young man running towards it from the opposite direction. No-one would remark on someone running for a bus. He got there at the same time as the other man, just as the bus door was opening, and standing close behind Jasper Felder, he reached forward and slipped his phone into the end pocket on Jasper's holdall. As far as he could tell, his action was unobserved. He then looked up at the side of the bus, pretending to do a double take, and frowning as he carefully read the number on the side. Everyone had now boarded the bus. Edwin took a couple of steps away from it, and now pretended to be absorbed in the laminated timetable on the bus stop. Why wouldn't the bus go? To his horror, the driver now called out to him.

'You getting on?'

Edwin muttered something, and turned away immediately. He was sure everyone on the bus must be staring at him by now. Finally he heard its doors closing, and the engine note changing as it began to move off. He couldn't resist a quick glance up as it left, and found himself staring briefly into the face of Jasper Felder, who was holding his dark glasses in one hand. His expression was inscrutable, and Edwin wasn't sure he'd even recognised him. Instinctively he raised a hand to check his hood was still up. It was.

A slightly dejected Edwin used the journey back to Lordship Lane to try and talk himself into a better frame of mind. Okay, Jasper Felder may now know that his movements were being scrutinised, but if he didn't find Edwin's phone, and the tracking software worked properly, then Edwin would be able to keeps tabs on him. It sounded like he was heading off to see a girl, maybe a Dutch girl, judging by the name Moeder.

Passing the bin near East Dulwich station where he had disposed of his sandwich carton earlier, his spirits took another dive.

Back in the office, having barely grunted at Parker on his way up the stairs, he listlessly set about having another look at Neville Northington's other bank account — the one Louise had tipped him off about. He was making sure he did this every day, just in case. As he typed his way, on autopilot, past the layers of security, he gloomily wondered if all espionage was this depressing. And when he finally accessed the overview, he initially thought he'd made yet another blunder. This was the wrong account, surely.

The balance stood at just over £420,000. Edwin clicked on the Transactions tab. One single deposit, today, for the full amount. The payment reference simply denoted it a transfer from another account. Edwin made a note of the number. He reached for his phone to use the calculator app, then remembered his phone was presumably still in Jasper Felder's holdall. He now felt even less sure about his decision to track Felder, in the face of this apparent confirmation of Northington's fraudulent dealings.

He reached instead for the calculator on the computer. He remembered that with Dave Clark he had worked out that a total of fifteen grand a day would be leaving the Connected Chain Bond system for each of the first two accounts. That would be thirty a day between the two. He divided 420,000 by 30,000. The answer was a beautifully clean fourteen. Fourteen days worth of money. Of course he couldn't at the moment prove where the money had come from, but if in a couple of weeks time another £420,000 was deposited, his theory would start to be fairly convincing.

Suddenly he felt pretty good about his espionage skills. And then he remembered that Father White's funeral was tomorrow. He had felt all along that he should go, and now he felt doubly sure. Who knew what clues he might pick up, what important snippets of information he might uncover, that a normal person would miss?

But he needed to sort out something more respectful to wear. He stroked his wispy beard thoughtfully. Maybe a trim, too?

Lunchtime had merged seamlessly into mid afternoon, and Trevor Turtall was weaving his way back to Haynes and Sharp after a trip to the Gents. His concentrated frown as he walked was replaced by a genial smile as he sat down again.

'I won't tell you what I just did — just to say it was a massive... relief.'

General laughter, dying down fairly quickly. A thoughtful pause, broken by Eddie Sharp.

'So, they tell me you work for Neville Northington?'

Turtall stared at him briefly. The well-known lawyer was even more red faced than he had been two hours ago, and the pauses in the middle of his sentences had grown longer. Sheldon wondered if Eddie had overdone the plying-with-drink routine. But then he replied.

'They tell... the... truth.'

'It's a shame that from what I've heard, his father's will has left him with nothing.'

Eddie was looking down into his drink with empathetic gloom as he said this, but Sheldon saw that the sharpness in his eyes never wavered for a moment.

Trevor Turtall was now looking round the room cautiously. 'Between you and me, that was one sweet... deal. Bear in mind who will still end up running the... company.'

He looked from Eddie to Sheldon and back again several times, with his eyebrows and one forefinger raised, establishing an elaborate sense of secrecy. 'And bear in mind what the inheritance tax rate is.'

Sheldon was surprised both by how frank Turtall was being, and at the fluent way he had spoken.

'Still,' Haynes said, 'it seems strange for a man to

effectively disinherit his children to save tax.'

'To be fair,' said Turtall, 'he was a strange man. But, entirely in confidence, Neville told me he and his father had a long chat about it, and he is quite happy, as he believes he has his mother wrapped around his little... finger.' Turtall beamed at his companions. 'But on the other hand, he got me to take a good look at the wording of the will, in case there was any chance it could be re-interpreted in his... favour.'

'Was there?' asked Eddie.

'It was sadly unambiguous,' said Turtall. He looked genuinely upset as he continued. 'We lawyers will starve, if people insist on this sort of... clarity.'

'Another bottle?' asked Haynes.

'If you... insist.'

As he made his way to the bar yet again, Sheldon struggled to conquer his dislike for the man they were entertaining. At least, he thought, as he ordered another bottle, and then, on an impulse, made it two, at least Neville Northington would be footing the bill.

CHAPTER 36

Jeanette put her phone down again. She sighed. She hated it when this sort of thing happened. Edwin seemed to have stopped returning her calls, though she was sure she had seen him lurking at Father White's funeral yesterday. So he wasn't answering her calls, yet he was still obviously snooping. Rather disconcerting, as she had him down as someone who was fairly up front about what he was doing. She had a few things that she wanted to ask him.

And now that Neville was pressing her for decisions on the future of the company, which apparently was now to be *her* company, the sort of inside information that Edwin seemed to be privy to would be very useful. She picked up her phone and tried dialling his number again. Straight to voicemail. Another sigh.

'Hunter?'

'Yes Miss Jeanette?' Hunter appeared in the doorway.

'Would you do something for me?'

Edwin was in his office, in a good frame of mind. He had slept well. Yesterday, before heading to Father White's funeral, he had spent a very enjoyable twenty minutes in the Blessed Hope Bakery sitting down with a cup of tea, and Bet had actually come out from behind the counter and spoken to him. She said she was just clearing the tables, but he wasn't so sure. It still gave him a warm glow, thinking about it.

Then, later on, he had managed to replace his phone with one that seemed to have absolutely every feature known to man. He had initially quailed before such a display of technology, but by the end of the day he had successfully customised the phone and email settings. He was so pleased with this achievement that the first call he made was to Dave Clark, in order to gloat. Dave had been, perhaps not surprisingly, unimpressed.

And then this morning, a package containing a whole new collection of Fantasy Element Compendium cards had arrived in the post, just as he was about to set out for work. He had put them in his backpack, and headed across the park with a light heart and a buoyant step.

So it came as a bit of a jolt when five minutes after settling down in his office chair, the brisk walk across the sunny park having raised his spirits still further, he was rudely interrupted by a grumpy Sheldon Haynes, who walked into his room without knocking, and stood just inside the door.

'Why don't you ever answer your phone, kid?'

Edwin was about to proudly indicate his shiny new purchase, when with some disquiet he remembered the circumstances in which he had lost contact with his old one. He didn't reply.

'I've been trying to talk to you for days, seems like. Straight to voicemail every time.'

Edwin managed a thin smile. 'Sorry.'

'Anyway, I wanted to tell you how I got on with Northington's lawyer. Fellow named Turtall.'

'Turtle?'

'Turtall. Ending in *a, l, l*. Anyway, he has confirmed that Tony Northington's will leaves everything to the wife, Jeanette. Including the company. Neville gets nothing and his sister gets nothing.'

'How does Neville feel about that?'

'Well,' said Haynes, 'according to Turtall—'

'Ending in *a, l, l*.' muttered Edwin.

'Ending in *a, l, l*,' said Haynes, 'Neville's not too bothered. Remember he's still currently running the company, and he thinks he has his mother twisted round his little finger.'

'There's another thing too,' said Edwin, suddenly remembering. 'The account I discovered in Neville's name, that he deliberately didn't tell me about? It's had a lot of money going into it recently. Over four hundred thousand. The amount fits in with what Dave and I reckoned was being siphoned out of the Connected Chain Bond in a fortnight. My idea is to wait and see if it happens again in two weeks time, and if the next sum fits with the figures as neatly.'

'That's a lot of money,' said Haynes. 'My idea would be to present Northington with the facts, and force him to confess.'

'What about Felder?' said Edwin.

'Felder?'

'Jasper Felder. I still feel very suspicious of him. I

mean, Northington's obviously very flaky, but Felder's was the most uncomfortable interview. More uncomfortable even than Molly Raestock's, and she turns out to have been covering for her boss.'

Sheldon Haynes stood, frowning, and Edwin took his silence for encouragement.

'I don't think we've spoken since I did some undercover work, and overheard him on the phone in a park.' As soon as he said this, Edwin realised it didn't sound very suspicious. 'He was saying things were turning into a bit of a nightmare,' he added.

Haynes raised his eyebrows a little. Edwin carried on, manfully.

'He seemed to be talking to a girl. Maybe a Dutch girl, I reckon, as he called her Moeder. What I've done is to place a tracking device on him, so we can see where he is, and keep tabs on him.'

'What sort of tracking device?'

'My phone. My old phone, that is.' Edwin waved his new phone briefly for Sheldon's benefit.

'It has a Phone Tracker feature. That's why I haven't been answering calls.'

Sheldon's eyebrows went up a little higher. 'And? Where is he?'

Edwin winced, and coloured a little. 'Not sure. But as soon as I work out how to use the software, I'll know.' He managed to contain his wince by an effort of will, and now smiled encouragingly at Haynes, who shrugged.

'Well, it's your investigation. I'm just being employed to keep an eye on you.'

'You're still doing it? You're still reporting back to

Northington?'

Now it was Sheldon's turn to redden. 'No, no. Of course not. I've not told him anything useful for ages. And like I just said, I think the best path forward is to confront him with what we now know. I wouldn't suggest that if I was somehow on his side, against you.'

'You might, if you knew full well that nothing could be made to stick. As you know, almost all the information we have has been obtained illegally, and wouldn't be of any use in court.'

'I didn't know that,' said Haynes, with a frown.

'What do you mean, you didn't know that?' said Edwin.

'I mean exactly that. I thought you got your information by courteously asking for it, face to face.' Haynes was now smirking.

Something inside Edwin snapped.

'Right!' he said. 'That's it. I resign.' He opened his backpack, and started putting his few personal items into it.

'You can't resign,' said Haynes. He sounded rather like an annoying older brother.

'Yes I can, and I have done.' Edwin was stuffing the final loose sheets of notepaper into his bag.

'Nope. I'm not your boss. And in this particular investigation, Parker isn't your boss either. You'd have to resign to Northington.'

Edwin zipped up his bag with a violent wrench.

'Well, so you say,' was his parting quip, delivered with the heaviest emphasis he could muster, to make up for its lack of any serious content.

He barged past Haynes, stomped down the stairs, past

a surprised Parker, and out into the street. After a moment's indecision, he headed to the minicab office along the parade of shops. One final journey on expenses.

Sheldon Haynes managed a wry smile as his colleague rushed out. They needed to sit down and talk. Give him some time to let off steam first. Then he'd call him. Though of course, he'd left his phone, somehow, with Jasper Felder. The wry smile was quickly replaced by a frown. Felder? Really? And Moeder? Struck by an idea, Haynes wandered over to Edwin's seat behind his desk, and idly opened up the translation app on his desktop.

Without taking his eyes off his unexpected visitor, Parker dialled the mobile number for Sheldon Haynes.

'Guy here wants to speak to young Edwin. Won't believe he's not here. Would you like to tell him?'

Hunter couldn't hear the reply, but Parker turned back to him and said, 'Mr Strong's colleague, Mr Haynes will see you. As it happens he's in Mr Strong's office just now. You go up the stairs, and turn left at the top. Then it's on the left.'

Parker disappeared back into his cubbyhole, and Hunter headed up the stairs, noting with displeasure the tattered carpet and dirty walls as he went. He turned left as instructed at the top, and knocked on the unmarked door.

It opened immediately, and Hunter recognised the man who had accompanied Edwin on his most recent visit to Hampstead.

'Do come in,' he said. 'How can I help you?'

His voice sounded tired, thought Hunter.

'I was really hoping to speak to your colleague, Edwin.'

'I'm afraid he's not in the office just at the moment. Is it anything I can help you with?'

Hunter noticed an alertness in Haynes's eyes that contradicted the tiredness in his voice. He hesitated a moment. He didn't want to have come all this way for nothing.

'Do you know when he'll be back?'

'No, I'm sorry, I don't. Would I be right in assuming you work for Mrs Northington?'

'Yes, you would.' Hunter disapproved of this sort of forwardness. But somehow he needed to orchestrate renewed contact between Jeanette and Edwin. Although maybe this other investigator would have access to the same information. But how to ask for it without compromising her position? He tried a tentative overture.

'In fact it's on her behalf that I'm here.'

'Yes, I'd guessed that.'

A facile smile appeared briefly on Sheldon's face. Hunter smarted at the comment, but continued.

'She is, well, contemplating a decision, and is hopeful that Edwin, your colleague, might have some information that would help her.'

'Well, maybe I could help? If you were to tell me what sort of information she needs? Won't you take a seat?'

Haynes, who had been standing beside Edwin's chair, now sat down on it, and began the lengthy process of winding his legs underneath him. Hunter moved towards the chair opposite him, and rested one hand on the back of it, but stopped short of actually taking a seat.

'Well the information *might* be, that is to say it *could* be, about the trustworthiness of her son. Neville.'

Hunter noticed the investigator's eyes light up at this point, and backtracked rapidly.

'But of course might *not* be. I'm probably speaking out of order.'

He let go of the chair, and moved away towards the door again.

'Stop,' said Haynes. Hunter found himself unable to disobey a direct command.

'Edwin wouldn't tell you this,' Haynes said, 'but I consider myself more of a free agent. So, without going into details, I can tell you that the investigation has uncovered enough dirt on Jeanette's dear son to... to build a dirty great pile of dirt. The really dirty sort.'

Hunter stood by the door, puzzled, as he tried to absorb this image. Eventually he shrugged, opened the door and said,

'Could you get him to ring Miss Jeanette when he returns?'

Haynes, who seemed trapped between the respectful urge to rise as a guest is departing, and the desire to maintain his hard earned convoluted position, mumbled something incoherent as he leaned forward a little and gave a half wave, in an ineffective compromise between the two. Hunter frowned, unsure how to interpret the strange twisting movement. Without saying any more, he walked out into the corridor, and down the stairs. As he passed, he proffered a quick 'Thank you,' in Parker's general direction.

CHAPTER 37

The minicab dropped Edwin at the bottom of his parents' lane. He got a receipt for the handful of twenties he'd given the driver. The car drove off and Edwin just stood there, listening to the sound of the engine gradually receding. As he did so, he consciously relaxed his breathing. He'd distracted himself during the journey by looking through the new parcel of cards that had arrived today — every time a stressful thought about Sheldon Haynes or Neville Northington popped into his mind, he carefully picked up a new card and examined it. And there were some great new cards.

He'd been hoping for some time to get a Peasant Depictor, and there one was. He had actually laughed out loud with delight in the back seat of the car when he'd spotted that one. Two more Polarising Troopers would come in handy as well. Another card on his wish list which had arrived in the parcel was a solitary, but very useful, Range Cadet.

He hadn't decided yet how long he would stay with

his parents — a couple of days, certainly — but he would make sure he got a few single-handed games of Fantasy Element Compendium in while he was there. He'd tried to show his dad the basics of the game a couple of times, with limited success. As Edwin stood in the quiet country road he chuckled at the recollection. But maybe he'd try again, and they could play a round or two together. If they used the rodeo format, that would be easiest.

He began the walk up the lane. He was struck again by the contrast with London. The silence, certainly. But also the quiet busyness that was responsible for the few sounds he could hear. The insects and birds either getting on with their routines, or enjoying their freedom from routine, he wasn't sure which. Perhaps an expert could tell him.

Did they worry about things? Were they struggling to decipher complex agglomerations of information that had deliberately been encoded to foil their efforts? Did they have such a thing as suspicion, or in a dangerous situation did they somehow bypass it, and move straight to terror? Did they conversely experience the sensation of trust? Edwin thought the higher mammals probably did, thinking of dogs he had known. They seemed to establish with their owners something very much akin to the relationships of trust that humans built.

And this brought him back to Sheldon Haynes. His pace increased very slightly, and his feet hit the gravel very slightly harder, as his mind brought up an image of his colleague, shimmering like a hologram in his imagination. This imaginary Sheldon Haynes spoke kindly and encouragingly to Edwin, and told him he was doing a great job, despite his lack of experience. And then Edwin watched as he picked up his hologram phone and rang a hologram Neville Northington, and told him every detail of what Edwin was doing, laughing as he described his ineptitude. The hologram Northington cackled maniacally and rubbed his hologram hands together with evil glee. And then in the periphery of Edwin's vision he saw, like a grey cloud, the spectre of Alastair Forth. This wraith-like figure was somehow intertwined with a representation of Gerry Kennedy, which had a plastic grin, luxurious waist-length wavy black hair and snakeskin cowboy boots. The two of them were muttering gloomy, fear-laden prognostications, and simultaneously facile denials of responsibility — glib excuses for things no-one had yet accused them of.

Disgusted by the shallowness of this scene, Edwin wrenched his mental gaze away, and his eyes immediately fixed on another figure, enigmatically leaning on the railing of a ship, looking down at the water. Effortlessly zooming in on the figure's face, he saw it was Jasper Felder. Not the cosmopolitan businessman of his Skype interview, but a young child, wearing clogs, and when he began to talk, rather than the Dutch Edwin was somehow expecting, what came out of his mouth was a string of zeros and ones.

Observing these apparitions as he walked along, Edwin now began to chuckle as he recognised the roots of the images his mind was conjuring up. As he laughed, the vision faded. He stopped walking, completely oblivious to his surroundings, and held his breath. As he did so, another scene was projected suddenly and glaringly into his awareness.

Amelia Northington, and her mother, Jeanette, were dancing round and round in circles, singing to a playground melody,

'They'll never catch us, we're far too clever.'

Molly Raestock was sitting on a smiling Hunter's knee, clapping in time with the rhythm, and in the background Louise Northington could be seen, furiously wrestling with a grimly determined Samantha Jones. Edwin got an uneasy feeling that there was someone behind him, and turned quickly to see a grey-haired priest at the bedside of a man who was clearly nearing his last breath. The priest was saying, consolingly,

'Don't worry. It won't be as bad as you think. Anyway, I'll see you soon.'

Edwin blinked and the images all disappeared. He suddenly felt very tired, and sat down by the side of the lane. The stress is getting to me, he thought. He sat there for a minute, recovering his wits, before looking around him and realising he had gone too far up the path. He could see his parents' turning just down the hill, but from where he now was, he had a completely novel view of the area. He stepped across the ditch and walked up the bank to the hedge, which he could just see over.

Spread out below him, glowing a luminous green in its fresh spring growth, he could see the whole valley, nestled in the embrace of the smoothly rounded hills on either side, and slanting ever so slightly downhill from east to west. There was no wind at all today, and in a couple of places he could see distant pillars of blue woodsmoke. The way the wooded section suddenly cut to pasture land on the opposite hill reminded him of the way some horses were partially clipped. It somehow seemed to accentuate the beauty of the curves it was following.

In the whole scene there was a deep sense of proportion, of coherence, of timelessness and yet of each second having a value. Edwin realised he couldn't see a single other human being. Not a Northington in sight, he said to himself, as he set off back down to the turning he had missed. He began to sing under his breath as he walked, to the same childish melody he had just imagined Jeanette and Amelia using, People are the problem, People are the problem.

He walked up to the door. No sound of badly played piano scales this time. No sound at all, in fact. He rang the doorbell, but there was no reply. He walked round the side of the house, but the elderly Fiesta wasn't there. Edwin felt irritated that no-one was at home, though he hadn't said that he would be visiting. He got out his new phone to ring his mum's mobile. She answered immediately, in some distress.

'Oh, Edwin, it's you! Thank goodness you've rung. I've been trying to get hold of you for ages. It's your dad. We're at the hospital now. They think he's had a heart attack.'

Jeanette Northington closed the door of the living room behind them, for extra privacy. Though as she closed it, she realised there wasn't anyone else in the house at the moment who might overhear them. Hunter stood stiffly to attention behind the sofa. Moving past him and elegantly taking a seat in the armchair nearest the door, she said,

'Won't you sit down?'

'I'm more comfortable standing, if you don't mind, Miss Jeanette.'

'Of course. Whichever you prefer.'

There was now a short and slightly uncomfortable silence, broken in the end by Jeanette.

'Well, let's get down to it,' she said with a bright smile. 'Did you get hold of Edwin?'

'I'm sorry to say I didn't, Miss Jeanette.'

Another pause, and her smile faded. 'Oh, that's a shame. Did you manage to find out any information at all? Anything about how I might contact him, perhaps?'

Hunter's face had gradually been reddening since he had entered the living room, and now Jeanette noticed.

'Are you all right, Hunter? Is anything the matter?'

He pursed his lips, and then sighed deeply.

'Well, Miss Jeanette, while I wasn't able to talk to Edwin Strong, I did have a brief conversation with a couple of his colleagues. Though first of all, I must tell you, the office premises where they are based are in really a very poor state of repair. *Most* unattractive. Anyway, despite that, from my conversation with his colleagues — the main one was that rather dishevelled fellow who came here with Edwin — I came to the reluctant conclusion that really, you'd be much better trusting your business interests to an independent advisor, than Mr Neville, even though he's your son.'

Hunter concluded his speech with another sigh, this one suggestive of a release of emotion. His colouring had now returned to normal.

Jeanette narrowed her eyes. 'You didn't mention to these people the specific reason I wanted to speak to Edwin, did you?'

Hunter's complexion immediately started returning to its former heightened shade.

'Well, no. I asked when he would return, and they said they didn't know, which seemed suspicious to me. I went upstairs and looked in his office — the disreputable looking one was there, but no sign of Edwin — and we talked, briefly... about... some... things.'

'Hunter, I can read you like a book.' Jeanette sat upright in her chair, and rested her chin in her hands, and her elbows on her knees. 'I can read you like a book, and it's fine, I understand. But do you really think I shouldn't trust Neville?'

'Really I do,' said a relieved-sounding Hunter. 'Though I'm sorry to have to say it.'

He came round from the back of the sofa, and sat in the armchair opposite Jeanette, who smiled.

'I think I will take a seat after all,' he said. 'The thing is, I talked to Father White,' here Hunter clumsily crossed himself, 'at the reception after your husband's, after Tony's, after your husband Tony's funeral.' Another, more superficial, display of respect for the dead.

'And the thing I came away from the conversation thinking, was that people were important, and that integrity was important. I would have to say that until that chat with him, I wasn't that keen on priests. But he seemed remarkably human.'

Across the room Jeanette raised her eyebrows slightly. Hunter didn't seem to notice.

'He started talking about a poem. Not a religious one, an ordinary one. The Cremation of Sam McGee, it was called. Do you know it?'

'I don't think so,' Jeanette murmured.

'It's all about a prospector in a frozen wilderness who promises to cremate his dying colleague, who's from the warm South, and can't stand the cold.'

'Tony was cremated,' said Jeanette quietly, with a slight twitch of her cheek.

'And he had to drag the corpse around with him for days till he found a suitable—'

'Father White was cremated as well,' said Jeanette in a slightly stronger voice. 'Thanks for your help, Hunter. I'll sit in here for a while on my own now, if that's all right.'

She nodded briefly at him, and as his years of training and experience kicked back in, he rose from his seat, made a slight and grave bow, and left the room silently.

CHAPTER 38

It had taken Edwin some time to get a minicab to come and pick him up — there weren't many drivers out, and they were all busy. Eventually a car arrived to pick him up from the same spot at the bottom of his parents' lane that he had so recently been dropped off at.

'It's the hospital you want?' asked the driver.

'Yes,' said Edwin. 'Main entrance I guess.'

He sat back in the seat, and tried to remember how old his father was. His fiftieth birthday had been just after Edwin had left for Bristol, so that must make him fifty-three? Fifty-four? Edwin felt very cold.

The minicab driver wished him well, as he dropped him off at the main entrance to the small hospital. The staff at reception were very helpful, and in what seemed like no time, Edwin was being ushered into a small room where his mum was sitting in a chair by the side of a bed on which his ashen faced dad lay.

As soon as she saw him enter, Sally Strong got up and hugged her son long and tightly.

'They think he's going to be all right,' she said. Her voice sounded unusually husky.

Over his mum's shoulder, as he returned her hug, Edwin looked at his father, lying there. He seemed to be sleeping, but despite his extreme pallor, his chest was rising and falling regularly. Sally took her son's hand, and led him to the chair at the bedside.

'You sit there for a bit, while I nip out. Talk to him. They say he may be able to hear us.' She turned and left the room, on rather unsteady legs.

Edwin watched her go, then eased himself down into the chair, and stared at his father's sleeping face. What a strange and sudden reversal of the roles of parent and child. Tentatively, he reached out to touch his hand. The skin was reassuringly warm, and as he quietly said,

'It's all right, Dad, I'm here now,' Edwin himself felt a sense of peace and relaxation appear, apparently from nowhere, in his chest. Maybe the roles of parent and child weren't reversed quite so easily.

Keeping his hand covering his dad's, he talked quietly. He talked about the new cards he had received that morning, which now seemed so long ago. He talked about his journey down from London in the minicab. It had been a Prius, and his dad was always interested in those hybrid cars and how they worked. And eventually, he began to talk about the case he'd been working on. He talked about the people he'd had to interview, and the unsettling situations he'd found himself in. He updated his unconscious father on the developments since they'd last talked.

As his monologue continued, it eventually got onto the subject of Sheldon Haynes. He talked about how

Sheldon had been engaged to keep an eye on his investigation, and how when he'd begun to understand what Edwin was dealing with, he'd then agreed to pull out of that engagement. He talked about how Haynes hadn't in fact done so, and about his fear that his work was still being relayed back to Neville Northington. As he talked, he realised that there was in fact a possibility that Haynes, as he claimed, simply hadn't got round to making the break. It would, Edwin presumed, be a rather stormy encounter.

And then Edwin remembered their plan for Sheldon to stay in place, to gauge Northington's reactions to any misinformation they might feed him. He remembered that they hadn't been able to think of any good line to test him with, and the plan had fizzled out. And eventually he found himself coming to the conclusion that he had been rather harsh judging his colleague so quickly. He resolved, once his father was definitely on the mend, to go back and patch things up at the office. After all, he hadn't formally resigned. Edwin gradually lapsed into silence. His dad hadn't moved at all, hadn't said a word, but Edwin felt as though they had had one of their enjoyable conversations, man to man. Curious.

Sally Strong had taken her time, freshening up, and getting a couple of sandwiches, and two cups of coffee. She was on her way back to the room her husband and son were in, when she came across the consultant who had been supervising Gareth's care, and who was also heading to see him. He was perhaps in his early sixties, tall and thin, with rimless glasses that he had a habit of taking off and cleaning while talking. Sally had found him very reassuring over the previous couple of hours.

'Mrs Strong,' he said, warmly. 'Let's go and see how that husband of yours is doing.'

Sally smiled. 'He seems very peaceful. I've left my son with him.'

The two of them entered the room, where Edwin was seated, quietly, still holding his father's hand. He looked up as they entered.

'Hello. I'm David Aylwick,' said the consultant, crossing the small room in a couple of strides, and shaking Edwin's hand. He took the chart from the end of Gareth's bed, and studied it as he moved towards the cardiac monitor unit by the wall. He compared a couple of readings on it with those recorded on the chart, and then seemed to be scrolling through a few settings on the machine. When he turned back to Sally and Edwin, he was smiling.

'It's as good as it could be, really. From all the indications, he has had a mild heart attack, but your prompt phone call, and the quick work from the paramedics should ensure that he makes a full recovery.'

'Oh, I'm so relieved,' said Sally. 'Will he have to take pills, and that sort of thing?'

As she said it, she realised it sounded silly, but the consultant answered her quite seriously.

'He will, at least initially, but in the long term, we'll see. Lifestyle factors are hugely important. But that's some way down the line now. He's responding very well to everything. We'll probably bring him out of his sleep soon, and see how he feels.' Aylwick smiled at Sally and Edwin, nodded, and slipped out of the room.

On a sudden hunch, Edwin followed him. 'Mr Aylwick? Thank you so much for looking after my dad.'

'It's a genuine pleasure. And I'm just doing my job. But I appreciate your gratitude.'

'If I can take the opportunity to ask a slightly irrelevant question, do you ever get patients who simply don't respond at all to any of your interventions?'

'Oh that's a completely relevant question! I've got to keep walking, but if you can...'

Edwin fell into step beside the consultant, and said, 'Let me put it a different way. What would you think of a case where the patient's heart had made no response whatsoever to the process of defibrillation?'

'No response whatsoever?'

'None whatsoever.'

'Not even a twitch?'

'Not even a twitch,' said Edwin.

Aylwick gave a dismissive snort. 'I'd say the equipment was faulty. Or the patient was wearing a special insulating vest.'

'Really?'

The consultant looked at him. 'Well obviously they wouldn't leave the vest in the way, if such a thing existed, but, electricity makes one twitch. The body conducts electricity. It might be too little, too late, or possibly even too much all at once, but there would be a reaction.' Aylwick stopped by the entrance to another ward.

'Thanks for your time,' said Edwin.

'No problem. Your father will be okay. But remember — never wear an insulating vest.'

And with a grin he'd gone.

That day and the next blended into one, in Edwin's memory. He and his mum took it in turns to sit with his dad, and occasionally they would be there together. As Mr Aylwick had suggested, it wasn't that long before Gareth was brought out of his sleep, and to the relief of his wife and son, he seemed almost his normal self, albeit rather groggy. There was a moment, just after he had regained consciousness, when no-one said anything, but Edwin was holding his dad's hand on one side, and Sally was holding her husband's hand on the other. Edwin made a conscious effort to capture that moment in his memory, as his dad gingerly moved his head slowly from one side to the other, looking up at them in turn, and smiling weakly.

When he wasn't sitting with his dad, Edwin had discovered a canteen, tucked away upstairs in the hospital, that had an amazing view over the surrounding countryside. The coffee was only just passable, but it was a wonderful place to sit and think. On his second visit, he remembered the new cards he had received that morning, and brushing aside a slight sense of disquiet that he wasn't actively thinking about his dad, or doing something practical to help him, he got them out and spent some time poring over them. They were just as good as he had thought, and after a while, he realised there was no reason why he shouldn't play a round or two of Fantasy Element Compendium.

The game required a phone app to generate random scenarios, and in the very first one he tried, Edwin's new Polarising Trooper enabled him to score a decisive victory very quickly. A lot of pent up emotion was released by his clenched fists, and his hissed 'Yes,' as the game ended.

Sheepishly he looked round to see if anyone had

noticed. The only person looking at him was the middle aged woman who poured the coffee. She smiled at him, and he made an apologetic and self-deprecating gesture back.

He shuffled the deck to play again. After a couple more games (one win, one narrow loss) he remembered that in one of the inside pockets of his backpack he'd put the cards he'd made himself, featuring characters from his investigation. He looked at his watch — there was time for one more game before going back to see how his dad was doing.

He carefully added his homemade selection to the deck, and shuffled the cards thoroughly. He primed the phone app to generate a scenario as the backdrop for the game. He pressed play, and quickly cast his eye over the salient points to bear in mind, even as the timer started counting down.

The initial confrontation saw Neville Northington up against a Tragedy Peasant. Not much doubt as to the outcome of that. The win moved Northington into something of a pincer movement however, as he ended up trapped between an Induction Trooper and Edwin's new Range Cadet. A nasty end, but Edwin felt little sympathy. There followed something of a long-winded war of attrition involving a combination of Peasants and Booster Peasants, that looked like leading to a stalemate, until suddenly the instruction was given to release Fox William into the fray. This tipped the balance decisively in favour of the Lowlanders, who carried the game into its final phase. Edwin winced a little as he saw that Amelia was now embroiled in a battle of strategy with The Sine Carter.

Two new cards were now drawn, but as they turned out to be one of his new Polarising Troopers, and an Insulating Trooper, they cancelled each other out. With less than a minute to go, in what was surely the last move of the game, he realised that both Amelia and her adversary were isolated from the other players. Quickly he scanned their attributes. For obvious reasons he had given Amelia a Special Skill of running electrical circuits safely under water, and he suddenly saw that the Sine Carter relied on his Remote Taser function for much of his destructive power. This didn't work at a great distance, but was very effective within a few metres. So if they were both to be submerged completely, he reckoned Amelia could be considered immune to the mighty Tasering that was sure to follow.

Edwin used Amelia's Activity Blend to initiate Deluge and Strangulation (the preferred method of close quarters combat he had assigned to her character) in a two to one ratio. Twenty seconds to go. The Sine Carter responded, of course, with Remote Tasering. Though this would usually result in a conclusive victory, Edwin judged that in this case it would have no effect at all, beyond draining the last of the Sine Carter's defensive reserves, and rendering him vulnerable to Amelia's choke-hold. Ten seconds left. Unfortunately not enough time for Strangulation to take fatal effect, so the game resulted in a draw. But Edwin was pleased that he'd thought of the option, and that he would be able to exercise the move at an earlier stage in another game.

He looked at his watch. Time to go back downstairs and see his dad again, and give his mum a break.

CHAPTER 39

Gareth Strong was out of danger by Thursday evening, but the hospital wanted to keep him in over the weekend. Edwin and his mum took the opportunity to get a proper night's sleep, back at the cottage. And on Friday morning, Edwin announced he was going back to the office.

'But I'll be back soon,' he added.

'Of course,' said Sally. 'Look after yourself though, won't you? Make sure you have plenty of those nice custard tarts.'

'Yes, of course.' Then, with mock indignation, 'Mum! Leave me alone!'

He headed off down the lane to where the car to the station was due to meet him, and Sally went to check on the hens, and then to ring their nearest neighbours to thank them for looking after them.

On his way back to Parker Investigations, Edwin made a point of picking up a selection of coffees and pastries from the Blessed Hope. Joyce was behind the counter. When it was Edwin's turn to be served, she addressed him in a stage whisper.

'She's not in today. Visiting her Mum. I'll tell her you called.'

Conscious yet again of his cheeks reddening, Edwin said, 'Can I have three black coffees and three custard tarts, please.' He put his hands in his pockets, and stared intently at the hygiene poster in the corner. Joyce chuckled to herself and turned round to get the coffees.

Back at the office, without saying a word, Edwin handed a coffee and a custard tart through the doorway to Parker, who stared at him blankly for a minute, briefly scratched his nose with a finger, and accepted the offering with a grunt. At the top of the stairs he turned right and came to Sheldon Haynes' office door. He took a deep breath, and knocked.

'Come.'

Edwin entered. 'Sorry to be an idiot. Here's a coffee and a custard tart.'

'Don't mention it. Thanks. Talking of tarts, where did you get it? Only joking! I know you worship the ground she walks on.'

Edwin frowned, and said crossly, 'Why does everyone think I—'

'Never mind, never mind,' said Haynes. 'Look, when you weren't here — I hope you had a nice time, by the way — Jeanette Northington's butler, or whatever he is, came here trying to get your advice on whether she should trust her son.'

'And you told him..?'

'I'm afraid I gave a rather negative character reference for Neville Northington, but then I think he realised he'd said too much, and scarpered.'

'Interesting,' said Edwin. 'I didn't have a nice time, by the way. My dad has had a heart attack, and I've been visiting him in hospital.'

'No! I'm sorry. Will he be okay?'

'Yes. He's out of the woods now, apparently. He has responded well to all the treatment.'

'Unlike the other poor bastards you've been dealing with,' said Haynes sympathetically.

Edwin became more animated. 'Yes. And I took the opportunity to quiz the consultant. He emphasised the point your medical man made, that patients always respond to treatment in *some* way.

'And another thing I've just remembered this minute. The text I got from Amelia when Father White died. She said something rather curious — "I don't know what to do". Why on earth should she say that?'

He was pacing up and down in the office now, taking an occasional bite of custard tart, and blowing flakes of pastry on the floor as he talked.

'I didn't see her close up at the funeral, but she seemed rather more upset than her mother. You would have expected that to be the other way round, wouldn't you?'

'You went to Father White's funeral?' said Haynes.

'Yes, yes, but that's not the point. Why was she so upset, and why the strange text, as if...'

Edwin's voice trailed away.

'Well?' asked Haynes, impatiently.

'She'd had a recent visitor,' said Edwin slowly. 'when I interviewed her. The cetohyde glass was empty, on the draining board. Cetohyde is apparently poisonous. I don't know what the symptoms of cetohyde poisoning are, but I think now would be a good time to find out. And a good time to find out if Father White was her visitor.'

'Yes. I see what you're thinking. Are you just going to ask her?'

'That's the way I operate,' said Edwin.

Haynes sniffed dismissively. 'If you can't get a satisfactory answer out of her, just let me know.' Suddenly he perked up. 'Oh, yes. There's another interesting thing. Felder has gone across to Holland on the ferry.'

'Holland? Do you mean the Netherlands?'

'Same difference. Anyway, he's gone there. He's in Amsterdam, and hasn't moved about much since he arrived.'

A slow smile spread over Edwin's face. 'You hacked into my phone!'

'Yup. The Find My Phone feature works nicely.'

'And,' said Edwin, 'remember I told you he seemed to be talking to a Dutch girl called Moeder? It all fits.'

'Yes,' said Haynes. 'About the name Moeder. How shall I put this? It's Dutch for Mother.'

Edwin closed his eyes and slowly nodded his head.

'I'll do some research on cetohyde,' said Haynes. 'While you ring Amelia.'

Edwin hesitated. 'I'll have to go to my office to get her number. I don't know why my new handset hasn't updated my numbers automatically.'

Frowning at his phone, he left his colleague scrolling through his own contacts.

But before he could ring Amelia, and in fact before he could even get to his office, an email from Dave Clark buzzed its way onto his phone.

Hi Ed.

Sorry for the electronic message trail, but I can't talk as I'm on a bus.

You'll be interested to know that the swipe sensor in the hospital on March 6th picked up

huge amounts of information from everyone who passed.

There are some curious electronic signatures that I have since deduced to be from

pacemakers, and one from an electronic tag from the prison service.

But the bit you'll really want to know is that at about 1.30 pm, the Northington

International office swipe card belonging to Neville Northington passed the sensor, and at

about 2 o'clock it passed again, presumably going the other way.

More cash soon?

Cheers,

DC

In his room now, Edwin sat down heavily on his chair. He had completely believed Samantha Jones's confirmation of Neville's story, and also Molly Raestock's telling of the background to this episode. Now the ground seemed to be shifting under his feet. It wasn't fair.

Suddenly ringing Amelia seemed an easier option than sitting down and thinking through this new revelation. He found her number in his notebook, entered it in his phone, and pressed Call. She answered almost immediately.

'Hello? Who is this?'

'Hi! It's Edwin. Edwin Strong.'

A brief silence, then a slightly strained, 'Oh. Hello, Edwin.' Now a more relaxed, 'That's the way James Bond introduces himself, isn't it?'

'What do you mean?' said Edwin.

'You know, what you just said. Edwin. Edwin Strong. He says, James. James Bond.'

'Isn't it Bond. James Bond?'

'No. Yes. Maybe. Actually I'm not sure. Anyway, nice of you to ring.'

Edwin could almost sense her smiling now. Shame, he thought. Here goes, he thought. 'Look, I'll get right to the point. That time when I stayed over at yours—'

'Oh, don't worry about it. Not everyone stays in touch, and I've a feeling I bundled you out of the house pretty abruptly in the end.'

'Yes,' said Edwin. 'About that. I was wondering—'

'No, seriously, no need to worry. It's very sweet of you to ring though.'

'Actually I was concerned about something else—'

'Oh. The phone call? No! I was mistaken. I thought I overheard you talking about something suspicious you'd discovered at Northington International, so I rang Neville about it. But he just laughed, and said he knew all about it.'

Now it was Edwin's turn to be taken aback. Amelia continued.

'Sorry for telling tales! But he's my brother. Blood is stronger than water and all that.'

Edwin seized the opportunity. 'So is cetohyde.'

'So is cetohyde, what?'

'Stronger than water. That's what I was ringing to ask you about. Remember the glass I nearly drank from? And you stopped me in a hurry? And it looked like someone else had drunk from it?'

Edwin paused. Amelia said nothing.

'And I asked if you'd had any recent visitors, and you said you might have?'

Still silence from Amelia.

'Might your recent visitor have been Father White?'

What was that sound that Amelia just made? Edwin pressed the phone harder to his ear, and frowned with concentration.

'Any visit from a priest is totally confidential,' said Amelia after a couple of seconds, in a voice that Edwin considered slightly unsteady. He moved in for the kill.

'I'll take that as a yes, then. A simple no would have been enough otherwise.'

Even as he spoke, Edwin regretted the pompous tone he seemed to have adopted. There was a muffled, choking sound in his ear, and then, very slowly, and very, very quietly, Amelia began to talk.

'I swear,' she whispered, 'I swear I didn't mean to kill him. He must have opened the wrong cupboard. And obviously I hadn't cleaned the glass out properly. And I had I no idea it was *that* poisonous. No idea at all. You've got to believe me.'

The muffled, choking sound started up again.

Edwin did believe her. He completely believed her. But after his experience with her brother, and how he'd believed *him*, he didn't trust that his belief settings were accurately calibrated.

'Okay,' he said, in a voice that was intended to be calm and dispassionate. 'I'm afraid I've got to go now. If you find you've anything else you need to tell me, you've got my new number now.'

He ended the call.

He had only met Father White briefly, on the occasion of his being announced as the investigator taking the case. And he hadn't particularly stuck in his memory. But everything he had heard about the man since, had painted a picture of someone who was inoffensive, kind-hearted and who had integrity. Edwin could magnanimously overlook the apparently irregular nature of his relationship with Jeanette Northington. By any standards, he was a man who didn't deserve to die.

He wandered back into Sheldon Haynes's office, in a bit of a daze. Haynes was on the phone. His face was completely blank. As soon as his call finished, Edwin blurted out,

'Neville Northington definitely visited his father just before he died, despite the statements of Samantha Jones and Molly Raestock.'

Sheldon's face remained absolutely impassive. He said,

'Jasper Felder's mother is still alive, and lives in Amsterdam. Jasper is staying with her at the moment. Sadly his father recently died.'

Edwin wasn't really listening. He interrupted with,

'And Amelia Northington killed Father White.'

No reaction from his colleague. In fairness Edwin felt obliged to add,

'Though it was a terrible accident.'

'Felder's father recently died,' continued Haynes, 'because his father was Tony Northington.'

CHAPTER 40

Sheldon had used the two biggest mugs in the kitchenette to make some scalding hot, strong, sweet tea.

'We've both had a shock,' he explained as he handed one to Edwin.

They nursed the comforting brews in silence.

'Let's piece this together carefully and logically,' said Edwin, after a while. 'Let's write it all down. And let's make sure we've got cast iron evidence for every little bit of the story.'

Haynes nodded his assent, and said, 'How do you want to record it? Narrative, or spread-sheet?'

'Narrative,' said Edwin, with a flicker of interest.

But Sheldon's lip curled downwards. 'You'll do the writing then?'

'Cool,' said Edwin. 'We'll jot it down roughly first, and check the evidence is there.'

He thought for a minute. 'Actually, on second thoughts, for this bit, a spreadsheet would be much clearer. I'll turn it into liquid prose later.'

Haynes raised his eyebrows, but then shrugged. He straightened his legs out from under him, and after a moment's consideration lifted them onto his desk in front of him and crossed his ankles. He carefully took another sip of tea, and pulled a tatty notebook from his pocket.

'Cunning disguise,' said Edwin, pointing at the cover of the book which bore the pencilled title, Horses.

Haynes looked at the cover. 'Sorry. Wrong book.'

He fished around in the same pocket and produced a similarly scruffy notebook with the legend, Investigations, on it. He grinned. 'Is that better?'

But Edwin was busy leafing through the papers he'd just taken out of the folder in his backpack.

'Right,' he said eventually. 'Why don't we start with the day of Tony Northington's death?'

'6th March,' said Haynes briskly. 'Plenty of evidence for that.'

'Very funny. Are you going to put this in the spreadsheet, or shall I?'

Sheldon responded by twisting his monitor round on its stand, and pushing the keyboard and mouse over to Edwin's side of the desk. Edwin looked with distaste at the layer of grime on the keys, then began the process of opening a new document.

'Right,' he said, after a bit of fiddling. 'I'm going to start with the information Dave just sent me, while it's fresh in my mind. One thirty pm, Neville Northington enters his father's hospital ward, two pm he leaves it. Evidence For — his Northington International office swipe card was picked up by the hospital sensors. Then I'll have another column, Evidence Against — Samantha Jones says he was visiting her from just before eleven till, let's see, just after four. And Molly Raestock confirmed in a general way that he had gone to visit Ms Jones.'

Edwin frowned. 'Though I could have sworn Molly was telling the truth. Then again, I suppose all she knew was that he wasn't in the office. And Sam's story could be mostly true, apart from her not mentioning that he left for a couple of hours in the early afternoon.'

'What's your gut feeling?'

'My gut feeling is that both women were telling the truth,' said Edwin slowly. 'I don't think either of them had anything to gain by what they told me, and Molly had already obviously been relieved to retract the statement that she had been put up to by Neville.'

'Well, leave the columns as they are for now. Maybe talk to them again, and probe more deeply? No offence.'

'None taken,' said Edwin. 'Maybe you should talk to them. Anyway, your turn now. Jasper Felder is the son of Tony Northington?'

'Yes. And it was through talking to Molly Raestock that I got the information. I seem to have caught her in a very candid mood today. Apparently Northington always refused to acknowledge him, but Felder had a DNA test done which was quite conclusive.'

'Well, that sheds a very different light on things. Assuming that to be true, we'll have to re-jig the family tree. And if he was a rejected, illegitimate son, there just might be a bit of motive there.'

'There just might be,' said Haynes.

Edwin started tapping away, creating columns and inputting details from his notes.

'We'll soon get to the bottom of this,' he muttered, as

he leafed through his stack of loose pages.

At lunchtime Jeanette got a call from Neville. Her initial response when she saw who was calling, was to ignore it, but she knew that sooner or later she'd have to talk to him. Neville had been pushing her for answers to some questions to do with managerial issues. Jeanette guessed that what he wanted was for her to tell him to just do what he thought best, and then one thing would lead to another, and before she knew it he would somehow have managed to effectively edge her out of it altogether. She sighed. Blame the parents, people said. They were probably right. But she took the call.

'Hello, dear.'

'Please don't call me Dear,' said Neville. 'It's unprofessional. Have you come to a decision about my proposed management structure?'

'How is Louise?'

'She's fine. I can take care of most aspects of running the company without needing to constantly request your input, and in fact that would become rather easier if you could see your way to agreeing with the suggested changes.'

'And little Josh?'

'Yeah, yeah, he's fine.'

There was a pause. Neville was obviously waiting for an answer. Jeanette, who was in her kitchen, looked out into the back garden. There was a pair of blackbirds hopping around at the far edge of the lawn. There were fresh green shoots everywhere she looked. The annual cycle of growth, death and renewal was continuing its long-term narrative. Maybe it was time to give Neville what he wanted. But then another thought crossed her mind.

'You know, dear, I think I'd still like a little more time.'

'Oh, please, Mother! How's that going to help? You know what the best thing to do is. I've told you!'

'Oh, I'm sorry — I've got to go. I think there's someone at the door. Speak soon. Love to the family.'

Jeanette felt bad as she ended the call without even waiting for Neville to reply. She was habitually transparently honest, and she had to do some nimble wriggling to convince her conscience that there might very well be someone at the door, who was just about to knock, any minute now.

Meanwhile, Edwin Strong and Sheldon Haynes felt they were making considerable progress. The spreadsheet Edwin had been creating was bursting with information. Haynes had gradually become more and more animated, and was now pacing round the room as they batted ideas back and forth.

'Have we got too many suspects,' asked Edwin, 'or are we too suspicious? Have we set our suspicion threshold too low?'

'It's just part of the job.' Haynes stopped his pacing for a minute, yawned, stretched, and then continued talking, with his hands resting on the back of his head. 'In normal life you wouldn't suspect any of these people of anything in particular, but because of the circumstances, and the fact that we have, or you have, been engaged to snoop around, it's inevitable, and appropriate, that we're more unbelieving than is normally psychologically healthy.' His hands dropped back into his pockets, and he resumed his prowling round the small office.

Edwin was impressed, and distracted from what he was doing. 'Have you ever considered lecturing?' he said.

'I used to lecture a bit.'

'Really? What in?'

'Never mind. Have we established yet what the symptoms of cetohyde poisoning might be?'

'No. Have you got a go-to poisoning contact?'

'Very funny. Though as it happens, I do.' Haynes had his phone out and up to his ear before Edwin could make a witty reply. As Haynes stared into the middle distance waiting for his call to be answered, Edwin was left muttering to himself, Speed dial! He's got a poisons expert on speed dial!

'Jackie, hello!.. Yes, same old same old... Yep, intern's still here... And you?.. Look — what do you know about cetohyde?.. What would happen if, say, you drank some?.. Just touched the stuff?.. And for argument's sake, injected it into yourself?'

Edwin shifted uncomfortably in his seat. Had he any calls he needed to make? To his computer expert, perhaps? A thought struck him, and catching Haynes's eye, he took out his own phone, and slowly and deliberately used one finger to speed dial seven.

Dave answered immediately. 'Ed, mate!'

'Are you still on a bus?'

'No, I'm at home. Did you get my message about the cash?'

'Yes. That's fine. I'll get it to you. But tell me — you've managed to source data from the swipe cards in the hospital where Tony Northington died. Do you think you could get hold of CCTV images from the same day?'

On the other end of the line Edwin could hear Dave chuckling.

'Depends on how new the system is. Ironically, a really old system would be impossible, as the images would all be stored on tapes. But their swipe technology was bang up to date, so I might be able to do something. I'll have a go. Can I get the money today?'

'Bring your CCTV images to The Plough tonight, and I'll have the cash. Deal?'

'Deal. See you later. About nine?'

'About nine.' Edwin ended the call.

'I like the way you're thinking,' said Haynes, whose own phone was now back in his pocket.

'Thanks,' said Edwin. 'I tell you what though — I'm hungry. Do you want me to go out and get a couple of sandwiches?'

'Yes, that's a good idea,' said Haynes. 'Do you want to hear what the symptoms of cetohyde poisoning are?'

'Curiosity trumps hunger. Yes please. I want to hear now.'

'Jackie's going to send me a whole load of information, but the basics are that — wait for it — the consequence of ingesting cetohyde in any quantity is heart failure.'

Edwin closed his eyes, as Haynes continued talking.

'Apparently this is because cetohyde is a brilliant insulator, and if it makes its way anywhere near the wrong part of the heart, the electrical impulses that regulate the heart rate are interrupted, either temporarily or permanently. And the tragic thing is that conventional treatment won't have any effect, as the insulating properties of the liquid, in the wrong place, simply shield the heart from outside assistance.'

Edwin's head was now in his hands.

'The more you took,' continued Haynes, 'the more likely you'd be to die, but there's a huge amount of luck involved, as it has to get to the right place, or the wrong place, to do the damage.'

Edwin looked up now, with a frown. 'But surely it would leave a chemical trace, that any medical investigation into a suspicious death would uncover immediately?'

'If you tested for it specifically at the time,' said Haynes, 'then yes, of course. Its astonishingly pronounced insulating properties would flag it up immediately. But as its base ingredients are natural by-products of blood plasma, you'd be very unlikely to come across it accidentally.'

'I wonder is it too late to perform this specific test now?'

'After cremation? I should think so, don't you?'

'Of course,' said a crestfallen Edwin. 'And even if we did discover that Tony Northington died of cetohyde poisoning, that won't tell us who administered it.'

'Though it points the finger rather at Amelia, doesn't it?' said Haynes.

Edwin nodded. 'I'm not hungry any more.'

'Why don't you act on the off-chance that Ms Raestock is still in a communicative mood, and see if you can get any more specific detail about what she knows about Neville's movements on the sixth of March? We need to start turning over every single stone.'

'Okay. I'll ring her,' said Edwin.

'Tell you what. Have you ever actually been to Tony Northington's old office?'

'No, I haven't.'

'Right,' said Sheldon Haynes, taking charge. 'I'll get my box of tricks, you grab some sandwiches on the way, and we'll buzz up there now, and see if we can learn anything the old fashioned way. Don't ring in advance, just turn up. Sometimes works.'

'Okay. Let me just save this spreadsheet. There. That's not going anywhere.'

CHAPTER 41

It was three o'clock in the afternoon by the time Edwin Strong and Sheldon Haynes arrived in Barter Street. They got security to ring Molly Raestock, who arranged for them to be issued with visitor passes, and admitted. Haynes, who hadn't been in the building before, looked around him with interest as they crossed the third floor foyer. Samantha Jones was on neither of the reception stations. A slightly tense looking Molly greeted them, and ushered them both into her office.

Edwin explained briefly why they were there, as he and Sheldon sat down on the proffered chairs.

'Is Neville in?' he added.

Molly shifted uncomfortably. 'No, not just now.'

'Officially, or unofficially?' he asked quietly.

'Unofficially,' she replied, even more quietly.

'And, just out of interest, is Samantha Jones off sick?'

'Yes. She's not been very well lately,' said Molly, with a straight face.

'Tell me,' said Haynes. 'What exactly is it that makes

Neville's absence unofficial?'

'I'd rather not say. But since it's you two gentlemen asking, I suppose I have to tell you.' She looked at Edwin enquiringly.

'You do have to,' replied Haynes. She kept looking at Edwin, who nodded in confirmation.

'Well,' she said, 'the trouble is it rather breaches our health and safety regulations, but he simply leaves his swipe card here. It's probably in his office right now. I could check if you like? He has to leave the door unlocked, or it would look rather odd. So, anyway, if there was a fire, the system would say he was still in the building, and the firemen might risk their lives trying to find him. I've tried to warn him, but he just laughs. He has an understanding with the security guards, that if he's "forgotten" his swipe card, they simply buzz him out and in, as he places his wallet on the reader, for show.'

Edwin was now sitting bolt upright in his seat. 'So let me get this clear — any time he leaves the building *unofficially*, he leaves his swipe card here?'

Molly seemed slightly disconcerted by the intensity of his tone, and the way he exchanged a glance with Haynes.

'Have I said something wrong?'

'No, but this is extremely important to clarify. Does he *always* leave his swipe card here if he's out of the office unofficially?'

'Yes. As far as I know.'

Another glance exchanged.

'Okay. That's very useful to know. Can we have access to Tony Northington's old office now?'

'Of course.' Molly Raestock seemed relieved to have

a change of topic. She led the way across the foyer. 'It hasn't been used since he died,' she said as she turned the key in the lock.

'Perfect,' murmured Haynes, behind her. Edwin noticed his colleague's fingers twitching on the bag he had brought with him. Edwin didn't know exactly what was in it, though he'd noticed it hadn't set off the metal detector in the Northington International entrance.

'No-one's really had the nerve to come in here and start clearing the room out, to make it their own.' Molly moved over to the window, and raised the blinds. 'Obviously to start with, Mr Tony was only off sick, and then he was hospitalised for a while, so by the time he finally passed away, everyone was used to him not being here, and to not coming into his office. I think Mr Neville would like the room, but even he hasn't quite felt up to making the move. It would be quite a statement, and Mr Tony was a big personality.'

Sheldon Haynes had been prowling round the room, as Edwin stood near the doorway. Having let some light in, Molly hovered uncertainly. 'I'll leave you to it then, shall I?' she asked.

'Thanks,' said Edwin. 'We know where to find you if we need anything else.'

Molly turned and shut the door behind her, as Haynes knelt on the carpet and opened his bag. Edwin watched with interest, as he took out a small plastic magnifying glass, a pot of powder, a small brush and a rubber bulb.

'Is that a child's detective kit?' he asked, incredulously.

'Yep,' replied Haynes, as he stood up holding the magnifying glass. 'But I got rid of the box it came in.

Didn't want to look amateurish.'

'Indeed not,' said Edwin.

Haynes started looking round the room, starting with a careful examination of Amelia's Life's Bright Idea artwork. The office didn't seem stuffy or un-cared for. It seemed to have been hoovered recently, and all the surfaces had been carefully dusted.

'Tony Northington was last here just before Christmas,' observed Edwin. 'I never met the guy, but I can understand why Neville didn't want to move straight in here. I almost feel his father's about to enter the room.'

Haynes had now got as far as the water cooler. 'You often get that in places connected with people who have recently died. A presence lingering. And as everyone seems to say, he had a very big personality.'

His tone of voice changed. 'Ah. This is interesting.'

'Found some fingerprints?' asked Edwin, wandering over, and putting on hold his own, rather less scientific, scanning of the room.

'Quite the opposite. On this water dispenser there are absolutely no signs that anyone has ever touched it.'

'Maybe it's been dusted?' Edwin was now peering at it too.

'Yes. Look. You can see where the top has been dusted, as far as the edges. But with something that's handled regularly, unless it has been very deliberately cleaned, you'll always get some sort of marks. And who would bother carefully polishing a water dispenser?'

Haynes now pulled the unit out from the wall, using the fabric of his bag to keep his own fingers away from it. He peered at it intently from several different angles.

'Nothing at all,' he muttered.

The plastic water bottle on top of the unit was only half full, so without much effort he was able to lift it out of its fitting, and place it the other way up, on the floor. He knelt down beside it, again with his glass.

'That's better,' he said. 'Here. Pass me the powder and the brush, will you?'

Edwin did so, and Haynes used the brush to dust a little of the fine powder onto the very top of the bottle, where it had been resting on the bottom part of the dispenser, when it was inverted in use.

'You have to be careful not to put too much powder on, or the print will clog up. Little by little. There we go. Now I'll just carefully blow some of the excess away, and... there you have it. Several nice clean prints, obviously left by whoever fitted the bottle to the base of the unit.'

Edwin was impressed. Haynes got out his phone, and took photographs from very close up, and from every angle.

'Okay — that'll probably do,' he said eventually. Blowing away the remains of the powder, he then replaced the plastic bottle in its original position.

'I'd like to take away some of the contents of this drinking fountain. Have you got something I can put some in?' he asked Edwin.

'No. Molly might be able to find us a container.'

'Let's ask her in a minute. I want to try something first.'

Sheldon Haynes filled one of the small plastic cups from the holder on the side of the unit, and took it over to Tony Northington's old desk. He glanced around the room, and seeing a four-socket mains adapter on a shelf, plugged the desk lamp into one of the sockets. He then connected the unit to the mains, and turned the lamp on. Taking the cup in one hand, he slipped back into lecturing mode.

'Water conducts electricity, so if this is water and I pour it into this live electrical socket, it will create a short circuit, the fuse will blow, and the lamp will go out. On the other hand...'

Haynes slowly and carefully poured the contents of the cup all over the live sockets. The lamp remained lit. Edwin nodded in understanding. The two investigators looked at one another, and simultaneously exchanged the same, single word.

'Cetohyde.'

The Plough was packed. Friday night was always busy, but after a lovely spring day, and with the evenings remaining light for longer and longer, any pub with any sort of an outside area was going to be full.

Sheldon Haynes had been there for some time, being joined after about an hour by Dave Clark. He and Haynes had hit it off straight away, the catalyst being Dave's frank admiration of the older man's powers of observation. They had begun a sort of party game, taking it it turns to pick one of the crowd of punters, and impress the other with a deduction about them. Sheldon's conclusions were founded on a combination of observation, intuition and experience, while Dave Clark relied on the fact that almost everyone in the room was accompanied by at least one electronic device with some sort of remote connection capability, and that many of them were inadequately secured.

Sheldon was buying rounds with no regard for the cost — he sensed that the bountiful expense account of The Northington Era might be drawing to a close, and he wanted to avail himself of any remaining opportunity to benefit from it.

Dave spotted Edwin first. 'Right. I bet that guy who's just come into the bar is a private investigator.'

'A private investigator with an unsecured phone?' Haynes was indignant, as he tried to see where Dave was pointing. 'I wonder if I know him? Maybe you should tell him that... Oh, I see. It's Edwin. Edwin! Cheer up. What can I get you?'

Edwin made an attempt at a smile, as he joined the others. 'Oh, I'm not that fussy. I'll have whatever you guys are having.'

Haynes thrust a twenty at Dave. 'You get this one.'

As soon as Dave had gone, Haynes said quietly, 'You all right?'

Edwin nodded. He looked genuinely upset.

'At least we've got an answer,' said Haynes.

'Yeah,' said Edwin. 'I really wish we hadn't though. All this investigating business is fine in theory — exciting and thrilling, even, in theory — but as soon as you connect with the real people involved, it becomes so appallingly personal. You can find yourself in the position of ripping whole chunks out of the fabric of people's lives.'

Haynes tried to be positive. 'Still, you're bringing truth to light, aren't you? Truth is supposed to be better than lies, or fakery, or even being slightly misleading, isn't it?'

Edwin was looking down at the table, and pressing

his lips together tightly.

Haynes was genuinely alarmed that he was going to start crying. He cast around for a cheerier topic. 'Your friend Dave Clark is a good guy.'

'Yep,' said Edwin.

'We've been playing a game where you have to deduce something about a stranger in the pub.'

'And then use the information to devastate them?'

Sheldon winced, but now Dave was back with a tray. There were six small glasses of a potent looking liquid on it.

'Is everything okay?' Dave asked, looking in alarm at Edwin's face.

'We're just talking through a couple of things,' said Sheldon, reassuringly. 'It's often very unsettling getting to the end of an investigation, and it's sometimes hard not to feel implicated in whatever is uncovered.'

'Heavy,' said Dave, opening his eyes dramatically wide. 'Luckily I've just purchased several doses of a highly effective antidote. Edwin — here you go. The medicine is most effective if you knock it straight back.'

He pushed two of the shot glasses across the table to his friend. Edwin silently nodded his thanks, and slowly, almost reluctantly, picked up the first glass, raised it in the air, and examined it critically in what light was coming from the vintage fittings in the ceiling. To Sheldon's relief, he seemed to be recovering his normal demeanour.

'Thank you, Doctor Clark,' he said. 'This looks like just the business. How do you rate my chances of recovery?'

'Fair to middling,' replied Dave. 'But if you don't take

your medicine like a man, the prognosis will deteriorate rapidly.'

Edwin's eyes opened wide. 'Well if there's one thing I don't want, it's my prognosis to deteriorate.'

He seized the glass nearest him, and downed it in one. After a short gasp, the second one followed it. With a smile, Haynes pushed his two glasses in front of Edwin, who immediately knocked them back.

'You know,' he announced, 'I do believe I'm starting to feel better.'

At eleven thirty, Haynes was shepherding Edwin and Dave out of the Plough. Their communal mood had swung both up and down during the last couple of hours, and had finally found its point of equilibrium in a slightly melancholy contentment.

'Before I go,' said Edwin expansively, 'I'd like to say that when I began this investigation, I was a naive, fresh-faced, idealistic youngster.'

'So was I,' said Haynes. 'So was I.'

Edwin swung round to stare and frown at him. Then his face relaxed into a smile.

'Joke!' he said, with evident glee. 'But what I was going to say was... it's gone. Probably I was going to say, oh, I don't know. Something deep, anyway. I know that much. But then, it might just have been the medicine talking. Good night, guys. You got your money, Dave?'

Dave nodded, winked, and patted his jacket pocket. Edwin turned to Haynes again.

'And I'll see *you* tomorrow. Two o'clock. Don't be late.'

Raising a hand in farewell, Edwin Strong left

Sheldon Haynes and Dave Clark at the corner, outside the Plough, and began his long, careful, walk home. Haynes watched him till he was out of sight, and then turned to Dave.

'I wouldn't exactly say I'm still thirsty, but I know a place just down here, which may still be open. Fancy a final drink for the road?'

Dave Clark looked impressed. 'Well deduced,' he said.

CHAPTER 42

Jeanette Northington rang the bell, and seconds later Hunter was in the room.

'You rang, Miss Jeanette?'

She liked being called Miss; it made her feel much younger than her 61 years.

'Ah, Hunter. Amelia is coming round shortly, and so is Miss Raestock from the office. So too are Neville and Louise, and Alastair Forth will be bringing Gerry with him. I'm also expecting Edwin Strong, and his colleague, Mr Haynes. Jasper is unable to be with us, but I believe we'll be connected to him by Skype. Would you be able to bring us some refreshments at about three? I'm guessing, perhaps unrealistically, that we'll have finished with whatever needs discussing by then, and will be able to relax a little.'

'Yes, Miss Jeanette.'

Jeanette looked round the room. 'And also, I think we'll need a couple of extra seats in here, if you would be so kind?'

'Certainly, Miss Jeanette.'

'Oh, and Hunter, Father White's brother, Harry, is expected to call as well. Though I don't really know what time he will be arriving.'

Jeanette had spent the morning trying to compose herself for this gathering. It felt like it was going to be one of those set-piece finales where everyone gathers in one room, and the detective, who is foreign, or has some sort of interesting foible, ticks off one by one the various clues and then springs his conclusion on the assembled company.

She had read those stories, and thoroughly enjoyed them, but she hadn't quite grasped till now the sickening emotional undercurrents that would accompany such a process. Especially in those denouements where those involved were intimately connected.

'Hunter,' she continued, after a short pause, and with a voice that wasn't altogether steady, 'I'd be grateful if you could stay with us as well, if you would?'

'Of course, Miss Jeanette. I'll go and fetch those chairs now.'

Jeanette wandered over to the window. Just now, she really missed Tony. She savoured, for a moment, the bittersweet feeling of self pity, but very shortly she was aware of a rather disrespectful thought creeping into her consciousness. She almost laughed out loud. Could it really be that she only missed him because of all the trouble his unexpected death had caused? Surely not. That would be so... unprofessional. She stifled a giggle.

Just in time to rescue her from a spiral of ridiculous notions, she spotted Amelia coming up the drive. Jeanette bustled out into the hallway just as Hunter appeared with the first of the extra chairs for the living room.

'I'll get this,' she said to him as she opened the door. 'Amelia, darling! Bang on time.'

'Mother.' Amelia walked straight in. She was just crossing the threshold of the living room when she turned back. 'I'm sorry. I meant to give you a hug.' She hugged her mother briefly but tightly. 'Living room, is it?'

'Yes, dear,' said Jeanette, concerned that Amelia didn't look at all her usual self, but pleased with the display of affection. Out of the corner of her eye she saw another figure turn in at the gate. Molly Raestock. She walked with her usual efficiency up the path to the door, but now Jeanette could see that she looked tired and slightly agitated. Buoyed by her contact with Amelia, she reached out to Molly as she came through the door and grasped her hand warmly with both hands.

'Come on in. This must be very hard for you.'

Molly just nodded. Then she leaned in closer and hugged Jeanette with her free arm.

'Thanks,' she said. 'I can only imagine what *you* must be going through.'

Over Molly's shoulder, Jeanette could now see Alastair and Gerry getting out of a cab. Alastair looked, even from this distance, unhealthily gaunt, and his dark eyes were now complemented by dark bags under them. Gerry looked his usual striking self, but as he greeted Jeanette on his way into the house she noticed he lacked his customary sparkle.

Hunter was welcoming people into the living room, and offering them refreshments. He was worth his weight in gold, she thought.

Before Jeanette could shut the door, two more cars drew up outside. One was a cab, containing Neville and Louise. The other parked up just across the road, and Edwin Strong and his colleague Sheldon got out.

The four of them arrived at the entrance to the drive at the same time, and walked up it in silence together. There followed an elaborate stalemated game of exaggerated courtesy at the door, which was broken by Neville saying, 'All right. After me, then,' and walking into the house, nodding briefly at his mother before entering the living room.

Everyone else was here now, and Jeanette went down the drive a little way to get a good look in both directions before returning to the house and slowly closing the door. She leaned against it for a minute, before taking a deep breath and going to join the others.

Sheldon Haynes was setting up a new-looking laptop on the coffee table, where most people would be able to see it. Before long Jasper Felder appeared on the screen. He looked composed, and was smartly dressed in a shirt and tie. He greeted those in the room calmly, and in his slightly accented English explained that he was currently visiting his mother in Amsterdam. A silence gradually descended.

Edwin cleared his throat nervously.

'Are we all here?' he said, looking at Hunter, who stared impassively back.

'I've asked Hunter to stay while we talk, unless anyone has any objections?' said Jeanette.

A murmur of assent ran round the room, but Neville

immediately bristled and said, 'Are you saying you want the least discreet man in the Cross Keys to stay and listen to our confidential conversation?'

'If Hunter goes, I go,' said Jeanette with a rare flash of anger.

'If Hunter stays, *I* go,' said Neville, standing up.

'Sit down!' said Louise sharply. Neville glared at her angrily, but slowly sank back down onto his seat.

'I always change the names,' Hunter muttered.

'Right,' said Edwin brightly. 'We met here not that long ago, when I was engaged to investigate the tragic death of Tony Northington. Since then I have spoken to you all individually, and to some of you on more than one occasion.'

His gaze moved from one person to another round the room, unable to rest for long on anyone without remembering something disquieting.

'I've also had expert assistance to help me decipher the story told by the objects and networks that we all spend so much of our lives interacting with. I've reached certain conclusions, and I'm sorry, but they make distressing telling. First of all, the very sudden, and completely unexpected death of Father White since I last saw you all, contains the key to the whole story.'

Everyone had their eyes riveted on Edwin. Except for Haynes, who was fiddling with his phone.

'The long and the short of it is that Father White died as a result of swallowing a tiny quantity of cetohyde, which by the smallest of chances found its way round his cardiovascular system to his heart before it had a chance to be eliminated from his body. Cetohyde is a plasma-based liquid which is an effective electrical insulator. If it gets into the wrong part of the heart, this insulating property interrupts the electrical signals that keep it beating. Being derived from blood plasma it is also virtually undetectable, unless tested for specifically.'

Amelia, who had already been sitting with her face resting on her hands, began to shake with silent sobs. Jeanette ran forward and knelt in front of her daughter, cradling her arms round her.

'This happened as a result of a tragic accident,' continued Edwin unsteadily, 'but it gave us a hint as to the method which was used to kill Tony Northington.'

Gasps exploded around the room. Neville jumped to his feet.

'Who did it?' he shouted. 'Who killed him?'

He started to approach Alastair belligerently. Haynes sprang to his feet, and clamping Neville's shoulder in a vice-like grip, slowly but forcefully pushed the other man back into his seat, where he sat, glowering. Haynes returned to his phone. Hunter's hands, which had clenched into fists at Neville's outburst, gradually relaxed.

'The method used was to fill the water dispenser in Tony's office with the cetohyde, which for that purpose was taken out of the art installed in the room.'

Amelia, whose eyes were now a startling red, and whose cheeks were blotched with the same colour, now looked up incredulously.

'My art? My art killed him?' She was whispering hoarsely. Jeanette kept her arms round her.

'Well—' began Edwin, vaguely.

'No,' said Sheldon Haynes in a commanding voice, and suddenly standing up. 'Your art did not kill him.

Someone else killed him using the one thing that had brought peace and beauty to your father's life in his final weeks. Someone else killed him slowly and in stages, by feeding him the cetohyde in his drinking water. And then when he became ill enough to be hospitalised, he continued the corrosive treatment during his visits to the hospital, by adding cetohyde to the contents of your father's drip.'

Amelia's head was back down in her hands again, and her sobs were no longer silent. Haynes continued talking.

'He made huge efforts to conceal his identity, but left incriminating fingerprints on the water fountain, and was observed entering and leaving the hospital ward on CCTV. Also, despite attempting to cover his traces by means of using a swipe card that wasn't his, the other cards he carried still left an electronic trail.'

Everyone in the room was staring at Haynes. Even Felder, who had so far seemed the most relaxed, was now leaning forward and peering intently. Edwin's phone buzzed. He glanced at it quickly. A message from Dave Clark, who they had left sitting outside in his dad's car.

Problem with the Skype feed.

Edwin looked up at the laptop screen. The feed looked fine. He could see Felder clearly, and he was obviously following what was happening. He ignored Dave's message, and concentrated on what Haynes was saying.

'The murder went hand in hand with fraudulent activities which, though we've nipped them in the bud, will still have amassed illegal profits of about a million pounds.'

Amelia's sobbing intensified. Neville jumped to his feet again, shouting, 'I knew it was him!' and this time got to Alastair before Haynes could react. He seized Forth by the shoulder and tried to pull him off his chair. But Hunter was right behind him, and planted his left fist firmly in Neville's left side. This winded him, and spun him round far enough so that his chin was now an easy, quivering target for Hunter's right, swung with considerable force. He crumpled into a heap on the floor.

Hunter rubbed his hand briefly with the other one, blew on his knuckles discreetly, and made his way back to his position by the wall.

'I might not change the names this time,' he murmured.

Haynes had stopped talking momentarily. Jeanette rather helplessly suggested getting a wet towel to revive Neville.

Louise said sharply, 'He'll be fine,' and turned back to listen to Sheldon Haynes.

Edwin's phone buzzed again. Another message from Dave.

Huge problem with the Skype feed.

Edwin glanced again at the screen. It still looked fine. Probably Dave's just worried that the screen's refreshing at less than the optimal rate, he thought. He shoved the phone back in his pocket, and refocussed his concentration on Haynes.

'There's no easy way to say this, but in fact the murderer, and the fraudster, was Tony Northington's son.'

Amelia shrieked and leapt up to direct a well aimed

kick at Neville's prostrate form.

'No, no,' said Haynes urgently. 'Tony Northington's illegitimate son, Jasper Felder.'

More gasps from around the room. Haynes was now getting his phone out, as Edwin began to talk again. Everyone else was now staring at the image of a stony-faced Felder on the small screen.

'He is currently in Amsterdam, at his mother's house.'

Edwin now turned to talk directly to Jasper Felder. As he did so, Haynes moved to the corner of the room and began speaking into his phone.

'But I have to tell you, that thanks to my colleague's international contacts, your mother's home is completely surrounded by police, and even now, they will be knocking at the door.'

Haynes put his phone down. 'They're going in,' he said, with a rare gravitas in his voice.

Everyone's eyes were glued to the Skype image of Jasper Felder. He returned the concerted gazes calmly, and after a minute, began to smile.

'I'm sorry,' he said. 'There's been a bit of a misunderstanding. Tony Northington was no father to me. No father whatsoever.'

The smile now became a rather distorted, and increasingly ghastly grimace.

'I repeat — he was no father to me. In fact, the man's been dead to me for a long time. And if perhaps I killed him once, I would point out in my defence, that he denied my existence many times. As if abandoning me as a baby wasn't enough, he rejected the DNA evidence I presented him with as an adult. So I've simply taken the step of rejecting his DNA in turn.'

Edwin's phone buzzed yet again. He instinctively took it out and glanced at it. Dave, yet again. This time the message was more specific, and as Edwin read it his face fell. Jasper Felder continued speaking, and with every word Edwin nodded resignedly.

'There's been a misunderstanding about my location too. The Korps may even now be ransacking my mother's house, but I'm afraid I'm well beyond their jurisdiction. I've had a tough time, guys, in case you're tempted to think harshly of me. I've been rather up and down recently, and felt I needed to get away for a bit.'

Felder now stood up, and took his laptop to the window of the room he was in. He pointed the camera out the window, displaying a view with a few log cabins in the foreground, then land sloping away down to broad meadows with a river at the bottom, and on the other side, hills leading up to snow capped mountains in the distance.

'As you can see, I've managed to find somewhere nice and remote. But I mustn't keep you. Give Neville a kick from me.'

He reached towards the screen, and the image disappeared.

There was a moment's silence, then everyone began to talk at once. Except for Neville Northington.

Hunter had displayed impressive reserves of poise as he continued to serve refreshments to Jeanette's visitors. Apart from discreetly forgetting to refill the glass of the man who had accused him of being indiscreet, he was courtesy personified. Jeanette thought she noticed the corner of his mouth twitch upward at one point, when he first saw the extent of the bruise developing on Neville's chin, but otherwise she couldn't fault his etiquette. Alastair, who seemed to be looking more relaxed already, went out of his way to thank him for his service, and quietly pressed a bundle of notes into his palm when he left later, with an apology for the commonness of the gesture. And Molly Raestock's eyes seemed to follow Hunter round the room.

A lot of talking and exclaiming went on that afternoon, interspersed with some explaining, from Edwin and Sheldon. They were joined after a while by Dave Clark, who had been invited in as soon as Jeanette had realised that another member of their team was sitting quietly outside in a car.

Once Neville had recovered his senses, he joined in the conversation in a rather chastened mood, but was unable to resist telling everyone that he *knew* something had been going on, and it was a good thing he'd insisted on the investigation. He and a grim Louise were the first to leave, aiming to hail a black cab in the street.

'Wouldn't like to be him right now,' observed Sheldon cheerfully, clutching a large glass of Chateau Lauriol.

'No indeed,' added Alastair. 'Nor on Monday morning when we start to review the implications for the company.'

'For *my* company,' said Jeanette, quietly, but firmly.

'For your company,' said Alastair, nodding.

'But don't forget,' said Haynes, 'it was Felder who had set up the skimming software in Neville's office, while he was unofficially out of the office. Our evidence is clear on that point. And the huge sums of money only started appearing in his account later — my assumption is that Felder was trying to frame him.'

Later, as Alastair was lavishing the cash on Hunter, Gerry was saying goodbye to Jeanette.

'Thank you for having us,' he said, as he kissed her on each cheek.

'You sound like a child leaving a birthday party,' she said. 'Thank you for coming.'

Amelia, after she had slaked her considerable thirst, and come back from a long phone conversation with Ben in the garden, seemed disposed to make an evening of it. She became absorbed, with Sheldon Haynes and Dave Clark, in an elaborate and whimsical version of their deduction game, which took as its subjects characters from history. Her artist's eye enabled her to draw all kinds of conclusions.

Molly had disappeared, and Jeanette came across her in the kitchen, bathing a rather embarrassed Hunter's knuckles under the tap. Jeanette smiled, and turned away, almost bumping into Edwin, who had come up behind her.

'I'm afraid I have to go,' he said, hesitantly.

'Thank you so much,' Jeanette replied. 'I know there will be lots of things to get my head around, but it's like a window has been opened, and suddenly I'm able to breathe some fresher air.'

They stood awkwardly in the corridor.

'Off anywhere nice?' asked Jeanette.

'A meal.' Edwin blushed. 'With a friend.'

He nodded, turned, and let himself out the front door. But he didn't close it behind him. Jeanette walked across the hall and just as she got to the door, Harry White reached the top of the path.

She stood in the doorway, framed by the warm light from the kitchen down the corridor behind her, and smiled.

'Sorry I'm late,' he said. 'Did I miss anything?'

POST POST SCRIPT

Edwin clutched the brown paper parcel in his left hand, as he rang the bell with his right. If it hadn't been for Molly Raestock's confusion about left and right, he thought to himself, he never would have got involved in this business.

Hunter opened the door with a smile, and indicated the living room. Edwin wondered if things would have turned out very differently if Sheldon Haynes had taken charge of the investigation on his own.

Jeanette was sitting in the armchair immediately inside the door of the living room, and as soon as she saw Edwin, she silently reached out for the package. He placed the heavy and slightly flexible parcel on her outstretched hands, and took his own hands away rather reluctantly.

'I feel a bit bad,' he said. 'It was Neville, after all, who commissioned the investigation.'

'Oh, don't worry,' said Jeanette calmly. 'He'll be kept in the loop.'

She tested the weight of it. Edwin stood near her, slightly awkwardly.

'A good few hours reading here,' she said, with a slight smile.

'I hope you enjoy it,' said Edwin. He shrugged, spread his hands out and briefly closed his eyes. 'What am I saying?' He opened his eyes again. 'You won't enjoy it. Of course you won't. But I hope you find some peace in it, or some closure, maybe.'

Jeanette nodded, and again smiled a little. 'Oh, I'm tougher than you think.'

'There's one other thing you ought to know.' Edwin shifted his weight from his left leg to his right. 'It will probably become apparent as you read this, but not all the methods I used to obtain evidence would stand up in court.'

Edwin watched for a reaction from Jeanette. There was none at all, so he blundered on a little. 'Yes, as I say, it's just unfortunate that some of our methods... totally unintentionally, of course... not quite above board, maybe.'

Still just a half smile in response. Time to change the subject a little.

'I imagine you've come to some sort of agreement with Neville about the future of Northington International?' said Edwin. 'Not that it's any of my business,' he added hastily.

'That's fine,' said Jeanette. 'You've spent a lot of time with it being your business. To answer your question, there's not a lot of agreement at the moment, but Neville is having to do as I say. It's my company now, after all.'

Now it was Edwin's turn to nod silently, as Jeanette

continued. 'He's behaving himself fairly well, so far.' Her smile now included her eyes for the first time. Edwin still found it slightly unsettling.

'And the Best — I mean the Connected Chain Bond?' he asked.

'I've got people working on that as we speak. By the way, would you be able to give me the contact details for your friend, Dave Clark?'

'Oh,' said Edwin. 'Would it be all right if I asked him first?'

'Of course,' said Jeanette calmly. 'Very right and proper. If he cares to get in touch with me through Molly, I may have some work that would suit his talents.'

'Will do,' said Edwin, slightly uneasily.

Jeanette now stood up and stretched her shoulders a little, rather like a cat would. She frowned. 'So. Jasper Felder. You say he's probably out of the reach of the law?'

'Let's just say the law would probably have to start again from scratch,' said Edwin.

'That Skype call — he clearly wasn't at his mother's apartment in Amsterdam?'

'Clearly not.'

'Where was he?'

Edwin shifted his weight back to his left leg.

'It's difficult to say exactly, but Dave says he must have been in the US, from the details of his wireless carrier.'

The smile slowly reappeared on her lips. 'Do you think you'd be able to find him?'

Closing the gate of Jeanette Northington's home carefully behind him, Edwin screwed his eyes tightly shut for a second, and then opened them wide. A shudder ran through him, and he took a deep breath. He shook his shoulders briefly, then took another deep breath. Finally he looked to the left, down the hill, and then to the right, up the hill. There was Bet, just coming down from the main road. He waved. She turned and looked behind her with a frown, then turned back to him with a grin. Edwin Strong began to relax.

The End

12743142R00226

Printed in Great Britain
by Amazon